For Sherri —

SILENCE ON MONTE SOLE

AVAILABLE NOW

THE HOWARD FAST COLLECTION
The Crossing
Moses
The Immigrants
Bunker Hill: The Prequel to The Crossing
2nd Generation

Helmet for My Pillow
By Robert Leckie

The Way of the Gladiator
By Daniel P. Mannix

Horizon: Ancient Rome
By Robert Payne

Horizon: Ancient Greece
By William Harlan Hale

Samurai!
By Saburo Sakai
with Martin Caidin
and Fred Saito

Fork-Tailed Devil: The P-38
By Martin Caidin

The B-17 The Flying Forts
By Martin Caidin

Thunderbolt
By Robert S. Johnson with Martin Caidin

When Hell Froze Over
By E.M. Halliday

The American Heritage New History of the Civil War
By Bruce Catton
Edited by James M. McPherson

The World War II Reader
By the Editors of *World War II* magazine

SILENCE ON MONTE SOLE

JACK OLSEN

ibooks
new york
www.ibooksinc.com

DISTRIBUTED BY SIMON & SCHUSTER, INC.

An Original Publication of ibooks, inc.

An ibooks, inc. Book

Distributed by Simon & Schuster, Inc.
1230 Avenue of the Americas, New York, NY 10020

Ibooks, inc.
24 West 25th Street
New York, NY 10010

The ibooks World Wide Web Site address is:
http://www.ibooksinc. com

Cover Design: Carrie Monaco

ISBN: 0-7434-3485-4

First ibooks printing January 2002

10 9 8 7 6 5 4 3 2 1

Share your thoughts about *Silence on Monte Sole* and other ibooks
titles in the new ibooks virtual reading group at www.ibooksinc.com

This book is dedicated to some who lived:

Livia Albertini
Nino Amici
Adelmo Benini
Sister Antonietta Benni
Corina Bertacchi*
Angelo Bertuzzi
Pio Borgia
Giovanni Bottonelli
Roberto Carboni
Carlo Cardi
Mario Cardi
Carlo Castelli
Guerrino Cavina
Gino Chirici
Maria Collina
Attilio Comellini
Raffaele de Maria
Gilberto Fabbri
Luigi Fornasini
Aldo Gamberini
Raphael Ciro Giobbe, M.D.
Renato Giorgi
Pietro Lazzari
Giuseppe Lorenzini
Giovanni Marchesi
Augusto Massa
Luigi Massa
Vittorio Massarenti, M.D.
Calisto Migliori
Giovanni Migliori
Anna Monfardini
Luciano Montanari
Laura Musolesi
Maria Negri
Vittoria Negri
Antenore Paselli
Cornelia Paselli
Bruno Pedriali
Susanna Pietrofiglio
Fernando Piretti
Gioacchino Piretti
Pietro Piretti
Amelia Pirini
Lidia Pirini
Mary Toffoletto Romagnoli
Ernesto Rosa
Gianni Rossi
Elena Ruggeri
Elide Ruggeri
Acacci Ruggero
Lucia Sabbioni
Adele Sasso
General Piero Stellacci
Luciano Testi
Leonardo Tiviroli
Maria Tiviroli
Antonio Tonelli
Antonio Venturi
Sereno Zagnoni
Mario Zebri
Pietro Zebri

*** According to customary Italian practice, married women are listed by their maiden names.**

And to some who died:

Luisa Acacci
Gaudenzio Acquaviva
Aldo Albertini
Francesco Albertini
Giuseppe Albertini
Maria Albertini
Orlando Albertini
Bruno Alvisi
Quirico Amaroli
Roberto Amaroli
Olimpio Ambrogi
Annamaria Amici
Iris Amici
Marisa Amici
Ettore Andreoli
Santuzza Angelini
Enrica Angiolini
Gabriella Angiolini
Giancarlo Angiolini
Giuseppe Ansaloni
Claudia Aprenzi
Primo Arienti
Anna Rosa Astrali
Gabriella Astrali
Ida Astrali
Alfonsa Bacci
Amedea Bacci
Enrico Bacci
Annita Baccolini
Calisto Baccolini
Claudia Baccolini
Federico Baccolini
Flavia Baccolini
Giuseppe Baccolini
Ruffillo Baccolini
Sestilia Baccolini
Amelia Baietti
Argia Baldanza
Arturo Baldazzi
Ezio Baldazzi
Divino Baldi
Giovanna Baldini
Giuseppina Balugani
Edmea Barattoli
Edmea Baravelli
Illuminata Baravelli
Raffaele Baravelli
Somiglia Baravelli
Alfredo Barbari
Mario Barbari
Rino Barbari
Maria Barbetti
Alfredo Barbieri
Amadeo Barbieri
Antonietta Barbieri
Arrigo Barbieri
Caterina Barbieri
Colombo Barbieri
Evarista Barbieri
Evaristo Barbieri
Ines Barbieri
Luigi Barbieri
Remo Barbieri
Vittorina Barbieri
Carlo Barnaba
Eliso Barnaba
Gino Barnaba
Clara Bartolini
Clementina Bartolini
Corrado Bartolini
Orvella Bartolini
Pietro Bartolini

Raffaele Bartolini
Ruffina Bartolini
Venusta Bartolini
Teresina Bartolucci
Nello Beatrisotto
Bruno Beccaccia
Roberto Beccaccia
Pietro Beccari
Bruno Beccaria
Renzo Bedetti
Arseno Beghelli
Giannino Beghelli
Carlo Bertucci
Riccardo Belletti
Vivilia Beltrami
Adelfa Benassi
Caterina Benassi
Giorgio Benassi
Mario Benassi
Orlando Benassi
Pompeo Benassi
Riccardo Benassi
Silvio Benassi
Evaristo Bendini
Giovanni Benelli
Adele Benini
Alberto Benini
Anselmo Benini
Armando Benini
Giovanna Benini
Giovanni Benini
Maria Benini
Mario Benini
Evaristo Benni
Gino Benni
Elisa Bernabà
Gelinda Bernardi
Mario Bernardi
Luigi Bernardoni
Maria Bernardoni
Elisa Bertacci
Giuseppe Bertarini
Ardilio Berti
Clara Berti
Amelea Betti
Armando Betti
Bianca Betti
Cleofe Betti
Cesira Betti
Francesco Betti
Fulvio Betti
Giambattista Betti
Giovanni Betti
Giovanni Betti
Giuseppe Betti
Laura Betti
Marisa Betti
Primo Betti
Ettore Bettini
Mercedes Bettini
Alfredo Bettocchi
Maria Bevilacqua
Nello Bevilacqua
Edma Bianchi
Edmo Bianchi
Luciano Bianchi
Arseno Bianconcini
Anna Bignami
Ettore Bignami
Ferruccio Boccato
Alfredo Bocci
Pietro Bolognesi
Romano Bolognini
Raffaele Bonafé
Agenore Bonaiuti
Agenore Bonaiuti
Bruno Bonantini
Pietro Bonantini

Amalia Bondioli
Silvano Bonelli
Leone Bonetti
Constante Bonfiglioli
Giuseppe Bonfiglioli
Pietro Bonfiglioli
Artemio Boninsegna
Filomena Boninsegna
Gino Boraggini
Clemente Borelli
Alfredo Borgia
Sesto Borsari
Stanislao Bortolotti
Trestano Bortolotti
Teresina Bortolucci
Candida Boscarin
Mario Boschi
Alberto Bovi
Oreste Bregolini
Armando Brighetti
Ernesta Brizzi
Livio Brizzi
Pio Brizzi
Antonio Brunelli
Marino Brunetti
Aldo Bruni
Augusto Bruni
Ettore Bruni
Ruggero Bruni
Bruno Bugamelli
Francesco Bugamelli
Adelmo Bugané
Amelia Bugané
Elvira Bugané
Federico Bugané
Fulvia Bugané
Italo Bugané
Maria Bugané
Mario Bugané
Marisa Bugané
Pietro Bugané
Primo Bugané
Renato Bugané
Roberto Bugané
Zaira Bugané
Renzo Bulgari
Renzo Buttelli
Enrico Burzi
Luigia Burzi
Maddalena Burzi
Marcellino Burzi
Renzo Buttelli
Gian Luigi Calanchi
Paolo Calanchi
Luigi Calisti
Anna Calzolari
Annita Calzolari
Antonio Calzolari
Argia Calzolari
Augusto Calzolari
Augusto Calzolari
Camillo Calzolari
Emma Calzolari
Francesco Calzolari
Giovanni Calzolari
Giuseppe Calzolari
Maria Calzolari
Natale Calzolari
Nella Calzolari
Ottavio Calzolari
Pierina Calzolari
Remo Calzolari
Ivo Camaiori
Clelia Camaggi
Cristina Camaggi
Alfonso Campori
Luigi Cancelli
Giuseppe Cané

Angelo Cantoni
Alvaro Capanni
Padre Martino Capelli
Alfonso Capponi
Edoardo Capponi
Ernesto Carata
Maria Carboni
Mario Carboni
Alberto Cardi
Augusto Cardi
Maria Elena Cardi
Gina Cardi
Giuseppe Cardi
Lucia Cardi
Maria Cardi
Walter Cardi
Maria Cardoni
Nerina Cardoni
Remo Cardoni
Arrigo Carolingi
Don Ferdinando Casagrande
Gabriella Casagrande
Giovannino Casagrande
Giulia Casagrande
Lina Casagrande
Lina Casalini
Pietro Casalini
Sergio Casalini
Tito Casalini
Walter Casalini
Edoardo Castagnari
Ernesta Castagnari
Franco Castagnari
Dina Castellani
Orfeo Castori
Avellina Catti
Giuseppe Cavalli
Estiva Cavallini
Giuseppe Cella
Isabella Ceretti
Maria Ceretti
Virgilio Ceretti
Cesarina Ceri
Giovanni Ceri
Giuseppina Ceri
Dino Cevenini
Enrico Cevenini
Giuseppe Cevenini
Antonio Chieffo
Amedeo Chinni
Giannetta Chirici
Ginetta Chirici
Armando Cincinnati
Bruno Cincinnati
Celestina Cincinnati
Dante Cincinnati
Dino Cincinnati
Francesco Cincinnati
Giancarlo Cincinnati
Giuseppe Cincinnati
Aristide Cinti
Laura Cinti
Maria Cinti
Antonio Cioni
Giacomo Cioni
Remo Cioni
Lucia Ciottolini
Giuseppe Collina
Tarcisia Collina
Alberto Coltelli
Aldo Comani
Alfiero Comastri
Bianca Comastri
Marcella Comastri
Marcellina Comastri
Fermo Comelli
Luigi Comelli
Alfonsa Comellini

Angelo Comellini
Argante Comellini
Livia Comellini
Maria Comellini
Don Elia Comini
Augusta Commissari
Cleonice Commissari
Ermenegilda Commissari
Filomena Commissari
Giovanna Commissari
Maria Celsa Commissari
Enrica Conti
Giovanni Conti
Augusto Coralli
Clelia Coramelli
Enrico Coramelli
Agnese Corticelli
Livia Corticelli
Luigi Costa
Burzi Evelina Crini
Lea Cristalli
Rino Cristiani
Fernando Cucchi
Aldo Cumani
Fernando Cumani
Albertino Dainesi
Alfredo Dainesi
Ruffina Dainesi
Salvina Dainesi
Giuseppe Daini
Guido Daini
Lucia Daini
Teresa Daini
Angelo Dal Cero
Noce Filippo Dalla
Vedove Alberto Dalle
Augusto Dall'Omo
Giorgio Dall'Omo
Agostino Dani
Alfonso Dani
Amelia Dani
Lea Dani
Maria Dani
Maria Amelia Dani
Pietro Dani
Esposti Adelma Degli
Esposti Adriano Degli
Esposti Cleto Degli
Esposti Ugo Degli
Esposti Walter Degli
Walter Degno
Orfeo Delfino
Giuseppe Delucca
Quirico Delucca
Duilio Dini
Celso Domenichini
Claudia Domenichini
Augusto Donati
Clarice Donati
Gino Donati
Artemio Dondarini
Enzo Dondini
Luciano Draghetti
Olga Druidi
Renato Druidi
Erminia Ecchia
Sergio Elmi
Giovanna Esperidi
Alfonso Fabbiani
Augusto Fabbiani
Leandro Fabbiani
Adelma Fabbri
Adolfo Fabbri
Alfredo Fabbri
Arrigo Fabbri
Elide Fabbri
Giovanni Fabbri
Giuseppe Fabbri

Luciano Fabbri
Luigi Fabbri
Maria Fabbri
Rosanna Fabbri
Silvio Fabbri
Federico Fabbris
Amabile Facchini
Duilio Faccioli
Franco Faccioli
Antonio Faggioli
Enea Faggioli
Goffredo Faggioli
Orfeo Faggioli
Oliviero Faggioli
Giovanni Fanelli
Bruno Fanini
Giovanni Fanini
Vittoria Fantazzini
Amelia Fanti
Armando Fanti
Attilio Fanti
Carlo Fanti
Claudio Fanti
Emilio Fanti
Francesco Fanti
Giuliana Fanti
Giuseppe Fanti
Maria Fanti
Renzo Fanti
Rosina Fanti
Augusto Fantini
Carlo Fantini
Imelde Fantini
Giuseppe Fantini
Massimo Fantini
Gastone Farina
Antonio Fava
Bernardo Felci
Adolfo Ferretti
Adriana Ferretti
Anna Ferretti
Aurelio Ferretti
Caterina Ferretti
Claudio Ferretti
Dario Ferretti
Ersilia Ferretti
Giancarlo Ferretti
Giuseppe Ferretti
Luigi Ferretti
Maria Ferretti
Martina Ferretti
Cesare Ferri
Eliseo Ferri
Livia Ferri
Giacomo Filigni
Maria Filocomo
Gina Fini
Luigi Fini
Maria Fini
Enrico Finocchi
Francesco Fiocchi
Adriana Fiori
Bruna Fiori
Cesare Fiori
Elvira Fiori
Enrico Fiori
Franca Fiori
Giuseppe Fiori
Lea Fiori
Maria Fiori
Suor Maria Fiori
Sergio Fiori
Antonio Fiorini
Bruna Fiorini
Carlo Fiorini
Sergio Fontana
Don Giovanni Fornasini
Giuseppe Fornasini

Rosa Fornasini
Iolanda Fortuzzi
Luigi Fortuzzi
Anna Frabboni
Chiara Franceschini
Enrico Franceschini
Lieta Franceschini
Lodovico Franceschini
Amadea Franchi
Alfredo Frascaroli
Giulia Frascaroli
Raffaele Frascaroli
Mario Fratti
Umberto Fringuelli
Alfredo Frondi
Giacomo Fuligni
Gaetano Fumicelli
Giancarlo Gabrielli
Emilio Galantini
Paolina Galantini
Marta Galli
Pasqualino Galli
Arrigo Galliani
Antonio Gamberini
Bice Gamberini
Bruno Gamberini
Cesarino Gamberini
Cleofe Gamberini
Gino Gamberini
Giuseppe Gamberini
Idalba Gamberini
Imelde Gamberini
Isora Gamberini
Lice Gamberini
Luciano Gamberini
Maria Gamberini
Maria Luisa Gamberini
Mario Gamberini
Roberto Gamberini
Rosina Gamberini
Wilma Gamberini
Emilio Gandolfi
Filomena Gandolfi
Giorgio Gandolfi
Giuseppe Gandolfi
Ines Gandolfi
Margherita Gandolfi
Maria Gandolfi
Severino Gandolfi
Sofia Gatti
Giuseppe Gavioli
Gino Gelli
Erminia Gentili
Maria Ghelfi
Alfredo Gherardi
Angelo Gherardi
Anna Gherardi
Armando Gherardi
Attilio Gherardi
Clelia Gherardi
Enrica Gherardi
Enrico Gherardi
Luigi Gherardi
Mario Gherardi
Tina Gherardi
Vincenzo Gherardi
Vittorio Ghiacci
Adornella Giacomazzi
Gino Gianassi
Aristide Giddi
Florinda Gigli
Angelo Giorgi
Virginio Giorgi
Maria Giovannetti
Elide Giuliani
Pietro Giuliani
Agata Giusti
Ernesto Giusti

Fortunato Gnudi
Pietro Golfetti
Erminia Gottardi
Adelma Govoni
Romeo Govoni
Clemente Gragalli
Giuseppe Grani
Maria Grani
Mario Grani
Romeo Grappoli
Gianfranco Grasilli
Eleonora Grilli
Primo Grilli
Tommaso Grilli
Paolo Grimaldi
Giuseppe Guccini
Anna Guermandi
Amedeo Ianelli
Amos Ianelli
Giovanni Ianelli
Giuseppe Indovini
Maria Indovini
Augusto Iubini
Bruno Iubini
Emma Iubini
Giorgio Iubini
Giuseppe Iubini
Ines Iubini
Lucia Iubini
Roberto Iubini
Adalcisa Laffi
Antonio Laffi
Arduina Laffi
Armando Laffi
Armida Laffi
Arrigo Laffi
Arturo Laffi
Demetrio Laffi
Dino Laffi
Ernesto Laffi
Ettore Laffi
Fernanda Laffi
Francesco Laffi
Franco Laffi
Gabriele Laffi
Giorgio Laffi
Giovanni Laffi
Giuseppe Laffi
Italo Laffi
Lea Laffi
Marina Laffi
Massimo Laffi
Mirella Laffi
Natale Laffi
Pietro Laffi
Primo Laffi
Vincenzo Laffi
Luigi Lamandini
Luigi Lamandini
Giovanni Lamberti
Elvira Landini
Alfredo Lanzarini
Anna Lanzarini
Arrigo Lanzarini
Celso Lanzarini
Gino Lanzarini
Giuseppe Lanzarini
Lea Lanzarini
Leandro Lanzarini
Lucia Lanzarini
Rosanna Lanzarini
Vittorina Lanzarini
Vittorio Lastrucci
Ilia Lava
Paolo Lava
Umberto Lava
Gaetano Lazzari
Oreste Lelli

Duilio Lenzi
Sergio Lenzi
Eva Leonesi
Nella Leonesi
Alfredo Leoni
Anselmo Leoni
Armando Leoni
Mario Leoni
Nello Leoni
Rina Leoni
Carlo Lepri
Adele Lippi
Maria Lippi
Werter Lodi
Arturo Lolli
Carolina Lolli
Celsa Lolli
Dina Lolli
Elena Lolli
Elisa Lolli
Ettore Lolli
Fanny Lolli
Giovanni Lolli
Giuliana Lolli
Luigi Lolli
Nello Lolli
Olga Lolli
Riccardo Lolli
Tito Lolli
Aldo Lollini
Amedeo Lollini
Carlo Lollini
Agostino Lorenzini
Anna Lorenzini
Augusto Lorenzini
Clara Lorenzini
Marcella Lorenzini
Maria Lorenzini
Maria Luisa Lorenzini
Nerina Lorenzini
Pietro Lorenzini
Renato Lorenzini
Rita Lorenzini
Albina Luccarini
Anna Luccarini
Cesare Luccarini
Luigi Luccarini
Prima Luccarini
Rita Luccarini
Giovanni Lucchi
Giuseppe Lucchi
Clementina Macchiavelli
Fernanda Macchiavelli
Vincenzo Macchiavelli
Alfredo Machelli
Dina Machelli
Enrica Maria Machelli
Filomena Machelli
Francesco Machelli
Gino Machelli
Giuseppe Machelli
Maria Machelli
Rosina Machelli
Costantina Magnani
Ferruccio Magnani
Pasquale Mancarini
Dolores Mandorla
Roberto Mandorla
Teodolinda Mandorla
Amelia Marabini
Luigi Marabini
Pietro Marandoli
Zefferino Marcacci
Dante Marcheselli
Ersilia Marchetti
Alba Marchi
Angelo Marchi
Augusto Marchi

Dino Marchi
Elvira Marchi
Frediano Marchi
Giovanni Marchi
Iole Marchi
Irma Marchi
Luigi Marchi
Marino Marchi
Tomasina Marchi
Viola Marchi
Maria Marchioni
Paolina Marchioni
Don Ubaldo Marchioni
Enrica Marescalchi
Ettore Marmocchi
Alfonso Marzadori
Dino Marzadori
Enrico Marzari
Adalcisa Mascagni
Carolina Mascagni
Caterina Mascagni
Alberto Maselli
Ernesto Masetti
Armando Masotti
Anna Massa
Emma Massa
Maria Massa
Mario Massa
Mario Massa
Domenica Matorozzi
Roberto Mattarozzi
Augusto Mattioli
Gregorio Mattioli
Raffaele Mattioli
Angiolino Mazzanti
Giulia Mazzanti
Giuseppina Mazzanti
Romano Mazzanti
Sisto Mazzanti
Bianca Mazzei
Luciano Mazzini
Faustino Mazzoni
Malfalda Medici
Maria Medici
Massimo Medici
Alberto Melchioni
Aldo Melega
Dario Menarini
Alberto Mengoli
Francesco Mengoli
Giorgio Mengoli
Lucio Mengoli
Luisa Mengoli
Marcello Mengoli
Rodolfo Mengoli
Alberto Menini
Arturo Menini
Fedele Menini
Loriana Menini
Gaetano Mezzini
Gino Mezzini
Irma Mezzini
Laura Mezzini
Maria Mezzini
Anna Migliori
Armando Migliori
Dante Migliori
Enrico Migliori
Franco Migliori
Lina Migliori
Marino Migliori
Norina Migliori
Vittoria Migliori
Olga Migliorin
Dante Minelli
Domenico Minelli
Olga Minelli
Domenico Mingarelli

Maria Mingarelli
Angelo Miserazzi
Achille Moli
Luciano Monachini
Alberto Monari
Vittorio Monari
Augusto Monetti
Primo Monetti
Ivana Montecristi
Maria Montecristi
Nora Montecristi
Argia Monti
Clelia Monti
Emilio Monti
Fernando Monti
Lena Monti
Maria Monti
Maria Petronilla Monti
Primo Moretti
Elide Mormoni
Aldo Morotti
Francesco Moruzzi
Giuseppe Moruzzi
Pietro Moruzzi
Rosa Moruzzi
Bruna Moschetti
Dario Moschetti
Ferdinando Moschetti
Lido Moschetti
Maria Moschetti
Vittoria Moschetti
Paride Musi
Olga Musiani
Alfredo Musolesi
Amalia Musolesi
Bruna Musolesi
Maria Muzzarini
Carlo Musolesi
Cleto Musolesi
Dino Musolesi
Evangelista Musolesi
Giovanni Musolesi
Mario Musolesi
Pietro Musolesi
Germana Nadalini
Ildegarda Nadalini
Massimo Nadalini
Natalia Nadalini
Anna Naldi
Assunta Naldi
Maria Naldi
Adolfo Nannetti
Bice Nannetti
Guido Nannetti
Primo Nannetti
Sabattino Nannetti
Virginio Nannetti
Alberto Nanni
Armando Nanni
Augusto Nanni
Caterina Nanni
Celestina Nanni
Clara Nanni
Desolina Nanni
Elide Nanni
Enrico Nanni
Fedora Nanni
Franco Nanni
Gabriella Nanni
Gino Nanni
Giovanni Nanni
Giulia Nanni
Guerrino Nanni
Gustavo Nanni
Lucia Nanni
Marcello Nanni
Mario Nanni
Nerina Nanni

Pietro Nanni
Romeo Nanni
Silvano Nanni
Sofia Nanni
Telesina Nanni
Vittoria Nanni
Amedeo Nannoni
Giorgio Natali
Emma Negri
Gaetano Negri
Angelo Negroni
Ada Neri
Dario Neri
Dionigio Neri
Ermes Neri
Nello Neri
Amalia Nerozzi
Francesco Nerozzi
Primo Nerozzi
Maria Nicoletti
Ernesto Nodi
Domenico Oleandri
Franco Oleandri
Giuseppe Oleandri
Pietro Oleandri
Sirio Oleandri
Olga Olghini
Bruno Olivi
Teresa Olivi
Nazzarena Opali
Adriana Pacchi
Dario Pacchi
Giuseppe Pacchi
Luciano Pacchi
Maria Paganelli
Vittoria Paganelli
Ivo Pagani
Raffaele Paganini
Fiore Palandri
Bruno Palazzi
Martino Palazzi
Martino Palma
Elena Palmieri
Mario Palmieri
Nerina Palmieri
Riccardo Palmieri
Umberto Pancaldi
Ester Pantaleoni
Eberle Paoli
Giuseppe Paolini
Amelia Parazza
Cesarina Parenti
Orsolina Parenti
Sisfrido Pascolderoni
Giorgio Pascoletti
Alfonso Paselli
Anna Paselli
Cecilia Paselli
Claudio Paselli
Dante Paselli
Fedia Paselli
Franco Paselli
Genoveffa Paselli
Giuseppe Paselli
Ildebrando Paselli
Luigi Paselli
Malvina Paselli
Maria Paselli
Mario Paselli
Pietro Paselli
Tomaso Paselli
Virginio Paselli
Giacomo Pasini
Augusto Pasqui
Pietro Pasqui
Paolo Passarin
Luigi Passelli
Maria Passelli

Mario Passelli
Fernando Passini
Giacomo Passini
Mirka Passini
Evaristo Pedretti
Alessandro Pedretti
Aurelio Pedretti
Bruno Pedretti
Luigi Pedretti
Amilcare Pedriali
Franca Pedriali
Gabriele Pedriali
Luigi Pedriali
Armando Pedrini
Ferdinando Peri
Giovanni Pesci
Maria Petruzzi
Gino Piacentini
Ruggero Piccioli
Dolores Pierantoni
Enea Pierantoni
Walter Pierantoni
Angelo Pinelli
Domenico Piretti
Emma Piretti
Enzo Piretti
Maria Piretti
Maximiliano Piretti
Riccardo Piretti
Teresa Piretti
Virginia Piretti
Alda Pirini
Annunziata Pirini
Damiano Pirini
Giorgio Pirini
Giuseppina Pirini
Giuseppina Pirini
Marta Pirini
Martino Pirini
Olimpia Pirini
Rosanna Pirini
Sergio Piselli
Paola Pizzoli
Mario Poli
Romolo Poli
Ugo Poli
Stevio Polischi
Augusta Possati
Amato Possenti
Fernando Predieri
Medardo Predieri
Pompeo Predieri
Margherita Prini
Arturo Prospero
Alessandro Puccetti
Augusto Puccetti
Emilia Puccetti
Fernando Puccetti
Giuseppe Puccetti
Pasquale Puccetti
Luigia Quadri
Enrico Quercia
Alberto Raimondi
Ugo Rambelli
Oreste Rami
Luigi Rani
Ivo Rasini
Cirino Rausa
Gino Ravaglia
Quinto Ravaglia
Amedeo Remalti
Walter Reni
Francesco Ricci
Luciano Ricolini
Maria Luisa Ridolfi
Elena Righetti
Evelina Righetti
Mentore Righetti

Angela Righi
Cecilia Righi
Ersilio Righi
Gaetano Righi
Giuseppe Righi
Maria Righi
Ortensia Righi
Maria Righini
Armando Rigoni
Armando Rimaldi
Carlo Rocca
Luigia Rocca
Maria Rocca
Giancarlo Romagnoli
Umberto Romagnoli
Graziella Romanelli
Carlo Rondelli
Enrico Rondelli
Federico Rondelli
Enrico Rondinelli
Ada Rosa
Alberto Rosa
Armando Rosa
Clelia Rosa
Cleonice Rosa
Corrado Rosa
Ferdinando Rosa
Gaetano Rosa
Gemma Rosa
Livia Rosa
Ulderico Rosa
Angiolina Rossi
Anna Rossi
Antonio Rossi
Calisto Rossi
Carlo Rossi
Edoardo Rossi
Enrico Rossi
Gastone Rossi
Gemma Rossi
Giacomo Rossi
Giuseppe Rossi
Ida Rossi
Ivo Rossi
Olderina Rossi
Augusto Rosti
Ettore Rosti
Gilda Rosti
Giuliano Rosti
Laura Rosti
Pietro Rovigo
Ettore Rovinetti
Eliseo Rubini
Jonio Rubini
Livia Rubini
Maria Rubini
Anna Ruggeri
Attilio Ruggeri
Augusto Ruggeri
Giulio Ruggeri
Padre Mario Ruggeri
Lina Ruggeri
Maria Ruggeri
Aldo Rusticelli
Aldo Sabattini
Adriana Sabbioni
Anna Sabbioni
Bruna Sabbioni
Desiderio Sabbioni
Gaetano Sabbioni
Giovanna Sabbioni
Irene Sabbioni
Otello Sabbioni
Adele Sabulli
Francesco Sabulli
Umberto Sala
Aristide Salini
Elisabetta Salvador

Giuseppina Sammarchi
Raffaele Sammarchi
Rosa Sammarchi
Agostino Sandri
Alfredo Sandri
Anita Sandri
Adelmo Sandrolini
Fulvia Sandrolini
Osvaldo Sandrolini
Silvano Sandrolini
Alfredo Santi
Ida Santi
Giuseppe Santini
Rita Santini
Giordano Sartini
Corrado Sassarelli
Giuseppe Sassetti
Anna Sassi
Celso Sassi
Gianna Sassi
Graziella Sassi
Maria Sassi
Alfredo Scala
Augusto Scala
Angiolina Scandellari
Ettore Scandellari
Pasquino Scandellari
Adele Selva
Domenico Sensi
Adolfo Serenari
Anna Serenari
Celso Serenari
Ernesta Serenari
Ersilia Serenari
Giovanni Serenari
Angelo Serpentin
Amabile Serra
Anita Serra
Antonio Serra
Giulia Serra
Ines Serra
Maria Serra
Mario Serra
Albertino Sibani
Emilio Silco
Augusto Simoncini
Linda Simoncini
Valentino Simoncini
Giulio Siri
Antonietta Smerigli
Franca Soldati
Luigi Soldati
Primo Soldati
Vincenzo Soldati
Giovanni Soli
Gaetano Sordi
Aldo Stanzani
Antonio Stanzani
Emilio Stanzani
Guido Stanzani
Marino Stanzani
Ersilia Stefanelli
Gaetano Stefanelli
Gino Stefanelli
Marino Stefanelli
Amedeo Stefani
Egle Stefani
Elda Stefani
Marta Stefani
Walter Stefani
Felice Suppini
Giovanni Suppini
Gennarino Tafuri
Adriano Tagliavini
Domenico Tassani
Marx Tassoni
Teresina Tattini
Giuseppina Tavoli

Adalgiso Tedeschi
Anna Tedeschi
Antonina Tedeschi
Antonina Tedeschi
Paolo Tedeschi
Romano Tedeschi
Zeno Tedeschi
Augusto Teglia
Emilia Teglia
Giuseppe Teglia
Massimo Teglia
Italina Testi
Laura Testi
Lucia Testi
Alfonso Tiviroli
Luigia Tiviroli
Anselmo Tomesani
Nino Tomesani
Asso Tommasi
Antonio Tondi
Giacomo Tondi
Giuseppe Tondi
Giuseppina Tondi
Marta Tondi
Norina Tondi
Paolina Tondi
Pia Tondi
Alberto Tonelli
Alfredo Tonelli
Antonio Tonelli
Argentina Tonelli
Augusto Tonelli
Benito Tonelli
Bruno Tonelli
Eleva Tonelli
Enrico Tonelli
Gino Tonelli
Giovanna Tonelli
Giuseppe Tonelli
Maria Tonelli
Mario Tonelli
Vittoria Tonelli
Dante Tonioli
Giuseppina Tonioli
Amelia Tossani
Fernando Tossani
Pietro Tugnoli
Orfeo Tunisi
Luciano Vaccari
Antonietta Valdiserra
Augusto Valdiserra
Gaetano Valdiserra
Girolamo Valdiserra
Mario Valdiserra
Giuseppe Valeriani
Luigi Valeriani
Luigia Valeriani
Dino Vannini
Lodovico Vannini
Primo Vannini
Vito Vannini
Riccardo Vecchi
Ezio Vedovelli
Filomena Vegetti
Imelde Vegetti
Loredano Vegetti
Zefferino Vegetti
Adelmo Ventura
Aldo Ventura
Alfonso Ventura
Amelia Ventura
Anna Ventura
Argia Ventura
Armando Ventura
Assunta Ventura
Augusto Ventura
Clara Ventura
Enrico Ventura

Ettore Ventura
Francesco Ventura
Gaetano Ventura
Giuseppe Ventura
Ida Ventura
Letizia Ventura
Linda Ventura
Livio Ventura
Maria Ventura
Mario Ventura
Nello Ventura
Primo Ventura
Raffaele Ventura
Talemo Ventura
Teresa Ventura
Ugo Ventura
Vittorina Ventura
Adelmo Venturi
Alfonso Venturi
Alfredo Venturi
Ardilio Venturi
Assunta Venturi
Bruno Venturi
Domenico Venturi
Enrico Venturi
Francesco Venturi
Gaetano Venturi
Giancarlo Venturi
Giuseppe Venturi
Guerino Venturi
Letizia Venturi
Liana Venturi
Livio Venturi
Luigi Venturi
Maria Venturi
Mario Venturi
Martino Venturi
Nella Venturi
Riccardo Venturi
Vilelma Venturi
Virginio Venturi
Vittorina Venturi
Silvio Verati
Ezio Veronesi
Pia Verucchi
Ada Vetri
Lodovico Vicinelli
Luigi Vignali
Giovanni Vignudelli
Clara Vignudini
Aldo Visinelli
Fortunato Vitali
Ugo Vitali
Igino Volta
Ines Volta
Renato Zaccaria
Alcidemio Zagnoni
Augusto Zagnoni
Gino Zagnoni
Rina Zagnoni
Romano Zagnoni
Silvano Zagnoni
Teresa Zagnoni
Francesco Zanardi
Teresa Zanardi
Oreste Zanetti
Giorgio Zanna
Irma Zanna
Raffaele Zanna
Tonino Zanni
Celso Zannini
Domenico Zannini
Flaminio Zannini
Giovanni Zannini
Rosa Zannini
Emilio Zannotti
Giacomo Zannotti
Gino Zanotti

Tullio Zanotti
Albertina Zappoli
Lodovico Zappoli
Carmela Zassi
Iole Zassi
Oile Zassi
Umberto Zassi
Angiolino Zazzaroni
Ersilia Zazzaroni
Bruna Zebri
Bruno Zebri
Mathilde Zebri
Carlo Zecchi
Silvano Zecchi
Angiolino Zini
Gino Zini
Giorgio Zini
Luigi Zini
Emma Zuarzi

Author's Note

This is the true story of the massacre of Monte Sole: the events leading up to the massacre, the three days of killing on September 29 and 30 and October 1, 1944, and the aftermath, all as reconstructed from the memories of the survivors and the records of the period. I would ask the reader to beware of jumping to easy conclusions. Even though it will often seem so, this is not a book about German evil and Italian innocence. This is a book about the effects of war. There are no heroes and no villains. So long as there are wars, there will be massacres like Monte Sole and corruptible human beings, of all races, willing to carry them out.

JACK OLSEN

Rollinsville, Colorado
March 1, 1968

Preface

IN the summer of 1967 the mayor of Marzabotto, Italy, sent a letter to several hundred citizens and former citizens of his commune. A German war criminal had appealed for a pardon from a life sentence for atrocities committed during World War II in the isolated area of Monte Sole, within the township confines of Marzabotto. Under a peculiarity of Italian law and custom, the prisoner, once a major in the SS, was ineligible for a pardon until the victims of his acts had granted him forgiveness. It was to these victims—the *superstiti* (survivors of the dead)—that the mayor wrote:

TOWNSHIP OF MARZABOTTO
Province of Bologna

July 12, 1967

We are pleased to tell you that on Sunday, July 16, 1967, at 9:30 A.M. in the theater Moderno in the town of Marzabotto there will be an open meeting of the Town Council in the presence of all surviving relatives of the fallen who will be able to choose whether to concede or deny the pardon requested by ex-Major Walter Reder.

I am sure that you will want to be present to express your opinion as one of those so cruelly hurt by the loss of those most dear to you. More than anyone else, you have the right to decide if Reder merits the requested pardon.

All surviving family members have the right to vote. They may be assured that they will be able to express their opinion freely and secretly in a polling booth.

Hoping to be able to meet you at Marzabotto, I wish to express to you my best regards.

THE MAYOR
Honorable Giovanni Bottonelli

P.S. We ask you also if you would be so kind as to inform other relatives, acquaintances and surviving family members of this letter. Thank you very much.

On July 16, a hot, muggy Sunday, 288 of the *superstiti* of Monte Sole—some assisted by others, one in a wheelchair—cast their ballots at the little movie theater Moderno. Two hundred and eighty-two voted against acquittal; 4 voted to forgive; 1 vote was nullified; 1 ballot was blank.

Several hundred survivors of the massacre did not show up at all.

It was the saying of Bion, that though the boys throw stones at frogs in sport, yet the frogs do not die in sport but in earnest.

—PLUTARCH

Prologue

FIFTEEN miles south of the ancient walled city of Bologna in central Italy, almost at the northern tip of the jagged Apennine range, there is a mountain called Sole (Sun), where the remnants of a culture older than the Bolognese, older even than the Roman, existed until modern times. Monte Sole is the highest tip of a rocky, sandy massif topped by small mountains that rise like bits of icing from a cake. Although there are lesser peaks like Caprara and Termine and Abelle, the 2,000-foot summit of Monte Sole is the central geographical fact of the region. Sheltered by the high saddles and valleys of these minor mountains, the region of Monte Sole became an early melting pot of civilization, starting with the Etruscans who thrived in a town called Misa at the eastern base of Monte Sole. The Etruscans stayed for centuries, until barbarians destroyed the lower portion of Misa and took up residence themselves in the upper part.

From the time of Christ until the extinction of the mountain civilization in World War II, Monte Sole and its surrounding valleys were washed over by successions of conquering races. Some left their own genetic and linguistic influences behind, and some contributed a few scattered families, who remained to farm the difficult land when the main forces moved away to battle somewhere else. There were the Celts, blond and fair and blue-eyed; the Romans, shorter and darker; the Langobards, another Germanic horde; and in modern times the French and Austrian troops, always on the march in northern and central Italy. The very language spoken on the mountain, the so-called Emilia dialect, or *dialetto bolognese,* was older than Italian and closer to French in sound.

The simple people who toiled on Monte Sole at the time of World War II knew nothing of their origins, linguistic or otherwise. They only knew that there were old patriarchs on the mountain who could not make themselves understood in anything but dialect and that when these elders of the community went off to other regions to buy cattle or seed, they would remark on a strange tongue they heard and could only partially understand. The strange tongue was Italian.

The land that the people of Monte Sole had spent centuries trying to beat into submission, with indifferent success, was a ragged patchwork of terrains, most of them inhospitable. There were chalky gray hills of marly sandstone and clay shales with ugly fissures cut into them by centuries of runoff, and slab-sided limestone canyons with walls that dropped hundreds of feet. There were tilted fields of corn and wheat and grapes, sinuous stands of willow alongside brooks, jungles of brush so thick that only the thinnest shafts of sunlight could penetrate. Mysterious unused paths shot straight up the mountain, going from nowhere to nowhere, reminders of the footfalls of previous tenants of the area. In watered places, thick thorny vines filled the interstices between acacia trees, whose trunks bore spikes an inch or two long and a half inch at the base. Another thorny tree—*spinacristo* (spine of Christ)—produced instant stigmata on the innocent person who reached out for support. And after one had pressed through the entanglements of brambles and raspberry bushes, thorn trees and nettles and other prickly specimens, one would come upon a majestic chestnut grove, the tasty seeds covering the floor of the forest and filling the air with a woody perfume. Everywhere there were ginestra bushes with thin green leaves like spinach noodles. In ancient times the natives had woven them into clothes, and now they were dried and used for broomstraws. Here and there a straight line of poplars would mark the limits of a field, while scrub oaks fought for a foothold outside the border. As one climbed higher, trees would give way to scrub, and scrub to a few hardy weeds, and weeds to lichens and mosses. Underneath it all there were big patches of the characteristic gray soil of the region—the natives called it *tufo* —showing through like the underweavings on a threadbare suit of plaid.

Nothing could disguise the fact that the soil was poor: part clay and part sediment and part sand and capable of producing crops only because of a propitious combination of rain and sunshine and the coolie labor of the farmers. A bare few inches of humus overlay most of the barren sandy clay, and sometimes the underground water pressure would build up a head and spurt out of the soil in a fountain, throwing up a load of gray sand in the shape of an ant hill. When this happened in a *contadino*'s field, he would have to rake the sand evenly over the soil and apply and reapply the nitrogens and the manures that kept him perpetually in debt to the owner.

Centuries of experimentation had shown the farmers where to plant, and there was no discernible pattern. In some places the mountain would be tilled to within a few hundred yards of the top, like a boy with a bowl haircut. Long sweeps of wilderness were juxtaposed with patches of cultivated land, as though a deranged giant had scalloped out swatches of growth with a huge straightedge razor. Vineyards grew in thin strips around the mountain and suddenly quit in a fierce tangle of underbrush. Wheat was planted in vague rhomboids and trapezoids, orchards in swirls and crescents and circles, vegetables in tiny square patches, wherever the long years of trial and error had shown that something would grow. And every *podere* was bordered by wild rosebushes, tall poplars covered with triple tiers of leafy parasites, and the larger oaks and beeches with truffles growing on their roots like fragrant bunions.

The people who lived in this chiaroscuro setting were inbred and insular, and the most obvious effect of their tight bloodlines was shortness of stature. For the most part, Italians are shorter than northern Europeans, and the so-called Alpine type of Italian is even shorter than other Italians, but the people of Monte Sole looked up to everyone. A mountain man of five feet six inches was reckoned tall. A woman of the same height would attract stares. Once, in a valley below Monte Sole, a man had grown to six feet, and he was discussed for generations. They referred to him in dialect as the *gigant'* and thought of him as a freak.

But aside from their Lilliputian characteristic, the people of Monte Sole were of no generally predictable physical type, perhaps because of the melting-pot nature of their history. A couple would have two or three children of light skin, blue-green eyes and straw-colored hair and then produce a baby who was brown-eyed, black-haired and olive. This swarthy type of Italian was rare on Monte Sole, but every now and then one would appear, for all the world like a Southerner, a reminder that the Romans had swarmed up the river valleys below Monte Sole 2,000 years before and left genetic calling cards behind.

If one were forced to describe the physical type of the region in a capsule phrase, one would have to say that the mountain people most resembled miniature Teutons. In other words, they were more often light-eyed, light-haired and light-skinned than they were dark-eyed, dark-haired and dark-skinned. Except for the matter of their stuntedness, they were not far removed from that "perfect" racial appearance that so impressed Hitler and other amateur anthropologists of the modern era, a fact which made their subsequent extermination at the hands of the Nazis all the more ironic.

The people of Monte Sole were peasants, and their dress reflected their poverty. The men wore lumpy old trousers that broke over the shoe top, battered work shoes or climbing boots, besplattered vests and narrow-brimmed hats with bands of work sweat around them, not much different from the hats of the Tyrol, except that nobody on Monte Sole would have thought to put a brush or a bird's feather in the brim of his hat. The common cause of these narrow-brimmed hats in both Tyrol and Apennines was wind. The hot wind, *il vento,* came up from the south, and the northern wind, *il bore,* blew from Trieste in the winter and knocked down haystacks with its force. Some of the mountain patriarchs wore black neck-to-ankle cloaks, without arms, but for most there were no special clothes to fend off the winds. A man would save for a suit, and he would wear the suit to church and on festive occasions. Five years later he would buy another suit, and the first one would be worn at work. Special outdoor clothes, like mackinaws and parkas and overcoats, were almost unknown. When the weather became cold, one wore one's ordinary clothes, but more of them.

The women, as befitted their recessive role in the agricultural society, dressed in drab blacks and grays, only rarely getting up the courage to put on a spot of color. Certain young women of the area, during the general intoxication of the war period, had begun to discover that bright colors attracted men, and they would go about in garish outfits like blue socks, yellow skirts, red blouses and purple scarves, considering themselves overwhelmingly attractive, but that was as far as their sense of style had developed. The older women looked down on these multihued creatures and clucked that it was the war; what could one expect? Slacks, however, were not tolerated, war or no war. A woman who appeared in slacks would have been stoned down the mountain. As for the children, the girls wore simple dresses, and the boys wore short pants, whatever the weather, and whenever possible, both sexes went about barefooted to save on shoes.

The wonder was that this region of clammy gray soil, whose random nutrients were forever being leached down the mountain by the heavy rains, was able to support human beings at all, and yet there they were, the farm families of Monte Sole, huddled in their stone houses with their thick stone walls, tiny windows, primitive wood-burning stoves, built-in stone sinks, stand-up outdoor toilets, religious pictures festooning every wall, niches with candles burning in front of statues of saints, and everywhere Christs on the Cross. The people of Monte Sole raised chickens, rabbits and pigs. Some of the better-off farmers had cows, which were used alternately as milk producers and beasts of burden. A few kept sheep, whose wool the resourceful housewives converted into clothes for all the members of the family. Everyone grew wheat, corn and grapes, and some had small orchards of plums and apples. Alongside every house there was a stone barn, often larger than the house, and next to the barn a stone oven strategically placed on top of the chicken house on the theory that contented chickens produced more eggs in wintertime. All around the outbuildings one could see basic watering troughs chipped from stone or hewn out of logs, beehouses for honey, primitive farm wagons with thick wooden wheels, huge demijohns and vats for the wine, stuffed dead rabbits hanging from the trees as scarecrows or bits of shiny tin snippings suspended in the orchards in such a fashion as to twirl in the breeze and scare the birds. Every house had a roof of "cooked earth," terra-cotta, and every roof was littered with heavy rocks to hold down the tiles in the high winds. The dominant color was the faded umber of the plaster that covered every wall of the region.

Communications hardly existed from house to house, even as late as World War II. There were no highways or county roads, only narrow mountain paths, and travel was by oxcart or on muleback, but mostly on foot. In the rainy seasons or times of deep snow there was no travel at all. Telephones were unknown, and electricity was available only far down the mountain, where wires could be strung in from valley conduits. Most of the mountain people illuminated their rooms by kerosene lamps or candles made of oxfat, and the privileged few, like the owner of the store at Caprara and some of the landowning farmers, had begun to install *gassometri,* carbide lamps that threw a bright light and impressed the neighbors.

Sharecropping had been the normal style of farming in the region for hundreds of years. In Bologna there were records that dated back to the thirteenth century of absentee *padroni* who came to Monte Sole only to collect their share of the crops. One man, the Count of Aria, had owned twenty-two large farms around the mountain. When the feudal holdings were broken up and the land was redistributed, certain *grandi agrari* remained, and so did the *contadini,* the lowest members of the social structure, the simple peasants who would always be working for someone else. Except for a few rare individuals, the farmers of Monte Sole were still sharecropping at the time the local civilization was wiped out in 1944. The big landowners, like the Marchese Beccadelli, who lived in a villa near the town of Casalecchio di Reno, would come out every week to ride horseback across their *poderi,* exactly like the feudal lords of history.

The system was heavily weighted against the *contadino.* Most often, he could neither read nor write, and the accounts were kept by the *padrone.* At the end of the year the *contadino* would usually find that he owed money. If he expressed any objection, he could be thrown off the land; there were always other sharecroppers who would be glad to take over the *podere* for 50 percent. In the extremely rare case that a contretemps reached the court, the *contadino* would find the matter resolved almost automatically against him, especially during the regime of the Fascists, who in large measure were supported by people of the landowning class. Nor could the *contadino* get much satisfaction from the church. The standard practice of the big *padroni* was to deed a portion of their acreage to the Curia, the legal arm of the Catholic church, which then would install a local priest who would hire sharecroppers and function as a *padrone* himself. There were wide variations in the workings of this system, depending on the human beings involved, but for the most part the only brake on the behavior of the *padrone* was the possibility that the *contadino* would starve and put him to the trouble of finding someone else. To avoid this inconvenience, the *padrone* turned his back on certain traditional petty frauds of the *contadino:* hogs that were raised in hidden pens back in the woods and slaughtered secretly; supernumerary chickens that roamed the fields unseen by the *padrone;* false walls that concealed bottles of uninventoried wine in the basements; dozens of other minor larcenies that barely kept the *contadino* alive but stripped him of a sense of decency and flung him back to the priest for forgiveness.

It was still possible for the *contadino,* trapped in this system, to live a comfortable life, but only with uncommon good luck—for no matter how skillfully he bred his animals and planted his land and managed his harvest and cheated here and there, he remained at the mercy of the weather, which could wipe him out in a single day. Hailstorms hung heavily over the *contadini* and made every new cloud a source of terror. The storms would come whipping over the mountain in selective, local gusts, wiping out one crop, sparing the field that flanked it, destroying a crop farther down the mountain, and then like as not doubling back to ravage a few undisturbed vineyards near the summit. By the early years of World War II the *contadini* were able to buy crop insurance, and this kept them from being wiped out even while it helped keep them permanently impoverished. The customary practice on Monte Sole was to insure half the crop, and if a destructive storm came, the farmer could recoup half his loss from the insurance company and borrow the value of the other half from the *padrone,* repaying over the subsequent five or ten years or until the next big storm came along.

In the spring and fall there were killing frosts, and in the winter snow, sometimes six feet of it. The farmer would dig tunnels from his house to his barn to his outdoor stove and sometimes to his neighbor's house for the succor of conversation and shared misery. Inside the large *casa colonica,* a wood fire would blaze in the hearth, and acrid smoke would fill the clammy rooms. There was no central heat, and the few windows could not be closed without shutting out the sunlight. In the coldest times of the year the families would sit together facing the fire, choking and coughing and cursing the cold. There was a popular saying, earthy like most of the mountain expressions, to the effect that during January and February you could spot an inhabitant of Monte Sole by his blistered face and frozen ass.

Under such conditions, it would not do for anyone to fall ill or suffer serious injury. There was only one doctor for the whole Monte Sole area, and he had to climb to the farmhouses on foot. When there was snow on the mountain or when it was too cold, he stayed home. Every year there were deaths in childbirth. If someone broke an arm, it was splinted by members of his family, and the broken bones were allowed to unite haphazardly. Most of the cripples who hobbled around the mountain were farmers who had injured their legs and been unable to reach the doctor below. There were excellent hospitals an hour's train ride away in Bologna, but few of the mountain people ever dreamed of going there. Bologna was China. If someone contracted a serious disease like pneumonia or tuberculosis, he went to bed and died; it was as final as that.

And yet with all the strains and tensions of this demanding mountain life, there was hardly any mental illness. "We have no time to lose our minds," the farmers would say, although each summer there were cases of temporary insanity from exposure to the sun, and every now and then a farmwife would take off screaming for the woods, sobbing hysterically. There were a few cases of imbecility, perhaps bearing some relationship to the inbreeding on the mountain or perhaps only to the law of averages, but these unfortunates were grappled closer to the family and given simple jobs like feeding the chickens and slopping the hogs to keep them busy. They were loved as children, and no one was ashamed of them. In all the memories of the people of Monte Sole, only one such person had ever been sent away, a deranged man who kept tolling the church bells in Sperticano, thus upsetting the villagers' daily timetable. Before the man was committed, his family and the parish priest had tried everything to solve the problem, but nothing short of confinement could keep him from climbing the bell tower and swinging on the ropes. The whole village went into mourning the day the *carabinieri* took the man away "to the institute."

The church had a strong hold on the women of Monte Sole, but less on the men. The *contadini* would go shamefacedly to confession, hoping to ward off the next hailstorm or frost, but when it came to the everyday ritual of the mass and vespers, they would either stay home or come in by the side door for a social session, which in the cases of the unmarried men consisted of ogling the girls in the pews. The average *contadino* was not unaware that the church of rural Italy was itself a partner to the injustices visited upon him, but he was too frightened to break completely away and too unschooled to have another theory of life. A man whose whole year's work and whole life's savings could vanish in ten minutes of hail was bound to be superstitious, jumpy and frightened of the unknown, and while many of the *contadini* turned their backs on the priest, hardly any were willing to go so far as to break with the church. Nor, for that matter, did they affront the *strega* (the witch); there was one practicing in every part of Monte Sole. Again, the *contadini* could see no contradiction in praying in the morning for a bountiful crop and visiting the *strega* in the afternoon for a session of incantation and spells and the evil eye. Their lives hung by invisible threads, and they dared not risk offending.

For all his nervous grovelings toward God and witch, the *contadino*'s higher allegiance was to his family. The first birth in a young farm family was a royal event, and every new birth was cause for celebration, for it strengthened the security of old age and the stability of the farm. Blood loyalties were intense and fanatic. Fathers and sons walked with their arms around each other's shoulders. Sisters went everywhere hand in hand. Grandparents were assigned the best rooms in the homes and treated with elaborate courtesy. The dead were not really dead; they were only "away," biding their time with Saint Peter till the whole family could be reunited. The mountain cemeteries swarmed with the living, paying respects. Fresh flowers were placed on the graves daily. Women in black shawls walked through the gates, knelt and crossed themselves, and spent hours with the dead, recalling their kindnesses, disavowing their cruelties, and praying God that their souls were in heaven where they certainly belonged. Candles in short red jars burned in front of the graves, symbolizing the presence of God. Tombstones were kept polished, and grass was weeded and manicured. Every ten years or so, the bodies would be disinterred, the bones carefully placed in small sealed boxes and reinterred in niches in the wall, thus readying the *camposanto* (the hallowed ground) for more beloved dead. Funerals were held at night, and when someone from San Martino was being laid to rest, mourners would come from Caprara and Cerpiano and Steccola and Sperticano and all the villages around the mountain to join in the procession. At such times there would be a sense of oneness, of concord, among the people of Monte Sole, each marching slowly toward the cemetery, carrying a candle and a portion of the grief. There was little else to share.

Worship of ancestors and devotion to family, so common throughout Italy, were economic facts of the mountain life. A man without a family might become a man without an income. He could have twenty acres to farm, but who would work the land with him? There was hardly any labor pool on Monte Sole; one's family was one's labor pool. Curious contradictions developed. A young man and his fiancée might be deeply in love, but there would be absolutely no chance of marriage until she became pregnant, and this in the face of an ultramoralistic mountain code that went back less than 100 years to a time when the region was governed by the papacy and a father could be jailed for allowing his children to take part in premarital sexual relations. These old codes were strong, but the need for children to work the farms was stronger. A *contadino* who married a barren woman would soon be out of the farming business, inexorably forced off the mountain along with the thousands of others through the centuries who had been exiled to places like America and Switzerland and England. Thus need became custom: marriage followed conception.

In this, as in most matters involving men and women, the mountain society ran at the convenience of the male. From the nursery to the grave, the male of Monte Sole was brought up on tales of his own importance, his own magnificence. This was why he could spend all day in the *osteria,* drinking wine and playing cards, and come home without apologies. A bachelor, in particular, could do no wrong. It was assumed that he was going to be a woman chaser, and who could deny him the privilege? Someday the whole *podere* would depend on him, and the rest of his life would be drudgery. Implicit in the mountain attitude toward the sexes was a harsh truth: if the mother of a family perished, the family tree might be cut off, at least until the husband could find another mate. But if the father perished, there would be no one to work the farm, and the family itself would perish. The family was *immediately* in the hands of the glorified male.

A young unmarried girl would reach maturity and suddenly find herself in a combat situation. The fortress between her legs had to be defended with utmost care, and if it fell, the blame was hers. The man had merely acted in the expected manner. As a result, the young mountain woman was clever, careful and sly, known throughout the region for her skill at manipulating the opposite sex. Another result was a peculiar dual standard inside the homes. On the one hand, there were the old moralities and taboos dating to the times when church law was official law and resulting in the most superstrict control by the parents, especially over their daughters. But on the other hand, there were engaged pairs making love to a fare-thee-well in the woods, enjoying themselves and only hoping that the girl would get pregnant.

After marriage, romantic love died fast in the rigorous life of the mountains. It was assumed that the bride had worked her wiles on the poor male; she had won, and she could look forward to a lifetime of economic security, thanks to the grand fellow she had tricked into matrimony. Now her role was to bear children and run the home. If the *podere* were a fallow one, like most of those on Monte Sole, the husband and wife would have to endure all sorts of hardships together, and a certain closeness, more like a comradeship, would develop. But if there was any time for frivolity or relaxation, it was spent by the male. He was the one who went off to drink *grappa* with the boys, got into the *boccie* game, hunted rabbits from dawn to dark. Gradually the wife would find herself becoming more of a useful object, a farm implement. The *contadini* would sit around the inn and tell derisive jokes about their wives. "A terrible thing happened to me. My wife and my cow got sick." "What happened?" "Oh, nothing to worry about. The cow is well now."

Just as in the rest of Italy, these rustic Neros could not bear the thought of being cuckolded, and the two-finger symbol of the goat's horns was the biggest insult. But there was a difference between being cuckolded and subtly offering one's wife to another. This custom dated to feudal times—and feudal times were only yesterday on the calendar of Monte Sole—when barons exercised the right of the first night and spent the wedding eve with the bride while the new husband died a thousand deaths in his lonely bed. No longer was this privilege extended as a matter of right or law to the important men of the community, nor was the custom retained on anything like a grand scale in the folkways of the mountains. But there were significant vestiges of the right of the first night. Certain *contadini* would permit their wives to carry on with influential people as a means of getting ahead. And there were some farmers who simply *had* to look the other way. They could not afford to deny their wives to surrogate "barons" like the *padrone* who might throw them off the land; the priest who dangled heaven or hell before them; the storekeeper whose credit kept them alive; and later on, the Fascist big shots and the German soldiers. It took a prosperous *contadino* to resist the pressure from the "barons" with the powers of life and death.

But whatever the hardships of the life on Monte Sole, everyone seemed to want to maintain the status quo. The roles were old and comfortable. The *padrone* had a steady income. The *contadino* was king of the home, undisputed ruler of a housekeeper and an ever-increasing supply of farmhands. The wife learned to fit into this big confidence game and felt at home in it. And as long as the people were locked into their traditions, the priest remained in a position of power. When a couple became engaged, the *reverendo* would waste little time counseling against adultery but would strongly urge them to get married so that he could regain control. The implied morality of the area, as passed along from mountain priest to mountain priest, was that sinning is permissible, but sinners must go to the priest to have the situation adjusted. Few of the *preti* added to the educational or cultural level of the region. On Monte Sole, most of them came from the peasantry; they had been brought up under the system and were in many cases just as ignorant as the *contadini* they were leading. They were like everybody else on the mountain; no halos were clamped automatically on their heads at the time of ordination, no guarantee provided that they would not convert church funds to their own uses, seduce the admiring women of the parish, and suppress and distort to keep themselves in a position of power. Some did, and some did not. Early in the game, the typical *contadino* learned not to place too much faith in the priest, though he might place considerable faith in what the *reverendo* represented.

The one allegiance that superseded family, church, government and even the farmer's own self-admiration was the allegiance to the soil: the lifeless gray soil of Monte Sole that was kept productive only by the most terrible of labors. The *contadini* thought of the soil as their personal property. They resented the Fascists who wanted a share; they resented the Germans who tried to build watchtowers and dig trenches; they resented any outsider who violated what they considered to be their main heritage. They placed their trust in the soil because no matter what the hail or the frost or the cold did to them, they could still go back to the soil and recover. It was no mere accident that "Il Lupo," the leader of the Monte Sole partisans, stressed over and over to his men that the soil was theirs and the Germans were trying to take it. "This is your soil; this is your land," Lupo said. "This is your soil; this is your land. . . ." It was enough. The soil was the only thing the *contadino* knew that could not be corrupted or swayed or bought. He knew who really owned this soil, and it was not the strangers whose names were written on titles recorded in the *municipio*. The true owner was the farmer who had worked the same plot from childhood; who had trudged through its snow and fallen to its heat; who had learned where the truffles were, and where the mushrooms burst forth each September, and where to plant the grapes and wheat, and what to feed the pigs, and when. The true owners of the land were the peasants who played *brescla* in their houses with a deck of forty cards, cooked grainy bread in their stone ovens, threw *boccie* balls into the sundown, lost children in childbirth, carried loved ones with broken limbs down the mountain paths to the doctor and back up again when the plaster set. The true owners of Monte Sole were the *contadini* who could trace their ancestors back 400 years to the same piece of land.

The eradicators of this culture in 1944 had convinced themselves that the Italians of the mountain called Sun were runts and traitors, cowardly members of a cowardly nation, inferior animals in every regard. But the truth was that they were people, neither superrace nor infrarace nor ever likely to develop into either. They loved their children and hated their enemies and offered prayers to a God they dimly understood. They laughed and cried and tried to live as painlessly as possible. And when they walked, they cast a shadow.

Life

ANYONE who traveled the worn, rutted mule paths crisscrossing Monte Sole would sooner or later run into a cheerful little man wearing a gray cap with a thin red stripe and a short patent-leather peak and a tinny badge emblazoned with the figure of a bugle and the letters *PT* (for post and telegraph) over the words "Kingdom of Italy" and carrying on his back a brown leather bag that exuded the fresh inky smell of new mail and the sharp heady smell of old cheese. Angelo Bertuzzi was only thirty years old in 1944, but he had been hauling the mail up Monte Sole for many years and he prided himself on knowing what there was to know and keeping his mouth shut about it. All that mattered to the *postino* was the companionship of his fellow human beings, every one of his fellow human beings. It was widely reported on the mountain that if Mussolini, Hitler, Stalin, Churchill and Roosevelt were to make a miraculous appearance in Luigi Massa's *tabacchi* near the top of the mountain and begin a game of *brescla,* Angelo Bertuzzi would be the first to come bounding in the door, shouting, "Deal me in!" It was simply impossible for the postman to hate anyone, and this included the partisans, who had tortured and executed a few of his friends, and the Germans, who had tortured and executed hundreds of others, and the Italian Fascists, who strutted around the valleys in their black shirts and their pompous manner giving orders to anyone in uniform, even if the uniform was only a cheap gray cap with a thin red stripe.

Whatever animus the postman had in his heart was reserved solely for the war. It seemed to him that all the true values of the mountain area were being strangled. The old-time festivals, the old traditions, even the old friendships—all were being put under too much tension. How long could it go on before Monte Sole would be just like any other place in Italy? Already tons of grapes were dying because the men were afraid to harvest. The corn had been cut, but no one hauled the stalks and cobs into the villages for the annual cornhusking party, when everybody got drunk on fountains of wine and somehow managed to finish the job. Who was going to harvest a single kernel when a Blackshirt patrol might come over the hill and send every man in sight to slave labor?

As he began his day in the valley town of Sperticano, the postman longed for the times when carrying the mail had seemed to him a pastime instead of a job, and every householder welcomed him as though he were a son who had been missing for months. At five A.M. he would get up and go into the kitchen of his small house for a hearty breakfast of a glass of wine and a raw egg. The postman knew that sucking a raw egg was regarded a luxury by some of the people up on the mountain, but for him it was a necessary start for the long day. By ten minutes to six he would be dressed and pedaling madly on his bicycle toward the county seat of Marzabotto, two miles up the road, where he would meet the train from Bologna and pick up the mail. There were four postmen in the district, but only Angelo Bertuzzi was entrusted with the responsibility of getting the mail off the train. Then he would cycle to the main post office in Marzabotto, help divide the mail and pedal back to Sperticano. If the people of Monte Sole did not wonder at the speed and energy of this carrier of their mails, they did wonder about his audacity on the bicycle. Going to and from Marzabotto, the postman had to cross a narrow wooden bridge strung from two cables over the rushing river Reno. The bridge was two feet wide and always slick with river spray and usually swaying gently in the wind, and no one had ever seen the postman whirl over the bridge at anything less than top speed, leaving a sine wave of clacking boards behind him. "Mark my words, *Postein*," the parish priest, Don Giovanni Fornasini, had said, calling Angelo by his local dialectical title, "you are going to take a bath someday, and the mail right along with you."

Each morning the postman would distribute the mail around his home village of Sperticano in the Reno Valley, dropping back to his house for a light luncheon snack and a rest. When the noon bells chimed at Don Giovanni's church 100 yards away, Angelo would kiss his wife and two daughters good-bye and begin the best part of his day. In his alpine shoes, he would head up the steep path to Monte Sole. At one time it had been his practice to go first to the lonely church at Casaglia, up on the shoulder of the mountain near Cerpiano, and on the following day go first to the church in the village of San Martino, a mile around the mountain from Casaglia. This practice of alternating between the two churches had begun in a peculiar manner. The postman did not like to break rules, and he was well aware that his official route map instructed him to go first every day to the church at San Martino, and that was exactly the route he had taken for years, until it had become a matter of community relations. A new young priest named Don Ferdinando Casagrande had taken up residence in the rectory at Casaglia, and the postman had found the new *reverendo* somewhat on the distant side. Each day, after delivering at San Martino at one P.M., Angelo would arrive with the mail at Casaglia at about three, hand it over to the priest and get a grunt in reply. *"Buon giorno,"* the postman would say hopefully, and the priest would answer by shutting the door.

But one day the new priest did not shut the door. "Tell me, *Postino*," he said, "why is it that you arrive with my mail every afternoon at three, and yet the mail gets to the church of San Martino two hours earlier?"

"Oh, well, *Reverendo*," the flustered postman said, "it is only because those are my instructions."

"As a result of your instructions, I get my newspaper two hours later than the other priests," Don Ferdinando said, and firmly shut the door.

The postman worried about this new problem, but rules were rules, and he could not find a solution. One day after the three P.M. delivery at Casaglia the new priest stuck his head out the window and said to the departing postman, "Who would it hurt if you brought me the mail first once in a while?" The postman hurried away, embarrassed because he had no answer.

The next day he dumped the problem square in the lap of the priest at San Martino, Don Ubaldo Marchioni. There was a rapport between the two men, partially because San Martino was well served by the postman and partially because Don Ubaldo's father had been a postman in a small town to the south. When the priest heard out the postman, he said, *"Postein*, I see you are trying to please everyone, as usual. Well, here is your solution. Today you bring the mail first to me, tomorrow you bring it first to Don Ferdinando, and you carry on in that way."

"But that is against my instructions, *Reverendo,*" the postman said.

"Yes, so it is," the young priest said, "but that is what you should do all the same."

From that day on the postman began the alternation, and by the time Don Ferdinando had been transferred to duties in the valley region of Gardeletta, he had even learned to thank the postman now and then, at least on days when he received the first delivery.

Angelo Bertuzzi could not put his finger on exactly what happened to him as he climbed the mountain each day with his sack of mail, but there always seemed to be an exhilaration in the air that lightened the load on his back. It was a one-hour walk without rest up the narrow ox path from Sperticano to San Martino, and the postman would find himself hurrying and not knowing why. Just before coming into San Martino, the road ran through a thick stand of chestnuts and oaks, and every day he would flush rabbits and grouse and hear larks and nightingales. Just out of the glade, as he came into sight of the house called Little Hill of San Martino, he would hear the first sound of geese and ducks in the village ahead and the barking of a big German shepherd with whom he had never been able to effect a truce. "What can I do?" the postman lamented to the dog's owner. "He sees me every day, and every day he tries to make a meal out of me, and every day I am only saved by his chain."

"Nient' a faire," the owner said in the regional dialect. "Nothing to do."

Carefully skirting the dog, the postman would press on until he reached the outskirts of the village, where the air would be rent by a familiar cry. *"Whay, Postein!"* an old man would call from the second-story window of his home. "Come in and have a little wine."

The ritual was daily and invariable. The old man, Gisetto, was the patriarch of a family of eight that lived in the big farmhouse. His family frowned on his heavy drinking, but gave him little else to do except feed the animals twice a day. Gisetto needed a social excuse to drink, and every day the postman provided one. While the postman sipped one glass of the black wine of the region, Gisetto would down four or five. Then he would slap the postman on the back and say in a crackly wine tenor, "What a nice visit we have had, *Postein*. When will I see you again?"

"Who knows?" the postman would say. "Maybe tomorrow?"

And so the amenities were observed. There were the inevitable doom criers in the area who warned the postman that it was not a good practice to lose time drinking with the old peasant Gisetto while the mailbag was still full. The people of the mountain liked to talk in proverbs. *"Chi va con lo zoppo impara a zoppicare,"* they would tell him as he strolled away from the old man's house with the fragrant aroma of black wine on his lips. "Whoever travels with a cripple soon learns to limp."

"Chi va piano, va sano e lontano, ma chi va forte, va incontro alla morte," the postman would say. "Whoever goes slowly goes healthy and far, but whoever goes fast goes toward death." And for good measure, he would add, *"Scarpe grosse, cervello fino,"* which meant: "Thick shoes, quick mind." In other words, the old Gisetto with his thick peasant soles was no mental cripple. The postman knew that underneath their mean trappings all the people on Monte Sole thought of themselves as brilliant thinkers descended from the Etruscans and the Romans and the Celts, so *"Scarpe grosse, cervello fino"* was not going to get him any argument.

After he left Gisetto's house, the postman would enter into the village of San Martino, which was really no village at all but a few farm buildings, a church with a tall, thin steeple, and a walled cemetery less than twenty yards square. Most of the fields around San Martino were owned by the Curia, and instead of splitting their crops 50-50 with the *padrone* like the other *contadini* of the area, the people who lived there split 50-50 with the church. Although this system was patently unfair to the farmers, it worked well on the San Martino farm for one reason: Don Ubaldo Marchioni. The young priest meticulously collected his church's share of the farm income and then just as meticulously handed most of it back to the *contadini*. To be sure, he lived in a pleasant enough rectory, where his immediate family also enjoyed free room and board, but this was a common practice of priests all over Italy. The vows of poverty did not preclude pulling one's family under the protective economic cloak of the church, and a priest who did not move his mother and father and sisters and brothers and a few uncles and aunts into the rectory would have been reckoned a fool. But in the case of the Marchioni family, living was frugal, and much of the church's 50 percent found its way back to the peasants. This was not true in every other parish. The postman had known of a nearby priest who was as hard on his *contadini* as the most vicious *padrone*. He would demand the last soldo of the church's share and would assess the tenant farmers 50 percent of all expenses no matter what they were. The *contadini* did not complain. They could see that their priest was living a simple enough life and assumed that the rest of their money was going to the Mother Church, where it would be used wisely. But when the old priest died, tens of thousands of lire were found hidden away in the rectory.

The postman knew nobody would ever accuse Don Ubaldo of stashing money away, just as no one had ever accused his predecessor, Don Antonio Cobianchi. There was barely enough to go around in San Martino, and a priest who insisted on his full 50 percent share of the crops soon would find himself being supported by a group of starved *contadini*. The village itself was a study in poverty: there were only a few stone barns and outbuildings and one three-story *casa colonica* where twenty-two members of the farm families lived at close quarters. The ground floor of the big farmhouse was given over to stalls; above that were kitchens, and on the top floor were bedrooms. The whole was made of fieldstone covered with a sickly brown stucco that was continually falling off, and the roof was of terra-cotta, the bright orange arcs of tile that cover half the roofs of Europe. In front of the *casa colonica* was a large open courtyard paved with cobblestones and serving as *boccie* court, meeting place and front yard. Down the road was the church, made of the same simple ingredients as the big house, but marked by a gracefully thin bell tower that overlooked hundreds of square miles of the Monte Sole area. The parishioners of the church of San Martino came from miles around, from little settlements with names like Le Scope (the brooms), Prunaro (plums), Il Palazzo (the palace) and Ca' dei Piedi (house at the foot), and since they were so scattered, the priests had installed a pair of oversize bells with a distinctive tone. No longer could anyone miss a mass and offer in excuse that he had not been alerted by the bells of San Martino.

The postman's first stop in San Martino was the church, where he would drop off the mail for the village, as well as Don Ubaldo's daily newspaper. To rest a bit and brighten his day, he would chat with the pleasant young priest. More often than not, Don Ubaldo would be waiting on the steps of the rectory, and sometimes he would even meet the postman on the path between San Martino and Gisetto's house, because he was always in a hurry for his mail. The two would chat about the latest news, and then the priest would go inside to study his paper. By now the news of the postman's arrival would have reached the children, and they would flock into the plaza for the *chicce,* little hard candies that he always carried in his pockets. "Go get them!" the postman would say, flinging a few of the candies into the bushes, and a mad scramble would ensue. Some days he would suggest a game of *mosca cieca,* like blindman's buff, with the winner hauling off a fistful of the candies. The trouble with *mosca cieca* was that there were so few places for the postman to hide, and the blindfolded children would find him too quickly. One day he arrived with pockets full of candy and a paper bag of *chicce* to boot, and announced that the winner of a game of *mosca cieca* would get the whole bag. When all the blindfolds were in place, he quietly climbed to the top of the big crucifix in the piazza. The crucifix was taller than the postman and six feet across at the top and made of thick timbers, and he knew he could sit up there forever and not be touched. Suddenly an angry voice upset the gaiety of the game. *"Whay, Postein!"* Don Ubaldo cried. "What kind of sacrilege is this?" The words gave the secret away, and soon the postman was looking down on a dozen blindfolded children screaming and shouting and jumping into the air like trout under a waterfall. "Here!" the postman said, and flung the bag to the farthest corner of the courtyard. He jumped from the crossbar, shouted "Excuse me, Father!" and raced off to the swift completion of his rounds.

Another day the postman was sitting on the steps of the rectory talking with Don Ubaldo when a boy of about five walked up and joined the discussion. "Well, well," said the priest, "it is our friend Agostino Lorenzini. Tell me, Agostino, is God in your heart today?"

"I have Him back home in my cart," the child answered.

"What?"

"God is back home in my cart."

The postman knew Don Ubaldo as a person of self-control and equanimity, but for a second it looked as though the young priest were going to explode right out of his cassock. He said in measured words, "Never let me hear you talk like that about God!"

Now it was the child's turn to look upset. "Did you not tell us yesterday—did you not tell us—"

"Tell you what?"

"That God was *everywhere?*"

"I am sorry, Agostino," the priest said. "I did not understand you." He turned to the postman. "Do you have any of those *chicce* you are always carrying around?" The postman produced a handful, and the priest gave them to the child and sent him off. When Agostino Lorenzini was out of earshot, Don Ubaldo said to the postman, "That child almost made a fool of the priest, eh, *Postein?*"

When he finished at the church, the postman would drop a few letters off at the various farmhouses, moving swiftly and quietly at the Calzolari house so as not to arouse the head of the family, who kept about sixty sheep. Lately Calzolari had been killing him with cheese, piece by piece. Whenever the postman would arrive, old Giovanni would shout, "Come in, come in, *Postein,* my wife and I have a piece of cheese for you." The postman realized that fresh cheese made from sheep's milk was a delicacy, but his taste buds did not agree, and every bite of the piquant strong cheese was an agony. As the summer went on and his trial by cheese continued, the postman tried two approaches: one was to slip up to the Calzolari house on tiptoe, drop the mail and rush away, and the other was to accept the gift, apologize that he had just got up from the lunch table and was stuffed to the ears, and deposit the sheep cheese in his mailbag with the promise that it would be enjoyed later. He did not know how long it would be before Calzolari would realize the truth. The postman worried about such things; he hated to hurt someone's feelings. Pride and children were all that the people of Monte Sole possessed. It was cruel to hurt either.

By the time he had finished with his deliveries around San Martino, the postman's climbing would be over. From then on all he had to do was follow the high ridge of Monte Sole, about 500 feet below the summit, delivering his mail en route. A mile or so around the narrow path on the shoulder of the mountain he would come to Caprara, the ancient seat of the ancient region of Monte Sole. It had been seventy years now since the authorities had wisely moved the county seat down to the busy valley town of Marzabotto, and all that was left of the lofty mountain village was a handful of weather-beaten houses and a store, the only commercial establishment in the whole mountain area. The residents divided the town into two places: Caprara di Sopra (Upper Caprara), and Caprara di Sotto (Lower Caprara), and the whole village, upper and lower and store and courtyards, occupied only a few acres, surrounded by infertile fields that the *contadini* worked on a 50-50 basis for absentee *padroni.*

Like the people of San Martino, indeed like all the people of Monte Sole, the Caprarans had nothing, but the postman never thought of them as poor. Their children would be running around the courtyard half-naked and barefooted, but they would be clean and fat and healthy. The villagers owned no bicycles or electric lights or iceboxes, and their financial reserves seldom exceeded a few lire, but they had bread, eggs, pork, chicken, wine, all they could use. In fact, they had so much to eat that they were always dropping delicacies into the postman's sack. There was a certain maiden lady named Clelia Rosa, daughter of a patriarch of the village, who made delicious *crescentina,* a pastry-and-ham delicacy that is baked between hot bricks. On those rare occasions when the lady Clelia was not at home, there would be a small package, still warm, sitting on the front porch. On it would be written in simple block letters POSTINO (the natives spoke in dialect but wrote in Italian).

In the fall, chestnuts abounded in the region, and the local women would grind them into flour and make sweet pastries. When the postman would arrive in the afternoon, there would always be a few women who had just pulled a trayful of the delicacies out of the oven and wanted him to sample them. When fall came, he would cut down on his lunch at home in Sperticano in case he would have to assist some of the housewives of the mountain with their samplings. "Just right!" he would always say, and there would be another batch for him the next day. His favorite, though he never divulged the fact to the other ladies of Caprara because he did not want to cause dissension, was a chestnut pastry called *mistocca* and made by the wife of Gaetano Venturi, a kindly lady in her forties who took a liking to the postman and did not want to see him go hungry.

It was also part of the postman's routine in Caprara to visit the house of a man called Lanzarini, who had a wondrous *cane da tartufo* (truffle dog) named Pronto. This wirehaired dog, white with brown spots, had been taught to pick up after Lanzarini, and although the dog sniffed out truffles for a living, he also would entertain for visitors to the Lanzarini kitchen. The master would hide his wallet and say, "Pronto, I cannot find my wallet," and the dog would run all around the room until he had sniffed out the missing article and carried it to his master. "Pronto!" Lanzarini would say. "Where are my slippers?" and within seconds the slippers would be deposited at his feet. The postman viewed all this as a circus in itself, a welcome divertissment on his route, and he would sometimes stay for fifteen or twenty minutes watching Pronto's act.

Then the postman would leave the village of Caprara, his stomach full and his need for entertainment satisfied and his mailbag as heavy as ever, and continue around the mountain, coming first to Poggio di Casaglia, where the family Laffi lived, and finally to Casaglia itself, which was not a village at all but a large mountain church combined with a comfortable rectory and a small piazza. The view from the church at Casaglia, especially if one took the trouble to climb the bell tower, was spectacular. It seemed to the postman that if just one faraway mountain were removed, you could see to Florence, fifty miles along the valley. He always stopped to rest his back and enjoy the scenery at the mountain church.

Lately, since Don Ferdinando Casagrande had been transferred to a valley parish below and another priest had died, there was no *reverendo* living at the lonely mountain church, but sometimes the conscientious Don Ubaldo would walk the mile from San Martino to say mass for the families who lived within walking distance of Casaglia. The only permanent resident of the old mountain church was a wizened little lady named Artimesia Gatti, who lived in a hut next to the rectory. For as long as anybody could remember, Artimesia and her husband had tended to the church. The old man had dug graves at the walled cemetery a few hundred yards down the road, but since his death, Artimesia had not been up to the task of gravedigging. She kept busy with certain other of her husband's chores, like ringing the bells for mass or vespers and again at high noon, and keeping the church and the rectory spotlessly clean. Although she was well past seventy, the old lady was a special favorite of the postman. She was so bent by old age that it was easy to mistake her for a hunchback, and walking around in that tortured shape, she did not clear the floor by much more than a yard, and yet she was as brisk and cheerful and active as a thirty-year-old. The postman would arrive in the afternoon and shout, "*Whay,* Artimesia!" The little old lady would be weeding her vegetable garden, or beating the nap off one of the rectory rugs, or enthusiastically performing some other chore, but when she heard the postman, Artimesia would drop everything and shout, *"Whay, Postein,* come in and suck an egg!" This was the ultimate in mountain hospitality, a nice fresh egg with a small hole punched in one end of it, and it was not offered to everyone. Of course, there would be times when Artimesia's few chickens would fall down on the job, and the postman would have to settle for a small piece of cheese. But there were also times, on feast days or on one of Artimesia's many anniversaries, when the postman would be served an egg whipped up in black wine: a mountain zabaglione. Carried away by the generosity of the old lady, the postman would say, "Artimesia, I swear you should find yourself another husband."

"Who would have me?" the old lady would say.

"Anybody who tasted this zabaglione!" the postman would say, and both of them would cry out with laughter. When he took his leave, the postman would circumspectly drop a few soldi on the dresser. Everyone knew that the old lady Gatti had no income, none at all. When there had been a permanent priest at Casaglia, she and her husband had been considered part of the family in residence and provided with a small income from church funds, but now that there was no permanent priest, she had only a few fruit trees, her vegetable patch and some chickens. She lived on the kindness of people like the postman.

After his pleasant visit with old Artimesia, the young postman would have finished his daily rounds. But it happened that the store at Caprara lay directly on the route home, and who was to blame him if he stopped in to rest his weary feet and perhaps slake his parched throat with a glass of the proprietor's *negrettino* wine? The *tabacchi* at Caprara bulked large in the life of the postman, as it did in the lives of almost all the men of the region. The local society was a patriarchy, although no one ever would have thought to put the matter in such terms. The wife was a worker, and the children, although they might be deeply loved, were assistants who would help run the farm and later provide for the patriarch's old age. They did not necessarily have to be played with, and wives did not necessarily have to be entertained. And so it was that every afternoon, when the sun dropped down behind Monte Sole, the *tabacchi* at Caprara would begin to fill with men. A lively game of *brescla* or *tresette* would be going on at one of the roughhewn tables, and a knot of men standing at the bar arguing the latest stupidities of the local government, and a few more men standing just outside playing *morra*, the uniquely Italian game in which fingers are thrown and numbers are shouted and tempers are lost. The *morra* players were always to be found outside the *tabacchi* because the proprietor would not permit them to play inside anymore. Since 1936, *morra* had been banned by the Fascists, because it aroused such rage that potential party members were being murdered in *morra* arguments. This national law did not prevent the men of Monte Sole from playing the game, but it made the proprietor force them out.

The postman had been in the habit of stopping at the *tabacchi* ever since he first took over the mountain postal route. As a man who placed companionship at the top of all virtues, he could hardly wait for the sun to go down and the crowd to assemble and wine to be drunk and jokes cracked and stimulating conversations begun. In the beginning, an old man named Amerildo Amaroli had owned the store, and the postman had developed a sort of unstable friendship with him. The proprietor, well into his eighties, would get angry when the postman showed up with no mail. "What do you mean, no mail?" the old man would shout. "I *always* get mail. I am Amaroli, first name Amerildo. Please check in your bag once again." The postman would go through the motions of checking, although he himself had sorted the mail in the early morning and knew there was nothing for old Amaroli.

"No, nothing," the postman would say, and Amaroli would accuse him of stealing the mail, losing it on the way, selling it to his enemies or just plain refusing to hand it over.

The only thing worse than showing up at the *tabacchi* without mail was showing up with mail. The old man, like many of the people on the mountain, could not read, and the postman would have to open each letter and read it aloud. If Amaroli took a special liking to a certain letter, he would ask the postman to read it two or even three times, and the next day he might ask the postman to read it again. One day the postman arrived with a single letter, but he felt like teasing the old man, and so he groped around in his brown leather bag and finally said, "No, nothing today, bearded one."

"What do you mean, 'nothing today'? Look again!"

"There is no use looking again. You are eighty years old. Who would write to you?"

Amaroli went red. "Who would write to me?" he shouted. "Well, let me tell you something. My name is Amaroli, Amerildo, and I am not used up yet!"

The postman pulled out the old man's single letter and slit it open and began reading. As he went from line to line, it was difficult to figure who was more surprised, the reader or the listener. The letter was from a seventy-year-old woman named Teresa Zenotti who was making it unmistakably clear that she admired the old man deeply. When the postman finished reading the letter, Amaroli did not ask him to read it again. "How did you meet this lady?" the postman asked.

"I knew her when I was a young man like you," Amaroli said embarrassedly. "I have not seen her for years."

The letters from Teresa Zenotti kept on coming, and soon they were arriving at the rate of about one a week, and to the postman's profound annoyance the old man decided one day to start answering. The postman would have to unshoulder his mailbag and laboriously compose long, affectionate letters to the lady in the valley. This went on for two years, until the letters had become so frequent and so lengthy that the postman had had enough. "No more!" he said to Amaroli as he completed a letter one day. "That is the last one I am writing, bearded one!"

"No," the old man said. "Write one more, *Postein.* Write that I want to marry her."

The wedding of the eighty-five-year-old man and the seventy-five-year-old woman was in the church of San Martino, and there were forty-four guests, and the postman sat in the first pew. The celebration went on all night, with everybody returning to the inn at Caprara and drinking up all the old man's wine and spirits. The next morning, as the postman wobbled up the mountain with his fresh load of mail, he passed the prostrate forms of several members of the wedding, sleeping among the weeds.

Not long afterward, old man Amaroli died, and the store's license was sold to a *contadino* of the area named Luigi Massa. For a while things were dead around the *tabacchi,* and indeed they never again reached the tumultuous heights of the night of the wedding, but little by little the social life of the store revived. There were, in fact, a few men who had taken the transfer of the store's ownership in stride, hardly missing a drink or a game of *brescla.* The leader of this nucleus of faithful customers was a man named Gaetano Rosa, who at the age of seventy was still regarded as the strongest man on the mountain. Gaetano was tall by the local standards, towering almost 10 inches over 5 feet, and he weighed more than 100 kilograms, or 220 pounds, much of it in a large paunch that stuck out from under the vest he always wore. As old Gaetano was fond of proving, the paunch did not yield when one touched it. Gaetano had black eyes and a black beard and a low, rumbling voice that some said had been produced by the progressive pickling of his vocal cords by the liters of *negrettino* he drank daily. The old man would arrive at the store shortly after breakfast and take up residence at a table in the corner. The first customer into the store would be expected to sit down and play him a game of *brescla* for a glass of wine. So would every other male customer of the day, including the postman. Gaetano Rosa invariably won these games, because not only was he the most experienced *brescla* player in the region, but he was also the one with the most card sense. So drunk that he could barely talk, with his nose bobbing down around table level, the old man could remember every card that had been played, and woe betide the opponent who took him lightly.

Sometimes, when there was no action, Gaetano would put his head in his arms and nap at the table. At lunchtime and dinnertime, he would remain in his chair and his wife or his daughter, Clelia, the same Clelia Rosa who provided the postman with delicious *crescentine,* would arrive bearing his food. Gaetano would eat, expel a small amount of gas and challenge somebody to a game of *brescla.* Thus he had been living out his years, but one day his relatives held a council of war and decided that the old man and his ailing wife were getting too far along in years to remain high in the mountains at Caprara caring for themselves. While the patriarch was enjoying himself as usual in the *tabacchi,* the family decided that it was time for Gaetano and his wife, Enrica Quercia, and his daughter, Clelia, to move down into the valley to the home of a foster son, the industrious Mario Zebri, who farmed a pleasant patch of land in a place called Colulla di Sopra (Upper Colulla), not far from the postman's home village of Sperticano. The plan made sense to everybody but Gaetano, who roared like a stuck ox when he heard the news. He announced that for thirty-seven years he had been the most respected farmer of Caprara, the *contadino* most trusted by the Marchese Beccadelli, owner of all the land in sight. Was it not true that the *marchese* chose Gaetano to go to the auctions and select animals not only for his own *podere* but for all the farms of Caprara? How would this land get along without him? What would the *marchese* say?

His family told Gaetano gently that the *marchese* already knew and approved of the plan, that the old man had worked long and hard and now deserved a rest in the home of his loving foster son down the mountain, and that he was no longer strong enough to farm a plot of land that was hopelessly worn out anyway. Gaetano said they would see about that. Everyone in the *tabacchi* speculated about what would happen. "He will not go," the postman said simply.

Piece by piece the family's few possessions were taken to Colulla by oxcart, while Gaetano sat in the *tabacchi* ignoring the goings-on. One night when the store shut down at eleven, Gaetano's usual time of departure, he lurched home to find that the family had moved and there was no bed for him. Gaetano slept on the floor and arrived at the *tabacchi* bright and early the next morning. He took his seat in the corner and remained there for ten more days and nights, playing *brescla* and drinking wine, while his relatives visited him in relays and begged him to come down to the new home. Finally, the family enlisted the help of the postman and the other habitués of the *tabacchi,* and they all agreed not to talk to the old man, for his own good. Gaetano endured the ostracism for another day and then without a word walked out of the *tabacchi* and descended to his new home. He ate one meal, wandered into the nearby village of Sperticano, shook hands with the proprietor of the local *tabacchi,* and asked if anyone would care to play him a game of *brescla.*

From then on, Gaetano Rosa was never seen in the inn at Caprara. He would putter around his foster son's farm in the mornings, giving advice and playing with his grandchildren. The children represented a new ingredient in his life; he had seldom seen them when he lived high above, and now he was seldom seen without them. His granddaughter Bruna, a child of six, was his favorite, and he used to say to her, "Help me into the barn, Bruna, because I am old and fat, and when I die, I will leave you my wallet." The little girl would lend a hand and say, *"Nonno, Nonno,* when are you going to die so I can get your wallet?" And the old man would feign righteous anger. Every day when the church bells at Sperticano would ring for high noon, Gaetano would say, "Well, I think I will go down to the *osteria* to get something to smoke," and no one would see him again until late at night, when the inn closed.

Even though the postman occasionally ran into Gaetano on his rounds in Sperticano, he missed the old man at the store in Caprara. The patriarch's traditional seat in the corner now went unoccupied most of the time. The new owner of the *tabacchi* was nervous about permitting card games on the premises and for a time had even cut off the hard liquor, until the postman made an arrangement with the *carabinieri*. There was wine available for consumption on the premises, but even though the postman was inclined to think the best of everyone, he could have sworn it was watered. And there were days when he was denied even the modest comfort of this inferior product. More and more often now, as the war months of 1944 went by, he would arrive at the *tabacchi* after his long day of exertion and find it closed. On such occasions, he would make the long walk back down the mountain shaking his head with annoyance. It was the war. If it did not end soon, Monte Sole would lose the last bit of character it had ever had.

The war nettled and annoyed the postman like the thorns of a certain bush that would settle in the skin and take up itchy residence for days that seemed like decades. A whole year before, word had come into the region that Italy had signed a peace with the Allies. The Italian soldiers were coming home. The Germans would leave, and the mountain could go back to its normal ways. There would be plenty of salt and sugar, no more blackouts, no more bombing raids, no more black-shirted Fascists and German patrols climbing into the mountain villages pushing people around. It was September 8, 1943, when word of the surrender was flashed throughout Italy, and the postman had never encountered anything like the scene that followed. You could stand in the valley below and trace the path of the news as it went by word of mouth from farmhouse to farmhouse. Each *contadino* ran out and lit a haystack as soon as he got the word. People rushed from their houses to dance and drink wine in the village squares, saving just enough strength to fall into the churches for prayers of thanksgiving in the evening.

Day followed day as the people of the mountain waited for the benefits of peacetime to wash over them. Nothing happened. All that had been in short supply remained in short supply. Blackshirts and

Germans resumed their pressure on the people, demanding their share of everything right down to the hindquarter of the smallest slaughtered lamb. A few soldiers of the mountain returned home, but they told stories of German troops encircling their units and placing them under arrest, and they warned the people that a true peace was a long way off. And sure enough, within a few weeks the radio was explaining everything. Italy had surrendered to the Allies, who were now landing in force far down the boot, but all the rest of Italy was in the hands of the Germans. Their former allies were now their captors, and the distinction was not long lost on the people of the mountains. The Blackshirts and Germans became worse than ever. In the past, they had treated the people of the region as comrades, albeit stupid and useless ones. Now they treated them with the disdain reserved for quitters, and soon the simplest of the mountain people, those to whom Fascism and capitalism and Communism had been only meaningless words, learned to hate the Germans and the Fascists. Despite official interdictions, there was another big celebration on the mountain on the first anniversary of the surrender. While German and Fascist patrols rushed from village to village to bully the celebrants, the mountain people lit big fires and danced in the squares. The fastest runners in each village would dart across the paths to warn others of the imminent arrival of the patrols, and as the soldiers appeared at each place, they would find only silence.

The postman did not take part. He was one of those on the mountain who still stood for peace at any price. He did not like to offend or annoy, and besides, he had not yet made up his mind about the Allied cause, as represented locally by the partisans. For many months it seemed to the postman that it was difficult to choose between the atrocities of the Germans and the atrocities of the Italian partisans. And the partisans kept him in continual hot water with the Fascist authorities. The postman, as an employee of the kingdom of Italy, carried a Fascist *tessera,* but this did not make him a Fascist. The high muckamucks of the local Fascist organizations did not seem to understand this, and they kept pressuring him to turn informer and tell them all he could about the partisans on the mountain he visited daily. At first, the postman would say that he knew nothing, which was more or less true, because the early partisan bands were small and frightened and stayed hidden in the deepest woods. But as the months went by, the ranks of the partisan brigade of Monte Sole swelled with returning Italian soldiers, deserting Mongols whose units had been drafted intact into the German Army, escaped Allied prisoners of war and certain anti-Fascist members of the *carabinieri,* as well as all young men of the area who did not want to be drafted into Mussolini's New Army or sent off to German labor camps. By the springtime of 1944 the partisan brigade had become a force for the postman, not to mention the Germans, to reckon with. It was no longer true that he knew nothing about them. He would see their leader, Mario Musolesi, nicknamed Lupo (Wolf) at command posts all around Monte Sole, but most frequently in the village of San Martino, where Don Ubaldo had become a sort of chaplain to the brigade. The postman knew where the partisan encampments were; he knew when they moved out to hide on adjoining mountains; he even knew some of their battle plans. If he did not see the partisans himself, he heard about their activity from his good friends, who were their close kin. And still he would tell the Fascist plenipotentiaries that he knew nothing and, by dint of this tedious repetition, seem to satisfy them.

Nevertheless, the postman was not accepted by the partisans. They looked on him as a lackey of the Fascists, and more than once he was told that he was under partisan surveillance and would be wise to keep his mouth shut. The postman did not need these suggestions, having kept his mouth closed for years as a way of life, and the situation became uncomfortable for him. He was watched with suspicion by the partisans on the mountain and the Fascists in the valley below. He feared for his wife and his two children and started each day's deliveries nervously. The postman knew well what the Fascists would do if they found he was holding out on them. Firing squads had been busy up and down the valley of the Reno ever since the Italians had changed from Allies to captives. The postman also knew what the partisans would do if he were caught giving information to the local Fascio. He remembered Dante Simoncini, a harmless rent agent of Termine, just south of Monte Sole, who had offended the partisans insignificantly—some said his only offense was ordering his teen-age daughter to stay away from a partisan gathering—and was buried to his shoulders in a cornfield and kicked like a soccer ball until his head tore loose from his body.

One day the partisans raided a *carabinieri* headquarters and killed a sergeant. The next day, as the postman trudged into San Martino, he found Lupo waiting for him. "Come here!" the Wolf said in a voice accustomed to command. "I have been talking to some of my friends in the village, and I am told that you knew about our raid before it began. Is that true?"

The postman could not stammer a single word.

"Never mind!" Lupo went on. "I *know* it is true. So you are a Fascist, and you carry a *tessera,* and still you keep our secrets?"

"I do not talk," the postman blurted out. "I do not talk about you. I do not talk about them." He pointed down to the valley.

"See that you keep it that way," Lupo said, and turned away.

From that day on the postman sensed a lessening tension. Slowly the partisans began to kid him about his *tessera,* or party card, and allow him to kid them back in his mild way. One day he was just leaving the deep woods by the house called Little Hill of San Martino when two men in German uniforms, their helmets pulled down to their eyes, jumped out and leveled their rifles at him. *"Su! Su!"* they said, and the postman raised his hands as high as he could. The Germans ordered him to march toward San Martino, and when the postman tried to object, they shouted *"Su! Su!"* again and waved their rifles menacingly. "Merciful mother, now it will happen," the postman said to himself as they passed the house and came close to San Martino. "If the Germans do not shoot me, the three of us will be killed when we get there." Several times he tried to tell his captors in sign language that San Martino was crawling with partisans, that they would all go down in a fusillade of bullets the instant they set foot in the village, but the Germans shoved him ahead with their rifle butts. Now they came to the fork in the road that marked the limits of San Martino, and to his horror the postman saw Lupo himself relaxing in the churchyard. The Germans and their prisoner marched straight toward the partisan leader, and one of the Germans counted cadence at the top of his voice. *"Eins! Zwei! Drei! Vier!"* The postman winced and waited for the first volley to cut him down, and then he saw that Lupo was laughing. A few other partisans came from around the church and joined in the laughter, slapping each other on the back, and pointing at the postman. When they had had their joke, Lupo said, "Look at the eyes of these Germans!"

The postman took a close look at the smiling faces of his guards, and for the first time he noticed that they had slanted eyes. "Merciful Mother," Lupo said, "did you ever hear of a German with slanted eyes? See how fine Caraton looks in his old German uniform." The postman had heard of Caraton, a Mongol officer who had deserted the Germans, and he blurted out that he was happy to make Caraton's acquaintance.

Lupo's little joke served to improve the relations between the postman and the partisans, and the pressures on the troubled mail carrier fell away, only to resume with the threatening letters. One day Lupo handed a letter to the postman and said, "Here, see that this gets to Mingardi." Lorenzo Mingardi was the secretary of the local Fascio and the most important Blackshirt in the area, and the postman dropped the note in Mingardi's mailbox before returning home that evening. The next day he was called to the *carabinieri* barracks to confront three angry Fascists: an official of the local *carabinieri,* a Fascist cop from Bologna, and Mingardi. "Where did you get this?" Mingardi said, handing Lupo's letter to the postman. The postman read the short message quickly. It said, "Improve your behavior, or we will take your head off."

"It must have been in one of the outgoing boxes on the mountain," the postman said.

"And so it went through the regular post?" the Bolognese Fascist asked.

"It must have," the postman said.

"Then why does it have no stamp?" Mingardi asked.

The postman thought fast. If the letter had been picked up in a mailbox on Monte Sole, it would have been taken to the post office at Marzabotto, canceled and then delivered. The fact that it bore neither stamp nor cancellation proved that the letter had been hand-delivered. How stupid he had been carrying the letter to Mingardi's house without thinking of the results! But how lucky he had been that he had not handed the letter to Mingardi personally! Now he had an out.

"Let me see the letter again," the postman said. He scrutinized it with mock intensity. "Hmmmmm, it has no stamp and no cancellation. It must have been carried to your mailbox by somebody else."

"Not by you?" Mingardi said.

"Certainly not by me," the postman said. "I only deliver mail that has been properly processed."

The interrogation went on for an hour. At one point the Fascist cop threatened to have the postman killed if he continued to refuse to tell the truth about the partisans. "You will have to go ahead and kill me," the postman said, his knees shaking. "I know nothing. I am only the postman of the mountain. Do not expect miracles of me." At the same time he was terrified that they would begin torturing him, and he would tell what he knew about the partisans, and then he would be killed the first time he went back up the mountain. It would have been a terrible squeeze for the bravest of men, and the postman did not delude himself: it was doubtful that he was the bravest of men. Finally, he was told that he was being given one more chance, that he was being freed on condition that he try to pick up some information on the partisans from his good friends on Monte Sole. "I will tell you all I hear," the postman said, "just as I always have. And if I am lying, you can take this away from me!" He held out his *tessera.*

The next morning the postman bought a sheet of violet 50-*centesimi* stamps, and from then on, whenever Lupo or the other partisans would give him notes for the Fascists in the valley, he would seal them in envelopes and apply one of his own stamps. To questions about the origins of the threatening letters, he could always say, "I got them in the box." Thus the postman walked the narrow bridge between two seething volcanoes, offending each as little as possible and not becoming committed.

One day late in September, 1944, he pedaled into Marzabotto to pick up the mail and found the little post office buzzing. "The Germans are going to make a reprisal raid on the partisans," one of the clerks said.

"What does that have to do with us?" the postman said.

"It is said they are going to take hostages, and that no man will be safe. We have decided not to deliver today."

The postman rode home, passing German convoys on the way, and in Sperticano he quickly learned that the local Fascists had disappeared during the night. No one knew exactly what was in the air, but all the men had decided to hide in the woods. It was men the Germans would be after. The women and children would be safe enough. The postman kissed his wife and daughters good-bye and put on his gray cap with the red stripe. One never knew when official business might come up.

When he first took over the mountain *tabacchi* after the death of old Amaroli, the *contadino* Luigi Massa found himself in practically continuous debate with the postman and his cronies. Although one of Luigi's five brothers was a storekeeper in Monzuno, across the Setta Valley and up the next mountain, this was Luigi's first adventure in the world of commerce, and he wanted to make his way slowly. He knew exactly what the store at Caprara had been in the past: a tobacco shop, drugstore, dry goods store, hardware store and tavern, all compressed into a small stone building high on the shoulder of Monte Sole. The trouble was that no matter how often he looked at his license, it still said the same: as the licensee of an official *sale e tabacchi,* Luigi was authorized to put up the big black sign with the royal crest and the Fascist symbol and sell only the nationalized monopoly goods of Italy: stamps, tobacco, matches, salt and quinine. This had been explained to him very clearly when he picked up his license in the valley town of Vergato. If he wanted to branch out and sell a few extra items like pots and pans, flour, lard and cloth, the state would look the other way, but the sale of wine or spirits was absolutely forbidden. So were serving drinks and playing cards.

"Old man Amaroli let us play cards," the postman said when Luigi announced that the nonstop *brescla* game was over.

"Old man Amaroli always kept a bottle of *grappa* or *crema cacao* or *sassolino* for us," the postman said when Luigi announced that hard liquor was out.

"Old man Amaroli let us play *morra* inside," the postman said when Luigi announced that he wanted the volatile game conducted on property other than his own.

The new proprietor took all this in his customary docile manner, but one day he came to his limit of patience. "Listen," he said, "I am not old man Amaroli. Take a good look at me. Do you see Amaroli, or do you see Massa?"

"We see Massa," the postman answered with a long face.

"Suppose you were up here playing *brescla* and drinking wine and the *carabinieri* arrested you," Luigi went on. "How would you like that?"

"If you do not serve the wine and let us relax a little at your tables," the postman said, "there will be nobody here for the *carabinieri* to arrest!"

The heart of the problem was that Luigi Massa was not cut out to be a storekeeper. All his life he had worked the land, and his attitudes were those of a *contadino*. No matter how much trouble the old-time storekeepers like Amaroli took to show the peasants that they were regular fellows, there was a deep chasm between the storekeeper class and the *contadino* class. The storekeeper was a member in good standing of the economic group that lived off the sweat and hardship of the farmers. To be a successful proprietor, one had to be able to make two and two equal five, turn ten liters of wine into eleven, and compute interest on a semiweekly basis.

Luigi was a gentle man in his forties, married with grown daughters, and he understood none of these techniques for growing rich in the midst of poverty. Because he did not comprehend the sweet uses of credit, Luigi abolished it. Instead of keeping endless accounts, he would make deals. A *contadino* would come in to buy some *pasta,* and Luigi would take a basket of eggs in exchange. Later he would exchange the eggs for a half bladder of lard, and the half bladder of lard a few days later for a stack of cut wood. He always kept hoping that someone would break into the chain with cash. But cash was in short supply on the mountain, and more often Luigi would wind up with vast overstocks of items like *prosciutti* and cheese, which he would have to take down to the valley to sell at wholesale prices. Now and then he would find himself the owner of two or three piglets, which he would feed and slaughter in the fall. To avoid giving credit, he would talk for hours arranging his deals, and one could never tell what was going to wind up in the *tabacchi.* "What good is a wagonful of broomstraws?" Luigi's wife would ask, and he would answer, "More good than a ledgerful of scribblings!" In the extreme cases where the customer had nothing whatever to offer in exchange, Luigi would fill his order and send him out to do chores around the *tabacchi.*

The alcoholic beverage problem was not so easily solved as the credit problem, but it was not long before things sorted themselves out in traditional Italian style. In the beginning, the pressure on Luigi had been so intense that he caved in quickly on the matter of the wine, which had been sold at the mountain store for as long as anybody could remember. "There are certain things you are going to have to sell unless you want to go out of business in your first week," the postman had warned him, "and the first three are black wine, red wine and white wine."

Luigi bought a stock of wine—normal, average, everyday wine, the black *negrettino* and the red *barbera* and the white *albano* of the region—and put it up for sale at high prices, hoping thus to dissuade the wine drinkers, who promptly screamed bloody murder. "Not only is this wine priced like champagne," the postman exploded, "but it is watered!" Luigi knew that his wine was not watered, but he also knew that it was not the best wine one could find in the region. Let them complain; soon he would be able to go out of the wine business. Everything was going according to plan until one night when his wife came running to the back, where Luigi was feeding the hogs, and said, "Come quickly!"

Just outside the door of the *tabacchi* Luigi could make out the figures of the postman and several of the *contadini* passing around a bottle of wine, playing *brescla* and having a loud enjoyable time.

"Good evening, Gigi," they called when he opened the door.

"What are you doing in front of my store?" Massa asked.

"We are enjoying ourselves outside just as we used to enjoy ourselves inside," the postman said.

"Where did you get that wine?"

"In the valley, and at a fair price, too. Here, have a sip!"

Luigi spurned the offer. "Well, you will have to play somewhere else," he said.

"Why?" the postman asked. "When you took over the *tabacchi,* did you take over the courtyard, too?"

Luigi slammed the door, and the battle was joined. For several nights he could hear the happy sounds outside the door of his store, while inside very little business was being transacted. Finally, he had a truce talk with the postman. "It is nothing personal, Gigi," the postman said. "But you have taken from us the biggest pleasure of our lives."

"What can I do?" Massa asked. "If I allow you your pleasures, the *carabinieri* will shut me down."

"Did they shut down Amaroli?" the postman asked. "Let me talk to the *marachale* of the *carabinieri* as one government employee to another, and we will see what can be done."

A few days later the postman called on Massa and told him that an arrangement had been made, that he could sell wine and spirits on the premises and allow the playing of cards, and there would be no *quid pro quo* involved. There was only one condition to this informal arrangement: if there were any trouble inside the *tabacchi,* any fighting or rowdy behavior or intolerable drunkenness, Luigi could not ask the *carabinieri* for help. How could the *carabinieri* enforce the drinking laws in a bar that officially did not exist? Luigi Massa would have to bear full and personal responsibility for the maintenance of law and order.

Luigi pondered the proposal. It did not rest well on his essentially timid and orderly nature to enter into such an agreement, but it also did not please him to go out of business. So he accepted, and soon the *tabacchi* at Caprara was humming almost as it had in years past. The *brescla* game went on all day under the general direction of the old man Gaetano Rosa, when he was not dead drunk, and the consumption of hard spirits was presided over by a *contadino* named Giovanni Migliori, known to all the region as Sassolein, which was dialect for *sassolino,* the sweet liqueur that the old Migliori bought whenever he could afford it. The rest of the time, Sassolein drank Massa's weak wine, shouting and complaining the second he entered the store that his glass was not waiting for him. No one ever saw Sassolein at night; he always managed to get drunk by sundown, and then he would go over the mountain to his home to sleep it off.

Soon Luigi was enjoying the best years of his life, with camaraderie and high spirits flowing nightly in the *tabacchi.* He was fond of telling his customers that the hard liquor in his cabinet was only for his immediate family, and when jaws dropped, he would say, "But the whole mountain is my immediate family!" and set up a drink. Not that it was all a drunken binge. Aside from a few veteran imbibers like Rosa and Sassolein, the mountain people had neither the desire nor the finances to indulge in a continuous bacchanal. They would show up at night and fill the *tabacchi* with talk and sip slowly at their wine. The hunters would tell tall stories—almost all the local hunting was for fat rabbits and hares and birds, but every few years someone would pot a boar, and this was just often enough to make boar stories credible in the bar. The older people would discuss their corn and their cattle and the price of salt, and a hard core would sit at a corner table playing cards. When the weather was good, the people would go outside to play *boccie,* repairing now and then to the inside of the store for refreshments. The brothers Lanzarini, Evaristo and Quirico, were the best *boccie* players, and when the two of them competed, bets were placed by everyone and the air was full of excitement. Sometimes Luigi wished that the people would take the game a little less seriously. *Boccie* was not like *brescla,* where a man made his cards a private matter an inch in front of his nose.

In *boccie* everybody could see when a player had stepped over the foul line, and everybody would get down on the ground to see whose ball was away, and sometimes the spectators would lose their tempers and blows would be struck. At such times Luigi and the postman, in their roles as the neighborhood's leading advocates of civilized behavior, would jump between the contestants and make them stop. And for the rest of the evening delegations would go back and forth from the homes of both families until a just and lasting peace had been secured. It was a tradition on the mountain: people could argue, and people could fight, but all such foolishness had to be settled by nightfall.

Sometimes the traveling chairmaker would show up at the *tabacchi,* and all the women of the surrounding villages would rush over to place their orders. Luigi never learned the chairmaker's name; all he knew was that the man had been a sergeant major in the army during World War I and that everybody called him *Ebanista* (cabinetmaker). *"Whay, Ebanista!"* Luigi would say when the man appeared, and set up a drink by way of greeting. Then the two men would go into the woods and cut two or three of the biggest mulberry trees they could find, dragging them back to the piazza of Caprara with oxen. Each day the *ebanista* would make six or seven chairs from this fine white wood, while the farm families stood around and admired his craftsmanship. When the last order was filled, the *ebanista* would pack up his tools and trudge down the path and stay away for another six months.

At other times, the little cobbled piazza between the two long farmhouses at Caprara would be the scene of loud games of *piastrella* among the children. Each child would put a soldo or two, worth less than a penny, on top of an upright brick and then pitch pebbles to see who could come the closest, with winner take all. There was a section of the piazza's cobblestones that was worn smooth by the years of *piastrella.* The parents did not object. All life was a gamble, and anyway, *piastrella* was good training for the later games of *boccie.* Sometimes the piazza would be the scene of a cornhusking festival. The *contadini* would drag a demijohn of black wine into the village and equip it with a tube and a spout so that no one would run dry while shucking the corn. And there would be dances that went on and on through the night to music from an accordion or clarinet or harmonica.

Just before the war, Luigi installed a *gassometro* in his store, and for weeks he had to light and relight the device to show everybody how it worked. The adjoining farmhouses were poorly illuminated by candles and kerosene lamps, both of which gave off smoke and yellow rays, but in Luigi's *tabacchi* the *gassometro* threw a flame that burned bright and white and clean. All he had to do was put a kilo of carbide into the brass canister of the gadget, pour in the water that slowly dripped across the chemical, and the *gassometro* would produce vast quantities of illuminating gas. By the time of the war Luigi had extended his *gassometro* system all over the house. Three tubes carried the gas into the *tabacchi,* and two more reached upstairs to the apartment where the Massa family lived. Every now and then Luigi would be confronted by a stranger who would ask if he would be kind enough to turn on the *gassometro* and demonstrate how it worked. "Stay around till this evening," Luigi would say. He had learned that a kilo of carbide would provide bright light from four until eleven P.M., or just about closing time. It was a convenient way to chase the all-night drinkers like Gaetano Rosa. The lights would start to flicker, and Luigi would pretend it was an act of God and say, "Sorry, my friends," and the *tabacchi* would shut down to the gentle hissing of jets.

Luigi Massa's worst troubles, like those of all the people of Monte Sole, began with the war and accelerated with each reverse suffered by the Fascists. In the beginning, when it had been difficult to tell that Italy was at war except for the absence of certain young men, Luigi would hitch up his old spotted mare, Nina, and make the three-hour trip into the valley to buy supplies and sell his overstock. In those early months of the war, business was better than good. He would buy spaghetti, macaroni, *pastina, tagliatelle, tortellini, cannelloni;* three or four grades of rice; olive oil and cottonseed oil; kerosene for those with lamps and candles for those who could not afford lamps. He would stock up on pots and pans, tableware, bolts of cloth, yarn and thread and needles, and the monopoly goods that were the store's reason for existence. In the summertime he would pile all this stuff into a cart, and Nina would struggle back up the mountain. In times of snow the horse could not negotiate the steep slopes with such loads—she was twenty years old in 1943—and Luigi would equip her with saddlebags and make several trips into the valley, riding through snow and ice and storms to keep his customers supplied.

But when the war was only a few years old, Luigi realized that it was no longer possible to satisfy everybody. Shortages developed in the valley warehouses, and he would be told that he could have his ten kilograms of salt only if he would agree to buy a box of cheap gimcracks that he knew he could not sell on the mountain. Tobacco would be available only if he were interested in slipping a small bonus to the wholesaler. For a time, Luigi worked within the system, keeping his oldest customers happy and turning away the newer ones. But gradually the screws tightened, and there would be days when no tobacco or salt would be available, and shouting matches would ensue with his customers, with Luigi insisting that he had tried his hardest to turn up the rare stuff and the old customers shouting that he was a war profiteer to whom friendships meant nothing.

Gradually Luigi found himself wondering what had propelled him into the business of running a store. His wife, Maria Comellini, owned a small *podere* called Poggio Comellini, and as the war shortages grew worse, Luigi began shuttling back and forth from the *tabacchi* to the farm, a mile away. He was returning to the ultimate resource of the *contadino:* the soil. No matter what happened to the *tabacchi,* the soil of Poggio Comellini would not fail them, and Luigi worked day after day to put in his crops. By skillful utilization of his wife and his daughters, he was able to keep the *tabacchi* open most of the time, serve a little wine, and provide the *contadini* with their traditional recreation hall.

Shortly after the beginning of 1944 Luigi began to be bothered by the partisans. He had known of the existence of a band of mountain men who were hiding on Monte Sole and harassing the Germans in minor ways like sniping and derailing freight cars, but so far they had lacked the strength to come into the open. By springtime the partisans had gained in numbers, and they would come into Luigi's store, three or four at a time, and help themselves. When he would object, they would explain that he ought to be glad to help them, since it was his freedom they were fighting for. Luigi did not know whose freedom was involved, but he did know that his business was headed toward bankruptcy. After the partisans cleaned out his stocks, members of the local Fascio would arrive and demand cigarettes, and when Luigi protested he had none, the Fascists would pull out their *tessere* and make threats and ask Luigi who he thought he was, holding out on the very people who were working to preserve his right to stay in business. Luigi became more and more confused and began spending days at a time at Poggio Comellini preparing for the worst. One night a band of armed partisans showed up at the store, and while two stood guard at the door, the others rifled all of Luigi's stocks of tobacco and salt. As usual, he took no action, but one of his customers reported the robbery to the *carabinieri,* and for days afterward Luigi was involved in filling out forms, looking at pictures he did not want to identify, and going through the motions of pretending to help the officials catch the culprits, knowing all the time that if they were caught, he himself would be assassinated by other partisans. The situation had become intolerable, and by summer Luigi was keeping only minimal stocks on hand, hoping that this would make the store less appealing to the partisans. But still they came, threatening Luigi and his family, promising to return later and spelling out in vivid detail what they would do if food and tobacco were not available. Finally, Luigi moved his family to the old farmhouse at Poggio Comellini and opened the *tabacchi* only sporadically, sneaking back by night to sell a few small items to his oldest customers.

One day toward the end of September, 1944, a *contadino* knocked on the door at Poggio Comellini and told the Massas that the Germans were forming up in the valleys below. No one knew why, but there were rumors that the SS was planning a great raid against the partisans. Luigi trudged the mile to his *tabacchi,* grabbed up a few personal possessions, and turned the little sign on the front door to the side that said CHIUSO (closed). "This time," he said to himself, "it is for good."

One day the Ruggeri children were working hard in the field, trying to bring in a wheat crop so they could go down the mountain to Vado for a fair the next day. As usual, Mario, the fifteen-year-old, was getting the most done, and the two family beauties, Elide and Elena, both of them nearly twenty, were chattering away and getting on his nerves. When Mario stopped to take a sip of wine, tilting his head far back, the mischievous Elide sneaked up behind him and tickled him under the arms. Mario jumped, and some of the wine went down the wrong pipe, and it was only after minutes of gasping for breath and rolling around and coughing and retching that he was able to breathe properly again. As soon as he had recovered, he took off after his sister, chasing her toward their home. Just inside the door Mario threw himself on the tiny Elide, grabbed her foot and began working on her bare big toe with a farm fork. "It is coming off. Off! *Off!*" he hollered, as Elide cried for mercy. Barely in the nick of time their mother, Cecilia, arrived and stopped the amputation, and the two young Ruggeris were sent back to the field mumbling at each other. An hour later Elide again tried to tickle her thirsty brother, but this time Mario got the wine down safely.

It was well known on Monte Sole that Elide Ruggeri had to be watched every second. She was short and pretty, with an upturned nose, light-brown eyes and a mole on her chin like an Indian beauty mark, and there was a liquid quality to her eyes that made her appear to be on the verge of tears. Her smiles, therefore, were the more surprising and attractive, like bright sunlight after rain, and enabled her to convince the unwary that she had decided to abandon her career as a prankster. She had not.

Her cousin Elena, who lived in the same house, was Elide's only competition for beauty queen of Monte Sole. Elena had a strong nose with the slightest scythe curve to it, glistening black hair in folding waves that came down to a widow's peak, and strong white teeth. She was one of the few on the mountain with a slight Roman look, and she was tall by local standards. Both the girls had firm figures from working outside in the fields every day.

Their fathers had farmed the same twelve acres of land on the slopes of Monte Sole since 1913, or long enough to learn their business, and consequently they had come close to becoming that contradiction in terms, secure *contadini.* No one who had to give back 50 percent of the harvest could ever become truly secure, but by the standards of certain other people on the mountain, notably Adelmo Benini and Antonio Tonelli and Augusto Massa and a few of the others who farmed near the Ruggeris, there was no doubt that the clan Ruggeri was rich. Every Sunday the two mothers of the family appeared in church wearing different colored neckerchiefs. Who could remember when they had repeated the same patterns two weeks in a row? On Monte Sole, this was ostentatious display of wealth.

The Ruggeri family benefited from a combination of good fortune and hard work. Their farm at Ca' Pudella was on the southern slope of the mountain, and it received a maximum of sunlight and a minimum of snow and hail. The land was not especially fertile—no part of the mountain could be called fertile—but the land at Ca'

Pudella was not rent by fissures or leached by wild-running streams, and when fertilizer was put down, it stayed.

There was also the matter of family enterprise. Years before, the two brothers and patriarchs of the clan, Giulio and Attilio, had decided that the only way to survive on the mountain was to pool everything they had and use it all in one big thrust at the land, and this meant that the families of both brothers would work together. Attilio and Giulio and their wives and their seven children shared the same house, ate at the same table, played in the same courtyard and tended to the same animals and fields. The mothers worked in the same kitchen, and it was a rare mealtime when they served fewer than eleven. The families occupied the same reserved pews (the two front rows on the right near the confessional) in the nearby church at Casaglia, and few people of the community knew or bothered to find out which Ruggeris were the children of Giulio and which Attilio. The main family contrast was between the two patriarchs. Attilio was an outgoing man who gave orders in the modern style: "Mario, would you do me the kindness of bringing up the pitchfork from the barn?" Attilio did a lot of smiling and bounced the little children on his lap. Giulio, the older of the brothers by five years, was the opposite. "Get the pitchfork!" he would say, and the child would break a leg to comply with the order. Giulio never smiled, and his favorite saying was *Il riso abbonda sulla bocca degli stolti*. "Laughter abounds on the mouth of idiots." He went about his daily chores as though the farm were skidding toward bankruptcy, and when German patrols would appear on the horizon and every able-bodied man on the mountain would run for the woods till the *rastrellamento* was over, Giulio would not make a move until he had finished his assigned task and then would walk slowly and with dignity into the brush. The differences between the two men even extended to their appearances. Attilio was tall and lean and wore a small, relaxed mustache, but Giulio was shorter and dumpier and wore a big handlebar mustache that overpowered his face and contributed to his look of sternness. "What Nazi soldier would have the courage to take old Guilio into custody?" the people of the community would ask, and the answer was always. "*No,* Nazi soldier."

None of the seven Ruggeri children had traveled far from Monte Sole, nor did they wish to. Elena's attitude was typical. She reckoned that she lacked for nothing. Someday she would marry, but there was no hurry. In the meantime she worked in the fields, and to her the farm at Ca' Pudella seemed like one great garden, with amber grain, fat purple grapes, healthy chickens and hogs, and more food than any eleven humans could have been expected to eat. Indeed, every August at the time of *Ferragosto,* the family would show off its largess by serving a dinner for twenty-five or thirty relatives. *Ferragosto* was August 15, the Feast of the Immaculate Conception, a day when Italy stopped and gorged itself, and none better than the people at Ca' Pudella. For days before the event, Elena and Elide and their mothers would be killing and plucking chickens and guinea hens, preparing rabbits, slaughtering a lamb, making *pasta,* baking desserts. The meal would start at twelve thirty, after everyone had gone to mass at Casaglia, and would last for four or five hours. The first course was *antipasto:* thick slices of *prosciutto, salami* and *mortadella* bologna, and heaping bowls of pickled onions, peppers, artichokes, green tomatoes, cauliflower and mushrooms. The second course was *tortellini:* envelopes of *pasta* filled with *mortadella,* pork and cheese and served in a chicken broth. Next came boiled lamb and beef and pork served with the Ruggeri mothers' own green sauce: capers, parsley, green olive oil, peppers and garlic, all cooked together with squash, zucchini and carrots. The fourth course was always chicken and rabbit, stewed hunter style in a tomato sauce, and the fifth was the same kind of meat roasted, plus pork and guinea hen. In Italian meals, the cheese course comes after all the main courses and just before the dessert, but at the Ruggeri feast huge slabs of cheese remained on the table throughout the meal. There were homemade Parmesan and bland *latticini* (cow cheese), as well as seasoned *formaggio,* and each course was supplemented by the diner's choice of cheese. The same was true of the wines, the family's own homemade black wine (*negretto* or *negrettino*) and white wine (*albano*), and there were no limits to age or quantity. *"Bevi del sangue di Dio,"* Attilio would say. "Drink of the blood of God." Every year a few members of the family could be counted on to topple backward from an excess of the blood of God, but somehow the wine never seemed to affect the children. They had learned early that wine made them sleepy, and they drank the favored liquid in moderation because they did not want to fall asleep and miss all the fascinating and mysterious remarks made by the elders at this annual reunion. Every year the same ritual would follow the last meat course: a smiling Attilio would enter the dining room with a trayful of cooked chestnuts, and the diners would applaud and cheer admiringly. "*Whay,* Attilio," someone would say, "you must have bought these chestnuts from the witch. There will be no chestnuts on the trees for a month yet." And just as though it had never happened before, Attilio would explain patiently how he had worked out a process of drying last year's chestnuts and then soaking them back into shape for the meal on *Ferragosto*. "How clever you are, Attilio!" guests would say, just as though they had not known his secret all along. The meal would end with the Ruggeri mothers, Cecilia and Teresa, making a grand entrance of their own, bringing in dessert after dessert while everybody clucked in amazement. There would be tarts, *mistocce,* Spanish spicecakes, *creme caramelle,* spongy rice cakes, big jelly rolls called *ciambelle* and *crostate,* jams and marmalades and breads. After everyone had spent another hour sampling all the delicacies, old Giulio would rise and announce sternly that it was time to milk the cows, and the meal would be over.

To girls like Elena and Elide, it seemed that there were always events like *Ferragosto* to look forward to, and the long hours in the field were made easier by ticking off the days. If they were not counting toward *Ferragosto,* they would be counting toward the corn husking festival in the village, or the arrival of the fair at Vado, or the coming of *Ottario,* the big annual church function, when a visiting priest would conduct eight days of prayer service leading up the Day of the Dead in November.

Except on such special occasions, the life within the Ruggeri family was harsh and stern, but no one complained, because no one knew of a different life. The word of the parents was absolute law, violated only rarely by the children. Elena was a timid girl, given to automatic and unswerving obedience, but her cousin Elide was always straining at the bonds of family discipline, and it seemed to Elena that more often than not her cousin would start the trouble and everybody else would get punished. There was not a bad bone in Elide's body, but she had an independence and an ebullience about her that seemed to lead inevitably toward disaster.

Of course, Elide was never openly disrespectful. The slightest act of disrespect toward the parents or, for that matter, toward any older member of the family was visited by immediate punishment. One day Elena and Elide saw their aunt walking up the path toward Ca' Pudella. The aunt had barely turned twenty, and both the girls were almost the same age, and they ran into the kitchen and said to Elena's mother, "Lucia is here! Lucia is here!"

The mother said, "Lucia? Lucia? Who is Lucia?" She ran to the window to see for herself. "Oh," she said. "You mean *Aunt* Lucia," and cracked both girls on the head.

This was not unusual behavior on Monte Sole. Everyone remembered the big church festival that had been held in Gardeletta some years before, when one of the married women of the region had said loudly to her mother, "Come now, Mama, do not speak nonsense." Without a word, the old mother arose from her chair, walked around the table and slapped her daughter hard across the mouth. Just as calmly, the old lady returned to her seat and resumed talking nonsense. The daughter, age fifty-seven, stayed silent.

In the Ruggeri family, the strongest prohibition was against dancing. Although the elders permitted dancing at public events when the whole family was present, they did not like to see the children go off to dances on their own, and this included "children" in their twenties, like Elena's brother Antonio. The result was a nonstop seething feud between Elide and her stern father. "I will jump out the window if you make me stay home," Elide would shout.

"You will not," Giulio would say. "I forbid you to dance, and I also forbid you to jump out the window." That was that; forbidden was forbidden, and Elena would listen to Elide cry herself to sleep. On a Sunday night long after the war had started, when there were restrictions and prohibitions on everything and dancing was one of the few pleasures left to the younger people, the family Laffi held a dance on the cobbled front yard of their farmhouse at Poggio, a skip away from the church at Casaglia. "We are going," Elide whispered to Elena.

"We are not permitted," Elena whispered back.

"We are going anyway!" Elide said.

The plot had been carefully worked out by Elide and her cousin Antonio, eldest of the seven children. The patriarchs, Giulio and Attilio, were away on this Sunday, visiting friends in the valley, and Elide announced to the mothers that the children were going to the church at Casaglia for the benediction. To make their story more believable, they dragged along Lina, Elide's six-year-old sister.

Having gained their freedom, the group hurried straight to the dance at Poggio, and after an hour of whirling and swirling the young Ruggeris heard a chilling sound. It was Cecilia Ruggeri, Elide's mother, calling across the 300 yards from their home: "Elide! Elide! I know where you are! You come home right now!"

Antonio said, "Keep quiet! Let her call," and the young Ruggeris kept on dancing.

Ten minutes later they heard the voice again, this time from the edge of the Laffi courtyard. "You come home right now," said Cecilia, and the hen-shaped little woman grabbed the children one by one and hustled them away. "When your fathers come home, you will hear more!" she told them.

The Ruggeri children, from twenty-year-old "Tonino" to six-year-old Lina, did not wait to find out what their punishment would be. As soon as they reached home, they put themselves to bed without dinner. Nothing more was heard about the incident.

The schooling of the children was meager, barely enough to teach them to read and write and add and subtract and to take the smallest children off the parents' hands during the busy times of the day. Both Elide and Elena had gone to the Catholic school at Cerpiano, a mile from their home, and extracted all the education they could, which consisted of academic learning from the ages of six to nine and subjects like sewing and cooking and knitting till the age of twelve, at which point their formal educations were at an end. It was none too soon for their fathers, Attilio and Giulio, both of whom entertained a deep hatred for Fascism and the Fascistic methods of indoctrination, some of which perforce had crept into the schoolbooks used at Cerpiano. "What is this?" Giulio would say, and hand one of the children's elementary textbooks to his nephew Antonio, who would read aloud in tones of mock pomposity:

> "Teacher," Bruno said to the teacher as she walked into the classroom, "Daddy bought a large new flag yesterday, with a lance at the top made of gold. Tomorrow we are going to put it on the balcony so that everyone down in the street can see it!"
>
> "I am sure you will! But tomorrow every balcony and every window will have flags. Do you know why?"
>
> "Yes, teacher!" the children shouted, jumping up.
>
> "Good, everyone! Now tell me, Bruno Sereni: What day is tomorrow?"
>
> "The twenty-eighth of October."

"And what is the twenty-eighth of October?"

"The anniversary of the March on Rome. The Fascists entered Rome in their black shirts and set things right. Then Il Duce arrived and said, 'All bad Italians who do not know how to do things right will have to go away. I am going to set everything right. *Viva Italia!*' "

"Good," the teacher said. "You have your own way of putting it, but you have said it correctly."

"I know the story, too," several children said.

"Of course you do. All of you know already what Fascism is and what Benito Mussolini has done for Italy. On October 28, 1922, he began his great work, and even though it is not yet finished, it has changed Italy. We remember this historic day with thanks, and therefore, every year we mark the date with great rejoicing. Listen, children: every window must have a flag tomorrow, even if you have to make it with paper."

"Yes, teacher! Hooray! Hooray! Hooray! *Viva!*"

While Tonino would be reading such material from the children's official textbooks, Attilio would begin to make typical farm noises of derogation, and this would be the signal for all the children to begin laughing, and sooner or later old Giulio would snap at them: "Shut up, all of you! There is nothing funny about these books! They are only disgusting!" And the children would nod their heads and agree.

By 1944 Fascism had proved itself a mammoth failure in Italy, but many years earlier it had proved itself a failure on Monte Sole. In the simple clarity of mountain life, the farm people could see that Fascism demanded taxes and tributes and unswerving loyalty and gave them nothing but bombast in return. There was no highly developed patriotic feeling on Monte Sole even before Fascism, nor any basis for such feeling. No state roads had ever crossed the mountain; no state schools or state hospitals or state institutions of any kind existed within miles. The *contadini* only knew what they could see, and what they could see was an avaricious central government reaching out for a pig here, a cow there, a hundred kilos of wheat here, and threatening dissidents with public beatings and jail. And who was gaining from these enforced contributions? Why, the fat cats in the valleys, who were growing big and corpulent and adding wings to their houses. Anybody could see that. When the Fascist recruiting drives came up the mountain, and children through the age of seven were urged to become Sons of the Wolf, and children of eight to fourteen to become members of the Balilla, and older children members of the Avanguardisti or the Young Fascists, most of the mountain parents would order their offspring to disappear for the day, to go pick chestnuts or dig truffles until the recruiters had left.

The people of Monte Sole, with hardly any exceptions, ridiculed and lampooned the Fascists. They would use Mussolini's name in place of the Deity's ("Holy Mussolini!") to show how great the leader had grown, or they would hold their fingers straight across their upper lips, give a Fascist salute, and make a loud raspberry, from one end or the other, to express their feelings about the alliance with Hitler. They would sit around for hours telling anti-Fascist jokes. "*Whay*, my friend," someone would say, "did you hear that Lanzarini's truffle dog has learned to sniff out Fascists?"

"How can you tell when he finds a Fascist?"

"He vomits!"

A man would recite both sides of a conversation. "How can we tell if the new bridge is good?" "Simple. You fill a truck with Fascists, and if the bridge does not fall down under the load, it is a good bridge." "What if it does fall down?" "Then it is a better bridge!"

The Fascists had "hymns" for every one of their children's groups, and not a single hymn escaped being parodied by people like the Ruggeris. The hymn of the Balilla, the group from eight to fourteen years, was based on the heroism of a boy of Portoria who, in the eighteenth century, had picked up a stone and thrown it at Austrian invaders whose mortar had become stuck in the mud. The hymn went:

Fischia il sasso, il nome squilla	The stone whistles, the name rings out
del ragazzo di Pordoia	of the boy of Portoria,
e l'intrepido Balilla	and the intrepid Balilla
sta gigante nella storia.	becomes gigantic in our story.
Era bronzo quel mortaio	The mortar that stuck in the mud
che nel fango sprofondò,	was made of bronze,
ma il ragazzo fu d'acciaio	but the boy was made of steel
e la madre liberò.	and set his mother free.

This was not, however, the version that was sung in the region of Monte Sole. The local people sang:

Fischia il sasso, il nome squilla	The stone whistles, the name rings out
di Arcibaldo e Petronilla	of Archibald and Petronilla,
che suneven la chitarra	who, playing their guitar,
a caval' d'una somara.	are riding on the back of a she-ass.
Poi arriva Bi e Bo	Then Bi and Bo arrive,
uno stronzo sul comò,	and make a shit on the bureau.
ma il ragazzo fu di acciaio,	But the boy was made of steel,
che con il cucchiaio	and with a spoon,
se lo mangiò.	he ate it.

Such parodies were standard fare for the Ruggeri men, though not for the ladies, who had their own milder barbs and arrows for the Fascists. It was not long lost upon the pompous, inflated members of the Fasci in the valleys below that the brothers Ruggeri had become outspoken rustic subversives. To the Fascist mentality, this meant that the family had to be harassed. Squads of police would make the long climb up to Ca' Pudella on the slightest pretext, bearing with them accusations that the brothers had failed to pay their taxes, had encouraged the singing of anti-Fascist songs and had acted against the government. But Attilio and Giulio were not stupid, even though they were largely uneducated, and the Fascists were never able to bring a formal *denuncia.* Then came September 8, 1943, and the surrender of Italy to the Allies. Antonio Ruggeri, nineteen at the time, had been serving in the Italian Army, and like hundreds of thousands of his comrades, he had dropped his rifle and headed home. The region of Monte Sole was soon glutted with such "deserters," many of whom became partisans, and no one paid them any attention. But Antonio was a special case. His presence gave the local Fascists a club to hold over Attilio and Giulio, and life became miserable at Ca' Pudella. In one month, the Fascists made seven full-scale raids on the Ruggeri home, always on the pretext that the family was harboring a deserter. They would slap the women around, dump barrels of flour and bottles of wine and insist that Attilio and Giulio return with them to the *carabinieri* barracks to fill out papers and answer questions. But no matter how severe the harassment or meticulous the search, the raiders never caught Antonio. There were plenty of high observation posts around Ca' Pudella, and he always had time to run off to the woods.

Two nights before Christmas, 1943, another raiding party burst in the Ruggeris' front door and demanded the deserter. "We do not know what you mean," Giulio said. "What deserter?"

"Very well," one of the Fascists said. "We will keep this woman in custody until the deserter shows up." They put handcuffs on Teresa, wife of Attilio, mother of Elena and Antonio, and took her down the mountain.

As soon as the raiding party was out of sight, Elena ran into the woods and found her brother, and the family began a discussion. Most of the women and children were crying over the arrest, but Elena felt only anger. "Look," she said, "I think this has gone far enough. This should be the end of it. Tonino, when they come up here and arrest our mother, then it is time for you to go back into the Army."

Antonio agreed, and the next morning the whole family marched down the mountain to turn the son over to the Fascist authorities and release the mother from her cell in the *carabinieri* barracks. The family, all but Antonio, was together for Christmas, and one week later, on New Year's Day, Antonio walked in the front door, to the surprise of no one. He had remained in the Army for as long as he could stand it, and now he was back on the mountain bearing forged working papers. He stayed a few weeks, or long enough for the Fascists to resume their bullying, and then he quietly slipped up the mountain to become a partisan. "I do not like to see my good nephew go," said the truculent Giulio, "but it appears that sooner or later a fight must be made."

"It has come to that," brother Attilio said. "A fight must be made." From that day on, the family Ruggeri looked to the partisans for their deliverance.

In his favorite dream, Adelmo Benini saw himself a genuine *marchese* on a big white horse, riding over thousands of acres of lush farmland, dispensing kindness to his *contadini*. "Guerrino!" Adelmo would shout at a gnarled and twisted old man pulling weeds in the cornfield. "Come over here! Now listen, Guerrino, you have worked long and hard for me, and I want you to go straight to my villa and spend the rest of your life resting. Yes, you heard correctly! To my villa! I never want to see you working again." Onward Adelmo would ride, dispensing banknotes to the *contadini,* throwing *chicce* to swarms of barefooted children and sending wives on vacation trips to Bologna, all expenses paid. The best part of the dream came at the end, when the "Marchese" Benini would return to his villa, eat a gallon of *polenta* with *cicciolo,* and fall into bed at nine o'clock. "Do not awaken me," he would say to his *contadino.* "I will be up around noon, or maybe later."

When Adelmo was a young man, he had made the decision that doomed him to a lifetime of hard work and sleeplessness and unfulfilled dreams. He came from Vallego, a settlement consisting of a few houses on the southwestern slope of Monte Sole and populated mostly by the family Migliori, of whom Sassolein, the champion drinker of the inn at Caprara, was a prominent member. The marriage of the handsome young Adelmo to the lovely daughter of Sassolein seemed preordained to the people of the mountain, and so it was arranged, and everyone waited for beautiful things to happen. But first it was necessary that the newlyweds make a living, and so they moved into the *casa colonica* at a nearby place called Possatore di Casaglia and began farming three acres of land owned by the Marchese Beccadelli of Casalecchio. "At least we will be free," Adelmo told his bride. "It is better than working inside a mill."

But Adelmo soon found that working in a mill would have been preferable. The land at Possatore, like most of the land on Monte Sole, had been squeezed dry and lifeless. Years earlier a farmer named Virginio Paselli had abandoned the place and gone to the valley to work as a laborer on the tracks of the *direttissima,* the express route to Florence and Rome, telling everyone that Possatore was hopelessly worked out. The Marchese Beccadelli enjoyed a reputation as one of the more reasonable *padroni* of the area, but Adelmo found that he was dealing with the land more than he was dealing with the *marchese,* and the land was unrelentingly harsh. Quickly it had defeated Antonio Tonelli, who lived with his wife and nine children in the other half of the big farmhouse. Tonelli had tried to work his own three-acre patch at Possatore, but when he found that his children were going hungry, he took a job in Bologna as a porter, eking out the equivalent of eight or ten dollars a week after travel expenses had been deducted and allowing his ancient uncle to putter around the land for what it was worth.

Adelmo had no old uncle to work the land for him, and by the time of the war years, the Fascists had made it so difficult for a *contadino* to leave his farm that the situation had turned black for the little Benini family, which by now included two pretty daughters, Giovanna (named for Sassolein) and Maria. The arithmetic of the matter was simple: Adelmo was able to grow about 1,800 pounds of corn each year, and most of this went to feed the hog. On an average, there would be a pound or so of corn per day to divide among the family. Wheat was the big crop of the people of Monte Sole, and by the most minimal standards it took 550 pounds of wheat per year to keep a person alive. When everything went right, Adelmo was able to bring in 4,400 pounds of wheat per year, half of which went to the *marchese,* and so his family of four was living on the edge of the minimum.

But that was in good years. In seasons of late frost or hailstorm, the family went hungry in proportion to the crop losses. Norina kept a small vegetable garden of tomatoes, peppers, celery, lettuce, beans and carrots, and none of this had to be split with the *padrone,* nor did mushrooms and truffles gathered in the woods in fall. But under the peculiar sharecropping laws of the *mezzadria,* the family had to give the Marchese Beccadelli half their chestnuts. Adelmo was permitted to keep a few animals of his own, apart from the 50-50 split, and there were always cows to be milked morning and night. None of the milk remained with the family; Norina would convert it daily into cheese, which Adelmo exchanged in the valley for salt, olive oil, fertilizer and other necessities.

As for wine, the "blood of God" that nourished the people of the mountain, Adelmo found that he could seldom make enough even to meet the family's personal needs. It seemed that every time his tiny vineyard would begin to burst with the pale-green *albano* grapes and he could imagine the rich taste of the new vintage, there would be a light rain followed by a parching hot sun, and the leaves would crinkle and wrap themselves into tight balls, leaving the grapes exposed to the heat. When this happened, the other farmers ran to the valley to buy a copper spray to save the crop, but Adelmo never had the money, and the blight wiped out his grapes year after year.

Sometimes Adelmo wondered what kept him going. On a typical summer day he would get out of bed at three A.M. Other farmers of the area could lie in bed till four-thirty and five, but they had helpers, and Adelmo worked alone. For breakfast he would enjoy a piece of bread and a few bites of sausage or *prosciutto*. Some of the local farmers liked to start the day with a glass of wine and a raw egg, but Adelmo seldom had the wine, and his eggs were put aside to be exchanged for staples. After breakfast, he tended to his cows, milking and feeding them and leading them to the stream 100 yards away for water and then mucking out their stalls. By now it would be five A.M., nearly daylight, and Adelmo would yoke two of his cows and head for the fields, where he would work till about ten. The cows had to be rested then, but Adelmo kept on working, unassisted, waiting with short patience for the church bells to toll high noon. The nearest church was at Casaglia, where the bells were pulled by the old lady Artimesia Gatti, but Adelmo would also hear the bells of the church at San Martino and the various churches in the valley. They all rang at different times, because it was not noon until the priest of each parish said it was, and most of the priests had cheap watches. There were days when Adelmo would run toward his house at the sound of the first bell, but this seemed to him dishonorable and always left him with a bad conscience. Usually he would allow himself to be governed by the bells of Casaglia.

The noon meal was the main one, the one that fueled the daily work, and Adelmo never could get enough of it. The entree was sometimes *pasta fagioli,* a sort of thick bean stew, or sometimes homemade noodles served without sauce and garnished with a slice of onion or a thin sliver of *prosciutto*. Adelmo and his wife called the noodle dish *direttissima* because it seemed to go from one end of the system to the other without stopping.

For dessert, they would have apples, if there were any, or grapes, if the blight had not yet struck, or a bowl of *radicchi,* a local green like chicory, with a bitter taste. Adelmo permitted himself a small glass of watered wine at only one meal a week.

After eating, Adelmo would rest until two, return to the fields with the cows, repeat the milking chores about six, and quit his daily labors when the sun went down at eight or nine. Dinner would be *radicchi* or cheese or sometimes a solitary fried egg shared with his wife. By now it would be nine-thirty or ten o'clock, and usually he would barely have the strength to take off his clothes and fall into bed. The next day began at three.

In the fall and winter, Adelmo's life was not much different. He had only one crop to tend, winter wheat, but he took on two extra jobs to support his family, and while the other *contadini* were staying indoors and catching up on repairs and social matters, Adelmo was out working the same old sixteen-hour day. There was a man in the valley who owned a thresher, and Adelmo would hitch up his cows and drag the machine from *podere* to *podere* threshing wheat for others. The *padrone* of the machine got most of the fees, but Adelmo was paid a percentage.

When all the wheat had been threshed and winter was about to grip Monte Sole, it was time to convert the hogs into the *prosciutto* and salami and headcheese and bacon that would sustain life till the next year's growing season. Most of the farmers did their own slaughtering, but there were always a few who did not know how or did not want to, and these would hire a free-lance butcher to do the job for them. Adelmo had taught himself this trade, and he was proud of his skill. He would spend two full days on each hog, collecting about five dollars for his work. This was half as much as a qualified laborer would make in two days, but Adelmo was being paid by other *contadini,* poor men like himself, and he had to settle for less. Adelmo tried to do his work so efficiently that the *contadini* would find it economical to hire him for the meat he saved them. He would lead the hog out of the stall, whip a rope around its feet, knock it down and stick it in the neck, twisting and turning the knife until all the veins had been severed. Then he would hang the pig head down and allow the blood to drain out, so that the flesh would become white and clean. Now the drained pig would be dumped into a tub of boiling water, and the bristles scraped till the skin was pink and smooth. Adelmo would hang the denuded carcass up once again, make a long slash down the belly, and take out the intestines, yards and yards of them, and lay them aside. Working quickly and deftly with his sharp knife, he would eviscerate the hog, separating the hams, or *prosciutti,* the rib meat that was used for bacon, the pockets of flesh from head and neck for headcheese, the spinal bits that went into salami, the shoulder meat that went into sausages, and all the other cuts. He would take every ounce of fat that remained and wrap it in cheesecloth and boil it off for lard, and when the last drop of fat had melted through the cheesecloth, there would be left a residue of meat and gristle called *cicciolo,* which was considered a local delicacy when served over *polenta,* the local cornmeal mush.

After he had ground up the various sausage meats, Adelmo would start to work on the intestines. He would drag them to a source of running water and begin washing, turning them inside out and washing again, repeating the process five or six times, and adding a final rinse in vinegar for good measure. When he was satisfied, he would ask the *contadino* for the necessary wine, salt, pepper and garlic and begin blending the sausages. Sometimes a *contadino* would give him a few bottles of low-grade *albano* or *barbera* for the sausage mixture, but Adelmo always counseled against this false thrift. "You should use only your best wine in sausage," he would say, "or you will pay the price for the rest of the year."

When the last hog had been slaughtered and winter had clamped down on the mountain, Adelmo would take whatever money he had made and go to the valley village of Gardeletta or Quercia to stock up on food. He already had the corn and wheat that were the mainstays of the winter diet, but even in a good year, he would have to buy staples. If the summer harvest had been normal, the family could last through the winter, keeping careful tabs on the weight of sausage remaining from the single hog Adelmo slaughtered for his own family each fall and watching carefully as the stocks of corn and wheat dropped lower and lower. It was always a harrowing process, sustaining life from one harvest to the next.

After a bad summer, of course, the family would face a season of chilly agony. If a crop had failed or come up short, Adelmo would redouble his efforts to make money with his threshing and his butchering, and in the valley he would buy a few barrels of salted herring, the cheapest protein foodstuff offered by the storekeepers. In bad years the *contadini* always fell back on herring. Sometimes the single meal of the day in the snowbound *casa colonica* at Possatore would consist of a salted herring each for the mother and father and one split in half for the two little daughters. This might be augmented in the early winter by chestnuts or mushrooms, but the supplies of these perishable items soon ran out, and the family would finish the season on the fish diet. Adelmo and his wife found that the salted herring provided their children with almost no resistance to disease, and since the house was full of drafts and dampness, the little girls spent as much time in bed as out. Sometimes Adelmo would have to carry one of the children on his shoulders to the doctor in the valley, and sometimes he would actually fear for their lives.

One winter, after Maria, the baby, had gone through a long period of fever and racking coughs (the doctor had drawn blood from her arm to relieve the congestion), Adelmo Benini and Sassolein's daughter sat down in front of the smoky fireplace and made the decision to leave the dead earth of Possatore. "No matter what we find, it cannot be worse than this," Norina said, and Adelmo nodded agreement.

But it was only a matter of a few days before the dream of escape evaporated. Adelmo went to the *municipio* to take out the papers permitting him to change his job. It was the dead of winter, and the Fascist clerk told Adelmo that he would have to stay put for at least six months under a new law passed by the Mussolini regime. "But that will be in the middle of my next growing season!" Adelmo protested.

"It is the law," the clerk said.

Adelmo would have quit the farm and waited the six months and then applied for work at the hemp factory in Pioppe di Salvaro or the paper mill at Lama di Reno, both only a few miles away and short of manpower. But in his talk with the clerk he had learned a few other provisions of the law. For example, even after six months' notice, one was not permitted to change jobs automatically; it was up to the local Fascio, which sometimes would decide that the community was not producing enough food and all the *contadini* would have to remain on their farms. Also, one was not permitted to leave one's land if there was any outstanding debt to the *padrone*. Adelmo laughed in spite of himself. One week after he and Norina had moved to Possatore, he had borrowed 100 lire from the Marchese Beccadelli to buy nitrogen fertilizer, and now, six years later, the 100 had grown to 200. It was true that one could violate the law that required clean accounts, but that meant running the risk of being blacklisted elsewhere and having all one's possessions taken over by the *padrone,* who would evaluate everything and render the final accounting.

Adelmo went home and told his wife that they could not move, at least for the duration of the war. "But we can run away to Bologna," his wife argued, "and you can get work there!"

Patiently Adelmo explained that they did not even have the train fare to Bologna, and that if they did, they would have no clothes for the children, no money to rent an apartment, and no legal status under the Fascist law. That night the Benini family went to bed without hope, and Adelmo said to himself that things could not get worse. He was mistaken. As the war went on, the Fascist government began to intrude more and more on the isolated people of Monte Sole, taking even from those who, like the Beninis, had almost nothing to give. Adelmo had to do his butchering at night, in clearings in the woods, because patrols of Blackshirts roamed the hills at slaughtering time, demanding the 25 percent that was the state's tax on hogs. There were all sorts of new levies: a small tax on a watchdog, a larger tax on a truffle dog, an exorbitant tax on a hunting dog. Luckily, Adelmo owned no dogs, having neither the food to feed them nor the time to enjoy them. At harvesttime, squads of enforcers would arrive with farm carts and haul away a portion of Adelmo's wheat and corn to square his tax bills. Adelmo never put up a fuss—too many of his friends had had their scalps laid open when they resisted the collection squads—and each winter the family had a little less grain to see it through. The final irony was that the government-issued shoes were barely adequate. The people of Monte Sole called them *così così* shoes (so-so shoes).

Italy's surrender in 1943 brought the promise of a halt to the Fascist tyrannies, and Adelmo and his little family joined in the big celebrations on the mountain. But when the Germans quickly seized control of the country, the situation worsened. High taxes were made higher, husbands were dragged out of their fields and sent off to slave labor, and squads of Blackshirts and German soldiers would show up at the farmhouses, drink the farmer's wine and make demands on everybody. One day a pair of German soldiers arrived at Possatore and helped themselves to food and wine. Norina stayed out of sight until Adelmo came rushing home from the fields. The Germans sat around for an hour or so, ogling the young mother, and then one of them asked Adelmo pointedly if he did not have work to do. No, Adelmo told them, his work was finished. The sitting contest lasted until late in the afternoon. Through all their months of shouting orders and committing indignities on the *contadini,* the Germans had never summoned the courage to remain on Monte Sole after dark, and when the sun started to go down, the two soldiers hurried off, muttering threats at Adelmo. "I am afraid they will be back," Norina said. "I am afraid of what they will do."

"They will have to kill me first," Adelmo said simply, and his wife knew that he meant it.

It was early in 1944 when Adelmo first learned that a band of irregulars was being formed, and he was excited beyond words at the news. His family had suffered under the king, Il Duce, the local

Fascists and the Germans. Maybe it would be different under the partisans. Adelmo's only regret was that he could not leave Possatore and go up the mountain to join Lupo and Gianni Rossi and the others who had decided to fight. He knew that such a move would condemn his wife and children to death. Even with him there to farm the land and protect them, the family barely survived.

One day a partisan showed up at the house, and Adelmo greeted him effusively. "Look," he said, "I cannot join you, and I have not enough food to go around, but I have a big barn where your men can sleep, and I can butcher for you and thresh your wheat and carry your messages."

From that day on there were almost always partisans in Adelmo's barn, much to the discomfiture of the Tonelli family, which shared the *casa colonica.* "This will come to no good, Adelmo," Antonio Tonelli told him again and again. "I have nine children to care for, and I want nothing to do with your partisans." But Adelmo Benini continued his dangerous liaison. He was carried away by the exhilaration of resistance, the heady fumes of comradeship, the feeling that for the first time in his life he was not merely existing.

One night in early September, 1944, when the partisans were away on a raid, Adelmo was awakened by a loud banging on the door of the farmhouse. "Go see what it is!" his wife said, but Adelmo was afraid. In these times, a knock on the door in the middle of the night could signify nothing but danger. Adelmo and Norina sat up in bed and listened, and soon they noticed that whoever was outside kept repeating a single word, and the word sounded like "Americans! Americans!" When he was positive, Adelmo ran to the door and opened it.

Four of the biggest, widest, tallest and dirtiest men Adelmo had ever seen bounded into the room shouting, "Americans!"

"Bene! Benissimo!" Adelmo said, and stuck out his hand, which was jerked ferociously by each of the visitors. There could be no doubt about it: underneath layers of mud and dirt and caked blood from long scratches on their hands and faces, the strangers were wearing the uniform of the American Army. Norina brought cheese and sausage, and the Americans managed to communicate in a painful pantomime that they had been en route to Germany on a prison train, that they had pulled the alarm and jumped out the window, that one of their comrades had been killed, and that they had headed

for the mountains because they had been told there were partisans there.

Adelmo installed the Americans in his hayloft, where they remained for ten days, or nearly long enough to eat him out of house and home. Altogether, they devoured one whole *prosciutto,* a fifteen-quart demijohn of wine that he had managed to borrow from a friend, and enough bread and *polenta* to feed the Beninis for a month. "I am proud to have them stay with us," Adelmo said to Norina one night, "but soon there will be nothing to offer them."

When he explained the situation to the Americans, one of them wrote out a note certifying that they had consumed large quantities of the food and wine of a certain Adelmo Benini of Possatore di Casaglia, and that this certain Benini should be reimbursed generously by the first U.S. Army fiscal officer to reach the area. *"Grazie! Grazie tante!"* Adelmo said, and went on to explain that the piece of paper did nothing to solve his immediate problem. Finally, he led the Americans over the hills to the temporary partisan headquarters at Prunaro, two miles away, and bade them an emotional farewell. The Allies were less than twenty miles to the south, and the partisans would slip the escaped prisoners through the lines at night.

Adelmo returned home with mixed feelings in his heart. There was less to eat in this harvest month of September, 1944, than in any September he could remember, with most of the crops rotting in the fields for want of manpower. But nothing so bad could go on forever. Adelmo knew that there were 1,200 armed partisans hidden about Monte Sole, and whole divisions of Americans and Englishmen just over the mountains to the south. When a new group of 15 or 20 partisans came to his house on the evening of September 28 and asked if they could sleep in his barn, Adelmo welcomed them generously. "I see you have brought a pig," he said. "Do you know how to slaughter him? No? Then I will see you early in the morning, and I guarantee you: you will enjoy your breakfast!" Before he went to bed, Adelmo sharpened his knife and laid out his ropes and his tools. They would have a banquet in the morning. The end of the war was not far off; they might as well start celebrating.

Sister Antonietta Benni, teacher of small children and lay nun of the Sisters of Saint Angela, saw life through enormous black-rimmed glasses that kept slipping down a nose that was too tiny for her face. By 1944 Sister Benni had been tolerating this architectural error for so many years that she poked her glasses back to eye level almost by reflex, as others brush back wandering locks of hair or rub at their noses or tug at their ears, and her warm brown eyes blinked through smudgy lenses oiled and reoiled hundreds of times a day by her fingers. Since Sister Benni was barely five feet tall and inclined to a slight plumpness, the total effect was that of a wise middle-aged owl, squinting with grudging approval at the world around her. This owlishness was heightened by her taste in dress. Although Sister Benni was a secular nun and therefore not permitted to wear the formal black habit of her order, she affected black in almost everything she wore —black shoes, black dress, black sweater and black shawl, only rarely setting off the black ensemble with a tiny pair of plain gold earrings worn through ears pierced in infancy. In her miniature house, consisting of two closet-sized rooms in the closet-sized mountain village of Gardeletta, there were always a few black cats running around, playing among the pictures of Pius XII, the statues of Christ on the Cross and the Virgin, and the sprays of violets and roses in front of the religious displays and niches.

Although Fascism and war had marched across Italy during Sister Benni's adulthood, neither had wrought any major changes in her way of life. She was aware that some of the children she had taught were now up on Monte Sole fighting as partisans, but she was not exactly sure what principles motivated them. Some of the priests had said that the partisans neglected their church duties, and others had said that the partisans evidently had forsworn the Ten Commandments for the duration. This was something Sister Benni could comprehend, and she hoped that these fallen souls would come to her after the war and explain why they had forgotten the moral lessons she had labored to teach them. For now, she simply tried to dismiss them from her mind. Her world remained bounded by the church down the road, which she visited twice daily for mass and vespers, and the little houses and huts of her native Gardeletta and the adjoining mountainside. These habitations furnished her, every morning at nine, with children of preschool age to be taught, molded and inspired, and who, in turn, taught, molded and inspired Sister Benni. She shared few of the interests of her peers in the mountain village. She took little part in the community activities, the cooking sessions, the games in the public square, the occasional dances, the wine festivals, the harvest celebrations.

Nor did she take part in the interminable conversations and speculations and gossipings that went on about the *strega* (the witch), who lived on the outskirts of town toward the village of Murazze. Not that Sister Benni took a position against witchcraft—that would have been too bold for any of the villagers, all of whom had been brought up on tales of the *strega*'s power. It was said that the *strega* could curdle milk, turn water to wine and wine to water, and double a cow's production. There was a witch in every village, and the one in Gardeletta was Letizia Testi. Letizia's husband was a shoemaker nicknamed Scarpecioli (Old Shoes), and therefore she became known by the same nickname with feminine endings: Scarpeciole. No one fooled with Mrs. Old Shoes; no one had challenged her since the next-door neighbor had poisoned the old witch's chickens. You could hear the story *sotto voce* from any resident of the little valley village. One day the witch's chickens had crossed through the fence and begun pecking away at freshly planted seeds in the neighbor's vegetable patch. This had happened before, and the neighbor was fed up, so she put out poisoned seeds and killed some of Mrs. Old Shoes' chickens. Instantly the *strega* knew what had happened and who was responsible, and she put a *malocchio* (evil eye) on the neighbor, who was in advanced pregnancy at the time. The child was born a few months later, sickly and stunted, and died after seven years of ill health.

It was commonly believed around Monte Sole that the *strega*'s favorite time for administering the *malocchio* was during mass, while the priest was saying the credo, and when the first words of the credo were heard, everybody would strain to see in which direction Mrs. Old Shoes was looking. One day the parishioners observed that the *strega* was staring hard at the pew of the Ruggeri family, who farmed a rich patch of land at Ca' Pudella, a mile or so up the mountain. To make her actions more ominous, the witch walked over to Cecilia Ruggeri after the mass, touched her on the shoulder and said, "My, how fat you have grown!" Signora Ruggeri was pregnant.

The whole Ruggeri clan, a dozen strong, raced up to their home and began taking steps to remove the curse. There were many techniques. One was to go to another witch and ask for help. The new *strega* would put a few drops of olive oil on the surface of a cup of water and make her magic incantations. If the oil spread smoothly and evenly over the surface, the curse remained. If the film of oil broke into droplets, the curse was gone. Sometimes it would take five or ten visits to the friendly witch to break the spell.

For men, there was a simple way to avoid becoming accursed, and that was simply to reach down and touch one's privates when a witch appeared. When Mrs. Old Shoes passed down the road in Gardeletta, one could see every man deftly reaching down his pants. Sister Benni had witnessed this often, and she also had witnessed a sacrilegious variation of the technique. Certain anticlerical men in town would wait till the priest had passed and then touch themselves. They regarded this as a clever comment on popery and the church. Once one of the priests was asked to double his efforts to save a highly sacrilegious man in the village, and the priest said, "How am I to save him when every time I come near him he touches his balls?"

The family Ruggeri had to take much more drastic steps to lift the curse on Cecilia. The pregnant woman made several visits to another *strega* on the opposite side of the mountain, but the film of oil held fast. Finally, the baby was born, healthy and fat, and christened Lina. After three months the infant weighed exactly the same as at birth. Cecilia went back to her new therapeutic *strega,* and again the oil film did not break. She hurried home and assembled the family in the kitchen. They made nine *pasta*-like *gnocchi,* tiny dumplings of flour, egg, potato and yeast. Each day for nine days one of the *gnocchi* was dissolved in water, and the resulting cloudy liquid rubbed on the sickly Lina. To everybody's relief, the curse lifted; the child began to gain weight.

Sister Benni had heard the story, and she did not doubt it for an instant, nor did she deny the *strega*'s powers. It was just that her own time was taken up by her devotion to the church. The way certain of her neighbors in Gardeletta carried on, you would have thought they had more faith in the *strega* than the priest, and this was where Sister Benni drew the line. When in doubt, she prayed. She did not run to the *strega,* and if she suspected that the *strega* had put a curse on her, she simply redoubled her prayers.

Of course, it was well known and believed by all, including Sister Benni, that the witch did have certain healing powers, and that these were passed on by the old Letizia to her daughter-in-law and protégée, Giulia Serra Testi, who also lived in Gardeletta. By the time of the war the second-generation witch had been credited with any number of healings. She had started with animals, and everyone on the mountain knew that Giulia Testi could make a sick pig get up and walk. Conversely, she could make a healthy pig lie down and die, although she was too good a person to use this power lightly. There was one family on the mountain that had been conducting a running feud with the Testi family, but so far the witch seemed to have the upper hand. Sometimes this mountain family would come down to the valley to grind grain, and since this was an all-day job, the family would have to bring along its cows for milking. Normally each cow would give between one and two gallons of milk, but the family members swore that as soon as they led the cows past Giulia Testi's house, the udders would go dry. When she was asked about this, Giulia Testi would shrug her shoulders and say that the mountain people were imagining things.

Sometimes the *strega* would make house calls, just like a general practitioner of medicine, and one of her specialties was relieving the mysterious aches and pains of the back. If her preliminary incantations did not "pull" the pain out, Giulia would ask for two pots, one large and one small, and a bucket of ashes. She would boil a few inches of water in the big pot, fill the smaller pot with ashes and carefully place it upside down in the bigger pot. While everyone maintained respectful silence, the witch would move her hands over the pots until all the water had been drawn out of the bigger one and into the ashes. Simultaneously the pain was supposed to be drawn out of the patient. If this did not work, the *strega* would ask for a scythe, and while the patient was prone, she would make various patterns above him with the blade. No one kept any records, but it was commonly believed that no ache or pain had ever been able to resist this ultimate step by the witch. In fact, her powers of healing were so respected that more than once the partisans in the hills had sent for her. Gianni Rossi, the vice-commander of the local partisan brigade and himself a native of Gardeletta, had often instructed his men to get the *strega*.

The pious Sister Benni did not look down her nose at the activities of the witch. She knew Giulia Testi to be a pleasant woman, the mother of three lovely daughters, all of whom attended the little *asilo* where

Sister Benni taught. Each morning promptly at nine the children would show up at the classroom, and each morning promptly at nine, to get things off in the proper spirit, Sister Benni would suggest a game of *giro, giro, tondo,* the Italian version of ring-around-the-rosy. Joining hands in the tiny room, the witch's daughter and Sister Benni and the other children would dance in a circle and sing loudly:

Giro, giro, tondo,	Around, around, in a circle,
Giriamo tutto il mondo,	The world comes down,
Gira la terra,	The earth falls down,
Tutti giù per terra!	Everybody on the ground!

And fifteen or sixteen children, ages three to six, and one secular nun, age forty-five, would fall to the floor with loud giggles and high-pitched laughter. "For charity!" Sister Benni would say as she scrambled to her feet, smoothing her black skirt and poking up her glasses. "What are all you *bambini* doing on the floor? Now it is time to play the woodcutter game."

The woodcutter game was one of a dozen different onomatopoetic singing games in which the children would try to duplicate the sawing sounds of the woodsman or the rapping of a carpenter's hammer or the clank and thump of a thresher. When the games were over, Sister Benni would lead discussions on subjects like: "What does the carpenter do? What does the thresher do?" It was Sister Benni's theory that children learned faster when ponderous schoolbooks were laid aside and the simple associations of village life were brought home to them. Thus she would hold up a picture of a grape and ask the children what it was. *"Uva,"* they would shout.

"And how do you say the first part of *uva?*"

"*U.*"

"And you have just learned a vowel!" Sister Benni would say triumphantly, turning then to pictures of an umbrella (*O* for *ombrella*), a tree (*A* for *albero*), and representations of the other letters. From there the students would go on to the rudiments of reading, but never very far past that point. Sister Benni only had the children for three years, and she did not deceive herself—most of the parents in the village regarded her as a baby-sitter, a handy custodian of the children till four P.M., a harmless old maid who enabled the mothers to help earn their families' livings in this most marginal of agricultural areas. The real educational process would begin at age six in the first grade at the local church, where trained teachers would school the children for another three years, at the end of which time they would be pronounced fit for their careers in farming and childbearing, the main concerns of the region.

Naturally, the preschool training period left many of the everyday disciplinary problems up to Sister Benni. "Go stand in the corner!" she would say to a miscreant. "We are not going to have any bad children around here." Now and then sterner punishment was required, and Sister Benni had no compunction about lashing out with her fingernails and knuckles to rap some second offender on the top of the head. Lately, with the coming of Allied bombers to the area, she found herself administering more and more smacks on the head. Through some obscure process which she did not try to understand, wartime seemed to be turning some of her best children sour. Little boys who were well on the way to learning their catechisms by heart would suddenly turn their intellectual energies to the construction of paper airplanes, which they would propel all about the room when her back was turned. More sophisticated craftsmen would throw spitballs or bombard the walls of the classroom with pebbles and peas shot from elastic bands. One day Sister Benni felt a minor sting in the seat of her skirt and, reaching around, extracted a paper airplane with a straight pin inset in the nose. When she took the problem to the priest, he told her not to worry, that the boys in her class were only imitating what was going on in the skies above them. She did not tell the priest about another disciplinary problem. Some of the children were singing bawdy songs, and teaching the words to the others. There was a song about Arcibaldo and Petronilla, sung to the melody of a Fascist march, and it was so off-color as to be unrepeatable even by adults. Sister Benni did not object to the implied insults to the Fascists in the song, although the Fascists had never bothered her, but she certainly did not approve of the language.

Far worse than these filthy secular songs, which only came to Sister Benni's attention by accident, were some distortions and contaminations of holy Catholic ritual. Certain children had learned a new version of the Hail Mary from some of the older children in the mountain village. During Allied bombing raids, they would chant:

Ave Maria, gratia pleina,	Hail Mary, full of grace,
Fa' che non suoni più la sirena.	Do not let the sirens sound anymore.
Fa' che non vengan' più gli aeroplani.	Do not let the airplanes come anymore.
Fammi dorma fino a domani.	And let me sleep until tomorrow.
Ese una bomba dovesse cadere,	And if a bomb should fall,
Vergine Santa! Stringimi accanto al tuo cuore,	Blessed Virgin, press me to your heart,
Misericordioso e santo.	Your blessed and merciful heart.

And there was even a slight variation on this variation:

E se una bomba dovesse cadere,	And if a bomb should fall,
Vergine Santa! Non nel sedere!	Blessed Virgin! Not on my ass!

Sister Benni did not know how to cope with such heresies, and she took to explaining them away (though never excusing them) by saying, with the rest of the people of the village, "It is the war; nothing is normal." Indeed, as the early months of 1944 went by, the situation in Gardeletta became violently abnormal. The village lay a few yards from the main railroad line, the *direttissima,* which ran in peacetime from Bologna straight to Florence, fifty miles away, and on to Rome. Now the rail line linked the German-occupied cities of the north with the front, twenty or twenty-five miles south of Gardeletta, and it had become a primary target for Allied bombers. To make matters worse, Gardeletta lay on a highway that also ran to the front, and local partisans operating from the mountains above had taken advantage of their intimate knowledge of the area to assault German troop convoys. Many of the partisans were closely related to the people of Gardeletta, and the situation grew volatile. There had already been murderous German reprisals, some of them on the traditional basis of ten Italians for each dead German soldier. This was one more reason why some of the people in Gardeletta did not approve of the partisan brigade. The irregulars made their raids at night, retreated back up the mountain, and left defenseless civilians to face the German wrath the next day.

With Allied air raids by night and tightening German pressure by day, Sister Benni discovered that her nursery school was rapidly dwindling in size. Alarmed parents were taking their children up to mountain refuges or sending them away to relatives in safer zones. News broadcasts told of Allied victories to the south, and by the spring of 1944 it seemed clear to everyone that the Americans and the English meant to push through the mountains to Bologna and the plain of the Po before the onset of winter. With the front moving closer and the *asilo* attendance down to a minimum, Sister Benni packed her black clothes and her prayer books and her pictures of the vowels and climbed one mile up the flank of Monte Sole to a place called Cerpiano, where her order maintained a children's refuge, a school and a small tenant farm. She was welcomed, and a dozen small children were placed in her care. It was not Gardeletta, and it was not home, but Sister Benni was learning to make the best of things. High in this mountain retreat, away from railroad lines and military operations and strategic areas, the nuns and the children would wait out the last few months of the war in safety.

When Fernando Piretti was a boy of three or four, his family had lived in a big house called Casa Veneziana at the bottom of the eastern slope of Monte Sole, between the old medieval village of Murazze and the busy little town of Vado. Their land, like the two communities, was watered by the Setta, which was too small to be called a river (*fiume*), too big to be called a creek (*insenatura*), and which was called, therefore, a torrent (*torrente*). Sometimes the *torrente* Setta was a torrent even in the English sense of the word, when heavy spring runoffs in the Apennines would flood the bottomland and carry thousands of tons of gray-brown mud north to the Setta's confluence with the river Reno, a few miles south of Bologna, and thence to the syrupy Po, where it would join with the mud from other *torrenti* and other *fiumi* and go roiling down the Po Valley. The Setta's unpredictability had caused most of the local farmers to give up on the rich bottomland along the torrent's banks. They built their homes a few hundred yards up the hill and farmed the slopes with oxen and cows that had to be trained to do their daily chores on the bias.

Casa Veneziana, the first home that Fernando Piretti could remember, was an old *casa colonica,* a farmhouse built to contain several families of *contadini.* It perched on the hillside directly above the *direttissima* and Railroad House No. 66, where a couple of families of track laborers shared living space. The railroad house, in turn, commanded a view of the road and the Setta. All that Fernando could remember about the people in House No. 66 was that one of the families was named Paselli and had a pair of twins of his age, and on very rare occasions he would be allowed to play with them.

For the most part, however, the Piretti children, four boys and two girls, did not enjoy the easy familiarities of the other children of the region. At three or four, Fernando did not understand what was wrong, and his father could not explain. The problem was that the father, Maximiliano Piretti, a mountain troll barely five feet tall with a fierce mustache, a sharp nose and an angry look about him, was a Socialist, and an outspoken one at that. In a country that permitted only one political party and muscled all others out of existence with bands of political toughs, Maximiliano's dedication to his own principles was downright suicidal. More than once he was set upon and bloodied; businessmen would firmly but politely refuse to do business with him; certain parents of the neighborhood would warn their children to stay away from the Pirettis and the crazy father. And still Maximiliano would tell all who would listen that Socialism was the answer for Italy, especially for agricultural Italy, and that Benito Mussolini was an ignorant ass who should be run out of office, along with the dummy king who sat behind him.

For years now, Maximiliano had felt the economic pinch forced upon him by such outspokenness, and the family had been surviving by selling off land. With the coming of the war and imaginative new taxes and sharply rising prices, Maximiliano found himself down to a few acres, and he redoubled his efforts to get a job. But the answer was always the same: "Go get a *tessera* [Fascist party card] and you can have work." There were war jobs available, but the inflexible Maximiliano had been branded by the local Fascists as unemployable, at least until he renounced Socialism. And when certain members of his big family would tell Maximiliano to stick his tongue in his cheek and go fill out a *tessera,* just as many of the others had done, Maximiliano would square his shoulders and explain that he could not bring himself to such hypocrisy. One day, when the war was young and little Fernando was four, his mother woke him up and told him that they all were going to move that morning to the home of Uncle Luigi Piretti, Maximiliano's brother, in the nearby village of Gardeletta. The last square foot of land at Casa Veneziana had been sold, and now the family of Maximiliano would have to depend on others.

Maximiliano found no more work in Gardeletta than he had elsewhere, and soon he was reduced to begging. Night after night he would come home and dump the contents of his paper bag on the kitchen table. There would be a few ends of bread, one or two apples, a half-spoiled cut of salami, some crumbly cheese, a handful of soggy grapes. Sometimes there would be nothing. Maximiliano, whose nickname in the ancient local dialect was Maxmein, was a soft touch himself. "Ah, there is good old Maxmein," another unfortunate of the area would say, and he would run over and put his arm around good old Maxmein and tell his troubles, and that night the Piretti family would go hungry. Little Fernando was used to it. At least he did not have to go out and help his father beg, as the older brothers did. He was left at home to play, when he could find someone to play with. The children of Gardeletta knew him, they all were pals, but if he ventured down the road toward his old home at Casa Veneziana or toward the town of Vado, he would run into packs of children who would say, "Get out of here! Your father is a beggar!" and Fernando would run home crying to his mother and ask her what he should do, and she would give him the same advice over and over. "Fernando," she would say, "you cannot do a thing about it. We need *everybody*. Even the people who insult us."

The happiest day that Fernando could remember was in early 1944, when he was almost nine years old and hardly bigger than a doll because the Pirettis were physically small in the first place and undernourished in the second. His father came rushing into the house, proudly displaying an old toy gun. Carefully, as though handling precious jewels, Maxmein showed little Fernando how it worked. You pulled back on the spring to cock the gun; then you put the cork in the end and pulled the trigger. The cork would pop out with a loud noise and hang by a string.

The next morning Fernando was sitting on a stone wall shooting his popgun and watching the cork arc out into space. When he heard his father come out of the house, Fernando scrambled to his feet to show off his gun, and just as Maximiliano came into sight, the boy dropped the popgun fifteen feet straight down the wall. Without a word, his father hit Fernando in the face.

Days later Maxmein put the boy on his knee and explained haltingly to him that he had never been able to bring home such a toy before, that he doubted if he would ever be able to bring home such a toy again, and that he had lost control of himself when he had seen what happened. On the other hand, Maximiliano explained, he could understand Fernando's carelessness. The boy had never had a toy. How could he know how to handle one? Maxmein said he was sorry.

But if there were no toys, there were other diversions for Fernando and his friends in Gardeletta. There were sticks to throw and trees to climb, there was the nearby Setta for swimming and wading and fishing, and there was Monte Sole. Now and then Fernando and his pals would go up the mountain hunting foxes and skunks. These were the two most hated pests of the community, and a boy who killed one could go from farmhouse to farmhouse displaying the pelt and collecting tribute from the farmers. There would be a piece of *prosciutto* here, a wedge of cheese there, an egg to suck, a sip of wine, all sorts of delicacies. The tradition was strong, and the boy who killed a skunk or a fox was a hero for weeks. Unfortunately, Fernando and his pack of friends had not been able to kill a fox or a skunk as yet, but they had seen tracks, and they knew that their first triumph could not be far off. Fernando would dream of seeing a fox, throwing a rock and hitting him right between the eyes, and then making the grand *giro* of the *contadini,* returning to the kitchen of his home at the end of the day dragging a sack of food that would sustain the Pirettis for weeks, or until Fernando had conked another fox between the eyes with his unerring aim.

But the most interesting diversion of all, to the young people of Gardeletta, took place every June 24, on the evening of the Feast of Saint John, when the natives of Gardeletta carried out a ritual imported from Brazil. Years before, the family of a girl named Palmina Betti had emigrated, like so many families of the Monte Sole area, to the New World. They had gone to São Paulo, Brazil, to work on a coffee plantation, and there the young Palmina had observed the natives showing their faith in St. John by walking on hot coals. Palmina noticed that the Brazilians were very exacting about the coals—they had to be made of oak that had burned for three or four days until the whole hot bed was covered with a blue-gray shifting of ashes. After a few years the Betti family became disenchanted with Brazil and returned to Gardeletta, where Palmina married a man named Rossi. She always remembered the strange custom of the Brazilians, and one year she prevailed upon her husband and other men of the village to build a fire of oak and keep feeding it for three or four days until the Feast of Saint John on June 24. With her wide-eyed neighbors standing around, Palmina Betti Rossi took off her shoes and walked across the coals. Then she repeated her act. "Run, run!" the neighbors shouted, but Palmina answered, "No, the slower I do it, the safer I am. But of course, I have faith in Saint John."

All of this had started in the 1930's, and by the time of the war the ritual was an old habit in Gardeletta. At first only adults had walked across the coals, but then Palmina's son Gianni, later to become a partisan hero, celebrated his tenth year of life by walking across the glowing bed, and from then on nothing could stop the children from having their turns. So many people came to Gardeletta to see the ritual and take part in it that the bed of coals had to be built up in the *boccie* court next to the village inn, where the men would burn tons of oak for several days before the ritual. One year the doctor of the region, Arturo Dalmastri, showed up in a big black Fiat sedan with several other officials and watched openmouthed. Palmina provided an explanation to the doctor and his companions. "It is widely known that you can do anything you want on the Feast of Saint John, provided you have faith," she said. The doctor did not express himself on the phenomenon, but there were certain other thinkers in the community, notably Maximiliano Piretti, who said that the scientific explanation was simple. There were five or six inches of light ash covering the coals, and this compressed under the foot of the walker to provide an effective insulation that shut out heat. This was why it was better to walk slowly across the coals, Maximiliano explained, because the ashes would then form a neat lining under the foot. The explanation mattered little to the children of the village. All they knew was that Saint John's Night brought hundreds of new faces to Gardeletta, and the whole village would glow with the light from the coals on the *boccie* court, and everybody would run around sipping wine and walking the coals. Even in this year of 1944, when there were hardly any men left in the village, they had carried out the ritual.

As it happened, the 1944 celebration of Saint John's Night was the final wartime *festa* in Gardeletta, although no one knew it at the time. By midsummer there was hardly an able-bodied man left in the village, and one result was that there was hardly any food to be shared. More and more the Pirettis went hungry, and Fernando would prowl the woods for chestnuts and mushrooms and truffles with diminishing success as others prowled the woods looking for the same edibles. The fields that rimmed the little mountain village had long since gone untended, the *contadini* up in the woods with the partisans or off in Germany as slave laborers or just plain hiding out. Men like Maxmein, fifty-three years old but able-bodied in the context of the times, had to rush for cover when the Germans came through rounding up laborers, and more than once he barely missed being picked up as a hostage. One by one Fernando's older brothers had said good-bye and gone away to join the partisan brigade—no one knew exactly where they were now, although they always seemed to come back to Monte Sole—and the situation in the valley village seemed more and more precarious, especially for the family of a Socialist beggar. If they did not die of malnutrition because of the food shortage, the Pirettis ran the risk of dying at night in their beds, when Allied aircraft came in low to bomb the bridge at nearby Vado and strafe the *direttissima.*

By midsummer, the Pirettis were spending more nights in the railroad tunnel shelter than in their sparse quarters in the house of Uncle Luigi, and when the partisans killed a German soldier on the outskirts of Gardeletta at the beginning of September, Maxmein told his family that it was time to flee. The Allied armies were only miles to the south and making steady progress northward. The Germans were becoming increasingly unpredictable. Maxmein could not go out to beg any longer, and even if it had been safe for him to leave the house, there was hardly anyone left to beg from. He told the family that he had heard of a refuge operated a mile or so up Monte Sole by the Sisters of Saint Angela. Surely the sisters would not turn away this family that depended on others.

The sisters did not turn them away. Mother, father, two teen-age daughters and son Fernando were given a room in the big farmhouse at Cerpiano, and the boy was handed a prayer book and told to learn his responses; there was a chapel connected to the big *palazzo* of the refuge, and there were visiting priests from the mountain area to say mass, but certain other niceties were lacking. At nine, Fernando was the oldest boy in the refuge. Quickly he learned his responses—there was little else to do except walk in the woods and play with smaller children—and soon he found himself a personage of renown in the mountain society: the one and only altar boy.

In the time that the family stayed in the refuge, Fernando also found that he was of interest to the German soldiers. When Nazi patrols visited the refuge, looking for the partisans who swarmed over the area but seldom came into sight, they invariably would go straight to Fernando and begin peppering him with questions in their faulty Italian. Where were the partisans? Did he have brothers in the partisans? Well, where had his brothers gone? If he knew nothing about the partisans, what could he tell them about the men of the area? Did he ever see any of them prowling around at night? How were they dressed? Did they carry guns? Fernando enjoyed every second of the inquisition, because it made him feel important and because one of the German sergeants always provided him with candies. He knew that no matter what he said he could not get his brothers and the other partisans in trouble, because he knew nothing. The partisans did not show themselves to the natives of the area any more than they showed themselves to the German patrols. They did not want to run the risk of giving away their locations to informers, and they did not want to subject their families to torture by the Nazis. On the rare occasions when one of Fernando's big brothers would come to the refuge for a visit, he would talk about everything except where he was hiding, and in the middle of the night he would slip away. Let the Germans question; Fernando had nothing to lose, and he was enjoying his first tastes of chocolate and importance.

Just down the hill from the Pirettis' old house at Casa Veneziana, the family of Virginio Paselli shared Railroad House No. 66 with the family of another trackworker. One night during the war, Virginio came home from his long day's work on the *direttissima* carrying a lamb in his arms. No one was surprised. Many of the poor people of Monte Sole kept a sheep or two. The fathers would truss the animals up once or twice a year, give them haircuts and turn the pile of wool over to the mothers to make into undershirts, sweaters and other soft woolly garments. When the sheep had outgrown its usefulness, it could always be slaughtered and eaten.

But when the lamb arrived at Railroad House No. 66, Cornelia, oldest of the four Paselli children, snatched it out of her father's arms and began petting it. Sister Giuseppina, fifteen years old, clapped her hands and said, "Oh, what shall we name him?" And the ten-year-old twins, Luigi and Maria, the youngest members of the family, jumped up and down with excitement.

"Just a minute," Virginio said. "This lamb will provide us with clothes and food. It is not a toy."

The four children looked shocked. "No one will eat this poor little thing!" Cornelia said.

"And no one will cut its pretty wool," Giuseppina said.

"We will see," said Virginio.

It has always been the impression throughout Italy that lambs and sheep do not say *baa,* as they do in Anglo-Saxon nations, but something that sounds like *tay-aaa, tay-aaa,* and so the lamb was named Tay-a and assigned a small lamb house next to the outdoor oven in the little garden behind the Pasellis' half of the dwelling. Hardly had the lamb grown into a sheep before it became evident that he was a barnyard prodigy. He learned to come when his name was called, and he licked the children's hands and wagged his tail and followed them around. But Tay-a's main virtue was that he could be ridden, at least by the twins, who were tiny dolls like all the mountain children.

It seemed to Cornelia that every morning began the same at Railroad House No. 66. When the sun had just begun to warm the thick stone walls of the dwelling, the twins would slip from their bed in their long nightclothes and yawn and stretch and lean out the window to call, "Tay-a! Tay-a!" The sheep would come bounding out of his house and stand under the window looking up at them, wagging his tail like a metronome. "Calm yourself, Tay-a," Gigi would say. "Soon we will go for a ride!"

Each of the four children dreaded the shearing days, and the sheep did not appear to enjoy the operation either. While Virginio held the animal tight and worked the shears up and down its flanks, the twins would circle around giving instructions. "Not so hard, Father!" "You hurt him!" "Oh, Father, how cruel!" All the children usually called their father *Babbo,* the Italian equivalent of Daddy, but when the sheep was being sheared, he was always Father.

One day Virginio carried the sack of wool into the house and told Cornelia, "Mercy, daughter, the twins do not seem to realize that we need this wool."

"Well," Cornelia said, "is it necessary that you be so rough, Father?"

"Whay!" Virginio said, his face showing mock alarm. "You, too?"

But later Virginio told Cornelia that he was pleased at his coup in getting the sheep. Tay-a was the perfect new addition to the family. He ate little, paid his own way, and provided fun and laughter for everyone. Virginio said he only wished he could say the same for the chickens.

In those days the Pasellis were frequently visited by a small boy named Leandro, who was barely out of diapers, and the twin Luigi used the sheep to tease him. Luigi would make friends with Leandro and then suggest that the child go for a ride on the sheep. When Leandro was firmly aboard, Gigi would stroll forty or fifty feet away and shout, *"Tay-a!"* The sheep would take off like a racehorse, and Leandro would scream and cry and hang on for his life.

"Never do that again!" the mother Angelina would say, wagging a stubby finger in Luigi's face, but nothing could stop the twin from repeating the same act as soon as Leandro had been lulled off his guard again.

One day the little victim came screaming into the kitchen where Cornelia was helping her mother prepare a meal. Cornelia took the child in her arms and tried to calm him, but little Leandro was not to be calmed. "What happened?" the mother said. "What is it, Leandro?"

"I . . . was . . . eating . . . a . . . prune," the child said between sobs, "and . . . I . . . swallowed . . . the . . . pit!"

"There, there," Angelina said, patting the boy softly. "Everybody does that. Nothing will happen to you."

"Yes, something will! Gigi told me! He said I will sprout, and he will plant me! What can I do? Gigi says I will soon be a tree!" It was hours before the mother and daughter could calm the small boy, and that night the twin Luigi went to bed early, missing both his supper and the evening session of storytelling by the father.

In those middle years of the war, Virginio would gather his children around him in the blacked-out living room of the railroad house and try to distract them, always ending by telling them not to worry about the bombings, that they would have to get far worse before they would be worth a single frown. Cornelia soon realized that her father's role on earth was to gentle the lives of others. When the family huddled inside the nearby railroad tunnel during the infrequent air raids, Virginio would say over and over, "Remain calm. Nothing to worry about. Nothing to fear." And in the tunnel, while hundreds of the mountain people cried at the sound of every bomb and shrieked at the fusillades from the machine guns, there always seemed to be an aura of warm dignity around Virginio and his little group. Cornelia, who had learned the routine, would say to her father: "Tell us again, *Babbo,* how you got bald."

"It was in World War I," Virginio would say, "when the Italians made their great stand against the Austrians at Piave in the Po Valley. Why, the bombardments made this look like a children's game! One morning I awoke in my trench, and there were shell holes in a complete circle around me, and part of the parapet had fallen down and covered my legs, and weeks later when I went to the company barber for a haircut, he looked at me and said, 'What do you want me to cut? Your hair is all gone!' And that is when I knew my hair had fallen out from fright. Yes, it is true! So you know there is nothing to worry about as long as you have hair." He would rub his knuckles across Gigi's brush cut and say, "No danger yet! Gigi is not bald!"

Although he lived and worked in the valley, Virginio Paselli was a mountain man by birth. His family had farmed Possatore di Casaglia, and as far back as anyone could trace, they had always been on the same *podere.* There was another Paselli in the area, the old patriarch Duilio, who could prove that his ancestors had been on Monte Sole for 400 years, and Duilio and Virginio were distant cousins. It was during the young manhood of Virginio and his brother, Giuseppe, that the family had begun to notice that the harvest at Possatore was decreasing sharply each year, and no amount of nitrogen or manure seemed to make any difference. Possatore was exhausted. One by one the Pasellis left their ancestral home, starting with Virginio, who married and went into the valley to work for the railroad. Giuseppe went next, finding work in the small town of Pianoro, and by the time World War II had started, the last Paselli was gone, and a succession of optimistic *contadini* had tried and failed to work the same *podere.* But times were difficult, and Virginio knew that there would always be men who were far enough down on the social ladder to challenge the barren land. Even in the middle of the war, two *contadini* were trying to make a living at Possatore, and Virginio could only feel sorry for them and their families.

Virginio Paselli was a miniature, like the others of the mountain. He was slightly taller than five feet, and he had intense green eyes that were the envy of his daughters. "What a waste," Cornelia would say to her father, "to give those green eyes to a man."

"Ah, but that is exactly how I captured your mother," Virginio would say, "and where would you be if that had not happened?"

Although he was no longer a farmer, Virginio was never able to rid himself of the *contadino*'s attachment to the land, and from the time Cornelia was able to walk, she found herself accompanying her father on hikes that went from one side of Monte Sole to the other. Wherever they went, from Quercia to Possatore to Casaglia to Caprara to San Martino and down the other side to Sperticano and Roncadelli and Pian di Venola, the little girl would hear the farmers shout, *"Whay,* Passlein!" using the dialect diminutive of Paselli, and Virginio would clap his friends on the back and sit down for long talks about the good old days. To Cornelia, the good old days were still with them. How exciting it was to cross the mountain with her father, to hunt mushrooms and truffles with him and pick chestnuts for the whole family! His nickname for her was Lela, and she always thought that she was her father's favorite child, although she had to admit to herself that one reason they were so close was because she was the only one big enough to keep up with him on his marathon hikes.

By late 1943 Cornelia had apprenticed herself to a seamstress, Iolande Veronesi of Bologna, and every morning she would leave Railroad House No. 66 in a high state of excitement. The electric train left the station at Vado at seven fifteen sharp, but Cornelia could never seem to get away from the house until the last minute, and she would have to pedal furiously to make it. One morning, when she was especially late, she tried a shortcut, riding on a narrow path alongside the tracks toward the station at Vado, but in the middle of a tunnel she heard the whistle of the Rome express and felt the rush of air and almost lost control of her bike as the train cleared her by inches. From then on she took the longer, safer way, twenty or thirty minutes by road. Some mornings she would be pedaling through rain or snow or drizzle, and she would say to herself, "It does not seem fair. I live on the railroad tracks, and I have to go to all this trouble to catch the train!" But as soon as she flopped down breathlessly in the third-class compartment and greeted her traveling companions and showed her pass to the conductor, her high spirits would return. She could hardly stand the excitement of being a young girl on a daily train ride to a glamorous faraway city (fifteen miles) that most of her friends had never even seen. In church, she said prayers of thanks that she came from a railroading family; otherwise, her apprenticeship would have been impossible. Since she rode the train free as the daughter of a railroad man and received a reduced bus fare under the Fascists' program called Traveling Reductions for Apprentices, the round trip to Bologna cost a few pennies a day. Even at an apprentice's salary of $1.60 every week, she was coming out ahead.

Cornelia would arrive at the home of seamstress Veronesi at eight A.M. and begin a fascinating day of stitching, embroidering and buttonholing, and if her teacher had withdrawn the $1.60 salary and beaten Cornelia every hour and made her work ten times as hard, the little country girl still would have been happy. To Cornelia, the Bologna home of Mistress Veronesi seemed like the center of world sophistication and culture. Cornelia was the only apprentice, and all the regular seamstresses treated her like a pet, taking time out from their own work to solve her problems and cover up her errors. The hours of the morning would fly, and at noontime Cornelia would open her lunch box to see what her mother had packed.

Usually the meal would consist of *pasta* in broth, kept warm in a small thermos, a slice of sausage or *prosciutto,* a piece of fruit and a lump of bread. But every once in a while there would be a surprise: a square of chocolate, a bit of chestnut-scented *mistocca* carefully wrapped in paper, or a few *chicce,* the traditional hard candies of the mountain. Cornelia would have only a half hour to consume her lunch, because she left each day at five thirty, a half hour before quitting time, to catch the train for Vado. And so her day would end in the same style it had started: running after a bus that would take her to the railroad station at the other end of the city and running from the bus to the station and out along the tracks to find the single door that was open in third-class so that she could swing herself aboard the moving car. An hour later she would be home spinning stories about the events of the day, and it was not long before her enthusiasm had communicated itself to every member of the family, including her father. Sister Giuseppina had long since announced that she was going to apprentice herself to Mistress Veronesi as soon as she got a little older, and one night, under the influence of Cornelia's vivid description of life in the big city, with its arcades and restaurants and thousands of busy people, old Passlein had said, "The way you talk, Lela, I wonder we do not all pack our belongings and move to Bologna."

"I wonder, too!" Cornelia said excitedly, and the family began discussions that went on for weeks and weeks and culminated in a decision to move to the big city. When both the older daughters were apprenticed as seamstresses, Virginio would apply for transfer. The only problem was the usual one, the war, and when the father mentioned his plan to the track foreman, he was told that his long years of service would certainly entitle him to consideration, but no transfers were being permitted for the duration.

"All right then," Virginio told his family, playing his usual pacifying role, "we will stay here till the war is over. It is not so bad. And I can tell you from my own experience in the Army: this war will not last long. Soon we will be free to move about as we choose."

But first, conditions had to get worse. By the spring of 1944 the Allies were bombing Bologna regularly, and sometimes Cornelia would have to sit on the train for hours while damage was being repaired on the line ahead. Soon her parents were asking her to interrupt her apprenticeship and remain safely at home till the war was over. One day when the family arose to the far-off sounds of bombs dropping on the city to the north, Virginio announced, "I no longer ask you, Cornelia. I tell you! When the war is over, you can go back to your apprenticeship." There was no use arguing. Her father did not often give orders, unlike most of the mountain men, but when he had made up his mind, he was inflexible.

At first, Cornelia was miserable, chained to the country home on the railroad tracks after her glittering life in the city, but soon the arrival of hundreds of refugees brought a new excitement to Monte Sole. Until now, her mother had never let her go to dances—she was barely eighteen—but with the coming of the refugees there were so many parties and dances in the various piazzas that her mother had to give in, and it seemed to Cornelia that she had never known such gay times. There was a sense of exhilaration that came with the war, and while the Allied aircraft stitched their sticks of bombs across the tile roofs of Bologna, the refugees in the valley danced and drank wine and tried to forget what was happening. It seemed to Cornelia that silliness and giddiness were the order of the day. She made friends with a lady refugee from Florence, the twenty-four-year-old wife of an Italian military pilot, and one day the two of them were bemoaning the fact that they had no phonograph. "I have a good one back home in Florence," the refugee said, "but of course, there is no way to get it now."

"Oh, but there is!" Cornelia said. The two young ladies borrowed the family's railroad passes and traveled to Florence, fifty miles away via *direttissima,* and fifty miles back carrying the heavy wind-up phonograph in their arms. They were lugging the thing into Railroad House No. 66 when Cornelia suddenly remembered something. "Records!" she said. "We forgot to bring your records!"

They put the phonograph down and opened the lid and found a single record on the turntable. On one side was "Ramona," and on the other, "Speak to Me of Love, Mariu." They played the two songs so often in the following weeks that the tunes became barely recognizable.

And then one day the gaiety ended. The Allies sharply increased their air raids on the *direttissima,* and all the refugees scattered. Some climbed Monte Sole to board with the *contadini,* and others returned to Bologna, realizing they were as safe one place as another. Around the railroad house there was a hushed silence, a feeling of impending catastrophe that even seemed to affect Tay-a, cowering and cringing in his lamb house whenever an airplane would appear. Toward the end of the summer the raids had grown so frequent that the Pasellis routinely hauled their blankets and their sheets into the railroad tunnel every night to listen to Virginio tell them that things were not as bad as they seemed against the background noises of bullets and bombs. Section by section, the tracks and bridges were shredded beyond repair, trains ceased running, and there was no longer any work for Virginio to do. With the end of the work came an end to his salary, and now for the first time the family began to feel the pangs of hunger.

On the morning of September 26, 1944, Virginio called his family together in the kitchen and delivered one of his calming addresses. "Children," he said, "the American soldiers are less than twenty miles to the south, and I can tell you from my own war experience that the front is soon going to pass through this valley. That is the way wars move: along valleys and roads. We are no longer safe here, and today we are all going to the refuge up at Cerpiano. We will have a pleasant time there with the sisters, and we will be safe from the war, and we will be back home in a week."

Cornelia's younger sister Giuseppina seemed elated by the news, and Cornelia thought of the trip as just another stroll up the mountain with her father, and the twin Maria acted pleased. But the child who was usually the most excited by any new activity, the prankster Luigi, was downcast. "What is the matter, Gigi?" Angelina asked. The child did not answer.

On the way up the mountain, carrying what they could and leading the sheep Tay-a, Gigi walked disconsolately within the family group, in contrast with other times when he would be running all over the place, picking chestnuts, and getting lost for long periods. After a climb of a few hundred yards the family reached the home of a neighbor, where they dropped off Tay-a, promising to retrieve him after the front had passed through. At Cerpiano, the six Pasellis were welcomed by the Sisters of Saint Angela and installed in a dormitory in the big house called the *palazzo*. There were already a dozen or so families in the refuge, some of them in the big house, some of them in the nearby dwelling of the *contadino,* Pietro Oleandri, and some of them camping in the barn. Sister Benni was in attendance, and the Pasellis recognized their old neighbors, the Maximiliano Pirettis who had lived above them at Casa Veneziana. "Well," said Virginio when they had dropped their heavy loads in the *palazzo,* "what is so bad about all this? We are on the mountain, and we are safe, and we are among friends." The girls chattered their agreement, but Luigi stood downcast and silent.

In his big farmhouse on the hillside between Quercia and Gardeletta, the old patriarch Duilio Paselli, distant kin of Virginio, had made another of his frequent promises to his favorite, Saint Anthony, and he wanted everyone to know about it. "I will announce my vow publicly," Duilio said to his large family after a bombing raid on the nearby *direttissima* had frightened them all. "I have sworn that if we get through the war safely, and our loved ones come back home unharmed, I will build a chapel at the gate of our property and dedicate it to Saint Anthony." Duilio had eleven children in all, but one of them was somewhere with the Afrika Korps, and two others were in military prison, and a few had married and gone to live elsewhere. Still, the old man's remaining household was as impressive as one would expect of the leader of one of the oldest families in the area. Under his roof, enjoying the fruits of his fertile *podere* in the valley, were his wife, two daughters, two sons, three daughters-in-law and three grandchildren, not one of whom had ever known a hungry day in the big farmhouse.

For at least four centuries the Paselli family had farmed in the area of San Martino, high on the mountain, but the land was poor, and when Duilio married Ester Pantaleoni, he quickly gave up the *podere* at San Martino and moved to Ester's property down the mountain. There he farmed thirty acres of nearly flat land, rich and dark, most of it in orchards and vineyards, with grapevines running from tree to tree, and juicy apples, pears, cherries and plums. From Duilio's vines came purple grapes that were so dark as to be almost black, and the wine they produced was a delicacy of the region. When you held a bottle of Duilio Paselli's *sangiovese* wine up to the sun, only the merest hint of red showed through, and the wine was rich and savory on the tongue. On the rest of his land Duilio grew overflow crops of corn and wheat, and his vegetable garden produced ten times more than his family could eat. By the standards of Monte Sole, Duilio Paselli was truly rich. Just before the war, on a Fascist holiday, his name had been included on an honors list of *Cavalieri del Lavoro* made up by Il Duce himself. By virtue of his hard work and his ancestry and his marriage to Ester Pantaleoni, Duilio Paselli was now officially a Knight of Labor. The old man looked the part. He had a circular patch of baldness, a floppy mustache and the face of a Mongol warrior, with eyes that slanted like a roof and twinkled in aquamarine. It was said in the valley that Duilio Paselli could stare down the devil.

But the old man was most renowned for his continuing arguments and reconciliations with his statues. All around the house he had saints in niches. There were three or four Madonnas a foot or two high, with fresh flowers at their feet, and statues of the favored Saint Anthony, and pictures of the Crucifixion. Some people bowed down to such things, carrying out the very idol worship that the Bible forbade, but Duilio Paselli was not of a humble nature. He thought of his saints and Madonnas and Christs almost as living things, partners in his work, and he carried on dialogues with them. When they were good to him, he gave thanks, and when they were bad, he lashed out at them in an angry voice. After a crop failed, Duilio stood in front of a statue of Saint Anthony in the barn and said, "What did you do to me? You are a traitor! I was so devoted to you." He threw a pitchfork and broke the statue in half. Soon there was the inevitable reconciliation and a repair job—the old man always felt bad after chastising one of his saintly friends—but later the statue in the barn had to face new perils. A calf was born weak and sick, and Duilio took the problem straight to Saint Anthony. "Dear Saint Anthony," he said, "please save the life of this new calf, because, Saint Anthony, if it does not go well for this calf, it will not go well for you." When the calf died, Duilio knocked the statue down and said, "All these years I have prayed to you, and look what you do to me!" He stood over the fallen statue and said, "You are a traitor, and a coward, too!"

These bouts between Duilio and the saints were legend on Monte Sole, but everybody forgave the old man. They knew he enjoyed his wine, sometimes a little too much, and sooner or later he would stumble out to the barn, cast a lantern on the statue of Saint Anthony and apologize profusely. Duilio was highly emotional, and everybody in the area figured that Saint Anthony would take that into consideration. When word went out that Duilio had promised to build a chapel to Saint Anthony at his front gate, provided that the family survived the war, everybody was pleased. After the trouble that the old man had given Saint Anthony, he certainly owed the saint a favor.

As the front lines moved up the valley toward his farm, Duilio Paselli became more and more nervous about the safety of his family, because he was a man who placed his loved ones above all else. He hated to think of leaving his fertile fields and so staunch a dwelling as the massive whitewashed Paselli *casa,* but the Germans had started disturbing them lately, asking questions about partisans and threatening to shoot anyone who lied. Then there were the reprisals: certain *contadini* had been taken away to Germany, and a few innocent men had been shot outright in retaliation for the acts of the partisans. Duilio talked the matter over with Saint Anthony and his other friends and finally decided to leave the *podere*.

Gathering up his big family and a few of his favorite statues, he made the long trek up Monte Sole to San Martino, where his ancestors had lived for nearly half a millennium, and knocked on the door of the rectory. Don Ubaldo Marchioni knew the importance of Duilio Paselli, Knight of Labor, and he invited him in immediately. "If this church is not safe," the young priest said, "then no place is safe. Come and be my guests."

A few miles southwest of the peak of Monte Sole a mountain called Salvaro thrust its peak almost 3,000 feet into the air, and in a sort of high valley between Salvaro and Monte Sole a belt of farm settlements had been slashed out of the thick woods. The region was connected by a steep farm road to the Reno Valley town of Pioppe di Salvaro, where a hemp mill had stood for years, and many of the farmwives and daughters augmented their families' meager incomes by working in the mill. In the late years of the war, when so many of the able-bodied men had vanished from the area, the mill had become a main support for the farm families of the region.

One of the men who had vanished was a young *contadino* named Mario Cardi, son of Augusto Cardi, who farmed for the Lelli sisters in a spick-and-span *podere* called Creda, a half mile up the mountain road from the mill town. When he turned nineteen, Mario joined the Italian Army, much to the annoyance of the young women of the region. Young Mario was no better off financially than anybody else, but he was regarded, nevertheless, as a blue-ribbon candidate for holy matrimony. For one thing, he was as strong as a horse, with the typical oversize hands of the mountain people, and for another, he was bold and brave and dashing by nature. When a task fell to Mario Cardi, it was carried out, regardless of peril or strain. That was one reason why Creda was such a neat, sparkling farm. Augusto and his sons were forever swarming over their barns, cleaning, painting, repairing, as though the whole *podere* were competing daily for a prize at the fair.

There was a charisma to Mario, a sort of pixie charm, that stemmed only partially from his appearance. His face was well chiseled, and his light-chestnut eyes were set wide apart over prominent cheekbones. He had wavy brown hair, and when he smiled, two big dimples formed in his cheeks. His voice was somewhat hoarse and heavy, and it lent interest to anything he said, however banal. Mario Cardi had the kind of charm that transfixed young girls.

And then all of a sudden he was writing from Africa, where he had been posted to the front. At an advance position near Tobruk, the British mounted a heavy attack on Mario and his seven comrades, and when the enemy fell back, the young soldier found that his comrades were dead. He held out till he was evacuated, but on the way to the rear lines his truck was strafed, and he was hit. After months in the hospital he was decorated with the Merit Cross and sent back to Italy to a soft assignment: guarding prisoners of war. Personally, Mario detested the duty, but unlike many of his fellow guards, who seemed to think that guard duty was a reward for service at the front, he did not spend his time growing fat and lazy. Mario had been taught by his father to take his military service seriously, and soon he had become one of the most respected guards at the camp at Udine.

One day in September, 1943, word swept the compound that Italy was getting ready to surrender, that it would all be over in a few days. Such reports were not uncommon among men who had little to do but talk, but the rumors always made the guards uncomfortable. At such times, certain of the 6,000 Yugoslavian prisoners tended to become frisky, eyeing the exits and subtly suggesting what would happen to some of the guards when the war was over.

On September 8, 1943, Mario Cardi and the other 700 guards of the prison at Udine heard a confirmed, authentic, undeniable report that Italy had surrendered. All hostilities were ended. The Croatian prisoners snake-danced and sang when the news reached them, and it was late that night before Mario and the other guards were able to establish order in the sleeping quarters.

The next morning Mario awoke to find that only 6 guards remained at Udine. All the others had fled during the night, headed for their homes and their families, and left their rifles and equipment lying all over the place. Already the prisoners were at the wire, proclaiming what they would do when the gates of the prison swung open.

Mario and his companions made an emergency call to the local *carabinieri* barracks. Italian soldiers might desert, but the *carabinieri* owed allegiance only to the king, and they were the most dependable and incorruptible force in Italy. Within minutes, the *carabinieri* began arriving, and after long negotiations with the informal spokesmen for the Yugoslavs, the gates of the camp were unlocked, and 6,000 prisoners trudged joyfully toward home. The guards hung around the empty compound for five or six days, and then they, too, packed up their barracks bags and left.

Mario arrived quietly at Creda, but soon his relatives and friends and neighbors assembled in the courtyard of the farm to pay him tribute. He was not only a war hero, but an eligible young bachelor and another hand for the fields, where there was a severe shortage of manpower. The partying went on for hours, and then Mario settled back to his old routine, helping work the fifteen acres of the Lelli sisters' farm. Another brother, Carlo, had a good job on the railroad, and four of the women of the family were employed at the hemp mill, and for a time the living was not unpleasant in the big farmhouse at Creda. But when German soldiers seized control of the country and Mussolini set up a new Fascist government in the north, things became worse than ever. The Italian Fascists, stripped of authority for a few weeks, came roaring back with vindictive new taxes, restrictions and demands on manpower. Every few days a squad of Blackshirts, sometimes accompanied by German troopers with machine pistols, would hammer on the doors of Creda and ask all sorts of questions about the men of the *podere:* how old they were and where they were working and why they were not in the uniform of the Mussolini New Army. At such times young men like Mario would be hiding in the woods; it was a steep climb up the road to Creda, and the Fascists would always be spotted before their arrival.

As the situation became more and more difficult, it entered Mario's mind that perhaps he should join the New Army; as a hero of the Regular Army, entitled to wear the blue-and-white ribbon of the Merit Cross, he would be welcomed and perhaps made a noncommissioned officer or granted other privileges. But by now Mario had found a fiancée, and even with the distortions and discomforts of the Fascist oppression, the life at Creda seemed preferable to returning to the old disciplines.

One day he climbed the mountain to see his friend Dante Simoncini, a land agent who was known throughout the region for his friendliness and hospitality. Three of Simoncini's daughters were home, but the father was off on business, and just as Mario had begun chatting with the girls, there was a pounding on the door, and four or five ragged-looking men burst in waving guns. One of them knocked Mario against the wall and said, "Stand still!" and the others began filling big sacks with food. This was Mario's first exposure to the partisans of Monte Sole, and he was not favorably impressed. When Simoncini returned home a few hours later and heard the story, he said to Mario, "If I had been here, there would have been none of this."

"I am not so sure," Mario said to his old friend. "The way they came in here, like wild men, nothing would have stopped them." A few months later he heard that Simoncini had been buried alive in a cornfield, and his head kicked off by the partisans. With that event the last thought of joining the irregulars was swept from Mario's mind. He adopted a personal policy of *attesismo* (wait and see), the policy of so many Italians of the period. Mario had grown to dislike the Blackshirts and the Nazis who came stomping up from the valley below, but not enough to send him into the arms of the mercurial partisans on the mountain. Even when the Germans grabbed three hostages at Creda and executed them point-blank, Mario remained a neutral. He had developed a new contempt for all military, regular or otherwise, and he preferred to wait out the war in his barn. Each night fourteen or fifteen young men of the area posted a guard and slept in the hayloft against the possibility of a *rastrellamento*. By day they watched for raiders and worked the fields and fled into the thick underbrush at the slightest signs of danger. It was not the most pleasant of lives, especially for a man who preferred to confront his menaces head on, but sometimes Mario would sneak off to be with his fiancée, and sometimes there would be whole weeks when the Fascists would not appear, and he could deceive himself into believing that life seemed almost normal.

Just over the hill from Creda was another *podere* called Steccola, owned and operated by the family Tiviroli, ancient inhabitants of the Monte Sole region. With its tall stone farmhouses jutting above the trees and its tile-roofed barns and hay shelters huddled around, Steccola looked exactly like a medieval village, and in a sense it was. The lords of the manor were Silvio Tiviroli, descendant of hundreds of Tivirolis at Steccola, and a man named Augusto Grani, who had been adopted by earlier generations of Tivirolis and now exercised the same authority as the others. Altogether there were about a dozen people living at Steccola. They worked a rich *podere* of fifty-nine acres, half in woods and half in fields, and even in the worst years of the war there was plenty for everyone. The Granis and the Tivirolis had an ideal arrangement: they were their own *padroni*.

The princess of the manor was only nine years old, but she knew her rights and demanded them. Maria Tiviroli was a golden-haired rag mop of a child, mostly skin and bones and hair and big hazel popeyes that commanded attention and blazed with anger and brimmed with tears when her royal needs were ignored. Her two blond braids were tended daily by her mother; they were always tied with white ribbons, and they hung to her waist, and at first glance she appeared to be composed almost entirely of eyes and braids—that is, until she opened her mouth and gave instructions in the voice of a drill sergeant.

As the baby of the family, little Maria had been led to believe that the world revolved around her, and the result was that she was well on her way to becoming a *marmocchia* (brat). When her sister, Gina, tried to teach her to read, Maria threw the book in the fire. When her brother Antonio insisted on taking a share of her chestnuts, she dumped them all in the manure pile. And when she awoke one night and her sister refused to accompany her to the dark outhouse, Maria wet the bed and the next morning put the blame on Gina. At twelve, Gina had learned not to tell. Nobody told on the princess. They would not have been believed.

Maria's older brother, Leonardo, was the only member of the Tiviroli family who had the *marmocchia*'s number, and he was away serving in the *Bersaglieri,* the proudly plumed military outfit that always moved in double time and numbered Benito Mussolini as one of its alumni. Maria went about the neighborhood bragging of the greatness of her brother, fighting heroically on the Russian front, but the instant Leonardo came home on a leave, she began to tremble. He thought nothing of telling her to shut up, ordering her into her room for punishment or making her perform the most undignified of chores, like blacking his boots or steaming the plume on his dress hat. And when she turned to her parents for comfort, to the same parents that she could usually manipulate with her little finger, she was told to do as Leonardo instructed. Slowly the little princess had to learn that in every family of Monte Sole the sons were revered above all others. She might be the princess, but sons were both princes and heirs apparent, the ones upon whom the parents' old age would depend. Leonardo could get away with almost anything, and one day he proved it by tying Maria hand and foot to a bed when she would not stop bothering him. All her screams and protestations counted for nothing, and her father told her simply, "You must have been very bad for Leonardo to do something like that to you." When she was released an hour later, Maria Tiviroli was less of a *marmocchia.*

In the summer of 1944, Maria was both happy and annoyed when Leonardo showed up at the farm. He announced that the war was over for the Sixth Regiment of *Bersaglieri,* and he exchanged his fancy uniform for the work clothes of the *podere.* In those days there were always partisans around Steccola. The place was well back in the woods, midway between the busy valleys of the Reno and the Setta, and every night the barns and outbuildings at Steccola would be crammed with armed irregulars. Leonardo did not take kindly to such troops—he was too recently a member of a highly disciplined military organization—but he expressed no objection to their presence, nor did he whine that the partisans were compromising the security of the *podere,* as some of the neighbors did. Leonardo knew that his father and the other relatives were strongly in favor of the partisans and that his own mother sewed their uniforms and his sisters, Maria and Gina, carried their messages.

Leonardo had been home only a short time when some of the partisans began pestering him about joining. At first he shrugged them off, though never in a rude way, and one day Lupo, the commandant himself, cornered him in the barn and gave him a vigorous sales talk. "This is your land," Lupo told him, falling back on the first passion of the *contadino,* "and all we are doing is trying to defend it."

"From whom?" Leonardo asked.

"From the Fascists and the Nazis who are taking it yard by yard."

Leonardo was impressed by the leader of the partisan brigade, and although he was still far from convinced that the Fascists were completely wrong and the partisans completely right, he agreed to join a formation encamped on nearby Monte Vignola. On a Tuesday morning he kissed everybody good-bye and went off again to war, and on the following Sunday he was back home for good. He told the family that he had found 300 partisans milling around two or three houses on Monte Vignola, and not one of them seemed to know what he was doing. A few were cutting up a calf, wasting sections of the meat with their poor workmanship. Some were dancing with a group of women, and others were stretched out snoring on the ground. The whole scene reminded him of a gypsy band, and his *Bersaglieri* training made it almost impossible for him to accept this clown convention as a military group. At nightfall the partisans had disappeared, and Leonardo had no idea where they went. When he asked for orders the next morning, he was told that the only standing order was to remain in cover and stay alive. After a few days the Germans staged a *rastrellamento,* and Leonardo found himself in the company of a wild-eyed partisan who thought he could lick the raiders single-handedly. "Come on!" Leonardo said to his companion as the Germans began working their way up the mountain behind heavy machine-gun fire. "Our orders are to hide, not fight!"

"But I just want to throw a grenade!" the partisan said. "Just one!"

"Listen, beethead!" Leonardo said. "I did not survive the Battle of Stalingrad to die on this hill with a *cretino* like you!" and he took off into the woods.

Hours later, when the firing had died down, he returned to the command post and found it deserted, and that same night he worked his way back to Steccola and announced his permanent retirement from World War II. "I am not saying that the partisans are wrong," he told his family, "or that you are wrong in helping them. I am only saying that they are wrong for Leonardo Tiviroli." The partisans continued to occupy the barns and haylofts of Steccola, but nothing further was said to Leonardo about joining. Like Mario Cardi and many of the other young men of the area, he would let the war get along without him.

Early one morning a group of partisans sat in the weeds alongside a road, speaking softly in their customary confusion of tongues (many nationalities had by now joined Il Lupo), and peering into the early morning haze that cut down visibility. The Scot, Jock, was arguing that they were wasting time in this Godforsaken area. Anyone knew that there were two important military roads leading from Bologna to the front: one paralleling the *direttissima* in the valley of the Setta, where Lupo and the headquarters company of the formation were already standing guard, and another down the valley of the Reno, where Rossi and his men should have been. Instead they were watching a back road that was little more than a cowpath. "Never mind, Jock," Gianni Rossi said. "If the Germans try to move through our zone at all, it will be on small roads like this one."

"What could they move on a road like this?" asked one of the two South Africans, Steve Hermes.

"Maybe we will see," Rossi said.

It was about ten in the morning when one of the Italians suddenly raised his hand and touched his lips for silence. The seven-man partisan patrol hunkered down and listened. There it was in the distance: the unmistakable *thunk-thunk-thunk* of an engine. Gianni Rossi made a gesture with his hand, and three of the men raced across the road to positions on the other side. The noise became louder, and then something big and dark lumbered over the rise and into view. It was a camouflaged amphibious command car, and it was moving slowly, as though not to make too much disturbance. Rossi and his men stepped into the middle of the road and watched the car approach through the sights of their Sten guns.

The command car slowed and swung to the side as though trying to find a way out. Rossi held up a hand to order the car to stop, and at that moment a German soldier on the front seat raised a pistol. Seven Stens exploded at once. The vehicle swerved and foundered. The firing stopped, but when a figure in the back seat of the car made a rapid movement, one of the partisans fired a burst that ended the action.

Now they had to work fast. There might be another German car, or even a tank, following behind to protect the amphib. It was hard to believe that such a defenseless vehicle would be sent through busy partisan country without protection, especially since so many enemy trucks and cars had already been ambushed. Rossi yanked a door open and saw that all the Germans were dead. There were a captain, a colonel, a lieutenant and a noncommissioned driver in the front. Behind them, dead from numerous bullet wounds but giving off the smell of gasoline, was a man in the uniform of the German Army Medical Corps. Rossi yanked the body to one side, and a box of wooden matches fell from the lifeless hands. On the floor next to the dead man was a small, opened bottle of gasoline, still leaking fluid, and next to the bottle a briefcase. Rossi looked inside and saw that the case was crammed with diagrams and drawings and pages of material in German. But a closer examination of the briefcase would have to wait.

"Go get every *contadino* you can find!" Rossi said to the three Italians in the patrol. "Tell them to bring their shovels and their picks and all their relatives, and tell them that if they refuse, they will be killed!" Soon there was a sullen group of several dozen *contadini* on the scene. Rossi pointed to a plowed field alongside the road. "Dig!" he said. He looked at his watch. It was ten thirty.

While the first group dug rapidly, more *contadini* arrived in response to the urgent command, and soon there were five or six dozen men flailing away at the coarse earth. When the hole was deep enough, Rossi ordered them to bury the amphibious command car with its occupants still inside. The earth was shoveled back in and the excess distributed evenly around the field. It looked as though a farmer had been plowing. The whole job had taken less than two hours. "Go, and keep your mouths shut!" Rossi said to the band of unwilling laborers. "If the Germans find that car, every one of you will be a corpse."

Back at partisan headquarters, Rossi turned the briefcase over to Lupo, but it was Giovanni Saliva, a *carabiniere* member of the brigade, who first realized what they had found. "These words," he said excitedly, pointing to a heading that topped every page, "mean Gothic Line. You have captured information about the Gothic Line!"

At this late stage of the war in Italy, the Gothic Line was the single most important military fact. Thousands of Italian laborers, many of them rounded up at gunpoint, had built massive fortifications across the spiny back of the Apennines from Pisa to Rimini. Working for two years, the Italians had used their classical talent for masonry to construct formidable piers and walls, gun emplacements, buttresses and watchtowers. The combination of Italian brickwork and German armament and natural Apennine cliffs and peaks made the Gothic Line the last logical line of defense against the American and British armies storming up from the south. The war in Italy would be over when the Gothic Line was breached, and both the Axis and the Allies knew it. Even the raggedy partisans of Monte Sole knew that inside information about the Gothic Line was of inestimable value to the Allied strategists.

"We will have to get this material to the Allies," Lupo said.

"Through the front lines?" Rossi asked.

"No, that is too risky for this package. We will go the other way. We will take it into Switzerland, and from there it will be simple to get it into the hands of the Allied command."

A partisan from the Alpine region of Italy strapped the papers to his belly and headed up the road toward Bologna and the north. Twenty days later, while the Germans were still searching feverishly all along the route of their missing amphibious command car and torturing a few *contadini* by way of soliciting information, partisan headquarters received a jubilant message from the Allied command. "Recent dispatches proved to be of extreme importance. Repeat: Extreme."

Gianni Rossi, the main executor of this coup, was the vice-commander of the partisan brigade, and he had been with Mario "Lupo"

Musolesi almost from the beginning. The two men had similar backgrounds: both came from the eastern foot of Monte Sole, Musolesi from the small town of Vado and Rossi from the village of Gardeletta, where he had distinguished himself by walking across burning coals at the age of ten. Both young men had been mechanics, and both had gone early into military service, Lupo into the Army, where he became a sergeant major of tanks in the African campaign, and Rossi into the Navy, where he served with no particular distinction. Like the great mass of the Italian military, they both came home in 1943 after the September 8 surrender, and like Italians everywhere, they immediately ran into the high-handed methods of Fascists and Nazis who were trying to whip the defeated nation into line.

Lupo and Rossi soon fled up to the woods of Monte Sole, where they found other young men living off chestnuts and mushrooms and making an occasional coin doing odd jobs. In those early months after the surrender, organized resistance had not entered the minds of the young men. Most of them were on the mountain for other reasons, the most pressing of which was that they did not want to be drafted into Mussolini's New Army, and they did not want to be hustled away to slave labor in Germany. There were others who had escaped from prison, both civil and military, in the general disorder of the surrender period; some career anarchists whose heads bore prices in the cities; some deserters from a Regular Army division that had been assigned to guard the *direttissima,* and some opportunists with motives less honorable.

Word soon began reaching the men on Monte Sole of tightening measures in the valleys below. Parents whose sons had deserted the Army were arrested and thrown into jail, and others were bullied and mistreated by Fascist goons. One day Lupo called together several of the motley bands, including the Army deserters with their old-fashioned Model 91 rifles, and suggested that they begin carrying out some military activities of their own, particularly against the Fascists who were terrorizing their relatives in the towns and villages below. The capacity of the twenty-six-year-old Lupo to command, to excite instant loyalty from others, may be measured by the fact that there was no word of discussion about who would take charge of the newly formed group, even though one of the Army deserters was a full colonel. Not only did Lupo have a quality of leadership, an intense persuasive way about him, but he knew the Monte Sole area from a lifetime of experience crawling over it. He appointed Gianni Rossi, twenty-two years old but also experienced on the mountain, as his second-in-command, and announced that the group would attack the Germans in the Setta Valley, along the *direttissima,* and also on the far side of the mountain, along the Reno Highway and the railroad line that went to Pistoia. Hardly had the decision been reached when almost the entire roster of the *carabinieri* of the nearby town of Castiglione dei Pepoli, several dozen men in all, arrived atop the mountain and joined the formation. There remained the matter of a name. "I have heard of a brave group of partisans in Yugoslavia," someone said, "and they call themselves the Red Star."

"Very well," said Lupo, who was naïve politically, even though he had once been interested in valley politics as a Fascist and still carried his *tessera.* "We shall call ourselves the brigade of the *Stella Rossa* [the Red Star], in honor of our new allies." No one objected, least of all the handful of Communists in the new group, and the brigade of the *Stella Rossa* was born.

From the beginning, Lupo and Gianni Rossi did not delude themselves that every member of the *Stella Rossa* was a heroic patriot, willing to lay down his life for the cause of liberation. In truth, it was difficult for any of the partisans, in those early days of 1944, to figure out exactly what they were for, although they were fairly certain what they were against. For every member of the brigade who had an honest and idealistic motivation, there were others who were going along for the ride, or evading the draft, or avoiding arrest on some trumped-up Fascist charge or other, or frankly seeking loot and plunder. The Communists in the brigade saw the war as a stepping-stone to a new Italy; their plans extended far beyond the end of hostilities.

But as the months went by, and the partisans engaged in their first encounters with the enemy, a sort of *esprit* began to develop, and out of a confused mélange of motivations the *Stella Rossa* slowly turned into a fighting unit with reasonably clear aims. The first skirmishes were cameos. Nervously packing their obsolete old Model 91 rifles and their Italian Army machine guns that could always be counted on to jam, the partisans halted a train near Grizzana, south of Monte Sole, and burned six cars of gasoline. A few days later a band of partisans blocked the railroad tunnel near Vado, and in the ensuing confusion, a few dozen Allied prisoners of war jumped off the northbound train. Most of them disappeared into the brush, but a handful joined the *Stella Rossa,* and not long afterward the brigade received another infusion of hybrid vigor: sixty Soviet Mongols deserted from the Germans and came up the mountain seeking allies. Led by a mammoth officer nicknamed Caraton, the Mongols had almond eyes and shaved heads and fierce scowls. The Germans had captured their division intact on the Russian front, complete with a Russian general, and put them in German uniforms, knowing that they were strongly anti-Communist. Now they were fed up with the Germans and looking for a new affiliation.

The augmented partisan brigade increased its range of action, and in February the first fire fight broke out when the partisans attacked a convoy of German trucks. Lupo and Rossi came away from the engagement with serious misgivings. The Model 91's had misfired, and the machine guns had jammed, as everyone had expected, and there was no question that the patrol would have been annihilated by return fire if they had not had excellent cover. "I do not care how much manpower we have in the brigade," Lupo said angrily. "We are never going to be able to do anything but derail trains and write threatening letters if we use these old weapons."

In the spring of 1944 the new Mussolini government announced that the high school classes of 1922-25 would be drafted forthwith, and another flock of young men headed for the peak of Monte Sole. Soon the brigade of the *Stella Rossa* was 1,000 strong, with weaponry that would have been insufficient for a company of regular infantry. Lupo sent men across the front lines to ask for help from the Allies, but his agents were told to return to Monte Sole and wait. "Return and wait!" Lupo stormed at Rossi one night. "Was a war ever won by waiting?"

In April an Italian in civilian clothes came up the mountain and paid a call at partisan headquarters. To a confused and suspicious Lupo he explained that he had been landed at Rimini in an American submarine operated by the Office of Strategic Services and that he was assigned to contact the partisans of Monte Sole. If he was an Italian, how did it happen that he was working for the American military? Lupo asked. The man explained that the OSS utilized anyone who could do the job, without regard to nationality, and that it included Italians, Greeks, Czechs, Slavs, even some Germans. Lupo asked the visitor how he could prove that he was an Italian. "Well, I am engaged to a girl who lives in Vado," the man said. He named the girl, and Lupo asked him to describe her.

"Perfect," Lupo said. "I know your fiancée. I come from Vado."

"I know you do," the Italian said.

The two men talked long into the night. The OSS agent outlined the techniques of partisan warfare. He instructed Lupo never to confront the enemy directly, no matter how uneven the battle appeared. He said that the essence of partisan warfare was to lash out and disappear, to nip and obstruct, and always to keep one eye on the exit. No longer could the *Stella Rossa* remain permanently around Monte Sole. The brigade would have to break up into three or four smaller formations, attack the Germans piecemeal, and stay in constant motion in a huge *giro* around the area. Thus the German countermeasures would always hit an area that the partisans had left. "Very well," Lupo said, "and while we are carrying out all these techniques, what are we to use for weapons and ammunition?"

The OSS agent outlined the complex program of air drops. Every night at eight thirty the partisans were to monitor Radio London. When they heard the announcer say, "The birds are singing," they were to send patrols to block off the narrow mountain road at Vado and Gardeletta, and between ten and midnight Allied planes would parachute supplies to the western slope of Monte Sole.

Twenty days later the partisans heard the code signal over Radio London, and that night Gianni Rossi led a patrol to the drop site. At first he could not believe his eyes as barrel after barrel of matériel floated down on the mountain. The men ripped them open and found dozens of Sten guns, larger Bren machine guns, automatic rifles, hand pistols and spare parts for all the weapons, plus case after case of ammunition. There were grenades and signal flares and plastic explosives and compasses and maps and everything the partisans needed, and the efficient Americans had even included a barrel of cigarettes and salt. At sunup, when the flames would not be conspicuous, the men burned the remains of the barrels and the chutes.

This first big drop was on May 20, 1944, and a week later the Germans mounted a full-scale attack to rid the mountains of the irregulars with their increasingly annoying old Model 91 popguns and their night raids on undefended railroad cars.

The Germans marched up Monte Sole from both east and west,

and the partisans waited in high brush, armed to the eyebrows with their new American weapons. When the Germans were full in their sights, they opened fire and drove the attackers all the way down to the bottom of the mountain. The disciplined Germans regrouped and came back up, and the partisans drove them down again. The fire fight lasted all day, with the partisans hardly counting a casualty and the brave German troops taking serious losses, and when the sun went down, the whole brigade of the *Stella Rossa* slipped off the mountain and headed for Pietramala in the pass of La Futa, a wild and desolate region where the enemy would not be looking for them.

Later the elusive partisans found out what happened after they left Monte Sole. The Germans had sent for reinforcements after the day long battle, and an artillery attack was begun before dawn of the next day. The panic-stricken *contadini* of Monte Sole thought the end of the world had come and huddled in their basements and shelters.

At San Martino, Don Ubaldo Marchioni had to call off the mass that was to begin the observance of Pentecost, and all over the mountain the peasants were terrorized by the heavy shells that fell around them. The bombardment lasted all day and a second day and a third, and just when the peasants of Monte Sole thought that their apocalypse had ended, machine-gun shots rang out and patrols of SS men swarmed up the mountain to apply the *coup de grâce* to the *Stella Rossa.* When they found no partisans, indeed hardly any able-bodied men at all, they took out their pique on the civilians. At Cerpiano, where the Sisters of Saint Angela ran their mountain refuge for children, a pack of SS men slammed open the door of the kindergarten and then fell back, looking embarrassed when they found themselves knee-deep in toddlers. They left, but later a larger group of SS arrived, fired their machine pistols into the air, smashed furniture and intimidated everyone. Finally, the Germans burned a few haylofts, executed some farm animals, and left the mountain after five days of wrathful display. Some of the SS officers informed the civilian population that the next visit would not be so pleasant.

When word reached the partisans of the raid against their relatives and their homes on Monte Sole, some of them were all for making a forced march straight back to the mountain and taking on the Germans directly. Cooler heads, notably Gianni Rossi and Lupo, won out after a long discussion. "We must not let ourselves be deluded by our new weapons," Rossi said. "We are still partisans. If we move against the Germans in force, they are going to wipe us out."

"That is exactly what the OSS man told us," Lupo said. "We will fight the Germans on our terms and in our way: in the way of partisans."

It was only a week later that Rossi and his patrol captured the German command car, and soon after, partisan headquarters listened to an inspiring radio broadcast from General Harold Alexander, commander of Allied forces in Italy. The general urged Italian partisans to fight the occupying forces, break down their communication lines and sabotage their retreat. "The liberation of Italy is well under way," the general announced. "In less than a month the strength of the German armies has been broken."

By mid-June the partisans were making systematic attacks on German troops and convoys, and the panicky Germans were answering with terror tactics. SS troopers grabbed eight members of a family named Musolesi and shot four of them, all brothers, much to the horror of Lupo, who bore not even the slightest relationship to this other family of Musolesis. On June 17, the German commander, Field Marshal Albert Kesselring, issued the first of several harsh warnings to the partisans. "The fight against the partisan bands has to be carried out with all means available and with the utmost severity," he told his troops in a publicized order. "I shall defend any one of my leaders who in his choice of methods goes beyond the usual normal reserve. The principle must be that it is better to make a mistake in the choice of means than it is to be neglectful and careless in carrying out this assignment. The guerrilla warfare must be attacked and defeated." To this, Kesselring added his oft-repeated philosophy that partisans were "illegitimate combatants" and were therefore not entitled to any of the treatment usually reserved for enemy soldiers.

Shortly after the Kesselring warning, Italian Fascists and German soldiers broke into the Musolesi home in Vado and placed both of Lupo's parents under arrest. The next evening, men of the *Stella Rossa* surrounded the Fascist headquarters in the nearby town of Monzuno and took twelve prisoners. They left a message saying that a dozen heads would be rolled down the mountain in the morning if Mario's parents were not released. The parents were freed, and the partisans sent their Fascist prisoners back home with a warning to keep hands off the innocent.

Within forty-eight hours there were placards all over the river valleys and as far north as Bologna. The Fascists were offering $16,000 each for the two archcriminals, Mario "Lupo" Musolesi and Gianni Rossi, and five to ten kilograms of salt to anyone turning in a partisan of the *Stella Rossa.* From then on the partisans had to confront menaces from within. In these desolate war years there was very little that certain Italians would not do for $16, let alone $16,000, and five to ten kilos of salt was a two years' supply for most families.

Every recruit who offered himself to the brigade now had to be viewed with suspicion. Whenever Musolesi and Rossi were not completely satisfied with the new member, they kept a personal watch on him, and sometimes he would pass the inspection, and sometimes he would be shot. One day a man named Amedeo Arcioni arrived at partisan headquarters at Ca' di Zermino, near the walled village of Murazze, and announced that he wished to become a partisan. Arcioni was welcomed, and because he was previously known to the leaders of the brigade, he was allowed to sleep in the same room with them that night. Four of them went to bed side by side: Lupo, the newcomer, Rossi and a battalion leader named Alfonso Venturi. In the middle of the night, Rossi heard a noise and noticed that Arcioni was standing up. "What are you doing?" Rossi whispered.

"Getting up to piss," Arcioni said.

Rossi fell back into a half sleep. A few minutes later he was reawakened. Arcioni had grabbed the knife that Lupo always kept above his bed and stabbed at the partisan leader. Lupo cried out, but before Rossi could grab his own gun, Arcioni landed on him, and all Rossi could see was the point of the knife dipping toward his head in a long arc. Just as the point dug into his scalp, Rossi grabbed Arcioni's wrists, and the two men twisted and writhed in a battle of strengths, with Arcioni trying to press the knife farther into Rossi's skull and Rossi trying to force it out. Through all the sounds of mortal struggle, Alfonso Venturi slept soundly on the hay alongside. Rossi reached out and kicked the battalion leader in the leg. Venturi jumped up, saw what was happening and pulled his gun.

"Shoot!" Rossi hollered.

"I will hit you!" Venturi said.

Rossi gave a powerful heave and turned Arcioni at a slight angle, and Venturi fired into the back of the traitor's head. Rossi felt the impact as bits of Arcioni's face splattered him. The other partisans thought their vice-commander was beyond medical assistance when they rushed into the room, but after the blood was cleaned away by a partisan doctor, all that remained was a quarter-inch puncture of the scalp. As for Lupo, he had been stabbed in the fleshy part of the side, and the doctor said that the wound was not serious.

The partisans soon learned to live with such treacheries, and whenever they were forced to appear in villages outside the Monte Sole area, they took pains to intimidate would-be local informers or to provide them with inaccurate intelligence to pass on to the Nazis. At night, when all the villagers would be in bed, the men of the *Stella Rossa* would march through in loud formations, using words like "battalion" and "regiment" to make their numbers seem dangerously large. After a platoon had marched down the main street of a village, it would double back and march through again, and all night long the commands would ring out: "Machine-gun company, right face!" "Artillery company, to the rear, march!" "All men present and accounted for, Captain?" "Yes, sir, Major!" The next day the local informers would tell the Germans that an army of partisans had been through during the night, and the Germans would dutifully pass the word along to their intelligence officers. Lupo and Rossi laughed when they read in a captured German document that the *Stella Rossa*'s strength was 2,000, or almost double its actual size.

By July, 1944, the brigade was operating at top efficiency, badgering the Germans and the Fascists and picking up an occasional tidbit of information to pass along to the Allies. The *Stella Rossa* had learned to function like a good lightweight boxer, hitting and moving and driving certain German officers to fits of annoyance. The whole Kesselring force knew that there was a strong partisan brigade headquartered at Monte Sole, but whenever the Nazis mounted a *rastrellamento,* they succeeded only in rousting out of bed a small army of ragged civilians—women, children and old men—and the next day another convoy would be ambushed, or a German officer sniped, or a patrol of Blackshirts forced to retreat down the mountain. German warnings were posted at both ends of the valley road entering the area of Monte Sole. ACHTUNG! they read. BANDEN GEBIETE. German soldiers were ordered to bypass the guerrilla area whenever possible.

But everyone knew that the Germans would have to come to grips with Monte Sole and the *Stella Rossa* sooner or later, simply because the mountain and its protectors stood squarely in the path of the coming Nazi retreat to the north. The partisans were average Italians, working-class and uneducated for the most part, but the military implications of their control of Monte Sole were not lost on them, and they made themselves as mobile as possible to escape annihilation by the Germans. The 1,200 men of the band were split into four formations of about 300 each, plus a small headquarters group. Each formation would carry out its attacks and then spin away to the nearest mountains, sometimes ranging as far as Modena, thirty miles to the north. Communications were poor, and weeks would pass when a formation was entirely out of touch with the others. Sometimes, in inevitable cases of mistaken identity, shots were fired by one formation on another, but luckily no one was hurt.

As the partisan activity increased, the frustrated German officers became more and more enraged. Kesselring was in the middle of the careful, controlled retreat that had been ordered by his superiors, and his chessboard campaign was exciting the admiration of the Allied General Staff, who enjoyed far superior forces and firepower. But Kesselring's brilliant defensive successes against the Allied Fifth and Eighth armies could mean nothing until the area to the rear of the German lines was neutralized. A classic retreat was being jeopardized by a tatterdemalion band of dirty, disorganized irregulars, stupid Italians whose very right to engage in warfare was not recognized by the imperious field marshal.

In the middle of the summer Kesselring issued another of his choleric orders about the partisans. "In my proclamation to the Italians I have announced that the fight against the gangs must be carried out with the most rigorous means," he said. "This statement is not an empty threat. All soldiers and military policemen have the right to apply the most severe means in cases of violence. Each atrocity is to be avenged immediately. Wherever bands of partisans gather, a percentage of the male population is to be arrested and, in cases of acts of violence, to be shot. If military personnel should be fired on from villages, the villages are to be burned. Perpetrators of deeds of violence and ringleaders of the gangs are to be hanged in public."

Shortly after the Kesselring order was circulated both to troops and civilians, the Germans roared into the small town of Pian di Setta, just south of Monte Sole, and began a *rastrellamento*. The irony was that Pian di Setta had meant nothing to the partisan operations. It lay precisely on the highway and the *direttisima,* and when the partisans found themselves in the vicinity of Pian di Setta, they made it their business not to tarry. Indeed, there were no partisans whatever in the area when the German raid began, so the Nazis contented themselves with burning barns, stalls and haystacks and intimidating the civilian population. But hours later, in the zone of Sasso Pontecchio, just to the north of Monte Sole, thirteen hostages were shot by the Germans, although once again no partisans had been found in the area. During both of these raids, most of the *Stella Rossa* had been hiding out in Malfolle, a tiny village to the southwest. Forty-eight hours too late, the SS men reached Malfolle and descended in full fury on the civilians. Eleven were taken as hostages, and one was shot trying to escape. When two others got away, the Nazis lined the rest against the wall and machine-gunned them. The bodies, some still twisting and writhing in the agonies of death, were heaved atop burning haystacks. Simultaneously, on the other side of the mountain in a place called Molinella di Veggio, seven hostages were executed.

Everyone waited to see how the partisans would react to the terror. Less than twenty-four hours after the executions, a German truck convoy entered the town of Pioppe di Salvaro, site of the hemp mill. The partisans were in Pioppe in force, having recently evacuated Malfolle, a quarter of a mile away, and they opened up immediately on the trucks. An hour later, ten of the vehicles were in flame, and dozens of German bodies lay about. Later in the day another formation of the *Stella Rossa* ambushed two German trucks in the Setta Valley and killed their drivers.

After these incidents, both sides began to engage in a battle of atrocities. Two German soldiers were axed to death in the woods near Rioveggio as they strolled with Italian girls. The Germans machine-gunned eleven residents of the town. The partisans ambushed a German truck, killed the driver and left another soldier for dead. When another patrol of partisans reached the scene later, they found a local doctor treating the wounded German. "Is there any chance he will live?" one of the partisans asked.

"I think he will," the doctor said.

The partisans emptied their Sten guns into the patient.

At about the same time two German soldiers were trying to buy eggs near a village called Gabbiano di Monzuno when they were captured by a squad of partisans led by a colorful figure who called himself Aeroplano. (All the partisans rechristened themselves with *noms de guerre* to protect their families.) While the Germans were holding their hands in the air in surrender, one of them was shot down. The other was taken to a partisan encampment where he pulled out his wallet, showed pictures of his wife and babies, and begged for mercy. He was strung up on a pole, head down, his hands pinned to the ground by knives, and left to die in the sun.

The partisans argued that such acts were in reprisal for German atrocities on the civilian populations, and the Germans argued that the executions of villagers were in reprisal for acts of the partisans, and soon the whole area of Monte Sole had become involved in a dialogue of death and torture. Civilian men began to hide in the woods by day, coming home only late at night when the Germans were afraid to show themselves on the mountain. Crops rotted in the fields while families went hungry. If the head of the family showed himself long enough to work in the fields, he ran the risk of being lined up against a wall and shot or sent to Germany as a slave laborer.

It was during this time of terror that Dante Simoncini, the land agent of Termine, was murdered by the partisans. Lupo and Gianni Rossi took no action, claiming that they were unable to find out who was responsible. But Rossi gathered his formation together and announced that the death of Simoncini could never be forgiven. "Look!" he said, rolling up his sleeve. "Do you see those scars? Who do you think treated them? Who do you think kept me from dying of loss of blood? It was Vittoria Simoncini, the daughter of Dante. She stayed with us all day long, tending to our wounded, at great danger to herself. And now we have repaid her by killing her father." Secretly, Lupo and Rossi suspected some of the harder-core Communist members of the brigade of the brutal killing. Simoncini was known as a neutral, and his home was frequently visited by hungry men of the *Stella Rossa.* But he was also an *affittario,* a collector of land rents, and the longtime holder of a *tessera,* the Fascist party card, and on both grounds he was anathema to the brigade's Communists.

By the middle of August, 1944, the area of Monte Sole had become almost entirely off limits to the German military. Hardly any traffic moved on the roads; the railroad line along the Reno had been wrecked, and the *direttissima* was barely in operation. The Allies had begun to bomb the railroad bridge at Vado and, after days of low-level attack, succeeded in dumping the center span of the heavy brick structure into the river. German engineers threw up a temporary steel span, and traffic resumed in a few days. Acting on instructions from the OSS, a small band of partisans crept into the railroad tunnel that lay above the bridge at Vado, released the brakes on a string of freight cars that had been shunted into the tunnel to escape bombing, and cheered madly as the cars bumped and creaked down the incline and finally derailed at the bridge in a shower of sparks and twisted steel. The stubborn Germans repaired the bridge in three days, and the stubborn partisans returned to the tunnel, killed the guards who had been detailed to watch the freight cars, and repeated their earlier triumph.

Heavy German patrols moved into the Monte Sole area from several directions at once, and the result was an all-day fire fight with casualties on both sides. Partisans, led by the Soviet Mongol officer Caraton, killed fifteen Germans of an advance patrol, including the SS major in charge of the operation, and toward nightfall the partisans trapped a group of Germans in a pincer and killed seven more. But for the most part the *Stella Rossa* fought in the only style that guaranteed survival: hitting and running. As they reassembled that night in their hiding areas away from Monte Sole, they counted heads and discovered that they had lost a dozen. There was general agreement that they would have to remain away from Monte Sole until the German pressure had lessened.

But within a few days new orders came in by way of an infiltrating OSS agent. The Allied lines had moved northward along the hills of Pistoia and then on to Porretta, and in fact, a man could walk from Monte Sole south to the front lines in just a few hours. The Allies wanted the men of the *Stella Rossa* to return to Monte Sole and secure the mountain. The reaction was mingled. Certain partisan officers pointed out that they had just been attacked on Monte Sole and would be asking for annihilation if they returned. Others said that the Allies were so close that liberation was only days away, and they might as well be back home on Monte Sole to celebrate the great day with their families. But the only opinion that mattered was Lupo's, and everyone knew what it would be. Lupo's favorite expression lately had become: "Orders are orders." He now called himself Major Lupo, and privately told his fellow officers that he had been assured that the *Stella Rossa* brigade would be taken intact into the Allied armies after the front had passed through. Now that the join-up was near, Lupo wanted to obey his orders to the letter.

The 1,200 men of the *Stella Rossa* made their way back to Monte Sole by various routes, splitting into groups of 30 and 40 and sleeping by night in the haylofts of the *contadini*. Within their units now were Fascist informers; there could be no doubt of it. Certain ones had been found out and executed on the spot, but others remained, and Lupo ordered the various formations to act independently of the mass, so that informers would only be able to inform about their own units. Nevertheless, two consecutive supply drops were tipped to the Germans, who waited until the first parachutes were billowing into the air and then swooped down on the mountain meadow, dispersed the partisan patrols and confiscated the matériel. Worse, a third drop was bungled. The partisans were in position at the meadow, but they gave an incorrect signal by flashlight, and the American pilots immediately concluded that the Germans had taken over the drop zone again. The pilots had been carefully briefed for such an eventuality, and they dipped down and strafed the area, barely missing some of the partisans.

The result of the three aborted drops was a severe shortage of ammunition and supplies, but for a time the lack of matériel was offset by the sudden cessation of almost all German activity in the Monte Sole area. The Germans were taking a pounding to the south, and all their attention seemed occupied by the worsening situation at the front. With the falloff in German activity on Monte Sole there came a corresponding falloff in partisan discipline, and some members of the brigade began to act as though the war was almost over. Every place except in the headquarters company of the superbly military Major Lupo, the partisans could be found dancing with the local girls and collecting favors for their heroic struggle against the enemy. One night Lupo received a visit from Vittorio Massarenti, a young Bolognese doctor who served as medical officer for one of the formations of the brigade.

"They act as if the war is all over," the disgruntled doctor told his leader.

"What can I do?" Major Lupo said. "The men are scattered all over the mountain. I cannot watch every man."

"It would not trouble me," Massarenti said, "if we were still in motion. But we sit here like targets. The Germans know we are here, and sooner or later they will wipe us out unless we move on."

"Orders are orders," Lupo said.

"You can disregard the orders and move off!"

"I am a military man. I take orders from superiors. My superiors say to secure this mountain."

"And do your superiors know that we no longer can trust anyone, that we have become a haven for Fascist spies?"

Lupo paused. He looked up at the young doctor and said, "That is a problem for us to solve ourselves."

"It is an insoluble problem," said the doctor.

A few days later Massarenti and Lupo and some of the other partisans were engaged in shifting caches of medical supplies, and the doctor ordered a young partisan named Cacao to pick up one of the packages a mile away. Cacao had blond hair and two adjoining gold teeth in a corner of his mouth, which made his smile appear lopsided. He had seemed to be a conscientious and brave partisan, and Dr. Massarenti was surprised to hear him say, "I cannot go. I have something else to do."

"What else do you have to do?" Massarenti asked.

"Just other duties," Cacao said. "I must—"

"I am canceling your other duties!" Lupo interrupted. "Do as the doctor tells you!"

Cacao hemmed and hawed and finally claimed that he had a pain in his side and he thought he might have a ruptured appendix. Massarenti examined him and said, "I can find nothing wrong with you, Cacao."

"Well, it hurts," the young partisan insisted.

"Look, we cannot stand here all day discussing this," Lupo snapped. He turned to Aeroplano, who was standing nearby. "Go get the package!" he said. "We will take care of Cacao later."

Aeroplano and two other partisans disappeared over the ridge and did not return. That night a villager came panting into the partisan headquarters high on the mountain and announced that Aeroplano had been ambushed and shot by the Germans. His body was hanging in the public square. Still Lupo found it difficult to believe that Cacao had been involved in the ambush. Several times Lupo had seen the slight young man in action as a member of Otello Musolesi's battalion, and he had noticed that Cacao attacked the Germans with a positive glee. He had been a partisan for five months, and he had had innumerable opportunities to turn traitor. As much as any of the common soldiers of the *Stella Rossa,* Cacao was above suspicion. Nevertheless, Lupo told Otello and Gianni Rossi to keep a special watch on the young man with the gold teeth. A few days after the watch went into effect, Cacao disappeared from his battalion. Lupo and Rossi and the other partisan officers assumed that he had been killed or captured by the Germans.

By September 10 units of the American and British armies were in sight of Rioveggio on the *torrente* Setta and Vergato on the *fiume* Reno, two small towns that lay in the southern shadow of Monte Sole. Advance Allied patrols along the Setta were foraging within two or three miles of Gardeletta, where people walked on hot ashes on the Night of Saint John, and on the Reno side the Allies were looking through field glasses at Vergato, the town where Luigi Massa and his ancient horse, Nina, went to buy monopoly goods for the store at Caprara. It appeared that the Allied soldiers would keep on slugging their way northward until they broke out at Bologna and the plain of the Po, only twenty-five or thirty miles away. This would mean the liberation of Monte Sole and its partisans and a massive retreat for the Germans.

Now it became absolutely necessary that the Germans neutralize Monte Sole by one means or another. Field Marshal Kesselring ordered a truce patrol to seek out the partisan leaders and attempt a settlement, a maneuver that had worked with certain other partisan bands. The usual procedure was to threaten horrible reprisals, but to promise to suspend all such actions if the partisans would lay down their arms till the front passed through.

The German truce patrol that marched toward the partisan headquarters did not complete its mission, and later the Germans claimed that every member of the patrol had been massacred by the *Stella Rossa.* The partisan command denied that any members of a truce team had ever reached the area. If German soldiers were killed approaching the partisan headquarters, it was simply because the *Stella Rossa* was in the business of killing Germans.

Kesselring was infuriated. He issued a final warning on September 17, sent it to all his men and ordered it published in the Bolognese newspaper *Il Resto del Carlino,* which had been taken over by the Fascists. He repeated his offer of five to ten kilograms of salt for each partisan brought in, dead or alive, and he said:

> The techniques and actions of the partisans have assumed a Bolshevik character. These low criminals of Moscow use their criminal methods to fight the authorities who have the responsibility of maintaining order and security in Italy. These people cannot be further tolerated. From now on we will act immediately and in the most severe manner. In some regions of Italy, the citizens not only tolerate but even help these delinquents. Localities where we find any verification of this fact will be burned and destroyed, and the people who help the partisans will be hanged in the public square. This is a last warning to those who are undecided. The majority of the population has realized the terrible danger of these bandits and the awful consequences their acts will have for Italy: the annihilation of every cultural value of the West, of religion, and consequently of the spiritual heritage of every proper person. These bandits wish to provoke with their continued fighting the foundation in Europe of a Bolshevik regime, synonymous with blind terror, the end of Italy and its years of civilization. This battle without quarter, for the destruction of banditry and delinquency, must therefore be carried out by the entire Italian population.

In their roving headquarters, which moved from night to night from one tiny Monte Sole village to another, the partisans were in a state of near euphoria. Any day now, the front would pass through, and there was every reason to believe that the *Stella Rossa,* Mongols and *carabinieri* and deserters and all, would be uniformed and assimilated into the Allied armies. Bologna would be a free city, and the war would be over in that part of Italy. Kesselring's ravings served only to reinforce the partisan joy. "When the cat is on fire, it makes the loudest noise," Lupo said.

One day a patrol brought in a sack of uncensored German mail, lifted from a truck ambushed in the valley, and the contents of the letters served only to strengthen the feeling that the end was near. Assisted by an OSS man and several of the German-speaking Mongols, Lupo and Gianni Rossi studied the mail and found that the morale of the enemy was at its lowest ebb. The soldiers wrote of the nightmare of Allied bombardments, of their own poor positions, of their lack of firepower to hold off the enemy. They spelled out broad hints that the battle of Italy was nearly at an end and asked their loved ones to pray for them in the retreat that was coming.

"This is exactly the time to strike!" Lupo said, but the trouble was that there was a shortage of targets. German soldiers and matériel were detouring around the area of Monte Sole, to avoid the partisans, as the whole German effort was concentrated on the grim situation at the front. The Italian Fascists were lying low in the valleys, behaving in their mildest manner. It appeared that Monte Sole had been forgotten. Lupo appealed to the Allies for permission to resume the brigade's old *giro,* moving in and out and around Monte Sole and striking the Germans wherever they could be found, but a quick reply told him to stay on the mountain.

Again Dr. Massarenti complained. "We have been on Monte Sole for two months now," he told Lupo, "and there is not a German soldier in Italy who does not know we are here. They have only to arm a battalion with mortars and machine guns, and they could wipe us out in hours."

"Orders are orders," Lupo said tediously. "The Allies know our position, and they must be planning to move through here very quickly. If the Germans attack us in force, the Allies will attack *them* in force."

"I wish I shared your optimism," Massarenti said. "It seems to me we have forgotten that we are partisans. Sitting up here on the mountain, we are acting like a victorious army. But we are not a victorious army, Lupo. We are still partisans, and our only defense is mobility."

Toward the end of September, disturbing reports began to reach the roving headquarters. Peasants climbed up Monte Sole to tell of German soldiers quietly setting up camps in the valley villages. There were hundreds of SS men, wearing the double lightning bolts and the death's-head patches of the Reich's specialists in mass murder. It appeared that the Germans were forming up for another *rastrellamento* against the partisans.

At about the same time, a man who said his name was Antonio arrived at partisan headquarters. He said he came from The Marches, to the southeast of Monte Sole, and that he had walked all the way to join up. Something about the man puzzled the partisan leaders. His accent did not match his biography, and the shoes in which he had walked dozens of miles appeared to be almost new. "I think, my friend," Lupo told the man, "that you are a spy."

Two partisans ripped the jacket off the newcomer's back and found that it was lined with Italian money, several thousand lire. Within minutes the man had confessed and, in a last effort to save himself, told the partisans that the Germans were planning to wipe out the *Stella Rossa* and scorch the earth of Monte Sole in a day or two. He said that he was a Blackshirt and that he had been enlisted by the Germans to make a final check on partisan positions. "Is that all you have to say?" Lupo asked.

"That is all there is to say," Antonio said.

"Take him outside," Lupo told his men, "and do not waste a bullet."

On September 25 word reached partisan headquarters that Lorenzo Mingardi, the Fascist boss in the Reno Valley, had warned Fascist refugees on Monte Sole to get off the mountain because the Germans were going to destroy it. Mingardi had told certain partisan informers that the order had come from the German high command to excise Monte Sole and its partisans with no further delay so as to secure the German retreat to the north. Everyone was to be killed. There were to be no exceptions. After delivering his warnings, Mingardi and his own family had fled north toward Bologna.

Lupo had heard innumerable such warnings in the past, and he persisted in his attitude that the burning cat was screaming. Nevertheless, he sent messengers scurrying over the mountain to tell his men to redouble their alerts and prepare to slip away at the slightest sign of German attack. Simply to pass the message took the better part of a day. The partisans were split into sections and distributed in almost every hayloft and barn on Monte Sole. There were thirty or forty at Adelmo Benini's barn at Possatore, another forty or fifty in the haylofts at Steccola, a headquarters unit of about forty at Cadotto, a strong force of fifty or so in the churchyard at San Martino, and smaller units everywhere. Because of the recent drop failures, the units were not well armed, but there was no anxiety. The war was almost over; if the Germans mounted a *rastrellamento,* it would be necessary only to flee up the flanks of Monte Sole and then to slip away in the night as they had done so often in the past. German soldiers did not remain in the area when the sun went down.

At dawn on the morning of September 26 the partisan headquarters at Cadotto was awakened by the visit of a shouting messenger. "It is over!" the man cried. "They are coming through the valley! The retreat has begun!"

As the morning went on more messengers came up the mountain.

Don Giovanni Fornasini, a partisan chaplain and pastor of the church at Sperticano, sent word that German units were headed northward in what appeared to be a disorganized mass. Some were driving cattle and sheep ahead of them, and some were dragging farm carts. A new detachment of Mongols in German uniforms arrived on the mountain, saying that the Allies had broken the Nazi line at every point and a general retreat had begun. Ten minor Fascists came to partisan headquarters by prearranged plan. They had been serving the partisans as informers, and their instructions had been to remain at their posts till the last minute. "The Germans are retreating at every point," one of them told Lupo. "We are liberated." A dozen or so *carabinieri* arrived at Cadotto with the same story. Like the ten Fascists, they had remained at their posts until the end was in sight.

It had been raining for two days, and the mountain roads were sticky with mud, but Lupo joyfully ordered a harassment of the retreating Germans. For two days, partisan patrols sniped and nipped at the enemy, but they were so low on firepower that they did little damage. There was only one pitched battle, and that was in Gianni Rossi's home town of Gardeletta, where two soldiers were killed. Partisan patrols brought back reports that the Germans no longer appeared to be retreating in a great disorganized mass. There were convoys of soldiers, to be sure, and sometimes smaller groups on foot, but this did not seem to add up to wholesale retreat. "Never mind," Lupo said. "They are through. It is only a matter of days."

By the night of September 28 the rains had become a deluge, and it was almost impossible to move about on the mountain. Inside the big farmhouse at Cadotto, some of the irregulars stayed up till early morning, drinking wine and telling jokes and gloating over the victory that was almost theirs. A few of the others, including Lupo and Gianni Rossi, checked the sentries and then dropped off to an early sleep. At about three o'clock in the morning, a young boy, soaked from head to foot and half-covered by mud, walked barefooted through the front door and told the few partisans who were still awake that SS troops were moving out of temporary encampments across the Setta, fording the river, and heading toward the base of Monte Sole. "We thank you for bringing us this news," one of the partisans told the boy, "and you can go back and tell the Germans that we will come down after the rain stops and dig their bodies out of the mud."

As the dawn of Friday, September 29, approached Monte Sole, the temperature took a sudden drop, and the rain came down like liquid ice. The sentinels were scattered about, some of them as far as 100 yards from the house, and their only shelter was the small outbuildings and haylofts that dotted the *podere.* Dressed in short pants and light shirts, the normal September attire of the region, the chilled watchmen pulled back into the doorways, and some of them snuggled under their haystacks and dozed off, secured by the very rain that made them tremble with cold. No one would be coming up the mountain on a night like this.

Death

JUST before dawn on the morning of Friday, September 29, Mario Cardi was chewing on the last half inch of a hand-rolled cigarette and wondering why he did not pin his Merit Cross back on and return to the Army. During the night it had alternated between chilling mists and heavy downpours, and toward dawn it had turned fiercely cold, and all he could do to keep warm was to rub his bare arms and legs and try to keep his mind off the temperature. Still, the old problem ran through his head. He supposed he preferred being here at home; the thought of returning to military regimentation was abhorrent. But on the other hand, home was not really home under these conditions. Here it was the time of the year when everybody on Monte Sole should have been a king, as rich as the richest *marchese*. No matter what the privations of the rest of the year, September brought free harvests that fattened all the stomachs. The truffles lay a few inches below the soil, begging to be disinterred and shredded atop steaming bowls of *tagliatelle*. Mushrooms popped up, and even though every *contadino* had long since learned the precise spots where the favored types would appear, there were still plenty of *funghi* left over by the time of the first frost. Ripe chestnuts fell from the trees, and wherever one looked on the mountain, there were little fires surrounded by knots of young men and girls roasting the paper-shelled nuts. And September was the time of the wine, when the bursting grapes would be crushed in the huge vats and the whole region could tell when a peasant had made his wine by the way he limped around on sore feet. The joke was that you could tell the winemakers by their purple feet, but Mario knew better. The purple color washed off fast, but the soreness that came from stomping on the stems of the grapevines lasted for a week, or until it was time to transfer the mix from the *begongio* in which the grapes are crushed to the huge *tino*, the larger vat that held up to a ton of fermenting wine. It was a process that always filled Mario and his father with pride of accomplishment, watching the mix as it seethed with life and sent up fat bubbles until exactly the right second arrived for transferring it to the glass *damigiane* and then studying the bottles for months until—*ecco*!—the wine was ready and could be matched with any in the neighborhood. Every social visit had to begin with a glass of wine, partly as a way of showing welcome and partly as a way of showing whose wine was best.

Mario sat cross-legged on the damp floor of the hayloft and shut his eyes, and for a moment he could almost smell the sweet Septembers of his childhood: the grapes in the open vats, the wood fires and the roasting chestnuts, the change in the very texture of the air as it began to take on the chill of autumn and work its peculiar properties on every living thing. And then Mario opened his eyes to the cold reality of the black night and laughed to himself. "What a joke!" he thought. The truffles are there, but who can afford a *cane da tartufo* to find them? The tax on a truffle dog would keep a man in ready-made cigarettes for three months, if there *were* any ready-made cigarettes to be kept in. And the mushrooms—why, it seemed as though they disappeared before they even came into sight, and so did the chestnuts. One hardly ever saw a full-blown mushroom anymore or a chestnut lying on the ground bursting its shell with sweet meat. The hills swarmed with men: a thousand hungry mouths were loose on the mountain. Nothing edible could last for more than a few hours. As for the grapes—and, for that matter, the wheat and the apples and the corn and the garden vegetables—most of them were rotting where they had grown. What with the Fascists and their taxes and the Germans and their raids and the partisans and their search parties, a *contadino* was lucky to remain alive.

Sitting in the predawn, Mario thought of the whole *podere* as a new kind of prison. Every day he went out to work the crops, while other *contadini* stood guard along the road, and at the slightest sound everybody would have to run for the woods. There was never a day when one could relax. At least the partisans had a few pleasant moments. They could sleep at night, protected by rings of sentries, and they had no worries about food. All they had to do was knock down a door and take it, as they had at Simoncini's house.

Mario spat into his hand and ground the last bit of the cigarette into soggy ash, out of respect for the hay that surrounded him. He had never seen a thicker night; he had no interest in ornamenting the dark with a roaring hayloft fire. Besides, he was standing guard for his usual sleeping companions: fourteen or fifteen young men of the area who had joined him in *attesismo,* the wait-and-see policy counseled by the church. Each night they assembled in the hayloft of the barn at Creda, and posted a guard, and slept fitfully.

Mario thought he heard a sound, and he raised himself to the narrow hayloft window and peeked out. It was like looking down a mine shaft. He told himself to relax. One was always hearing noises, especially on such dark nights. This one had been so soft as to be felt rather than heard, and he dismissed it from his mind and rubbed his skin against the chill.

But there was the sound again, a sort of rustling, this time from directly below the loft window. It was as though oilcloth raincoats were brushing against the side of the barn. Mario awakened one of his companions, holding a finger across the man's lips to keep him quiet. "Listen!" Mario whispered. "Do you hear that?"

The man listened for a few seconds. "There is someone in the courtyard," he whispered back.

Neither man was frightened. If there were someone in the courtyard at this time of the morning, it had to be one of the other *contadini* up early to begin his chores, or one of the young men of the area looking for the others, or maybe even some partisans making an early morning prowl for breakfast food. *"Cosa c'è di nuova?"* Mario called out. "What is new?" This was the traditional greeting of the area.

No answer came from below, and the rustling stopped. Mario stuck his head out the tiny window and tried to see, but all he got for his trouble was an eyeful of rain. The night was opaque.

"Maybe we were imagining," the other man said.

"Two people do not imagine the same things at the same time," Mario said. "I am going down to see."

The vertical wooden ladder that dropped to the barn floor below was usually creaky, but the humidity of the last few days had muted its joints, and Mario got to the bottom without a sound. He walked across the floor of the barn to the door, and as he looked again into the night, he thought he spotted a glint of metal across the courtyard near the bench. He made a mental note to tell the refugees in the house that they should not go sneaking around the courtyard before dark, or at least if they had to go out before sunup, they should announce their presence to the man guarding the hayloft. Once again he called out, *"Cosa c'è di nuova?"* and once again there was silence. Mario's annoyance grew. There was somebody out there, no doubt about it. Whoever it was—a chicken thief, a partisan scout, a *contadino* trying to be clever—Mario was going to teach him a lesson and catch this interloper. Keeping his eyes fixed on the spot where he had seen the glint of metal, he made his way along the wall of the barn until he came to the corner.

Just as he edged into the open, Mario felt something hard poke into his stomach, and entirely by reflex he grabbed it and shoved. A helmeted man wearing raingear and grenades shoved back, and Mario found himself pinned against the barn, wrestling a German soldier twice his size for possession of a machine pistol. After a few seconds of struggle, the soldier appeared satisfied to keep Mario pressed against the wall, and both men maintained their grip on the gun. While they stood locked in this absurd position, Mario heard approaching footsteps. "You coward of a partisan!" a vaguely familiar voice said in a hoarse whisper. "I have you now!"

Into Mario's short range of vision walked a man he had known as Cacao, a blond-haired, gold-toothed partisan who was always bothering the people of Creda for a bite to eat or a date with one of the girls of the *podere*. Now Cacao was wearing a German camouflage poncho.

"What is the matter with you?" Mario said to Cacao. "Do you not know me? Do you not know who I am?" He spoke loudly to alert the men sleeping in the loft.

"Keep your voice down!" Cacao whispered.

"I will not keep my voice down!" Mario shouted. "What the hell do you think you are doing? There are no partisans here!"

"Shut up!" Cacao said, still in a whisper.

"Look at me," Mario said. "Do you see a man who was ever in the partisans with you?"

Cacao edged closer. "Oh, it is you," he said, "the one with the four sisters. Where is Gigi?"

The only Gigi who lived on the *podere* was Luigi Valdiserra, an active partisan, some of whose relatives were asleep in the adjoining *casa colonica*. "You know better than I do where Gigi is," Mario said.

"Where is his family?"

"They went away. I have no idea where they went."

Cacao spoke in Italian to the soldier sharing the machine pistol with Mario. "He says Valdiserra and his family are gone. I know they are here. He is lying. We will have to kill him!"

When Mario heard the death sentence, he instinctively exploded into action. With a burst of energy, he wrenched the machine pistol away and held it on the two men. "Now who gets killed?" he said.

Cacao muttered a few soft words in a tongue Mario did not understand, and out of the fog came four or five German soldiers, all bearing machine pistols pointed straight at his stomach. As he watched openmouthed, they kept approaching till the snouts of their guns held him hard against the wall. He would have fallen from the pain, but the pressure of the gun barrels held him up, and he fought to get his breath. He dropped the gun, and the soldiers stepped away. "Sit down there!" Cacao ordered, pointing to a door leading to the stalls at the end of the barn. Mario sat, dazed and hurting, and a German soldier stood guard over him.

Just before dawn the friendly man that everybody called Rugi left the hemp mill with his co-worker Edoardo Rossi, and the two of them headed up the road that led toward Creda and Steccola and down the other side toward Cadotto, where the partisans were momentarily headquartered. Acacci "Rugi" Ruggero was so tired that he could hardly walk, but the rain seemed to revive him, as cold water reassembles the wits of a drunk. For two days and two nights now, Rugi had been on duty in the mill without sleep. The Allies had bombed the place, and although the fire had been brought under control, it still smoldered, and Rugi, normally a skilled mechanic, had had to stand fire guard, not only to protect the mill from a new conflagration, but to watch over the lives of the fifty or so bombed-out people who had taken shelter in the mill. It had been an uneventful night, this second in a row on fire duty, broken only by the appearance of the stationmaster of Pioppe di Salvaro, who had come in to chat and repeat the litany that was always on his lips these days. First he bemoaned the fact that he was a stationmaster without a station: the Allied bombing had ended all traffic on the railroad line from Bologna to Pistoia. Then he complained about the war in general. "For charity, Rugi," he said, "when will I see my sons again?"

"Have you not heard?" Rugi said. "The Allies are almost to Vergato."

"I will believe nothing until I am shaking hands with an American soldier," the stationmaster said, "and even then I will smell his breath, to see if he is a German spy."

When the stationmaster had left, Rugi had settled down to a long, boring night, and now, at six A.M., it was over at last. As he and his fellow worker trudged up the stony path toward the little mountainside home where Rugi and his wife and two daughters had taken refuge from the war, he turned to Rossi. "Come in and suck an egg with us before you go home to Creda."

"No, thank you, Rugi," Rossi said. "I barely have the energy to make it to Creda."

"A little wine and a raw egg will help you along the way."

"Molto gentile," Rossi said. "It is very nice of you, but I am going home."

At a crossroad the men parted. "When you see Attilio Comastri, tell him I will be up to Creda after I have rested," Rugi said. "He and I are going to look for chestnuts, though heaven knows where we will find any." Rossi waved and disappeared up the path toward Creda.

Attilio Comastri was Rugi's best friend. In the intensely male culture of Monte Sole the two were closer in many ways than they were to their wives. As young men living in the mill town of Pioppe di Salvaro, they had chased girls together, drunk together, got in and out of trouble together, and sat together for hours playing *tresette* or *brescla.* Attilio Comastri was a strong, shy, athletic man, and Ruggero was short and slight and voluble, a hazel-eyed miniature with heavy brows and a strong dialect that made him sound almost like a Frenchman, and their opposite personalities dovetailed perfectly. When Attilio went off to play in soccer matches, Rugi would be there to lead the cheers for his best friend.

Now both were thirty-five, married with families, and they still saw each other almost as often as in their single days. They worked together in the mill, met together in the *osteria,* played cards together and only regretted the fact that they no longer lived closer. When the bombing had begun, and the Germans had killed several hostages in Pioppe, both men had taken their families up the mountain, Ruggero to the home of his in-laws at Maccagnano, about a half mile up, and

Comastri to the farmhouse at Creda, nearly a mile from the mill. But whenever their shifts at the mill permitted, the men met and enjoyed each other's company.

Rugi was surprised to see his wife waiting for him at the door when he finally reached home. "Here, take these!" she said, thrusting a pair of climbing boots at him.

"What for?" he asked.

"The Germans are around! You are going to the woods!"

While Rugi was lacing up the boots, his father-in-law, Giovanni Righi, a lively man of almost sixty years, came running out of a room. "Quick! Quick!" the old man said. "The Germans are behind every bush!"

Rugi and his father-in-law jogged up the path toward the woods. Over his shoulder the exhausted Rugi could hear his three-year-old daughter, Luisa. *"Babbo, Babbo!"* she was calling. "When are you coming home to sleep?" Rugi waved good-bye and kept on trotting. Just before the two men detoured into the brush that would cover them as they crawled up the mountain, they saw a green glow intrude on the morning blackness. It seemed to come from San Martino.

Attilio Comastri was dreaming about the good old days when he felt himself being pummeled into wakefulness by his twenty-year-old wife, Ines Gandolfi. "What is the matter?" he said. "It is still early."

"Something is going on," Ines said softly.

Attilio listened. From the courtyard there came the loud sounds that men make when they are herding sheep, except that there were no sheep at Creda, and these sounds seemed to be in an undecipherable language that sounded harsh and gurgling. In the *casa colonica* itself, Attilio could hear loud knockings on doors and occasionally a splintering as though a door had been bashed in. He ran to awaken the others, and one by one they assembled in the little room at Creda: Attilio, his wife, their two-year-old daughter, Bianca, Attilio's twenty-three-year-old sister, Marcella, and various of his wife's relatives. Attilio was about to climb into his working clothes when there was a loud hammering and the door burst open. German soldiers carrying machine pistols began shouting, *"Raus, raus!"* and pointing toward the door. Attilio grabbed up his pants and started to struggle into them, but one of the Germans kicked him and knocked him over, and Attilio crawled down the stairs in his shorts and undershirt.

In the courtyard, barely lighted by a few flickering flashlights, he made out a strange sight. All the *contadini* and refugees were being herded out of the *casa colonica* at gunpoint. Some men were being dragged out of the hayloft above the barn and shoved against the wall by German soldiers. At one end of the barn Attilio thought he could make out the form of Mario Cardi, the tough war hero, sitting on the ground under the muzzle of a German gun. At the other end, he thought he saw two German soldiers hauling a kicking and struggling Edoardo Rossi into the middle of the courtyard. Comastri wondered what Rossi was doing here; he was supposed to be on guard at the mill with Rugi. If Rossi were here, it had to be after six o'clock, but to Attilio it seemed like three in the morning in this miserable cold rain that fell from the black void above. He cursed the rotten luck. That afternoon he had planned to go hunting chestnuts with Rugi, but by the time Rugi came up to meet him, he would be on his way to Germany and slave labor, along with the other able-bodied men. Already the Germans were beginning to sort them out. There were about 90 people in the courtyard, and the soldiers ordered them into the opening where the empty farm carts were kept. This opening was in the middle of the long barn and fronted on the piazza; it looked exactly like a small garage with the front door missing, and there were only two ways out of it: straight out the front, where something like 100 Germans were assembled, and through a little side door that led into the stalls. Attilio figured he might as well go into the shed willingly and forget any idea of escape. It was better to go to slave labor than to be shot dead at the hands of these Germans, all of them clutching machine pistols and wearing camouflage suits and clanking with the grenades that were belted around their middles, and all of them wearing the crossed lightning bolts, the "crooked 44," of the SS.

"Men on the left, women on the right!" one of the soldiers shouted in Italian.

Pressed tightly into the fifteen-by-twenty-foot opening, some of the women and children began to cry. There were two small carts in the room, and a few of the women tried to deposit their babies in them, but the Germans ordered them to hold the infants in their arms. Attilio and his wife and daughter managed to remain together in the middle of the dark shed and halfway back, behind one of the farm carts, and in the midst of all the hysteria he gripped his wife's arm and shouted, "Do not worry! I will be back!"

Just then a brilliant flare turned everything to scarlet, and as soon as the incandescence had died, two of the SS men came into the room and started to count. "As I expected," Attilio said in his wife's ear, "they are making up a group for slave labor."

"Then why are they counting the women and children?" Ines called out.

Pressed on all sides by what felt like tons of human flesh, Attilio pondered his wife's question, but he could not think of a logical answer. Then he saw that the Germans were wheeling a heavy flatbed farm cart toward the entrance to the room. On top of the cart a German soldier was fiddling with a machine gun.

At the entrance to the opening, Mario Cardi's brother, Carlo, showed his railroader's permit to an SS man, but the response was a fist in the face. Carlo staggered, and as he was about to fall, the SS man gave him a shove that propelled him inside. Somehow he managed not to drop his son, Alberto, who was sixteen months old and trembling with cold. Inside the shed Carlo looked for his wife, who was carrying their other child, fourteen-day-old Walter, but it was impossible to see over the packed rectangle of humanity. As he stood on his toes to look for his wife, it seemed to Carlo that he was looking over a raft of disembodied heads, floating on a pond of nightclothes. Everybody's head blocked everybody else's, and he was barely able to tell one from another.

At first it seemed odd to Carlo that there was hardly any noise, except for the guttural shouts of the Germans outside. It was as though each person in the shed had decided to maintain a perfect anonymity, so as not to draw attention. Carlo knew they were terror-stricken—he was frightened himself—and he realized for the first time that there is a fear that surpasses tears. A few of the babies were whimpering, but they would have been crying anyway. None of the infants had been dressed or fed.

Carlo did not understand exactly what was confronting him, whether the Germans intended rounding up the men for slave labor or whether they intended something worse. A scene intruded on his thought processes: he kept seeing the bedroom of the *casa colonica* where his wife and the two babies slept. The night before, an old friend had visited the house, and Carlo had taken him around the family's tiny living quarters and shown him all the improvements he had been making. Their last stop had been the bedroom. His wife and the babies were already asleep, and the visitor commented on how angelic they looked, and how lucky Carlo was to have such a family.

Now Carlo was standing in a herring pack of relatives and friends and refugees, under the barrel of a German heavy machine gun, and he could not get the bedroom scene out of his mind. He fought to regain control of himself, and then he remembered the farm cart in the middle of the room. He knew of the little door that led to the stall, and he thought that he might have a chance to wriggle to the door from underneath the cart. He handed his son to his oldest sister, Elena, who was thirty-one, and squeezed himself behind the cart. As he sat on the floor trying to figure his next move, his friend Quinto Marzari passed him down a cigarette. "Here," Quinto said. "You might as well have a smoke. It will be your last."

Mario Cardi was flung into the shed with his friend Mario Medici, who had been in the *Bersaglieri* until half his foot had been shot away, and now the two war veterans were squeezed together next to one of the farm carts. "What do we do now?" Mario said without expecting an answer.

"Do what you want," Medici said, "but I cannot run fast enough to get away even if I could get out of here, so instead of worrying myself to death, I will have a smoke." With that, the invalid hoisted himself on top of the two-wheeled farm cart, pulled out a cigarette and began smoking it as though he were taking a five-minute break from his farm chores. Mario craned his neck to see what was going on outside, and immediately he noticed that the 100 or so SS men who had originally swarmed over Creda were now reduced to 18 or 20, almost all of them carrying machine pistols. Four or five of the Nazis were struggling to push a heavy flatbed farm cart in front of the opening to the room, and when it was in position, Mario noticed the heavy-caliber machine gun mounted on top. His training as a prison guard told him it was not unreasonable that the Germans should mount such a formidable weapon to guard 90 people in the shed, but then he noticed that there were stacks and stacks of ammunition belts alongside, enough ammunition to fight a major battle. Mario wondered what in the world the Germans would be doing with all that ammunition, and in the same second he knew. To no one in particular, he said, "They are going to kill us."

Four or five of the SS men squeezed into the pack of human beings and began collecting everything of value, and a few of them wisecracked in what sounded to Mario like perfect Italian. "You will not need this wallet anymore, *Nonno*." "Here, *Signora,* let me have that purse. There is nothing to spend it on where you are going." "Give me those cigarettes. You will soon be rid of the habit." The one who searched Mario said, "Your big hero act outside, where did it get you?" Only one of the Germans seemed to be carrying out the search with any degree of seriousness. He was a young soldier, barely eighteen by the soft look of him. His face was white, and his lips trembled, and to Mario he looked as though he was about to pass out on his feet in this congestion of humanity.

Now the soldiers went out of the room and took up positions around the machine gun. They seemed to be waiting for something. The minutes went on, and all at once Mario became aware of an orange glow lighting up the sky. The Germans had begun to burn the *podere*. There could no longer be any question about what was going on. Creda, its buildings and its people, was going to be removed from the earth. Mario whispered to his friends Franco and Bruno Brizzi. "There is only one way to save ourselves," he said, "and that is to make a break for it."

"We would be killed," Bruno said.

"Some of us would be killed. But if we stay here, all of us will be killed."

"So you want us to tell everybody to run for it now?"

Mario paused. "No," he said finally. "Maybe they are just trying to scare us." He could not bring himself to tell his friends and relatives to run into certain death at the hands of the Germans, so long as there remained the slightest chance that he was wrong. He knew that he was respected, and he knew they would make the break if he ordered it.

For about the fifth time, Mario squeezed between the dozens of bodies to try the door that led from the little room into the stable, and for about the fifth time he could not budge it. He cursed the extra-large lock that his father had installed on the other side of the door.

He called Franco and Bruno. "Maybe if we all push together," he said, "we can worry this lock to death."

For long minutes they pushed and strained at the door, but it held firm. "What is happening outside?" Bruno Brizzi said, and Mario wriggled into a vertical position. He saw that the machine gun was unmanned on top of the four-wheeled cart, but it was flanked by two SS men with machine pistols. As Mario watched, a bright green flare lit up the sky in the direction of San Martino. As though on command, the women and children set up a loud wailing and lamenting. The SS man with the pale face, the one who looked like a frightened boy, climbed on the cart and positioned himself behind the machine gun. While Mario watched in horror, the young soldier gingerly gripped the handles. Mario heard several loud commands in German, but nothing happened, and then the young gunner took his hands off the weapon to wipe at his eyes. Instantly another SS man jumped on the cart, knocked the young soldier to the ground and began taking a position behind the gun.

Mario dropped down. "Holy Mother!" he said. "This one is going to shoot!" Franco and Bruno and Mario put all their strength into an attack on the reluctant lock, and just as it gave way and the three of them hurtled into the dark stable, they heard the first bursts of machine-gun fire.

Leonardo Tiviroli peered through one sleep-encrusted eye at the little window in his bedroom and realized that he had violated the first rule of his family's feudallike *podere* at Steccola. He had overslept. There could be no doubt about it. The glow of sunlight was already coming through the window, and so was the heavy pounding of rain. The former *Bersagliere* groped for his trousers and pulled them over his ankles and realized suddenly that the glow of sunlight and the sound of heavy rain could not coincide. Half out of his pants, he hobbled to the window and saw that Creda, only a few hundred yards down the road toward Pioppe di Salvaro, was a big fireball. His first instinct was to run and give the alarm, but something held him at the window. When one has been looking out of exactly the same window at exactly the same scene for two decades of dawns, one develops an instinct about minor changes; they are felt more than seen. Now Leonardo's skin crawled. He looked down toward the barn, where forty partisans were sleeping, and found nothing amiss. Then his eyes swept across the ridge, up to the house called Le Scope (the brooms), after the good broomstraws that grew there. When he had decided that his instincts were failing him, Leonardo saw a movement behind the hedges of Le Scope. In a half-crouch position, four German soldiers passed his line of vision in a gap in the hedges 400 yards away. He saw that they were carrying weapons heavier than mere rifles and that grenades were hanging from belts around their middles. He gave the alarm.

The partisans swarmed out of the hay like ants from a broken hill, pushing and shoving and arguing among themselves, and the four Germans melted back into the underbrush. A partisan shouted, "Attack!" but another leader said, "Keep your mouth shut! Our orders are not to confront the Germans."

The argument continued, and the scene reminded Leonardo of the four days he had spent with the partisans and how they had acted like a gypsy band. The loud discussion went on for another five minutes, with everyone talking at once, and then the whole group headed into the brush and up the side of the mountain. "Where are you going?" Leonardo asked one.

"To Zone X, our emergency zone," a partisan answered.

"Where is that?"

"On top of Monte Sole."

The two families of Steccola assembled and decided that the Germans were staging a big raid and that as usual they would be looking for able-bodied men. "You must go into the woods," one of the mothers said as she distributed crusts of bread and cheese to sustain the men through the day. Finally, they were assembled for flight: Leonardo, his brothers, Giovanni and Antonio, his father, Silvio, and two members of the other family that worked the *podere:* Silvio Tiviroli's cousin, Augusto Grani, and his son, Francesco. Old Augusto was especially annoyed. It was the twentieth birthday of his daughter, and the family had worked for weeks preparing for the celebration. "Well, we will have our party after dark," Augusto said.

Just before the male exodus from the farmhouse, nine-year-old Maria, the blond stringbean with the long pigtails, began to cry.

"Stop that!" Leonardo said, and Maria stopped out of respect for the one member of the family who had always been able to keep her in line.

"Where are you going to hide?" Maria asked, wiping her eyes.

"We will tell you when we get back home," Leonardo said, "and do not forget to behave yourself." Maria promised.

Before the dawn of Friday a partisan named Pietro Lazzari and his squad leader, Lolli, left their vigil at a farmhouse called Ca' di Dorino and walked 300 yards through the rain to the new headquarters of the *Stella Rossa* at Cadotto. It was Lolli's idea. "We will get the latest word," he had said.

At Cadotto, a big *casa colonica* surrounded by six or seven outbuildings that housed some thirty civilians and forty partisans, the two men chatted with the sentry and went inside for some bread. When they came back out, the weather seemed even worse. The rain poured down, and a puff of low-lying cloud had cut the visibility to only a few yards. They had just started back toward Ca' di Dorino when they heard the soggy sound of footsteps, and out of the gloom came a dozen Germans with a police dog on a leash. For a few seconds, the two groups stared at each other, and then Lazzari fired a burst from his Sten gun. The Germans took cover and began to return the fire, and then more Germans appeared out of the haze, and Lazzari and Lolli were beaten back toward the farmhouse. Gianni Rossi, second-in-command of the brigade, stuck his head out the window and shouted, "What is happening, Lazzari?"

"The SS!" Lazzari shouted over the gunfire. "Where is Lupo?"

"Getting dressed."

Within minutes, the partisans had fled from the farmhouse, firing as they ducked up the side of the hill toward Monte Sole. But the Germans had infiltrated a ring around the headquarters, and ten of the partisans, including Lupo, were killed during the retreat in the fog. A few civilians got away with the partisans, but four families were left behind in the farmhouse. When the last shot of the skirmish had been fired, the Germans posted guards at each door and set the house afire. As the inhabitants climbed higher and higher to escape the flames, the Germans took potshots at them at the windows, and some who jumped were killed from the fall or the gunfire or both.

Aldo Gamberini, one of the *contadini* of Cadotto, watched the destruction of the farmhouse from Ca' di Dorino, where he had fled when the first shots were fired, twisting and darting across the fields as bullets zapped into the earth around him. At Ca' di Dorino, he fell exhausted in a ditch near the road and lay there, trying not to make a sound. While he was hiding, he heard noises and looked up through the haze to see the Nazis herding the women and children of the *podere* at Il Palazzo along a mountain path not ten yards away. He wondered why the Germans would want to make prisoners of a bunch of women and children, but his thoughts were interrupted by something brushing against his leg. Gamberini looked down and saw his dog, Mascherino (Little Mask), and instantly he began a mad search through his pockets for his knife. The knife was nowhere to be found—he must have dropped it while running—and Gamberini took the dog in his arms to strangle it. But Mascherino only whimpered slightly; he was in no mood to bark, and the two of them lay quietly in the ditch while the Germans marched by. Minutes later Gamberini heard a great outcry from the direction of Steccola, where the column had headed, and then nothing.

Still he lay in the ditch, until all he could hear was the screaming of the farm animals that had been left to die in the flaming barns and the occasional loud crunch of a building collapsing into its own ashes. He knew that the *casa colonica* at Cadotto was a total loss, and that everyone in it was killed. He had lost seven children, his wife, a granddaughter, a sister and two brothers. For a while he was torn with a desire to see their bodies once more, but then it occurred to him that the sight might be more than he could bear. He cast one final look toward the smoldering pyre of Cadotto and headed into the woods, shielding his eyes as though to shut out the day.

When the firing started at Creda, Carlo Cardi was crouched behind the heavy wooden farm cart almost exactly in the center of the open room. At first the screams and the gunfire were almost equally loud, but as the bursts went on for long seconds, the other sounds died down, and all he could hear was the heavy machine gun's ponderous booming interspersed with short rapid bursts from the machine pistols. The firing stopped and started, stopped and started, until the ninety people in the room were knocked flat, and then there was a short pause. Carlo felt pain in his thigh and arm, but he sensed that he was not mortally wounded, and he began slithering through the bloody bodies toward the side door that now hung open to the stable. As he twisted and turned on his belly, he caught a glimpse of his wife and infant son Walter lying nearby. Dina was covered with blood and motionless. Walter lay sobbing and hiccuping next to his mother's body. For a moment, the sight of his own flesh and blood drew Carlo up short, and then, just as he started to resume his tortuous journey toward the door, he heard his father cry out. "Stay, Carlo!" his father was saying. "Do not leave me!"

Before he could reply Carlo saw a movement at the front of the shed. It was still more dark than light outside, but there was an amber glow in the air, and as he lay motionless on the pile of dead and dying, Carlo could make out the shape of a soldier holding a pistol. Slowly, as though on a range, the German began firing into the bodies. After five or six shots, he put his pistol back in the holster and climbed up behind the machine gun. Carlo burrowed under some corpses just as a new burst began. This time the firing period was shorter, but it was followed by grenades that were tossed atop the dead. After the grenades, there was more machine-gun firing, and after the machine guns, more grenades, and finally the Germans threw in a half dozen incendiary bombs to finish the job.

Now the shed became as bright as the inside of a forge, and a great blast of heat seemed to choke off the remaining air. Carlo looked up and saw that life remained. A few children were screaming. A boy of three or four years was sitting in front of Carlo, his face half-covered by a hat, and he was alternately sitting up and lying down, clutching his arm. Carlo looked again toward his wife. She was covered by a sheet of bluish flame, and the baby, still crying, was beginning to burn next to her. His sister, Elena, was in a half-erect position, her back toward the machine gun and Carlo's other son at her breast, and the two of them were surrounded by leaping fountains of orange flame in the rear of the shed.

Carlo had seen all he could bear. He was sorry he had not died with his family. He felt dismayed that he had been permitted to live. But a sudden irrational wave of hope came over him as he lay on his side gasping and choking in the acrid fumes of the incinerator. He saw the situation with what seemed to him like total clarity. All he had to do was get up and walk, walk straight into the machine gun and into the woods where the Germans could not find him. He pulled himself unsteadily to his feet, and felt the sharp pangs in his wounds. Teetering like a drunk, he slipped and slid across the wet bodies and out the opening. No one was at the machine gun as he lurched by, and in the smoke and haze he did not see a single German as he rounded the big farm cart and headed across the courtyard for the woods. He started to run, but all at once clouds of red and black passed across his eyes; he felt as though he were in a dream, running down a street of fresh poured tar with all the demons of hell in pursuit. It seemed to him that his feet were moving, but that the rest of him was disconnected and useless. Just then he heard a shot and felt a terrible pain in his foot. A bullet had lanced from the heel to the instep. Somehow this fresh wound woke Carlo up to what was happening, and he kept on running till he was several hundred yards from the piazza of Creda. As the danger diminished, the pain increased, but he managed to make it almost to the top of Monte Salvaro, the next mountain over from Monte Sole. There he turned and watched. Through a momentary clearing in the clouds he could see the whole *podere* of Creda burning and other fires beginning to billow up from adjoining farms. It seemed as though the earth were on fire and that sooner or later the flames would consume the whole mountain. Carlo had no idea what to do. His wounds had begun to throb, and there were scenes that he kept trying to push from his mind. He sat down and smoked a cigarette.

Attilio Comastri wondered why the machine gunner was aiming so low, and just when he realized that it was to hit the children, the soldier cut loose with a long burst. Attilio was hit in the thigh and fell instantly, and as he lay on the floor of the room, bodies thumped on top of him. When the shooting stopped, he looked for Ines, and found that she was lying dead across his body. He looked for his sister, Marcella, and found that she, too, was in the stack of bodies pinning him to the floor. She was trying to talk, but Attilio could see that she was beyond help. Then the firing started again, and Attilio lay under the bodies and prayed that his end would come quickly and painlessly. He stayed through successive waves of machine-gun fire and grenades, and when the firing finally stopped, he saw that two of his friends were also alive under the stack of bodies. He called out to them, but suddenly there was a loud explosion, and fire seemed to break out instantaneously in several parts of the shed. "We survived the gunfire," Attilio murmured. "Now we are going to burn alive."

Frediano Marchi, one of the living, said hysterically, "I will not die like this!" As Attilio watched, Frediano clambered to his feet. There was a short burst of gunfire, and he fell dead. Then a German entered the smoky opening and began kicking at the bodies. Attilio closed his eyes and tried not to breathe, and he heard several pistol shots ring out, but apparently the German did not see him under the bodies of his loved ones. There was another pause, and then more incendiary bombs were thrown in, and the whole place seemed to flare up at once. Attilio burrowed into the pile of bodies, using them as insulation, and prayed. There was an intense heat, and lying under his wife and sister, soaked in their blood, Attilio decided that the simplest and easiest way out was to stand up as Marchi had and get it over with. Then he heard a voice: "Come! We must get out of here!" Attilio turned and saw twelve-year-old Remo Venturi creeping along the bodies toward him.

"Remo," he said. "You are not dead?"

"No, I was only hit in the side. Come on! We must get out!"

"But how?" Attilio whispered.

"A lot of people got out the door to the stable. All we have to do is wait till the smoke gets thick."

By now the hayloft and the wooden beams above them were burning, and as the two survivors talked, a pair of the heaviest supporting beams crashed down in a fiery crisscross toward the front. Behind this perfect screen Attilio and the boy crawled across the bodies and through the side door to the stable. There were eight stalls inside, in two rows of four each separated by a narrow corridor, and only the first stall on the right was unoccupied by cattle. Attilio and the boy tumbled into the empty stall just as the Germans broke open the door from the outside and piled into the stalls looking for survivors. There were several others in the room, and one was caught in the corridor when the Germans entered. He turned and ran toward the empty stall, and just as he reached it, there was a volley of shots, and the man fell dead on top of Attilio and the boy. They remained inert as long as they could, but the man's body had begun to burn with a green flame, and finally Attilio had to take a chance on giving their position away. He reached around and grabbed the man's belt and slid him off to one side. But burning hay continued to drop from the loft and sear the man and the boy, and they ran across the smoky corridor and ducked into a stall that was already occupied by an ox. The animal began kicking at them and rolling its eyes and trumpeting its panic, and Attilio quickly untied the beast and shoved it out of the stall, where it ran up and down the corridor stepping on bodies and bumping into the other animals. It seemed as though every beast in the stable had gone crazy, and any minute Attilio expected the Germans to return to see what the noise was about.

From their new position across the corridor from the empty stall, they could see the body that had fallen on them and they recognized the victim as one of the Valdiserra brothers, some of whom were partisans. Attilio wondered why the body burned with a bright green flame. As the two of them watched, Valdiserra's head seemed to puff up from the heat, and all at once it broke open, and both of them looked away. "If we stay here, we are going to be found when the Germans come back for the animals," Attilio said. "I think we should wait and then try to get away."

"But how can you go like that?" the boy said.

Attilio looked down at himself. He was wearing only charred bits of shorts and undershirt, and every inch of his body was stained with remnants of other human beings. "Just a minute," Attilio said.

He stepped into the corridor and studied the dead. From the body of a man he recognized as Giuseppe Righi, he took a pair of pants, but he left the old man's shoes when he found that they were full of blood. From the body of a refugee named Pietro from Pioppe di Salvaro he took a dry pair of shoes. From a man whose name he remembered as Fransconi or Frascaroli he took a bloodstained shirt. When he was fully dressed again, he motioned to the boy, and the two of them tiptoed to the door leading to the outside.

"If the Nazis are still out there," Attilio said, "it will be quick and painless. So we will open the door and run as fast as we can toward the woods."

Remo nodded his head. "I will do what you say," he said. "You are older."

They burst out the door and into a chilling mist that obscured everything, and they ran up the mountain till they dropped into a clump of sodden brush and weeds. When they had regained their breath, they peered down toward the road and saw a patrol of twenty Germans moving off in the haze, headed toward the next *podere*. The soldiers clanked as they moved, from bobbing grenades and bombs belted to their waists, and it seemed to Attilio that they were lifeless, automatic, more like robots than men. "Come," he said to Remo. "We must make our way to the front lines."

Between the time that Mario Cardi and his friends broke the lock on the little door and the time that the machine-gun bullets had begun to hit those in the middle of the open room, eight or ten people had managed to slip into the stable. In broadest daylight, the stable was lighted only by small vents near the roof line, and now it was pitch-dark inside and out. The room was not more than twenty feet square, and as the long bursts of machine-gun fire continued from outside, the people who had escaped ran about the stable in circles, bumping into oxen and cows and one another. Mario and his friends Gino Gandolfi and Bruno Brizzi huddled together in a corner, listening to gunfire mow down their loved ones and at the same time trying to soothe a frightened cow that threatened to crush them against the stone wall. After a few minutes, the shooting stopped, but soon a pair of Germans opened the outside door of the stable and began pouring a steady stream of fire into the shadows inside. Mario recognized the sound of the Schmeisser machine pistol, a deadly little weapon that fired bullets so fast that it sounded like somebody ripping a paper across a dotted line: *Brrrp. Brrrp.* He and Gino and Bruno flattened their bodies into the hay and offal on the floor, while the cows and oxen strained and heaved at their lashings and mingled their bawling with the screams of the people dying in the other stalls. Then the firing stopped, and there were a couple of loud explosions, and the hay in the stable caught fire. Mario jumped out of the stall when the flames began licking at him and searched for a way out. He could go back into the little room where he had come from, or he could go out the door where the Germans had just thrown the bombs, or he could stay inside and burn to death. There was a hole in the ceiling that led to the loft, and many times Mario had stood up there forking hay down to the animals, but now the whole roof was ablaze, and balls of burning hay periodically floated down to the floor.

Mario threw himself on the corridor stones to find some cool air and realized that he was lying on human beings. He studied their faces in the light from the fires and recognized his mother and his twenty-one-year-old sister, Lucia. Mario crawled under their bodies to escape the heat that was scorching his face and listened to the diminishing screams from the other room and the periodic bomb bursts that were still going off. Then he realized that the door to the outside had been opened again, and the Germans were back in the smoke-filled stable looking for survivors. He felt a hand grip his ankle, and he made himself go limp all over. His body was dragged a few inches, but he neither breathed nor stirred, and he felt the hand let go. The Germans remained near him for a few minutes more, firing random shots, but then the heat drove them back out, and when he was positive they were gone, Mario slid out from under the bodies, wiping the blood from his eyes so that he could see again. To his surprise, Gino and Bruno joined him in the smoldering corridor. Both had escaped death by hiding in one of the stalls, and the pawings of a terrified ox had kept the Germans from coming after them. The three young men decided to make a break out the side door while it was still dark and smoky. The alternative was to stay in the stable and burn to death or be captured later when the fires cooled and the Germans came for the animals. They were moving on their hands and knees toward the door when a voice cried out from one of the feeding troughs: "Mario! Save me! Help me!"

Mario recognized the voice. With Gino, he crawled right through the legs of a cow and reached his twenty-four-year-old sister, Maria, wounded by machine-gun fire. The two men lifted her from the trough, where she had been doubled up painfully, and laid her flat in a corner of the stall. As they worked, bits of burning wood and hay snapped around them, and now and then a piece of hot rock would snap off the wall. Mario looked at his sister's wounds—a hemstitch of holes from shoulder to shoulder—and he realized that nothing could be done. "Be calm, sister!" he said. "We are just going to see if the Germans are gone."

He and Gino backed out of the stall to the corridor, where Bruno Brizzi was standing watch, and the three of them edged toward the door. As they were about to make their break, Mario heard something behind him. He turned to find Maria, blood streaming down her nightgown, her eyes bulging and her body quivering. "Where are you going?" she said, and when Mario took another step toward the door, she almost screamed at him, "You are leaving without me."

Mario lost control. He grabbed his sister by the arms, as though to shake her, but instantly he could see the pain flash across her face. He watched horrified as she slid bonelessly to the floor. Gino beckoned, and the three men shot out the door and across the field. They ran downhill in heavy fire until they were several hundred yards from the barn and out of range. There they crouched in a ditch, and a few minutes later they were joined by Quinto Marzari and Pietro Macchelli. When his breath returned, and his panic subsided, Mario stepped out of the ditch and started toward the barn. "Where are you going?" Marzari called.

"I am going to get Maria. I left her up there, and she told me not to leave her to burn."

"Stay!" Macchelli said. "Maria is dead."

Mario stopped. "How do you know?"

"We saw it happen, Marzari and I," Macchelli said. "We came out of the stable right after you, and your sister was trying to follow you, and she almost made it to the hedge when a German shot her in the back. We ran right past her. Her body is up there now."

After a while Gino and Bruno and Mario slipped from their hiding place and went toward the church of Salvaro, about a mile away. The going was slow; Gino was wounded in the hip, and all three were burned. Finally, they knocked on the door of the church, and the monsignor, Firenzio Mellini, opened it and fell back. "For charity!" he said as he looked at the three blood-streaked men. "Go away! You will get us all killed!"

"We need help, *Monsignore,*" Mario said. "Gino is wounded."

"I do not know you," the priest said, his voice rising like a woman's. "If the Germans see you here, we all will be shot."

"Father—"

"Go to the woods! Go to the woods!" The door slammed shut.

The three men limped up the road and into the woods, heading for a little house where a refugee doctor named Mario de la Valle had been staying to escape the bombings. They found the doctor on his way out the door. He told them that a partisan messenger had reached him, and he was on his way to a dozen wounded men who needed help in the nearby woods. The doctor looked quickly at Gino's wound, told him that it was not fatal, and handed the three men a loaf of bread. "That is all I can do for you now," he said. "Go hide in the woods, and I will see you later." The three men limped into the brush and up the flank of Monte Salvaro, and as they climbed, they could see the glow of hundreds of fires on Monte Sole.

"Mario," Gino asked wonderingly, "can you make a mountain burn?"

"The Germans are doing it," Mario said.

* * *

It seemed to Acacci "Rugi" Ruggero that he and his father-in-law had been sitting in the woods in this punishing rain for days now, and for his own part he did not intend to put up with such agony a second longer. "Now I go!" he told old Giovanni.

"Are you crazy?" Righi said. "You will be killed."

"Look, *Babbo,* I have been on guard duty in the mill for two nights without sleep, and my skin is clinging to my underwear, and I would just as soon die at the hands of the Germans as stay here and die of discomfort."

"No!" the old man said hysterically, and grabbed Rugi around the shoulders, and for a moment the two pulled and tugged at each other. Finally, Rugi broke loose and jogged down the mountain. "Wait!" Giovanni said. "Wait for me!"

When Rugi's wife opened the locked front door to their wild knocking, she began to sob. "You will both be killed!" she said. "Go back to the woods! The Germans are all around!"

Rugi fell into a chair. "Not me," he said. "I am exhausted."

Other relatives joined in the discussion, but Rugi hardly cared what they said. At last his wife grabbed his hand and pulled him to his feet. "Rugi!" she said, almost screaming at him. "Listen to me! For charity, listen to some sense! The Germans never hurt women and children, we know that. It is you and *Babbo* they want!"

Rugi felt his father-in-law pulling him through the open door, and he realized that it would be less tiring to allow himself to be led away than to stay in this tower of Babel. "I will go," he said, "but you must promise me one thing. You can see in both directions down the road, and the second you spot any Germans, take the baby and hide."

"We will, Rugi, we will," his wife said. "Now go!"

The two men made their way several hundred yards up the mountain, to the edge of a deep wooded area. From there, they could not see the house, but they could watch a stretch of the road. Rugi did not know how long he had dozed when he felt himself being shaken. "Look!" Giovanni said.

Rugi heard the voices of five or six men speaking in a familiar tongue, and as he peered through the woods toward the road below, he saw a patrol of men in German uniforms, all of them carrying machine pistols and belts of grenades and bombs. "Those are not Germans!" Rugi said. "They speak *dialetto bolognese.*"

"No, they are not Germans," his father-in-law said. "They are something worse. They are Fascists."

The patrol disappeared around the bend headed for the house at Maccagnano, and soon the two men began hearing the bawlings of their farm animals. A wisp of smoke rose from the direction of the house, and there were more mingled screamings, and several times Rugi jumped to his feet. Each time his father-in-law pulled him back. "Stay down, Rugi!" the old man said, tears welling in his eyes. "You cannot help them."

In ten or fifteen minutes black smoke was billowing from the house, and the animal noises had become frenzied. "We must go now!" Rugi said. "We must see if we can save something."

"It is too late," Righi said. "There is nothing to save. They are all dead."

Rugi grabbed his father-in-law by the lapels of his tattered jacket. "You crazy man, you crazy old man!" he screamed. "Why do you say such a thing?"

"Because I heard the shots," Giovanni said.

Rugi allowed himself to be led over the mountain to the church at Salvaro, where their old friend Monsignor Mellini hid them both in the sacristy along with another hundred or so men of the region. Later they were joined by Giovanni's brother, Celso Righi. "I know exactly what happened," Celso said. "I was watching from close up." He covered his face with his hands and began to sob.

At that exact instant Rugi gave up all hope for his family. "Do not tell me, Uncle," Rugi said. "You do not have to speak."

Five minutes down the path from Creda the family Sasso lived in a handsome stone farmhouse called Prunaro di Sotto. The parents were very old, and there were two grown sons, one a deaf-mute. There were also two grown daughters, Adele and Graziella, and Graziella's own children, Gianna, five, and Annarosa, three. With them in the *casa colonica* was a young married girl named Albertina, awaiting the birth of a child.

Adele Sasso awoke on Friday morning to the sound of shooting and the flicker of fires up and down the valley. Quickly she alerted the other members of the household and shooed the males into the woods, as she had done a dozen times before. "Thank God the partisans are not here!" she said to Graziella. The sisters had mended clothes for the men of the *Stella Rossa* and both of them had carried messages and treated the wounded.

As the sun came up and the women could see that Nazi soldiers were crawling over the valley and the ridge and setting fire to everything that would burn, they began carrying their belongings out of the house and into a nearby air-raid shelter cut into the hill. Five-year-old Gianna was hauling an oversize loaf of bread across the yard when four soldiers burst into the clearing and herded everybody into the house at gunpoint. The soldiers were accompanied by a man in a green camouflage poncho, and Adele was surprised to hear that he spoke the Bolognese dialect perfectly. One of the soldiers went up the inside stairs of the house, and the man in the poncho stationed himself at the front door. The German shouted down something that Adele could not understand. "He says he found medicine," the Italian said. "You have to do with the partisans, *vero?*" No one answered, and the man pushed his helmet back, exposing his blond hair, and smiled, showing two gold teeth, and Adele realized that she had seen him somewhere before. He waved his machine pistol first at one and then at another, clicking the safety off and on, until he had terrified everyone in the room. "Now you are afraid, right?" he said, smiling his golden smile.

Adele was trembling, but she said in as bold a voice as she could muster, "One need not be afraid when one has done nothing."

"You know what my comrade upstairs said?" the man continued in the local dialect. "He said, 'Kill them all!' "

Adele could see his knuckles whitening on the machine pistol, and she blurted out, "You cannot kill us! It is wrong. Think of your own wife and children!"

"We have no concern with who you are or what you are," the man said. "We are here only to kill you." He approached the four adult women and the two little girls and began kicking and shoving them into the narrow hallway of the house. When they were all enclosed in this small area, Gabriella made a break for the kitchen door, dragging little Gianna behind her. The blond man shot the mother in the face and then shot the little girl, and both of them fell to the floor, with Gianna still holding the bread. Then he turned and began firing indiscriminately. The pregnant Albertina went down holding her stomach. Adele grabbed her mother, and the two of them fell together. Three-year-old Annarosa dropped to a sitting position in the middle of the corridor, her arms outstretched, and screamed.

When the shooting stopped, Adele was aware that she was unhurt except for a bullet hole through her hand. She lay still and listened to the soldiers smashing everything in the kitchen. Little Annarosa continued to scream, and Adele heard the clomp of boots down the corridor, a single shot, and then silence. After a while the noise subsided in the kitchen, and Adele climbed to her feet, separating herself from the blood-soaked body of her mother. She crept to the window and saw the five men walking in single file up the hill. She ran to an upstairs bedroom on the opposite side of the house, lowered herself to the ground by a rope and sprinted like a madwoman into the woods. Even as she ran, it seemed to her that she could hear the echoes of gunfire from every direction, and she thought that there must be a great battle going on.

It had just begun to get light outside, and the men had disappeared into the woods, when Maria Tiviroli, the nine-year-old blond girl with the pigtails, heard her mother call out, "Hurry up, children! We go to the shelter now." All summer long the families Tiviroli and Grani had worked to hollow an air-raid shelter out of the mountain behind Steccola, and inside they had stored medicine and cots and candles to see them through the raids that were expected any day now. But this morning the shelter would be used for another purpose: the glare in the sky around Steccola had told the elders of the family that a major *rastrellamento* was in progress, and although the Germans had never harmed any of the women or children or old men, the family had decided to go into the shelter to be on the safe side.

Maria could not understand why some of the older women were crying, why she had not been given a bite to eat, and why no one would listen to her as she went from adult to adult protesting her discomfort. There were seventeen or eighteen in the shelter: Maria's mother, sister, grandfather and all her cousins from the Grani family, a few neighbors, and some refugees from Bologna, and not a single one of them would pay the slightest attention to her. Then there was a noise at the entrance to the shelter. Maria turned and saw several Germans with machine pistols, and her hunger drained away.

The Germans stepped inside and indicated by hand signals that they wanted everybody to walk over the ridge toward Prunaro. When the group got outside, Maria saw that Steccola was afire, and then she realized why no one had paid attention to her. From the front of the shelter they had been able to see the Germans arrive and begin lighting the buildings. She hurried to her mother's side and clung tightly to her skirt as the Germans shoved them along the path. All at once the procession stopped, and there was loud talking in German, and Maria turned and saw that her grandfather, Alfonso Tiviroli, a *contadino* of eighty-two years, had fallen. When the Germans kicked him with their heavy boots, the old man struggled to his feet, took a few more steps and fell again. While Maria held her breath and tried not to scream, she watched two burly Germans pick the old man up by the arms and the legs, swing him back and forth three or four times, and sling him toward the top of a haystack that was burning with bright flames of orange and blue. Maria saw her grandfather's hat fly off and his heavy black greatcloak swirl in the air, and then he fell into the flames in a cloud of smoke and sparks.

The Germans hustled them along and slapped a few of the women who insisted on watching the *nonno*'s short death struggle. In the confusion, a refugee whom Maria knew only as Lucia fell with her baby, and a German lashed her across the back with the barrel of his gun. As she lay on the ground, crying, another German gently helped her to her feet, brushed off the child and led her back into line.

Now the leader insisted that the pace was too slow, and Maria found herself almost running as she tried to keep hold of her mother's skirt. Just ahead her sister, Gina, was walking fast, looking over her shoulder to make sure that her mother was there. When they reached Prunaro di Sopra, just up the hill from the Sasso home at Prunaro di Sotto, the Germans ordered them to form a line alongside the house, and around the corner came some more Germans and a slight man wearing a green poncho. Maria recognized him as Cacao, a partisan who had often visited them at Steccola with the brigade of the *Stella Rossa*. He looked at the line of people and began strutting up and down, pointing certain ones out. "This one sewed for the partisans," he said. "This one ran messages. This one washed. This one made the uniforms." There was a shocked silence from the line until Cacao stepped in front of Maria's mother. "This one—"

"Look," Signora Tiviroli said, "we helped you when you were at our house. We took care of you. We even sewed your pants when they were ripped. Now tell the Germans to let us alone!"

Cacao ignored the demand, and out of the corner of her eye Maria saw that the Germans were mounting two heavy machine guns next to the path. She felt faint, and she drew closer to her mother. A laughing German walked along the line and pointed to the death's head on his uniform, and another German pointed toward Steccola, ordering them to return home. The group had taken only a few steps when the shooting began.

Maria felt a searing pain in the fleshy part of her hip, as though someone had stuck a white-hot poker in the front and out the back, and then she fell. When she came to, she was lying under a steady drip of blood from her mother's body. No matter how she twisted, the blood kept raining on her hair; her pigtails were drenched with it, and she had to wipe her eyes to see. Out of a crack of visibility she saw a German boot, and then she heard several pistol shots. She watched through slitted eyes as an eight-year-old refugee girl named Paola crawled out from the mound of bodies, and a German stepped over and shot her in the head. There were a few more shots, and then silence.

Soon Maria became aware that someone was moaning. "Oh, my baby!" the voice was saying over and over. "Oh, where is my husband?" Maria recognized the voice as the refugee Lucia, and she wanted to help the lady, but she did not know how, nor was she sure that the Germans had left for good. When Maria finally wriggled out from under the body of her mother, she saw that Lucia had rolled a few feet into a bush and died. Maria took her mother by the shoulders and said, "Mother! Mother! Wake up!" But her mother's head wobbled like a puppet's.

Hardly aware of the wound in her hip, Maria wandered into a nearby field. When a German patrol came over the ridge toward her, she dropped into a hole in the ground and let them pass. Then she walked toward the brook, hoping to find some of the men of her family, and to her surprise she saw her cousin, nine-year-old Giuseppe Grani, leaning back against a grassy bank, still dressed in his brown Sunday suit, a peaked cap and his silver and blue confirmation medal. He looked as though he were catnapping, but as Maria walked up, she saw the round stain just under the medal. A few paces farther she spotted something waving gently in the stream. It was the long hair of her sister, Gina, lying head down in the water. The children must have run when the firing started; they had covered 200 yards.

As Maria slid down the bank to try to help her sister, she heard several shots from the ridge above, and she sprawled flat. After a few more shots, the firing stopped, and she crawled on all fours into the brush. She wandered toward Steccola, always keeping out of the open, and looked in at the refuge, but there was no one there. She was torn between a desire to find her father and brothers and a need to stay with her mother's body. She walked back across the ridge until she found a vantage point in the weeds where she could watch both Steccola and the bodies, and she lay down exhausted. But she could not get comfortable; her hip flashed with pain and her braids had turned into long, stiff boards of coagulated blood. She had a packet of pictures of the saints in her pocket, and she alternated looking at the bodies and Steccola and the saints until she dozed off.

Luigi Fornasini had dared to sleep at home in Sperticano that night, although everybody in the family, including his brother, Don Giovanni Fornasini, had told him it was foolhardy, that he should have remained on the mountain while there was so much German activity along the valley roads.

Like everybody else around Monte Sole, Luigi was counting the days till the Allies would close the twenty-mile gap between the front and the mountain, and the *contadini* could be rid of the oppressive control of the Germans and the Fascists. No acts of the Americans and the British could match what was going on, with his poor brother having to rush all over the area to intercede for hostages and the Nazis and the Blackshirts coming right into the churches to make up their work parties for Germany and stringing up bodies in village squares as object lessons for the partisans. It was after a few such bodies appeared in Sperticano that Luigi's family—his wife and his mother and his daughter and his brother, the priest—had recommended that he take the family's twenty sheep and wait out the war higher up on Monte Sole, where at least he would have a chance to break for the woods if the German patrols appeared. Don Giovanni made arrangements with the priests of the mountaintop, Don Ferdinando Casagrande and Don Ubaldo Marchioni, so that Luigi would have a place to sleep. When an overpowering urge to see his family came over Luigi, he would walk down to Sperticano after dark and get up before daylight the next morning to make the one-hour walk back to San Martino and the flock.

Now it was Friday morning, September 29, 1944, and Luigi was just approaching the church at San Martino, feeling a little ashamed. It was almost eight o'clock, and mass was over, and this was the day of the Feast of Saint Michael the Archangel. He was certain that Don Ubaldo would rebuke him in his usual sly way: "Good morning, Luigi, I see you are too late for mass. But perhaps our Heavenly Father makes a special case of the brother of such a good priest, *d'accordo?*"

As he stepped around the corner of the church, Luigi saw that an energetic conversation was taking place on the steps among Don Ubaldo and Don Ferdinando and a few of the *contadini* of San Martino. Luigi did not want to intrude, and as he stood quietly on the edge of the excited group, he learned that Don Ubaldo had just said mass, that the Germans had been raiding around Creda and Steccola and the other valleys below for several hours, and that the priests were worried about the consecrated host that remained in the church.

"When the Germans arrive, the host must be gone!" Don Ferdinando said excitedly.

"They would desecrate it," Don Ubaldo said. The *contadini* nodded their agreement.

The discussion went on, and finally Don Ubaldo waved his hand in the direction of Casaglia, a mile around the ridge. "We will go to the big church at Casaglia," he said. "We will all be safe there."

"Let me walk with you," Luigi said to his friends, the two priests.

"No, you go ahead," Don Ubaldo said. "Don Ferdinando and I are going to consume the sacrament before the Germans arrive to desecrate it." The two priests disappeared inside, and Luigi walked toward Casaglia, trying to piece his thoughts together. As the brother of a priest, he was familiar with ritual, and he knew that consuming the host was a drastic step, almost an ultimate one. He wondered if the two priests were not going too far, if they were not being a little hysterical. The Germans had been on the mountain plenty of times before, and they certainly had acted with cruelty and recklessness, but they always had exempted churches and women and children from their actions. Luigi wondered what the priests knew that justified the steps they were taking.

Along the road he ran into his old friend Luigi Casalini—a draftsman of Sperticano who also had taken refuge on the mountain—and a partisan whom both knew only as Socialista. The partisan told of a great raid by the Germans and pointed to a wound in his side that was leaking blood. "We must get you some medical attention," Luigi said.

"Never mind me," said Socialista. "There are others who are worse off."

A short distance down the road the three men came to a fork marked by a six-foot wooden cross set into a stone base. To the right lay the ridge route to the church of Casaglia, and to the left an ancient path that led straight to the top of Monte Sole. A partisan with a Sten gun slung on his shoulder stood at the base of the cross, and when Luigi tried to turn toward Casaglia, the partisan said harshly, "No! Up the mountain!"

"I have to get to the church at Casaglia," Luigi said. "I am the brother of Don Giovanni Fornasini."

"Even if you are the brother of the Holy Ghost," the partisan said, "you are going to the top. That is the only safe place."

The three men began to trudge up the steep path, and it seemed to Luigi that in this crazy world of war and confusion everybody had suddenly gone mad. But when they reached the peak of Monte Sole, he could see the fires reflected in the haze below.

It was dark and rainy when nine-year-old Fernando Piretti awoke. There was an unusual amount of excited chatter going on around him in the refuge of Cerpiano, where he and his Socialist father, Maximiliano, and the other members of his family had been staying for several weeks. Quickly he jumped out of bed and into his short pants and ran to see what was going on. Half-dressed *contadini* were standing in little groups, talking hurriedly and pointing down the mountain, where one could see what looked to be the orange glow of fire pushing through the mists. "What is it, Father?" Fernando said when he spotted Maximiliano.

"Nothing," Maximiliano said. "Just the Germans."

Fernando had never known a more exciting scene. People were rushing about with armloads of clothing and food, disappearing into the woods, and talking and gesturing frantically. Every now and then a *contadino* would burst into the courtyard, and everyone would gather around to hear the news. Fernando learned that the soldiers of the SS were on the way up the mountain in great numbers. They had gone first to the old partisan headquarters at Ca' di Zermino, where they had threatened to shoot all the *contadini,* but had finally let them go after setting the place on fire. "It is a bad *rastrellamento,*" one of the men said, and another said, "Yes, but not so bad that they are killing."

But soon another out-of-breath man arrived with worse news. As the Germans made their way up the mountain, fleeing *contadini* were running parallel to them in the high brush and woods, never letting the Germans out of their sight, but never exposing themselves either, and they were witnesses to every incident. It was true that the people at Ca' di Zermino had been released, the newcomer said, but a few paces farther the Germans had shot seven people without a word. If they had not killed at Ca' di Zermino, it was only because they had some special reason, perhaps because they did not want to alert too many others with gunfire.

Now the people at the refuge began to shake with hysteria, but to Fernando the whole scene was unreal and, therefore, not frightening, almost a welcome relief from the dreary day-in, day-out existence at Cerpiano, where there was not even another boy of his own age. He hopped from group to group, listening to the talk. Another man arrived with the news that all the people at Le Scope had been killed, that Creda and Steccola and Cadotto and Prunaro and Vallego were ablaze, and that the partisans had broken formation and were fleeing in every direction. "They are the ones who told us to come up here so they could protect us," Fernando heard a disgruntled *contadino* say, "and now they leave us to the Germans!"

When the news of Le Scope and the fires in the southern valley reached Cerpiano, several of the elders decided that everyone would have to hide. "But where?" one of them said.

"In the air-raid shelter," a teacher said.

"But if the Germans come here and find the place is empty, they will know we are hiding nearby," Maximiliano said, "and the air-raid shelter is too easy to find."

Finally, it was decided that the able-bodied men would flee up the mountain toward the deep woods, and the women, children and old men would remain at Cerpiano. There was simply no way to hide so many people, and the Germans had never bothered the helpless. Everyone packed a suitcase of valuables, because they could not be sure what was going to happen. Fernando hoped that the Germans would veer away from Cerpiano, so that the rest of the families would calm down, but if the Germans had to come, he hoped that they would be led by the sergeant who had spoken to him before. It had been a long time between chocolates.

Not everyone was content to stay at Cerpiano and wait. Virginio Paselli, the railroad trackworker, told his wife and two teen-age daughters and ten-year-old twins that his war experience had provided him with a sort of sixth sense about such things and that Cerpiano was no longer safe. With the coming of misty daylight they could see down the mountain from the refuge at Cerpiano, and wherever there had been a farm, now there was a bonfire. Tiny dots that nearly blended into the background could be seen making their way toward the refuge: Virginio said they were Germans in camouflage suits. There was a distant stuttering sound that Virginio said was machine guns and heavier, sporadic explosions that he explained were mortar shells. He remembered the sound from the Battle of Piave, in World War I, when he had lost all his hair.

"The place to be is the church at Casaglia," Virginio said. "There will be many people there and a priest, and the Germans will not bother you there. I will hide in the woods with the other men, and we will meet here after dark."

The walk to Casaglia took twenty minutes down a long, dark path hooded with dripping vines and trees and over a stream and up a steep rocky path that ran through a grove of chestnut trees, and the Pasellis were splattered with mud when they arrived at the cobbled piazza of Casaglia. Dozens of people milled about, clutching their cardboard suitcases, embracing the men who were going off to hide, and chattering together about the fires and the gunshots from below. From every direction more people headed for the majestic church of the mountains. Virginio was right; soon there would be at least 100 people sharing the asylum of Casaglia. The priest of San Martino, Don Ubaldo Marchioni, who sometimes visited the pastorless church to say mass, stepped from the main entrance, raised his hands and said in gentle tones, "Have courage. We will pray together. We will say the rosary. Let us pray together. Have courage, and we will say the rosary." The disorganized group began to slip slowly into church.

Lidia Pirini had awakened that morning to the sound of distant explosions, and once again she told herself that her father had made a wise decision moving the whole family up from the valley town of Murazze to the shelter at Cerpiano. Plainly, the bombardment was beginning below, and none of her friends in Murazze would be safe.

Lidia was fifteen, a pretty girl of striking colors: golden-brown hair, rich amber eyes, and skin the color of fresh milk. She was a happy girl, though given to certain childish fears, and she had managed to make the best of the week they had spent at Cerpiano. She did not suffer from the lack of companionship that disturbed some of the others. There were more than a dozen Pirinis at Cerpiano, including her mother and father and little sister, Marta, and big brother, Francesco, and eight cousins and four aunts, and on top of that she was related more or less distantly to almost everyone in the refuge.

Lidia rolled out of her cot on this drizzly Friday morning just in time to hear somebody shouting instructions in a panicky voice. "Get your clothes!" the man was saying. "Hurry! Hurry! They will be here any minute!"

Lidia ran down the corridor and out into the courtyard, where she asked Dario Mazzanti what was going on. "The Germans are headed up here," he said. "They have been killing down below."

"Killing what?"

"Everything."

Lidia ran back to the house and awakened the family, and it seemed as if less than five minutes had gone by before everyone at Cerpiano was dressed, and the men were hurrying into the woods, and the others were hiding themselves all about the refuge like Easter eggs: some in the big *palazzo,* some in the *contadino*'s house alongside, some in the nearby cave that doubled as air-raid shelter, and a few in the little chapel that was connected to the *palazzo* by a common wall. Lidia found herself in the damp and unlighted basement of the *palazzo,* where twenty or thirty people jammed together, sobbing and praying and leaning on one another. In the confusion Lidia had lost contact with the other members of her family, and she became panicky. Whatever was going to happen to her, she was not going to let it happen in this clammy, spooky basement. She pushed and shoved her way to the staircase, almost knocking several people down in her anxiety, and ran into the open. There was hardly anyone around, but the German troops were plainly visible less than 500 yards away and climbing fast. The rain had stopped, and the fog had thinned, and Lidia could pick out eight or ten familiar farmhouses that were spewing black smoke and red sparks into the morning air. Quickly she turned and ran across the fields that led to the stream and the bottom of the gulch and up the path to Casaglia. As she was picking her way across the brook, she was overtaken by her fifteen-year-old cousin, Giorgio Pirini, and the two of them ran together to the church. They tiptoed up the aisle to get as close as possible to the priest. He was saying the rosary in Latin, and Lidia was comforted by the familiar words.

The Ruggeris were up and around at five A.M., as was their custom, but before they could even sit down to breakfast, there were loud knocks on the door and warnings from their neighbors that the Germans were burning in the valley. "What will we do?" Elena asked her stern uncle.

"What will we do?" Giulio said, his handlebar mustache shaking with annoyance. "Why, our chores, of course!"

It was Giulio's turn to work in the barn and Attilio's turn to work on the wine, and the two brothers went about their duties as though nothing were happening, while the women and children stayed in the house, trembling with each new sound. At eight o'clock someone knocked on the door and said that the old men and women and children were taking refuge in the church at Casaglia, and all the able-bodied men were hiding in the woods, and the Ruggeris had better move if they did not want to be trapped in the house by the Germans. "All right, all right," Attilio said, and assembled the family on the porch. "I will lead you to the church."

"I will finish the cows," Giulio said.

Elena walked by her father's side as they headed toward Casaglia. "Elena," he said, "I wonder if it is wise to go to the church. Somehow I think you all would be better off in the woods."

"No, *Babbo,*" Elena said. "There is no place on earth safer than the church."

"Elena, listen to me for once," Attilio said. "Come with me into the woods. Stay away from the church. I have a feeling."

"But the church is where we belong, *Babbo,*" Elena said.

At a fork in the road, the father kissed each member of his family good-bye and disappeared into the brush, and the rest of the Ruggeris went on to the church at Casaglia and took their customary places in the two front pews on the right. Don Ubaldo was on his knees facing the altar, saying the rosary in Latin, when several bursts of machine-gun fire rattled the church windows. At once the congregation began to moan and cry out, and Don Ubaldo quickly turned and said, "Stay calm." Elena could see that Don Ubaldo was not calm himself. "Have courage," he said, "the saints will protect you." But the priest's hands were trembling, and he nervously pushed at his black-rimmed glasses. "We are all safe here. This is the house of God."

Noises began to come from outside, and Elena was aware of shouts in a strange tongue. The priest raised his voice, and the people began to weep and moan, and a dozen or so slipped quickly to the back door that led to the woods and the meadow and the nearby orchard. Elena found herself in the middle of this pack at the door, along with her fifty-seven-year-old aunt, Maria Menarini, and her thirteen-year-old cousin, Giorgio Menarini, and when someone flung the door open, they ran. Elena heard shots at close range as they raced across the slippery grass clearing to the orchard, but once they were inside the shelter of the trees, the shots stopped. At the end of the orchard, they had to negotiate a wheat field in order to reach the greater safety of the woods, and when they were in the open field, the shooting resumed. Elena saw that soldiers were firing on them from the road, 200 yards up the hill. Gasping for breath, the three dodged and twisted their way across the field and finally sprawled safely into cover. "Who else got away?" Elena asked her Aunt Maria when she recovered her wind.

"I can see nobody else," Maria Menarini said. "We are the lucky ones."

The family Paselli sat in the middle of the church on the left, and out of the corner of her eye Cornelia Paselli, the eighteen-year-old seamstress and lamb fancier, could see all the way into the bell tower vestry, where paralyzed old Vittoria Nanni sat in a wooden chair. The bell tower entrance was the traditional gathering place for the men, who would usually stand throughout the service, while the women and children occupied the pews. But this morning there were hardly any males in the church, except for a few elderly ones, and Vittoria's relatives had left her in the bell tower vestry in their haste to take to the woods. The paralyzed woman scraped and bumped her chair to the edge of the vestry, and Cornelia could see her straining to hear the comforting words of Don Ubaldo.

When loud voices came from the piazza, several people jumped up and ran out the back door of the church. Cornelia stayed with her family, but now there was loud gunfire from outside, and the priest interrupted himself to look around. Just as he had resumed the service, there was a loud hammering on the door, and two German soldiers burst in. *"Halt! Halt!"* they said, and Don Ubaldo turned and walked slowly down the aisle toward them, still reciting in Latin. *"Heraus!"* one of the soldiers said, and began directing everyone toward the piazza, where six or seven soldiers stood with machine pistols and another wore a portable tank on his back with a hose and nozzle leading from it. Cornelia stationed herself as close as she could to Don Ubaldo, so that she would hear the conversation with the Germans. It entered her mind that she and her family should take advantage of the momentary confusion to slip into the brush that adjoined the piazza, but she was overtaken with curiosity about what was happening, and anyway no harm would come to them so long as they stayed together and listened to the priest. Don Ubaldo was having a spirited talk with one of the Germans, and although it was a compound of German and Italian and gestures, Cornelia thought she understood. The soldier was ordering the priest to conduct his flock to Ca' Dizzola, a farmhouse not far away, where he said the SS had set up a temporary headquarters. The priest argued that there was no reason to take these women and children and old men to any German headquarters, and the soldier said that orders were orders, and the priest said that he was not going to be a party to such a ridiculous action, and the German drew his pistol, cocked it and said he would shoot the priest on the spot.

Led by Don Ubaldo, nearly 100 people from infants to the crippled and the old made their way slowly and hesitantly until they reached a fork 300 yards down the road. The left path led to Ca' Dizzola and Cerpiano, the right path to the little walled cemetery of Casaglia. Cornelia thought once again how simple it would be to take two steps to the left and vanish into the brush, but she also realized that if her whole family tried to slip away, one or two of them might be shot. She knew that the Germans were not at all reluctant to fire at escapees, as proved by the fusillade of shots when the people had run out the back door of the church. She wondered if any of her friends had been hit. She thought not. Most likely the Germans had fired in the air to frighten them. Still, Cornelia felt it better for the family to remain with the priest than to face the risk of being shot by some trigger-happy soldier.

As the group reached the fork in the road, a new squad of Nazis came double-timing from the direction of Cerpiano and Ca' Dizzola and ordered the procession to halt. There were seven or eight of them, and Cornelia could see that they were dressed in the same forbidding style as the others. Each one carried a machine pistol and a belt of grenades, and on their uniforms they wore the double lightning bolts and death's heads of the SS. Some of them were dressed in long camouflage raincoats, and all the helmets were festooned with leaves and twigs. To Cornelia, they looked like a delegation from another planet, and for the first time it occurred to her that she should be frightened. She looked at her mother and sister and the ten-year-old twins, and told them not to worry. Little Gigi's face was green, and his twin was trembling in the cold morning air and the terror. Cornelia's fifteen-year-old sister, Giuseppina, looked at the ground, but the mother, Angelina, was staring hard at the Germans almost as though daring them to start something. In spite of the situation, Cornelia had to smile. Now a loud conversation began in Italian. "Where are you taking these people?" a German officer asked Don Ubaldo.

"To Ca' Dizzola," the priest answered.

"Why?"

"I was ordered to take them there."

The German sputtered and fumed and looked as though he might strike the *reverendo*. "That is absolutely impossible!" he said. "No one could have given you such an order!"

"The one who told me is back at the church."

"We will go see!"

The officer directed one of his men to set up a machine gun to guard the parishioners, and while Cornelia stood wondering what was going on, the Germans walked back toward the church, shoving Don Ubaldo ahead of them with the barrels of their guns. Now Cornelia thought more seriously about escape, but under the sights of the machine gun there was no chance. For twenty minutes the group remained at the fork in the road, and then a few German soldiers returned from the direction of the church and said to Cornelia at the front of the line: *"Heraus!"* They pointed toward the cemetery.

Cornelia played dumb. *"Cosa?"* she said.

One of the Germans gave her a shove. *"Raus!"* he said. *"Avanti!"*

At last, feeling the numbness of fright, the eighteen-year-old girl led the procession toward the iron gates of the cemetery, where another soldier was busy shattering the lock with the butt of his gun. The Germans now appeared to be in a hurry, and they pushed and kicked at the people as they went through the narrow opening. One old lady had opened her umbrella against the rain, and she was having trouble keeping up with the throng. When she reached the gate, a German soldier held out his arm and escorted her gallantly inside. Then he returned to his duties at the gate, hurrying the others with his boot.

When everyone was inside, one of the Germans signaled them to line up in rows against the wall of the tiny burial chapel, with small children in front. The crowd twisted and surged like a single living being, and in her position at the rear of the group against the wall, Cornelia thought she was going to be mashed to death. A few were crying, and some were screaming at the others to take it easy, but the people on the outer edges would not stop pressing to get into the middle, and everyone was being squeezed. When the German soldier saw that he could not form the group with military precision, he shrugged and began setting up a machine gun just to the left of the entrance and about ten yards in front of the nearest person. Cornelia heard someone shout, "Children, say your act of contrition!" Just then an old lady burst out of the pack and threw herself on one of the Germans.

"I have to see my daughter!" she cried. "I cannot stay here, I must see my daughter!"

Cornelia recognized the woman as a refugee from Bologna, a well-to-do lady of about fifty, tall and regal, with a silk handkerchief tied around her neck. Cornelia heard her own mother, Angelina, call out, "Why do you try to get away? We are all finished. It is over now."

The woman from Bologna continued to pull at the German, and the soldier who had helped the old lady at the gate grabbed her by the hair and flung her to the ground. The woman hit with a thud and lay motionless, and the soldier straddled her and fired a bullet into her chest. "You see?" Angelina Paselli cried angrily. "It is useless to try to get away. See what happens? You will just be the first to get shot!"

Now a hush came over the people, and from that second everything seemed to Cornelia to take place in slow motion. It was almost totally quiet in the little walled cemetery, except for the muffled sobbing of children whose mothers were trying to cover their mouths to silence them. The gunner inserted a belt of ammunition into the machine gun. He knelt and cranked something, and Cornelia could hear a clicking sound, like an oversize watch being wound. She wondered what the gunner was going to do with the belt of bullets that hung from his neck, and why the other Germans had slipped outside the gate, and why Don Ubaldo had not returned. When the loud roar and the flashes of light began to spit from the mouth of the gun, Cornelia went right on musing. "What a strong odor that gun makes!" she said to herself, and when the bullets slammed into the wall of the chapel and showered her with plaster dust, she said, "What a heavy gun this must be! What a powerful weapon to break the plaster right off the wall!" Then the people around her seemed to surge into violent motion, and she felt her feet being lifted from the ground and it was as though she were in a packed city bus that had suddenly flipped on its side. The air was full of cries and screams, and Cornelia felt her legs and her feet rise in the air and her head bump down on the ground. There was a thump-thump as bodies began to fall on her, and she felt a splash of heat on her right side. She pushed her hand through the layers of flesh that surged over her and touched her hip and drew back a handful of blood. Cornelia felt no pain, and she realized that she was being warmed by the blood of others.

The Germans wasted no time in flushing everyone out of the hiding places at Cerpiano. Sister Benni was in the cellar of the *palazzo* with the others when she heard the heavy boots stomping through the halls above them. A murmur of fear went through the people, but Sister Benni said, "Calm yourselves, we have done nothing wrong."

"But what if they burn the house?" someone asked.

"There are two exits down here," Sister Benni said. "If we cannot use one, we can use the other."

The Germans sounded like the hounds of hell upstairs, and some of the people in the basement began to pray. When one of the older women raised her voice in supplication, an old man called across the room in a stage whisper, "Who are you praying to, *Signora,* God or the Germans?"

"I am asking the Virgin to save us," the woman answered.

"Well, ask her more quietly," the man said.

The basement was pierced with a broad shaft of light from above, and the shadow of a soldier fell over the people at the bottom of the steps. *"Raus!"* a loud voice called. When nobody moved, the German banged his gun against the side of the door and repeated, *"Raus!"*

Behind him another voice said in Italian, "Everybody up! Everybody up!"

Someone shouted, "Are you going to kill us?"

"Niente kaput!" a German said. "Nobody killed!"

But as soon as the last person had walked up the stairs and assembled out front in the wet, the Nazi attitude changed from conciliation to righteous anger. "Yes, you will be killed," one of them said. "You are all partisans!" As though to underline the threat, a long burst of machine-gun fire came from across the gulch at Casaglia, 500 yards away. The firing stopped and started several times, and then there were explosions.

At a break in the noises, the teacher of the school at Cerpiano, Maestra Anita Serra, pointed to the children and babies shivering in the cool morning air. "Those are partisans?" she said.

The soldiers ignored her.

Maestra Serra, a forceful woman of thirty-one years, walked up to the nearest soldier and shook a finger in his face. "What is the matter with you?" she said. "Are you blind? Can you not see that we are all women and children here? No, I lie. There are a few old grandfathers, and a man with braces on his legs. Look at them!" She swept her hand toward the trembling captives. "Look at your dangerous partisan band!"

The German shoved her away, and another said, "In five minutes all will be killed!"

The soldiers led the group, twenty-four refugee women, three teachers, nineteen children and three men, into the tiny Chapel of the Guardian Angel that had served the old owners of the *podere* as a private oratory before the Sisters of Saint Angela had taken over the place. The chapel was large enough to accommodate an altar and a large family, but now there were forty-nine people crammed inside and they pressed against one another trying to make room. A sort of mass hysteria seized the group, fed by the Germans who were shouting, *"Tutti kaput! Tutti kaput!"* as though they were playing a game at a party.

Sister Benni called out from the center of the pack, "Do not worry, everybody. There is no danger."

"You cannot hear what they are saying?" somebody called.

"Yes, I hear," Sister Benni said, "but what can they do? They will search the *contadino*'s house and the *palazzo* and the barns and they will find nothing, no guns, no ammunition, no explosives, and then they will have to let us go."

One of the German officers stuck his head in the door and said in Italian, "All right, you partisans, prepare to die!" He stepped back, cackling with laughter, and a groan went through the chapel.

"Say your act of contrition!" one of the teachers called out, but it was only the children who obeyed her. The others watched as the Germans pulled a heavy machine gun just outside the door. A soldier climbed into position behind the gun, and the people nearest him shoved backward into the mass to get out of the line of fire, but the German made no effort to shoot. Instead, he stood guard over the entrance, while around him several of the other soldiers squatted on the road and began opening wooden crates. Each crate seemed to contain a dozen or so metal cylinders wrapped in paper, and the Germans stacked them in neat piles around the machine gun. A soldier wearing corporal's stripes held one up at the entrance and shouted gleefully, "Bombs!"

Sister Benni heard a man call out, "Wait! Stop! You cannot do this!" It was a well-to-do man of about forty named Federico Fabbris, and he had squeezed his way to the door to hold out something that looked like a card. A German examined the card and said, "If you are a member of the Fascist Party, what are you doing in this partisan zone?" Before Fabbris could answer, the German shoved him back into the crowd. "Shut up!" the soldier said. "If you were a good Fascist, you would not be here!"

Fabbris fell back, but he kept on shouting. "Listen!" he said. "We are not poor. We have plenty to give you. You can have everything we own!" The German turned away. Now the pyramids of grenades were getting higher, and the people sitting nearest the door passed hushed progress reports over their shoulders to the others. "They are still unwrapping." "The machine gunner is lighting a cigarette." "They opened another crate." Many of the reports came from Pietro Oleandri, the seventy-four-year-old *contadino* of Cerpiano, who sat nearest the door holding the hand of his great-grandson, seven-year-old Sirio Oleandri. Pietro passed the reports calmly enough until he saw several of his cows running loose on the road, and then he said excitedly, "Holy Mother, the cows are out!" A few minutes later, he said, "My cows are in the *erba medica!*" The *erba medica* was a small fenced area of the pasture where Pietro had planted certain therapeutic herbs that were cut and dried and measured out to the animals during the winter. "They must not eat all the *erba medica!*" Oleandri said, scrambling to his feet. "It will make them sick." Before anyone could stop him, the old *contadino* was halfway out the door with Sirio by his side. There was a volley of shots, and man and boy fell in the doorway, still holding each other by the hand.

"They killed them!" someone whispered near the door, and the message passed through the room from ear to ear: "They killed them." "They are dead." "They lie dead at the door." "They killed them." Sister Benni crossed herself when the message reached her. "If they do not even spare the *contadino,* there is no hope," she said to herself, and began her act of contrition.

Now there were loud voices in German outside and the crack of a single shot, and another message passed from ear to ear to Sister Benni. "A German soldier threw down his rifle and ran," she was told, "and the others shot him. His body is lying next to the *contadino.*" The Germans began engaging in heated discussions among themselves, and wine bottles were passed about, and in all the confusion a forty-eight-year-old woman named Amelia Tossani slowly opened the side door of the chapel. A burst of gunfire ripped across her chest, and she fell dead, blocking the door. Just outside, the captives could see a young SS man coolly blowing smoke from the tip of his machine pistol, and a new hysteria gripped the room. Children began to cry and hide their faces in their mothers' breasts, and women started screaming, and the murmur of acts of contrition filled the room.

As though to end the alarm, the Germans shut the main door where the bombs were stacked, and Sister Benni said to herself, "Now it comes!" A tinkle of breaking glass came from the single window in the front wall, and seconds later there was an explosion. Sister Benni heard a high-pitched scream above the frightened roar of human voices, and she saw smoke and smelled something sharp and pungent. She was rising to her feet to see what was happening when she felt a ping in her arm. Her knees gave out, and she slipped to the floor, rolled on her back, and lost consciousness.

Antonio Tonelli, the watchman whose family shared the *casa colonica* at Possatore with the family of the impoverished young farmer and hog butcher Adelmo Benini, had gone early to the church at Casaglia. His neighbor Adelmo, the one who foolishly entertained partisans, had got up at five A.M. to slaughter a pig for one of the bands that were always hanging around the other half of the *podere* and immediately had given the alarm that there were fires in the valley below. The partisans had vanished up the mountain, and all the civilians had gone to the church at Casaglia: Antonio Tonelli, his wife, his uncle, his brother and his nine children. With them went eleven members of the family Sabbioni, refugees from Murazze who had taken shelter at Possatore, and Adelmo Benini and his wife and two small daughters. At the church they had found Don Ubaldo standing at the front entrance, ordering the men to disappear into the woods, and when they had put up an argument, Don Ubaldo had told them angrily, "Look, get out of here! If you stay, you are only going to make trouble for your families."

Now Antonio and his old uncle and his brother, Mario, were hiding in the weeds on Monte Sole directly above the church at Casaglia, and nibbling at a bag of bread the uncle had carried with him. They had been hearing distant gunfire, mostly from the direction of the town of Pian di Venola, where a strong partisan force had been hiding, and they had seen a few German patrols move toward the church, but so far as they could tell, no shots had been fired nearby. Then all at once there was a loud burst of small-arms fire squarely from the direction of the church, and Antonio felt an instant panic. Ignoring the shouts of the other two, he sprang from his hiding place and ran down the mountain toward the ridge road, tripping and lurching until he reached the ditch alongside, 100 yards or so from the church. He heard running footsteps coming around the bend, and he stretched out in water up to his neck, and to his surprise found that there were eight or nine other men in the ditch with him. He did not know exactly how long he stayed in the water, but it was no more than thirty minutes. The German patrol ran by, and then another, and there was frequent firing from the church and sometimes a loud shout in a foreign tongue. When he could stand it no longer, Antonio pulled himself out of the ditch and began to run down the road toward the church. "Where are you going?" one of the others called.

"I must see what happened to mine," he said.

"You are only going to get killed," the voice called after him.

As he trotted along, Antonio almost tripped over the body of a *contadino* he knew, and he saw the bodies of two other men, one of whom he thought he recognized as a partisan doctor. He sidestepped the bodies and kept on toward the church. As he came into sight of the old stone building, he saw no signs of life, but on closer inspection he noticed a rivulet of blood dripping down the steps of the bell tower entryway onto the cobblestones. Antonio gingerly stepped inside, and he saw the bodies of two more of his friends, sprawled next to an old woman he recognized as Vittoria Nanni, a cripple whose sons always carried her to church in a wooden chair.

Antonio could not see the altar from the bell tower entrance, and he did not want to step into the puddle of blood that lay in the vestry, so he backed out of the entrance and walked around toward the piazza and the main entrance. He found one of his wife's shoes flanking the oaken door, and he shoved his way inside with a feeling of dread. The church was smoky, but Antonio walked straight down the aisle until he came to a sprawled and burning body with its hands stretched out toward the altar. Antonio fell to his hands and knees to get below the heat, and he could see that there was plainly nothing to be done. Every inch of the body was burning with a bright blue color, like the flame from a gas oven. Antonio crawled around to the side for a better view and looked into the smoking eyes of Don Ubaldo.

Antonio could feel his heart bumping in his chest as he backed away and looked at his own flickering shadow on the walls of the burning church, and he ran as fast as he could out the bell tower door, slipping and sliding on the blood, and into a ditch across the road. He was holding his head in his hands and gasping for air and wondering what was happening when he heard machine-gun fire from the direction of the cemetery. He rushed toward the sounds, and when he was about 100 yards from the cemetery, he ducked into the brush and ran up the hill to a place where he could see down through the rain to the inside of the walls. He saw that the Germans were circling the cemetery in a group of about six, beating the bushes and shouting as though looking for someone. When they passed out of sight behind the far wall, Antonio rose to his feet and ran as fast as he could to get closer, and when the first helmets bobbed back into sight from the other corner of the wall, he grabbed a tree and threw himself behind it. It was an acacia tree, and one of the spikes tore into his palm, but

Antonio felt nothing. His line of sight now ran straight into the cemetery, and in front of the burial chapel he saw what looked like a big stack of wash. Then he watched a head pop up and heard an outcry, and he knew that he was looking at what was left of his family and all the others who had been in the church. Even as he watched, his teeth biting into the back of his hand to keep from screaming out, the Germans began lobbing grenades over the wall, and Antonio backed dazedly up the hill, unable to comprehend any further. Like a wounded animal, he wandered through the woods in the general direction of his home.

Cornelia Paselli found herself under a crisscross of bodies, and when the machine-gun firing stopped, she heard her mother calling, "Cornelia! Cornelia! Are you alive?"

"Yes, Mama," she whispered, "but do not talk. Be quiet."

"Are you wounded?"

"No, Mother. For charity, be still!" Cornelia whispered. "The Germans are there."

Then the grenades started, and Cornelia felt a sick hollowness in her stomach as she heard more screams and the splat of the metal shards tearing into flesh, living and dead. There were ten or twelve loud explosions, and then silence, and once again the first new sound Cornelia heard was her mother's voice. Now Angelina was making a roll call, asking each of her children to respond. Cornelia heard her say, "Giuseppina, are you alive?"

And the sister answered, "I am covered with blood. I am dying, Mama!"

"Be brave, Peppina!" Cornelia called. "You will not die."

"Silence!" the mother said. "Listen for the twins. See if they are alive."

Cornelia strained to hear under the bodies, and she thought she could make out the sound of the twins crying very softly. Soon the sound died away. *"Gigi è morto,"* her mother called. "Gigi is dead." A few minutes later, Angelina called, "Maria, Maria!" When there was no reply, she said, "You see, Cornelia? Maria is gone. She does not answer anymore. Now both the twins are dead."

Cornelia heard another voice calling her name. "Help me get loose, Cornelia!" someone was saying. She turned and saw her friend Lidia Pirini, the pretty fifteen-year-old from Murazze, the girl with the amber eyes, lying under a dead woman's legs and holding her hip with both hands.

"Stay still, Lidia," Cornelia said. "Wait till the Germans are gone, and then I will come help you."

"I do not know if I can stand it till then."

"You will have to, Lidia. I am sorry."

An old woman raised her head from the mound of dead, and Cornelia recognized her as the grandmother of the little boy Fernando Piretti, who had once lived in the big house above them at Casa Veneziana. "Help me, Cornelia," the old lady said. "I hurt. My fingers have been cut off."

Before Cornelia could answer, she heard her own mother, Angelina, say, "How can she come help you, *Nonna?* If she moves, the Germans will kill her, too."

Giuseppina began to cry loudly, and Cornelia slowly extricated herself from the pressure of bodies and tried to crawl to her sister's side. Giuseppina's head was covered with blood; it had matted around her eyes and dripped over her face. Cornelia said, "Oh, Peppina," tried to stand up, and fainted.

When the shooting started in the cemetery, Elide Ruggeri tried to pretend that nothing was happening. She absolutely refused to let herself believe that she was going to be killed, and she would not give the Germans the satisfaction of getting a single bleat out of her. All around her people were falling and screaming, and Elide said to herself that they were fools. Her position was to the right of the gunner, between the end of the chapel wall and the upraised new grave of a priest of Quercia, and as the long left-to-right traverse of machine-gun fire reached her end, Elide felt a chill in her right hip, as though a piece of ice had been rubbed against it, and she sank to a sitting position even as she slipped her hand down her dress and felt a wet hole in her hip. As she fell, bodies collapsed on top of her, until she was lying in a sort of shelter made of human flesh. She heard muffled explosions, but in this cave of corpses they seemed to represent no danger, and she thought she might even be hearing things. Blood dripped down, and her leg was pressed under a heavy body, but she lay motionless and quiet till all the noise had stopped. She had just begun to drag herself into the clear when she glanced toward the front gate of the cemetery and saw a German approaching with drawn pistol.

As he slowly walked across the ten yards of *camposanto,* Elide sprawled out and tried to play dead, but she bumped a four-year-old girl, who sat up and began screaming and wiping at her eyes. The German marched over to the child and shot her in the head. Then he stood over Elide and said in halting Italian, "Come now, you are not dead." He crouched down and stared at her intently. "It is remarkable!" he said. "You look exactly like my fiancée back in Germany." Elide opened her eyes and saw a blond man of about thirty, wearing a poncho, helmet, full field pack and the insignia of an SS officer. "Never mind," he said. He grabbed her under the arms and slid her out of the pile of bodies. He lifted her gently and carried her to the wall, where she would be slightly sheltered from the rain, and laid her down on a blanket he took from his pack. "Wait here till we come back," the German said, putting his face close to hers. "Do not worry. You are not dead." Then he returned to the bodies, fired a few more *coups de grâce,* and disappeared out the front gate with a gallant smile and a wave of the hand.

Lucia Sabbioni was fifteen years old and beautiful, with chocolate eyes and glossy black hair and an aristocratic nose as straight as a ruler, and now she was lying under a pile of bodies, her mind in a jumble. There was a hole the size of an apple in her hip, where a slug had torn the flesh away, and scattered about her body were ten or twelve shrapnel wounds, but even through all the pain and confusion, one thought pursued her compulsively. They had all gone to the church at Casaglia that morning after the *contadino* Adelmo Benini had spotted the fires in the valley, and when they were inside, Lucia and her five-year-old sister had been able to think of nothing but getting out. They had been jammed in the sacristy with another fifteen or twenty young people, and as they looked out the back windows that commanded a view of the meadows and fields, they had seen fifty or sixty German soldiers slowly forming a massive semicircle below the church. Through the morning haze the soldiers looked like supernatural beings: their helmets came down to their eyes, and in the distance some of them appeared almost headless. Around their bodies hung grenades and guns and hand bombs, and one of them was covered from head to foot with some kind of thick coveralls and a mask, and on his back was strapped a small tank. Lucia and Irene began to cry at this strange sight, and they bolted out the main entrance of the church and started running up the road. But they had hardly gone ten yards before the voice of their father, Renato, a stonemason from Gardeletta, came out of the weeds. "Get back inside!" he said sharply. Renato and the girls' brother, Giuliano, eighteen, had been hiding in the bushes along the road with other men, and the two sisters shamefacedly returned to the church. Not two minutes later the first Germans banged on the door, and it was too late to get away.

As she lay in the pile of bodies, aching all over and waiting for death, Lucia could not stop thinking about the coincidence that had positioned her father exactly on the path she and her sister had taken. If only he had gone the other way, or up the mountain, or down the meadow. If only the two girls had used another route, or if the whole family had gone to another refuge, or if they had not left their home in Gardeletta in the first place. She could trace the chain of coincidence in any number of directions. They would still be safe at home if it had not been for one stupid American pilot who had not been able to tell a simple country bridge from a military target. The Sabbionis lived alongside a small stone bridge that had absolutely no strategic value; it was used solely by the *contadini* and their farm animals to get across the *torrente* Setta. One day an American attack bomber planted its load squarely on the bridge and shattered windows in the Sabbioni house. When Renato came home that night, he looked at the damage and announced that the whole family, from the seventy-year-old grandfather, Desiderio, to the two-year-old daughter, Bruna, was going up the mountain to a safer place. He made a deal with the *contadini* Antonio Tonelli and Adelmo Benini for cheap room and board at Possatore, and the next day the family made the climb. Altogether, they had been at Possatore for two months.

Lucia looked around her at the corpses. Somewhere in this stack were four of her sisters, her brother and her mother. There were occasional stirrings as the wounded began to free themselves, but no one who moved was of her family. Lucia tried to slide a body off her legs, and discovered that it was her mother. Nazzarena Opali Sabbioni, thirty-six years old, had been in the very front of the group when the firing began, and now Lucia could see that her skull had broken open. Alongside her sprawled the five-year-old Irene, her face smashed in and her arms cut off by the sawing effect of the bullets. Directly on top of Lucia lay a heavy woman whose body had acted as a shield. Lucia tilted the body's head and discovered that she owed her life to Cleofe Betti, the middle-aged wife of a shoemaker from the valley below.

Gradually the survivors of the cemetery massacre began to make themselves known, and Lucia could hear voices as people cried for their loved ones. She called softly to the other children of her own family: "Adriana! Bruna! Giovanna? Otello?" But somehow she knew in advance that there would be no answers. She lifted the dead that lay on top of her and tried to stand, but the pain in her hip forced her back to the ground. She made several more attempts to get up and hop away, but the leg on the wounded side would not support her. She was sitting in the rain moaning softly to herself when some of the survivors appeared in front of her. Lucia recognized Imelde Vegetti and her fourteen-year-old daughter, Bianca, another married woman named Clelia Monti, the eleven-year-old Maria Buganè, and two young women of Vado. Then another blood-covered figure worked its way out of the bottom of the pile and joined them, and Lucia recognized Vittorio Tonelli, the eight-year-old son of their co-host at Possatore.

"We are going to leave as soon as it is safe," one of the Vado women told Lucia.

"Oh, take me with you!" she begged.

"How can we take you with us when you cannot even stand up? We will all be killed."

The group of the living huddled together and tried to make plans, but no one wanted to move until they were certain the Germans were gone. "I will go see," the Tonelli boy said. He walked to the gate and peeked out. Then he disappeared around the wall just as several rifleshots came from 500 yards across the ravine in the direction of Cerpiano. Minutes later he returned. "They are gone," he said.

The group trudged toward the entrance. Lucia called out, "Take me with you! Oh, please take me!"

The young woman from Vado, whom the others had been calling Vittoria, walked back to Lucia, hefted her into a piggyback position, and carried her out like a baby. Tears of gratefulness mingled with tears of pain on Lucia's face as the blood-soaked band of survivors headed down the western slope of Monte Sole. They had gone less than 100 yards when they came to Casetta di Casaglia (the Little

House of Casaglia), where Augusto Massa farmed for the church, and as they walked past the far end of the barn, they saw a group of German soldiers. *"Halt!"* one of the Germans shouted, and the survivors stopped.

Vittoria, still carrying Lucia, began speaking quickly in a mixture of Italian and German. As best Lucia could understand, the woman was telling the Germans that she and the other woman from Vado had worked for German occupation forces in another city and that they had credentials to prove it, although the credentials were not with them at the moment. The German looked dubious, and Vittoria said, "All right then, do you want to hold us here while you check on us?"

The German talked with some of the others and finally came back and said that the women could go on. They continued down the path, but they had only taken a few steps when there was a series of clicks behind them. "Run!" Vittoria said, and the women jumped into the high weeds that separated the path from the deep woods. Lucia fell from Vittoria's back in the sudden movement, and she lay in the brush listening to the volleys of gunfire and waiting for the shot that would put an end to her misery. Suddenly she felt someone grip her by the ankle and pull her roughly into the woods. She thought she would faint from the pain, and she closed her eyes and bit her lip till it added to the blood that covered her. At last the agonizing trip came to an end, and she opened her eyes and saw that Vittoria had pulled her into a narrow clearing in the woods with the others. *"Zzzzzzt!"* Vittoria said, the local equivalent of *ssshhhh,* and the five females lay quietly listening for pursuit. They had remained thus for the better part of an hour when a noise came from the direction of the road. Someone was approaching, and the women held their breaths. When the noise was almost upon them, one of the women sprang up and said, "Hold your fire! We surrender!"

A man crawled into the clearing on all fours. "Oh, it is Toni!" Lucia said. "It is only Toni." Antonio Tonelli joined the women, and immediately a Greek chorus of sympathy went up.

"Poor Toni!" Clelia Monti said. "They killed all yours!"

"No, not all," Lucia said. "Little Vittorio is alive back in the cemetery."

"Alive?" Antonio said. He seemed to be groggy or half-asleep.

"Yes, your son lives, Toni," Lucia said, "but do not go for him now. There are Germans everywhere."

"Germans everywhere," Tonelli repeated vaguely, and wandered back into the woods.

Giuseppe Lorenzini, thirty-five, had been hiding on the mountain for several hours, ever since he had awakened in the house at Casoncello to the sounds of gunfire and the eerie flickerings of distant blazes, and he only wished he had picked out a hiding place with a better view. He had hardly had time to jump out a back window of his house and sprawl into a ditch before a patrol of SS men had come to the door and ordered everyone out, his wife and his two small sons and nine or ten other relatives. The Nazis set fire to the place, and then they marched Giuseppe's loved ones off toward the *podere* of San Giovanni.

Now he was up here in the brush, looking over acres of wheat fields, and San Giovanni was obscured from his sights by a nearby hillock. The Germans were all around, and he could not improve his position. As he lay in the weeds cursing the situation, Giuseppe heard a series of war whoops and shouts, and he looked down the mountain to see a patrol of SS men. He had heard the SS before, and they seemed to have some sort of private communication consisting of whoops and shouts, and Giuseppe had noticed that they even talked to one another in a kind of canine manner, barking and spitting their orders. Now he could see that they were entertaining themselves by chasing an old man down a path. As one soldier gave chase, another doubled up the mountain to cut the old man off, and to his horror Giuseppe realized that the German was heading toward his hiding place. He ducked his head and lay motionless, and soon he was looking through a single bush at the muddied boots of a German soldier. But by now the German concentration was fixed on the old man, and Giuseppe breathed again when the boots moved off. He rose to his hands and knees and saw that one of the Germans had sent the old man flying with a blow from a gun butt. As the old man lay moaning on the ground, the two soldiers took turns firing bullets into his head. Then they marched off toward San Giovanni.

Alfredo Comellini, thirty-nine, one of several owners of the big farm at San Giovanni, lay in the weeds in the rainy morning, listening to gunfire from all directions. He had the fleeting hope that somehow the raiders would bypass his *podere,* and just then he saw two SS men with machine pistols come out of the woods from behind the barn. As Alfredo held his own lips with his fingers to keep from crying out, the two Germans walked up to his blind cousin, Ildebrando Paselli, and sent him sprawling with a single burst of gunfire. Two other men, Edoardo Castagnari and Alfredo's uncle, Pietro Paselli, heard the shot and ran to release the animals before the Germans could ignite the barn, but they, too, fell quickly. Then more soldiers arrived and split into groups to round up the residents of the *podere*. A dozen or so were marched out of the three big houses with their hands in the air. Several dozen more were flushed from an air-raid shelter on the hillside, and another eight or ten were led to the site by soldiers. Alfredo recognized almost everyone, except for a few of the refugees. When the entire group was assembled—it looked to Alfredo like forty-five or fifty people—the Germans positioned them carefully in front of the manure pile, with children in front, and began to set up three heavy machine guns. When the shooting started, Alfredo looked away and held his ears. It seemed to him that the firing went on steadily for fifteen minutes. When the final echo had died away, and he dared to look again, he saw that the mass of bodies lay motionless on the manure. Alfredo caught a flash of black and white at the far edge, and he remembered that a nun, Sister Maria Fiori, had been hiding in the refuge along with nine members of her family. "The Lord works in wondrous ways," Alfredo Comellini said to himself. The witch of Gardeletta, Giulia Serra Testi, was dead in the mound with her three daughters.

Amelia Monari, thirty-eight, the wife of Alfredo Comellini, waited where her husband had left her, in the refuge at Villa Serena, a short distance up the mountain from the village of Quercia. With her were her two boys, Giovanni, seven, and Marko, three, and forty others who had come up from the Setta Valley to elude the raiding SS men. At about ten in the morning a patrol of Germans arrived and ordered everyone out of the refuge and into the courtyard of the big house. Amelia noticed that the Germans, most of whom seemed to be sixteen and seventeen years old, were accompanied by an acquaintance of her husband, Raffaele Sammarchi of Ca' Saligostro, who was carrying a rotating spool of heavy wire on his back and a field telephone on his chest and seemed to know all about the Germans. "These are not bad boys," Raffaele confided to Amelia and a few of the others as the group was being lined up in the courtyard. "They ordered me to carry this field telephone, but they were not cruel about it. They will not hurt you."

Amelia allowed herself the luxury of believing that Sammarchi spoke the truth, and indeed the Germans seemed gentle and considerate as they led the group of refugees into the stable of the villa, handed them a few wheels of cheese to share, and locked the door. After a while the door opened again and Amelia could see that one of the Germans was talking on the field telephone. The refugees were ordered to reassemble on the cobbled courtyard, and as Amelia was leaving the stable, she tripped and dropped her three-year-old. A young German soldier with the strong smell of alcohol on his breath helped her to her feet, picked up the baby, patted him on the back and handed him to his mother. "How can you be so good and so bad?" Amelia asked, and they both laughed pleasantly at her little joke.

In broken Italian, the Germans told the refugees to hand over the contents of their suitcases and turn their pockets inside out. When Alfredo had run off that morning to hide in the woods, he had left the family fortune with his wife, and now Amelia was forced to give the Germans 40,000 lire in cash and six postal orders for 6,000 lire each, or a total of several thousand dollars. When all the money and jewels and watches had been collected, one of the Germans cranked up the field telephone again, and after a short conversation, three heavy machine guns were mounted on the edge of the courtyard. Just then a new SS officer made his appearance on the path, and two young women with babies in their arms sprang from the pack and ran to his side. "Why, mothers, what are you doing here?" the officer asked, shaking the hands of the two women enthusiastically. "Just yesterday you were with us at Ca' di Marsili."

The young mothers explained that they had taken refuge in the shelter at Villa Serena when they had heard gunfire at Ca' di Marsili. "Well, that gunfire was not for you," the officer said. "That was for the partisans."

"Then why are your men setting up machine guns?" one of the women asked.

The officer engaged several of the young soldiers in short discussions, and then he picked up the field telephone. After an impassioned five-minute conversation, he waved the two young mothers abruptly away and said to the group, "We are leaving you here for now, and we are going off to engage the partisans. If we find a single bandit hidden around here, we will return and shoot you all." The machine guns were stripped, Sammarchi was helped into his heavy harness, and the patrol marched away from Villa Serena up the hill toward San Martino. As soon as the Germans were out of sight, everyone began looking for a hiding place. Later, Sammarchi's body was found face down in the mud twenty yards from the church of Quercia. He had been shot in the back.

Twelve-year-old Gilberto Fabbri, the baby of his family, had started the morning with the refugees of Villa Serena, but when he heard gunfire in the distance and saw that some of the surrounding *poderi* were being set afire, he decided that he wanted to be with his big brothers, three of whom were partisans of the *Stella Rossa.* His brothers had guns, and they would protect him from anything, including a division of Germans. Gilberto ran out of the shelter and began asking everyone he could find if they knew where the partisans were hiding. Miraculously, he managed to avoid the Germans, running into brush whenever he saw them near, and by the middle of the morning he had climbed up to a partisan group near Caprara, the little village where Luigi Massa ran his mountainside *tabacchi.* A voice cried out, "Gilberto!" and the young boy ran to the side of his brother, Leo. "Gilberto!" his brother said, "you must get away from here!"

"Where are you going?" Gilberto asked.

"To Zone X, our escape zone," Leo said. "To the top of Monte Sole."

"Take me!"

"No!" Leo pointed down the slope to a narrow black slit in the side of the mountain. "That is the air-raid shelter for Caprara," he said. "Go there and wait till I come for you."

The shelter was crammed with fifty or sixty people, most of them from around Caprara, and Gilberto felt alone among the strange faces. His home was in the valley town of Vado, and he would not have been on Monte Sole at all except that the Allies had been bombing the railroad bridge at Vado, and a week earlier his family had decided to take shelter at Villa Serena. Now they were caught in the middle of a *rastrellamento,* and his relatives were scattered over the danger area. The three big brothers were fleeing with the partisans. His sister, Maria, was at Ca' Beguzzi with her husband, Dante, and Gilberto feared for both their lives; he had heard from several people that Ca' Beguzzi had been one of the first places destroyed. He was not sure where his mother and father were, and various other cousins and in-laws were in different refuges around the mountain. Gilberto wished he were back in Vado, air raids and all. At least he would not have to sit in a clammy, chilly hole in the ground listening to strange babies cry and mothers wail and old men say their beads.

Gilberto sat in the shelter for four hours, or until about two in the afternoon, and then he decided that anything would be preferable to staying here another second. He got up, but something made him sit down again. Leo had ordered him to stay. Leo would be coming back for him, and if he was not here, Leo would be worried. But would Leo want him to spend the rest of his life in this dingy hole? Leo was an understanding brother; maybe Gilberto could leave and run to the top of Monte Sole, and once he was there, Leo would protect him. Gilberto was considering all these possibilities when the first Nazis appeared in the entrance way. *"Raus!"* they shouted. *"Raus!"* Gilberto followed the others out of the shelter. When he got a good look at the Germans, his heart began to pound. They were dressed in camouflage suits covered with brown and green and black markings that made them look like giant upright caterpillars. They wore helmets covered with netting, with branches and leaves stuck into them, sometimes obscuring their faces. Each of them bore a machine pistol or a rifle and a thick belt from which a dozen or so grenades and bombs dangled. With each step, the Germans made a metallic noise, and it flashed through Gilberto's mind that he had one advantage on these mechanical men: he could outrun them. But could he outrun their bullets?

The Germans lined them up in the big courtyard at Caprara, and the women began crying and hiccuping, and a few threw themselves on the ground to ask for mercy. Another twelve or fifteen Germans came up the hill and joined the group, and by the time they finished a long palaver with their comrades, the group had remained standing on the courtyard for the better part of an hour. Then the Germans became loudly decisive. *"Avanti!"* they shouted, and began shoving the people toward the doorway of one of the row houses.

Gilberto and the others were following a German officer into the house when a woman threw herself on one of the soldiers and began pleading for mercy. "Look!" she said. "See my three little sons! You would not hurt them?"

"Nienti bimbi kaput, niente donne kaput," the German said. "No children killed, no women killed."

"Then why do you put us in this house?" another asked.

"Niente kaput!" the officer said in a high-pitched shout, and began kicking them through the portal. At the back of the house was a small kitchen, and when all had been stuffed inside, the women began screaming and the children hugged their mothers' skirts and cried in terror. Gilberto watched as a German soldier opened the window looking out on the vineyard, and when he saw this, Gilberto began slipping between the pressed bodies to get as far from the window as possible. Around him people were whispering and sobbing, and a few were holding debates. "They are going to kill us." "No, they will not kill us!" "Yes, they will!" Gilberto had almost reached a big wooden closet in the rear of the kitchen when something flew through the window and landed near him. He saw that it was about as long as a wine bottle, with an enlarged gray bulb at one end, and instinctively he turned sideways to the object. There was an explosion, and Gilberto felt shards of hot metal tear into his body from the ankle to the head. He fell among the other wounded and saw more of the same objects landing in the room, and as explosions went off all around him, he noticed a different type of bomb rolling on the floor, a larger one, almost round, painted red.

The Germans were shooting at anyone who appeared at the window, and soon a stack of bodies had formed sill-high. As Gilberto watched, three or four people jumped out, and he could hear a volley of shots with each departure. He thought that he might as well die in the open, and he ran up the incline of bodies and jumped six feet through the air to the ground. Just in front of him the Germans were wrestling with a woman, and a baby lay alongside, screaming. Gilberto heard shots, but he kept running across the yard until he reached the edge of the vines. Two others were running with him, and as Gilberto jumped into the leaves, he heard the Germans clank by in pursuit of the others.

Gilberto burrowed his bleeding body deeper into the vines, and he saw that a young girl was doing the same a few feet away. As he lay concealed by the leaves, he saw the Germans rope the young mother to a tree, place the baby in her arms, and lob grenades at them till both were only bits of shattered flesh. An elderly woman in a black dress ran across the fields that widened toward the brush a few hundred yards away, and she gasped for breath and stumbled as she ran. A Nazi followed a few yards behind, laughing and waving his pistol at the old lady, as though to encourage her flight. As Gilberto watched, the woman moved slower and slower, and finally fell to the mud of the field, her hand grasping her throat. The German grabbed her by her white hair with his free hand, turned her head slowly toward him, and shot her twice in the face.

Gilberto looked back toward the house and saw the figures of two children appear in the window of the kitchen, but they went down in a fusillade of shots. Now there were six or eight bodies lying stacked outside the window, to match the bodies that lay stacked by the window in the inside, and after about fifteen minutes there was no more movement from the kitchen. The Germans remained outside, their guns pointed at the window, for a short time, and a detail went inside the house with machine pistols drawn.

Gilberto heard shots, and then the Germans regrouped and marched off, babbling excitedly and crowding around their officers like a victorious soccer squad. Gilberto looked for the young girl who had hidden in the vines with him, but she was gone. His whole right side felt afire; he touched the wounds lightly with his fingers and found that there were at least twenty depressions gouged out of his legs and side by the shrapnel. His right eye was gone. When the Germans were out of sight, he pulled himself slowly out of the hedge and limped away in search of his brothers.

Sister Benni opened her eyes and wondered what she was doing under an immovable pile of human beings. From all around her came a chorus of moans, screams and hysterical outcries, and for a moment she thought she had died and gone to hell. The air was filled with the smell of gunpowder and excrement, and she saw that she was lying next to an altar that was mottled with bits of human gore and blood. To herself, she said aloud, "Are you alive, or are you dead?" Just then she heard a childish voice cry out, "Is Sister Benni alive? Where is Sister Benni?"

She recognized the voice of one of her little pupils of the *asilo,* and all at once Sister Benni remembered what had happened, although she could not figure out how she had crossed ten feet of floor to get from the middle of the chapel at Cerpiano to this place behind a curtain of the little sacristy next to the altar. Quickly, she said, "*Zzzzzzt!* I am alive, but do not call my name!" It seemed to Sister Benni that her name would attract the Germans, who then would stomp in and single her out for immediate execution. As it was, the door to the outside had been opened again, and she could hear German voices in relaxed conversation. There could be no doubt that the soldiers heard the screams and cries coming from the chapel, but they did not respond. Sister Benni had no idea how many grenades had followed the one that had caused her to faint, but at a guess it seemed to her that at least half the forty-nine people in the oratory were dead, and half the others dying.

For all Sister Benni knew, she might be the only person in the chapel who was not mortally wounded. Her thigh ached sharply, but she reached down with her uninjured arm and found that there was no wound. Perhaps she had bruised her thigh when she fainted. Her left arm tingled with a thousand little pinpricks, but that was mainly because it was poking straight up in the air between two heavy bodies, like a piece of wood in a vise. She could see blood dripping from a small wound in the upraised elbow, but she felt no pain, only the tingling sensation. Sister Benni did not try to pull her arm down for a better look. She felt that her only chance to survive lay in playing dead.

Thus she lay for at least an hour, until she heard the Germans move off, leaving behind a single sentry who stood in the doorway looking toward the outside, as though he knew that no one in the chapel could menace him any longer. The loud moaning and crying began to diminish, as one by one the mortally wounded died or lapsed into final coma, and soon Sister Benni could begin to make out sounds from the adjoining *palazzo*. First, she heard a few notes played on the little harmonium with which the teachers entertained the children in the evening, and then she heard the squeal of a mouth organ and a raucous marching song by a chorus of five or six, followed by what sounded like several men making Indian war whoops. From then on there was a steady obbligato of gay noises from the adjoining building. Sister Benni guessed that the SS men had already looted the wine cellar and were now gorging themselves on the food that was stored in the pantry.

Soon she became aware of a single voice from the middle of the chapel floor. "Oh, help me, help me!" a woman was saying. "Oh, please, get them off me!" Sister Benni thought she recognized the voice of Anna Frabboni Fabbris, the forty-two-year-old wife of the landowner who had shown the Nazis his *tessera* and begged for mercy.

"Be brave, *Signora!*" Sister Benni called. "You must carry on the best you can."

"Oh, but I am in pain," the woman said. "I cannot stand it. I hurt. My husband's body is lying across me."

"But, *Signora,* we are all in the same position," Sister Benni said.

Soon Sister Benni heard the wealthy woman say, "Ines, you *work* for me. At least *you* can come and help me."

Sister Benni heard Ines Barbieri, a thirty-two-year-old woman who worked on the Fabbris land, say softly, "*Signora,* how can I come and help you? I am blinded, and I have my baby in my arms."

At this, the Fabbris woman began screaming at the top of her lungs. *"Zzzzzzt!"* Sister Benni said, and again: *"ZZZZZZT!"* But the woman's screams only grew more shrill, and the sentry turned from his outward stance and peered into the room. Soon he shut the door, and the room darkened, and the woman's outcries grew so wild and violent that Sister Benni thought they must be audible all the way down to Gardeletta. In a few minutes the door sprang open, and a hatless soldier with rolled-up sleeves stood backlighted in the doorway. He shouted something incomprehensible, and when the screaming continued, he picked his way between the bodies until he reached the hysterical *padrona.* There was a single shot, and the noise stopped, and Sister Benni could hear the German grumbling to himself as he walked out of the room. The party noises from the *palazzo* had died away, but in a few minutes they resumed.

Sister Benni heard a child pleading, "Stay alive, Olimpia. Stay alive!" and a weak answer from the other side of the room; "If you knew how much it hurts me, Fernando, you would want me to die. You would understand." Sister Benni tucked her head under a body and tried not to hear.

When Cornelia Paselli regained consciousness, she looked at her wristwatch, the cheap one she had bought to assist her in making the train to Bologna each morning, and saw that it was two o'clock. The cemetery was almost completely quiet now. A steady rain thrummed down on the tombstones. Cornelia looked around and noticed that a few had left, although seventy or eighty remained, almost all of them dead. Her sister, Giuseppina, lay to one side, breathing heavily, her head encrusted with blood, and Cornelia began wiping the blood away with her handkerchief. At last she reached the wound and discovered that it was minor. "Peppina," she said, shaking her sister. "Peppina! It is nothing! You are all right!"

"What will I do?" their mother, Angelina, moaned. "What can I do? I cannot move my legs."

"Be calm, Mother," Cornelia said. She examined herself, and when she was able to stand, she found that she had only a slight flesh wound in the thigh. Then she hobbled over to her mother and said, "Stay calm, Mother, we will take care of you. I will get help as soon as it gets dark." She looked for her mother's wound, but all she could see was a line of shredded cloth in Angelina's skirt just above the knee. Cornelia lifted the skirt and saw a row of red slits where the bullets had cracked across her mother's legs like a deadly dotted line. Blood was oozing from each of the holes, and Cornelia realized that her mother had been losing blood steadily for four hours. Quickly she ripped off her own sweater and applied a tourniquet high on each of her mother's thighs. The two daughters dragged Angelina out of the mound of the dead and over to the cemetery wall, where they were surprised to find their cousin Elide Ruggeri lying in the rain on a blanket. "There is not much shelter here, Mother," Cornelia said, "but soon I will bring help, and we will get you to the hospital at Bologna." The two girls sat alongside their mother, comforting her, but they noticed that she was not always conscious to receive their consolations.

Once she awoke and looked around at the scene in the tiny cemetery. "Oh, my children!" she moaned. "When *Babbo* finds us like this, he will die of a heart attack!" Another time she opened her eyes and said, "The twins are dead. Cornelia, Peppina, look over there! The little ones are gone!"

Cornelia could stand the waiting no longer. "Peppina," she said, "if I wait until dark, I will find no one to help, and Mama is still losing blood. I will have to go now."

She got up and walked to the mound of bodies. "Can you help me now?" Lidia Pirini called, and Cornelia worked till she had cleared the bodies off the pretty girl from Murazze. "Do not worry, Lidia,"

Cornelia said. "I am going for help." She went to the side of the grandmother who had called out before, but the *nonna* had slipped back into the pile, and Cornelia could see that she was not breathing.

"Cornelia!" her mother called weakly from the wall. "What are you doing?"

"I am going for help, Mama," she said, hurrying back to her mother's side.

"You cannot go!" her mother said, gripping Cornelia's arm. "They will kill you!"

"Mama," Giuseppina said, "do not worry. I will stay and take care of you while Cornelia goes for help."

"No," Angelina said. "We must remain together. Cornelia will be killed if she leaves."

Cornelia turned away and headed for the single gate of the mountain cemetery. "Where are you going?" her mother shouted hoarsely into the heavy rain.

Cornelia stepped over the body of the refugee woman who had begged to see her daughter, the woman whose death had signaled the massacre. "To Cerpiano," she called back, and walked out the iron gate.

Antonio Tonelli was dimly aware that he had bumped into some women in the woods, and he remembered that they had tried to tell him something about his family. Was it that one of his nine children was still alive? Had they told him that little Vittorio was up there waiting to be saved? Or was it somebody else's child named Vittorio? Antonio sat in the bushes and tried to figure it out. He was no longer crying—a man of thirty-eight can cry for only so long—but his throat ached, as though he had been sobbing and retching for days on end, and it hurt him to swallow. He decided to return to the cemetery and see if he had heard the women correctly, but as soon as he reached the road on his hands and knees, he heard a German patrol swinging up the mountain, and when he doubled back and approached the road from another point, he heard more German voices. "What is the good of anything?" Antonio asked himself. "I may as well go home."

He reached the farmhouse at Possatore by a long crawl through the underbrush, and as he came in sight of the *casa colonica,* he saw two calves standing untethered in the front yard. Pigs were rooting around, and the chickens were out of their yard and pecking at the flowers. The house had burned, though not completely, since most of it was stone, and Antonio got a ladder and climbed to the second-story window leading to the bedroom. Inside, the beds were black and smoking. A bureau had been turned over, and its contents lay charred on the floor, and part of the roof had fallen in. Antonio climbed into the smoldering remains of the room and opened a closet. The contents were intact, and he took down a heavy cloak and a hat. He thought that they were suitable funeral garb, that they would lend distinction to his body when it was found. He did not know how he would die, but it seemed to him that his death was imminent. And anyway, he had no more reason to exist. He was finished with society, with civilization, and vice versa. They had provided him with a sixteen-hour-a-day job as a porter, a bare patch of dead land that was even inhospitable to weeds, and eight or ten dollars a week to support himself and his wife and his brother and his uncle and his nine children. Such a life would never have been bearable without the children, and now they were gone. His personal store of riches, the little ones who would secure his old age, were lying dead at Casaglia. Antonio put on the cloak and the hat, climbed back down the ladder, and headed off to the woods. Self-slaughter was unthinkable, but perhaps there would be no sin in courting death.

Elena Ruggeri and her aunt, Maria Menarini, and Maria's thirteen-year-old son, Giorgio, the three who had escaped from the church at Casaglia just before the Nazis had pushed in the front door, had spent the rest of the morning and the early hours of the afternoon huddling in the woods in a bottom of land below the church. Somehow the fifty-seven-year-old Zia Maria had managed to bound across a mile of weeds, woods, pasture and field and not drop her umbrella, which she found dangling from her arm when they pulled inside the thicket. The three of them crouched under the umbrella through varying degrees of rainfall, while from almost every point of the compass there came the incessant sound of machine guns. "It must be a battle between the SS and the partisans," Elena said.

"Yes," Aunt Maria said, "a very big battle."

They were standing alongside a small stream, where the trees and brush grew thickest and they could not be seen. They were not far from their own home at Pudella or the big *podere* at San Giovanni or the Laffi home at Poggio, but they had made up their minds that they were not going to venture out until the last gunshot had sounded. It was about two in the afternoon when they became aware of a voice calling, "Elena! Elena!" in the woods. They listened intently and recognized the voice of Elena's father, Attilio.

"This way, *Babbo,*" Elena said. "Over here!"

Attilio came into the thicket and threw his arms around his oldest daughter. "How did you find us, *Babbo?*" Elena asked.

"I watched you from my hiding place on the mountain," he said breathlessly. "All the men are up there. You ran from the back of the church and I saw you come out at the field, and I watched where you entered the woods. But I have not been able to reach here till now."

"What is happening, brother?" Maria Menarini asked.

Attilio began to cry, and Elena put her arms around him. *"Babbo,"* she said, "tell me, and we can cry together."

"They are all gone," Attilio said between sobs. "The Germans killed all of ours. I heard it and I saw it."

The family group drew together under Aunt Maria's umbrella, and for almost an hour Attilio sobbed out the story of the march from the cemetery and the machine guns and the grenades and how he and dozens of men like him had sat on the mountain looking helplessly at the whole scene. "I got up to run down the mountain to help," Attilio said with great effort, "and somebody pulled me back, and I realized that he was right, that I could do nothing to help your mother and all the others. And then some of the other men began to run, and we had to stop them one by one. They were just trying to throw themselves at the Germans, to give their lives away. They could not stand to be up on the mountain safe from the Germans while their families were dying down below. Afterward, when we could see that a few still lived, we could do nothing for them. Wherever we looked, there were Germans on the roads, and every barn was on fire, and we heard machine guns from San Giovanni and Caprara and practically everyplace on the mountain."

"But, *Babbo,*" Elena said, "where are the partisans?"

"They fought as best they could," Attilio said. "Some of them are trapped right now on top of Monte Sole, and the Germans could go up with their mortars and wipe them out easily. But the Germans seem to have no interest in the partisans. They seem to be after the women and the children."

Attilio started to cry again. "Women and children do not shoot back," he said.

After a while the little group of survivors began to hear a female voice wailing and screaming on the road a few hundred yards up the hill. "Where did they go?" the voice cried out. "Oh, where are they?"

"Babbo!" Elena said. "That is Albertina Laffi. I know her voice."

Albertina lived in Gardeletta, but she had been brought up in Poggio, where a big family of Laffis lived and gave occasional dances on their piazza. "I saw seven or eight of the Laffis die in the cemetery," Attilio said. "She must be looking for them."

"I must help her!" Elena said, and she sprang out of the bushes and headed up toward the road. As she was running across a field, a machine gun opened fire from nearby San Giovanni, a farm village down the hill that commanded a view of half the flank of Monte Sole. Elena sprawled on the soft earth and, with her nose almost digging a furrow, groped her way over a hump of land and out of the line of fire. Behind her in the thicket she heard her father cry out, "She is dead! They killed Elena!" She kept crawling toward the road, but she no longer heard Albertina, so she decided to head through the woods to the cemetery at Casaglia. She arrived at about four thirty in the afternoon and found a partisan crouching alongside the gate.

"What are you doing?" he said. "Are you trying to get killed?"

"No," Elena said. "I am only trying to find mine."

"I am sorry to tell you that they are in there," the partisan said.

Elena walked through the rain into the cemetery, and when she saw the bodies heaped in front of the burial chapel, she slumped to the ground, clutching her forehead. A partisan ran over and lifted her gently, and she heard a familiar voice crying out from the wall to the right: "Tell Uncle Attilio to come get me! Do not tell *Babbo!* He will be angry."

It was her cousin Elide, the pretty little prankster of Ca' Pudella. She was lying atop a tomb, on a blanket, and four or five partisans were busy dragging other survivors over to the same corner of the cemetery, where they seemed to be improvising an infirmary. Elena saw another of her aunts, Angelina Paselli, lying unconscious in a half-sitting position against the wall, while Angelina's daughter Giuseppina watched over her. The young Tonelli boy, Vittorio, was standing around apparently uninjured, but a five-year-old boy named

Vincenzo Soldati was lying on another tomb with bullet wounds in the shoulder and arm and a huge contusion on his head. Elena could not detect the slightest sign that anyone was alive in the mound of bodies in front of the chapel. She saw the young girl Lidia Pirini of Murazze lying apart from the others, but Lidia did not appear to be breathing, and the rest were jammed into a shapeless tangle of arms and legs and heads, some of them detached from the bodies.

Elena rushed to her cousin's side, but all she could think to do was rearrange the blanket. "Where are you hurt, Elide?" she said.

"In the hip," Elide said.

"Let me see." She screened her cousin from the others and groped for the wounds, and she found one in the top part of Elide's thigh and another in her hip. It appeared that a bullet had gone in and out. "Do not worry, Elide," she told her cousin. "We will get you home as soon as we can."

"Oh, please, Elena," Elide said, "tell Uncle Attilio to come for me now. I am in pain, and the rain keeps beating in my face."

Elena took her cousin's hands. "There is nothing to do but wait, Elide. I am sorry, but that is the situation. The Germans almost killed me when I was coming here. Nothing can be done until night."

"Please come!" Elide said.

"We will." Elena patted her cousin's hand, left the cemetery and ran all the way downhill to the place where she had left the others, passing one patrol of Germans so quickly that they only stared at her. *"Babbo! Babbo!"* she said. "Elide is alive in the cemetery!"

"It is a miracle," Attilio said. "But what can we do?"

"We must save her tonight," Elena said.

"We will save her if we can," Attilio told his daughter.

As soon as she got outside the cemetery gate, Cornelia Paselli looked both ways for Germans, and then she followed the walls around to the back. She knew that the path to Cerpiano would be alive with soldiers, and she had made up her mind to go through the woods on a beeline for help. But as she reached the back wall of the cemetery to begin her sprint down the gully and up the other side to Cerpiano, she heard a faint scream. She was tempted to climb the cemetery wall and tell whoever had made the sound to be quiet until she could get away. But then the cry came again, and Cornelia realized it was coming across the gulch from Cerpiano. She ran through the fifty yards of open field that lay between the cemetery and open woods and began working her way toward the sounds. As she got closer to Cerpiano, she could tell that there was more than one person crying out from the mountain refuge of the Sisters of Saint Angela.

Cornelia was torn between an urge to complete her mission of getting help for her loved ones at Casaglia and going to the aid of these new victims, among whom she now was certain she could hear children. But when she tiptoed to a vantage point and parted the weeds for a better look at Cerpiano, she saw that a sentry was on guard in front of the chapel, and a noise that sounded like a drunken men's chorus was coming from the *palazzo*. When there was no longer any doubt in Cornelia's mind what had happened, she backed off and began following the stream down the mountain toward Gardeletta.

The rain had let up, though there was still a slight mist, and she half-ran down the steep sides of the mountain, sometimes slipping and almost losing her balance. She stepped on sharp-edged rocks and ran through brambles, and her feet and legs were soon a crosshatch of cuts and scratches. Her hair was still caked with the blood of the cemetery, and her simple black dress hung in shreds from her body. But nothing could slow her. She felt a surge of energy, and it seemed like only a few minutes before she was approaching Gardeletta. She slackened her pace as she came to the edge of the woods, and down on the main road she saw another German sentry. With no more sound than a weasel, Cornelia retreated a few yards into the brush and back up the mountain till she was out of rifle range. If Gardeletta was unsafe, she would follow the railroad tracks north to the town of Vado, always keeping out of sight. She had gone a short distance when she recognized the house where her family had left the sheep only a few days before. Cornelia approached with caution, but there were no signs of life as she climbed up a steep path to the courtyard of the house. Then she saw the *contadino* sprawled dead in front of the door, and a few feet away a woman she had known only as Gigina. When she had looked closely to make sure that both were beyond help, Cornelia circumnavigated the house, calling, "Tay-a! Tay-a!" but there was no response. She remembered how the sheep used to run like a firehorse when he heard his name, and she assumed that he had wandered away into the woods. She felt sad at the prospect of never finding him. As she was leaving the house, she climbed down a stone wall to get back into the woods, and there she found Tay-a, hanging half over the edge. An involuntary shudder went through Cornelia's tired body. She did not have to touch the pet to know he was dead. His wool was soaked and lying close to his skin, and his head dangled loosely from his neck.

Cornelia began to cry, and it came as a shock to the eighteen-year-old girl to realize that she had not cried till now, not even when she had awakened to the nightmare scene at the cemetery. It was not that she loved Tay-a more than her family. It was difficult for her to comprehend fully the deaths of her twin brother and sister and the shooting of her mother and sister and the massacre of dozens of their friends. Her mind refused to accept the shock of so much death. But there was something infinitely clear and final about the body of the sheep lying before her eyes. With Tay-a gone, the family could never again be the same. For two years the sheep had symbolized their triumph over poverty, their limitless capacity to be content, even happy, with next to nothing. Now they would have to start over again, without Tay-a, without the twins, maybe even without their mother, Angelina.

The thought of her mother dying in the cemetery made Cornelia begin to run again, this time toward Railroad House No. 66. She was not sure what she would find there, only that she had to see for herself. She crossed the tracks to the house and started to enter when something made her pull back from the latch as though it were electrified. A force more powerful than reason told her that going into the house would be wrong, after all that had happened. There was something immoral, indecent, about returning to the hearth when the others were suffering far up on Monte Sole. She barely whispered, *"Babbo! Babbo!"* but there was no answer, and she knew without entering that the house was as empty as it had been two days before when they had left it for the false security of Cerpiano.

Now there was nothing to do but continue on to Vado, across the Setta and almost a mile away. She decided that she would be safer on the other side of the Setta, but she felt a panic as she stepped off from the shore to ford the *torrente*. The rain had filled the stream with gurgling, sucking whirlpools, and Cornelia had to keep telling herself that other lives hung on her courage. She was almost in the middle of the little river when she heard gunfire from a house on the other side called Villa Elvira. She hurried on, and the shots continued, and now she could see bullets cutting bubbly lines through the water around her. They looked like sparklers, and Cornelia stopped to watch. The sparklers died away, and she waited in water up to her waist. Behind her were ten yards of river and an open field. Ahead were ten yards of river, Villa Elvira, and German soldiers. She raised her hands in the air and began to walk backward. She might be shot as she walked, but there was no power on earth that was going to get her to head voluntarily toward the Nazis. She felt her feet reach the dry bank, and any second she expected a final bullet to catch her. But inexplicably no more shots were fired, and she turned and ran as fast as she could back across the open area and into the woods.

The sky was darkening, and Cornelia realized that she had to find someone soon if her mother were not to spend the whole night in the rain at the cemetery. She began to get a helpless feeling, as though she could walk to the ends of the earth and still find German sentries, German riflemen, German machine gunners. The whole mountain had turned German in a single day, and there was no place to run. Closer to Vado, she passed near an air-raid shelter that had been dug into the side of the mountain, and on an impulse she walked to the opening and called, "Signorina Serra! Signorina Serra!" thinking that one of her acquaintances might be there.

Instead a man's head appeared at the opening. "For charity," he said. "Be quiet! The Germans are around."

She recognized a fellow trackworker of her father, Virginio, and she went inside and found a group of a dozen or so sitting quietly in the dusk. She told her story quickly, and the others told her that similar massacres had been taking place all over the mountain. "All right, then," Cornelia said finally. "Will one of you go with me to help my mother?"

No one answered.

"Oh, please, please!" Cornelia said. "She is lying up there with bullet holes across her legs, and the rain is falling on her, and she has nothing to eat or drink. At least will you help me bring her some food?"

There was no answer.

"Then I will go myself," she said, and walked toward the exit. The trackworker was standing across the hole that led to the outside, and when Cornelia tried to pass, he refused to move. "Girl," he said. "What can you do for your mother now?"

"I must go," she said. "Let me go!"

"Be reasonable, my child," the man said. "The *rastrellamento* is still on. If you leave here, the Germans will surely kill you."

"And if I stay, they will kill my mother and my sister."

"What could you do about that?"

Cornelia began to cry. "I want to be with my mother," she said.

"Come, my child," one of the women said, taking her gently by the arm. "You sleep here on the straw tonight, and tomorrow we will try to help your mother."

"How would it hurt you if I went to my mother and my sister?" Cornelia asked in a voice choked with hopelessness and tears.

The trackworker took her other arm, and said, "Cornelia, we have been hiding in this refuge all day, and all day people have been coming here to tell us that the Germans are killing every living thing on Monte Sole. And still they have not found us here, and now night is falling, and for the first time it looks as though we have a chance to survive this *rastrellamento*. How can we let you go back up the mountain with our secret?"

Cornelia was led to a pallet covered with straw, and she fell on it, exhausted. But she was not able to sleep. She watched the narrow exit of the shelter as it changed from brown to purple to gray to black, and then it was night.

Fernando Piretti, the nine-year-old son of the Socialist beggar Maximiliano, lay under his mother's skirt and tried to figure if it was day or night outside the chapel of Cerpiano. He was unhurt, but his ears ached from the screams of the wounded around him, and his throat was sore from swallowing his own tears. Earlier, his thirteen-year-old cousin, Olimpia, had died in front of his eyes, even while he was begging her to live, and now he was trying to comfort six-year-old Paola Rossi, who lay moaning next to him with a slash across her eye socket from a piece of shrapnel. There were fifteen or twenty others who remained alive, including his mother and his teacher, Anita Serra, and the teacher of the *asilo,* Sister Benni, and some refugees whom Fernando did not know. An old lady had taken a bottle of medicine out of her suitcase and gone among the wounded administering capfuls. "Oh, give me some!" Fernando pleaded. "I am dying of thirst!"

"No," his mother said. "You must not take any, Fernando. It is medicine, not something to drink."

As the hours went on, the sounds of partying grew more and more raucous from the adjoining *palazzo,* and every now and then there would be a loud conversation at the door of the chapel, and someone would open it, look in and shut it again. Once the door was opened, and a drunken voice said in Italian, "Does anybody need help in here?" Immediately a woman began to scream that she was dying of pain. As Fernando snuggled under his mother's skirt and played dead, he heard the man shout, "What do you have to scream about? I will give you something to scream about. I will empty this gun in your face!" There was a series of shots and the squish of the man's boots as he walked back over the bodies, and then silence.

Now Fernando could tell it was nighttime, because no light came into the oratory when the door was opened. Several parties of Germans stumbled in and out, laughing and discharging their pistols, but by now most of the survivors had learned to make neither sound nor motion when the door was opened, and even after several visits by the roistering Germans there remained more than a dozen alive.

Fernando closed his eyes and tried to doze, but the sounds from the *palazzo* became so loud that it was almost impossible to sleep. The Germans would make their peculiar SS noises: cheering and shouting and roaring like wild animals. They would quiet down for a few minutes, then suddenly break into song, alternating between rousing marches and soulful laments and hymns. Fernando would sleep momentarily, only to be jerked awake by the next series of outcries. He thought it must have been about midnight when he heard snorting noises from the side door, where the body of the woman Amelia Tossani lay wedged. Over the din from the *palazzo,* Fernando had difficulty in figuring out what was making these new sounds, and he raised himself up to see. One of the *contadino*'s pigs had wandered to the back entrance, and it was nibbling at the corpse. Listening to the familiar sounds of a rooting hog, Fernando snuggled under his mother's skirt and fell into a deep sleep.

It was near midnight, and the moon had just slid into sight for the first time, when the poor *contadino* and part-time hog butcher Adelmo Benini got up the courage to slither out of the hollow chestnut tree that had sheltered him through the long day. He looked again at the little mountain cemetery of Casaglia, only about 100 yards down the slope from him, and he thought he could detect some stirrings near the mound of bodies that held his wife and his two girls. He feared that the Germans had returned, and he started to climb back into the chestnut tree, but hunger drove him to stay outside. As he slowly picked his way among the thorny acacia trees and the nettles and brambles of the mountain underbrush, he heard a voice. "How can I go on? How can human beings do such things? Look how I am reduced! Look what they have taken from me!" Adelmo recognized the voice of his father-in-law, Giovanni "Sassolein" Migliori, and he hurried through the woods to the old man's side.

"Adelmo, Adelmo!" Sassolein said, embracing his son-in-law. "They are dead, Adelmo. Every one of them."

"I know, *Babbo,*" Adelmo said. "I watched from the tree. I started to run down to stop them, but I was afraid, and I hid in a chestnut tree." Adelmo turned aside with shame, but Sassolein put his hand on the younger man's shoulder.

"You would only have been killed," Sassolein said. "They had machine guns and machine pistols and one of them carried a flame-thrower."

"I saw that, too, *Babbo,*" Adelmo said. "They brought Don Ubaldo back to the church and told him to say his prayers, and he was on his knees in front of the altar when they shot him in the back and set him on fire. I saw it all from my hiding place next to the church, and then I went up the mountain."

Adelmo heard a noise in the underbrush and turned sharply. "Do not worry," Sassolein said. "It is only my friend."

A young man materialized from the weeds and shook Adelmo's hand. "My name is Luigi Cesare," he said. "I am an Army pilot from Florence."

"What are you doing here?" Adelmo asked.

"I escaped from a German work crew at Rioveggio yesterday, and the priest was hiding me in the basement of the church. I left after they killed him, and then I ran into your father-in-law."

The three men worked through the patch of woods, looking for chestnuts and berries, but there were none, and Adelmo suggested that they awaken the nearest *contadino* and ask for something to eat. They knocked at a nearby house, but the farmer did not answer until they had almost broken down the door. "Here, take this and leave!" he said, handing each a small cup of milk. As they walked away from the darkened *casa colonica,* Adelmo appropriated a pick that was lying alongside the barn. The three men climbed up the mountain until they came to a small cliff just under the summit, and they used the pick to hack out an opening. They covered it over with branches and leaves and went inside to rest.

Elena Ruggeri and her father, Attilio, and Aunt Maria and Cousin Giorgio had bedded down for the night in the woods bottom not far from the Ruggeri house at Ca' Pudella when they heard the sound of someone approaching through the trees. It was Augusto Massa, the *contadino* who farmed Casetta di Casaglia for the church and whose brother, Luigi, ran the *tabacchi* at Caprara. Augusto and his two sons, Pompilio and Dante, sat down to talk, and Augusto said, "It has been a hard day, a hard day, Attilio. We have been hiding in a cave on the mountain since dawn. Thank God we are on our way home now."

It seemed to Elena that there was something strangely naïve about these words. "What of your wife and your little son, Mario, and the baby?" she asked.

"What do you mean?" Augusto said. "I left them in the church at Casaglia with the others." He gripped Elena by the arm and said, "Surely they are safe?"

"Sit down, Augusto," Attilio said softly, and when he had finished the story, softening it around the edges as best he could, old Augusto and his two sons walked off sobbing into the dark woods. "Be careful, Augusto," Attilio called. "The Germans are still killing."

"Does it matter now?" Augusto called back in a choking voice. Elena waited to hear her father's answer, but there was only silence, and the moans of the others faded into the distance.

Around midnight, the rain stopped completely, and the moon put in an appearance, and Elena tried to get some sleep, but as soon as she would doze off, she would see the mound of bodies at Casaglia, and she would sit straight up. Once she heard herself screaming into the night. "For charity!" Attilio said as he shook his daughter by the shoulders. "Try to stay quiet, Elena, or you will lead them to us."

Later she fell asleep, only to be awakened by her father's shaking her again. *"Zzzzzz!"* he said. "Listen! Do you hear your mother calling from the cemetery?"

Elena listened. "No," she said. "I hear nothing but the brook."

"Your mother is out there," Attilio said. "I hear her calling for us."

They woke up Zia Maria and Cousin Giorgio, and the four of them searched the woods bottom in enlarging circles, but they only succeeded in scaring themselves. "Come, *Babbo,* get some sleep," Elena said. "You must have been dreaming."

"She is out there, calling for us," Attilio said. Elena and the other two huddled back in their bivouac, and all through the rest of the night Elena could hear her father searching about in the brush.

The teen-aged Lucia Sabbioni and her fellow escapees from the cemetery at Casaglia lay on the weeds in their hiding place just off the road near Casetta di Casaglia, and every time Lucia would begin to sleep, she would be awakened by her own screams. "Lucia, you have to keep your mouth shut!" Imelde Vegetti said. "You will get us all killed!"

"But I cannot stand the pain," Lucia said. "I try to be still, but I lose control."

Vittoria, the Vado woman who had carried Lucia into the woods, had left with her friend to get help, and now there were just four of them: Lucia, Imelde, Imelde's teen-age daughter, Bianca, and the older woman, Clelia Monti. As the night went on and Lucia continued to scream, tense whispered arguments broke out, with Lucia trying to explain that her screams were involuntary, and the others telling her to be quiet or they would all be killed. At last, Imelde said, "One more scream, Lucia, and we are finished with you. We know you are in pain, but if you make another loud noise, the three of us are leaving."

Lucia bit into the tattered sleeve of her dress to keep from crying out. Wave after wave of fiery pain shot up and down the string of wounds in her legs and hips. She could feel blood oozing from the big hole in her side with every beat of her heart, and between the pain and the fear that she was dying, she found herself unable to stay quiet. She pushed her face into the soft humus to muffle the sounds, and lying that way for several hours, she passed into unconsciousness. But then she heard her seven-year-old sister, Giovanna, calling from the woods nearby, "Lucia! Lucia! Come save me!" Lucia had seen her sister's body just as they were leaving the cemetery, and even though the eyes were clear and open, the little face was full of holes. There could be no doubt that Giovanna was dead in the cemetery.

Lucia lifted herself on one elbow and tried to decide whether she had been dreaming, and then she heard a stick break in the shadows. "Giovanna?" Lucia said softly, and four men slipped into the little clearing. The other women jumped up as though to run, but Lucia could see that the men were *contadini* of the area.

"Did you see my sister when you were walking through the woods?" Lucia asked. "My seven-year-old sister, Giovanna?"

"She is dead in the cemetery with the others," one of the men said.

"I thought I heard her calling."

"We have just come from the cemetery," another said, "and there are a few people still alive against the wall, but there is no girl of that age with them."

Lucia fell back on the ground and paid no further attention, and soon she heard the *contadini* going on their way into the woods. Names and faces kept passing in front of her eyes, and she could not sleep. The faces flickered through her brain, and when she thought she had seen them all, they would pass again, and again: Bruna, two years old, and Irene, five, and Giovanna, seven, and Adriana, ten, and Otello, thirteen, and her dear mother, Nazzarena. She saw them all lying dead in the cemetery at Casaglia, and suddenly she realized that she was screaming again.

It was dark when Alfredo Comellini, one of the *padroni* of San Giovanni, crawled from his shelter to stretch his legs. He could see the ruins of his *podere* in the dull moonlight that followed the rain, and in the valley below fires still smoldered, casting up glimmers of orange and red. Alfredo walked in the opposite direction from San Giovanni, because he had noticed at dusk that the German machine guns were standing in front of the mound of the dead, and he assumed that the Germans were camped there for the night. As he walked through the fields, Alfredo thought he heard a man's voice coming from the mule path that ran between Calzane and Villa Serena. Keeping in the shadows, he made his way toward the road and recognized the silhouetted form of his friend Don Ferdinando Casagrande. Alfredo could not understand what the priest was doing walking in the moonlight, talking aloud. Don Ferdinando and his three grown sisters and their old father had been hiding in a shelter on the *podere* of the priest of San Martino, and so far as Alfredo knew, they had remained inside all day. He hurried to his friend's side. "Don Ferdinando," he called out, "it is me! Alfredo."

The priest stopped and turned his head slowly, and looked at Alfredo with the unseeing eyes of a sleepwalker. Alfredo asked, "What is the matter, *Reverendo?*"

"What is the matter?" the young priest mumbled. "*What is the matter?* I am a priest. I must administer the last rites. I must bury the dead. My sister is wounded, and we have nothing to eat, but I have taken this vow."

"Father—"

"Even if it costs my life, I must administer the rites. I must bury the dead. I do not know what to do. I have taken this vow."

Alfredo put his hand on the priest's shoulder and shook it lightly. "Don Ferdinando," he said, "go back to your shelter and rest. For charity, do not try to help the dead now. The Germans are all around."

"I must bury the dead. I have taken a vow."

"The dead are already dead. There is nothing you can do to help them tonight."

The priest stepped from under Alfredo's hand. "I must fulfill my vows," he said. "I cannot recognize obstacles." Alfredo let Don Ferdinando go off in the night, still muttering to himself, and he saw that the priest headed back toward his shelter.

Giuseppina Paselli wished that she could sleep, but every time she dozed, cradling her head in her arms atop a tombstone, her mother would cry out, "Peppina! Peppina! Where are you?" and she would have to convince her mother that she had not run away. It was growing more and more difficult to keep Angelina quiet. "Cornelia will bring help," Giuseppina would say, and her mother would scream out, "Cornelia! They have killed my Cornelia!" and Giuseppina would have to explain patiently to her mother that Cornelia was probably on her way with help right now, and soon Angelina would be in a clean white hospital bed in Bologna.

Once Giuseppina slept for a few minutes and woke up to hear her mother say, "Peppina, I just dreamed of your father. I dreamed that he was very close to us," and another time her mother called out, "Where are the twins, Peppina? Tell the twins to come back here this minute!"

A few hours before dawn, Giuseppina became aware of some heavy shapes entering the front gates of the cemetery. She peered into the darkness, but all she could hear was a sort of vague trotting sound. Her mother's eyes were closed, and she was breathing deeply, so Giuseppina left her station and walked a few yards toward the mound of bodies. She saw several pigs poking about, and just as she turned to go back to her mother's side, she heard a creaky old voice coming from the center of the dead. "You pigs!" said the voice of Artimesia Gatti, the ancient caretaker of the empty church at Casaglia. "Get out!"

In the blackness of the cemetery, Elide Ruggeri turned her head to escape from the rain that had started again after midnight, and as she turned, she thought she saw a German soldier standing next to the tiny burial chapel. She started to quiver, but then she realized that the soldier was only a sheet-iron cross, flapping in the wind. She was finding it more and more difficult to maintain her composure. In the morning, when the Germans had lined them up and started shooting, she had been totally unafraid, even contemptuous. If she had not been hit in the hip, she would probably have remained standing in the line of fire until the end, looking daggers at the gunner. But now the fearless young lady of the morning had turned to jelly. She trembled at shadows. She cried out in fear that the Germans would return. She prayed that someone would come rescue her, but she knew she had been forgotten. The night lasted a thousand nights, and when she heard hushed voices in the cemetery a few hours before the dawn of Saturday, she burrowed her head under her blanket, certain that the Germans had come to finish her off. Then she heard a man begin to cry and moan uncontrollably. Cautiously, she looked out, and saw her Uncle Attilio standing in front of the mound of the dead, his shoulders shaking and his hands pressed to his face.

"Zio!" Elide called. "*Zio!* Over here!"

Attilio continued to cry and fell to his knees, and Elide said, *"Zio,* be quiet! Calm yourself, *Zio*. Everyone is dead; there is nothing you can do. Take me away. I am wounded. Take me to the house."

Attilio stumbled to the tomb where his niece was lying in the rain. "Where is your aunt?" he said.

"She must be in those dead bodies over there."

"No, she is not. I heard her crying out last night."

"I do not think so, *Zio*. I am sure she is somewhere in the bodies."

Attilio lifted the tiny Elide piggyback style and called to Giuseppina Paselli, "I will come back soon, my niece."

As they started off, a voice came from near the bodies. "Can you help me?" someone was calling. "Can you help me, please? I am in such pain."

Attilio stopped, and Elide recognized Lidia Pirini, the young girl from Murazze. "Try to be strong," Attilio said. "I will save you if I can. Where are you hurt?"

"In the hip," Lidia said. "It feels as though the bone has been broken in the socket."

"I will try to help you later," Attilio said. "Remain quiet, and if the Germans come back, try to look like a corpse."

Elide clung like a monkey to her uncle's back as the two of them walked in total darkness 500 yards down the road to their home at Pudella. The house was intact. It had burned down years before, and Attilio and Giulio had rebuilt it almost entirely of stone. Elide and her uncle could see signs that the Germans had tried to wreck the house, but only the barn and the outbuildings were down. "You must not make a sound!" Attilio whispered to his niece as they approached the darkened house. "Since they did not burn it down, they may be inside sleeping."

But their house was empty, and Attilio placed his niece gently on a mattress in front of the cold kitchen fireplace. "I will go to the others," he said. "Do not make a sound!" An hour later he returned, this time with several *contadini* helping him. They carried Elide's aunt, Angelina Paselli, and the wounded five-year-old Soldati boy on rung ladders. Antonio Tonelli's sole remaining son, Vittorio, and Elide's cousin, Giuseppina Paselli, walked behind. By the time all had been made comfortable in the large kitchen of Pudella, it was daylight, and Attilio said, "I am afraid we will not be able to go back to the cemetery and help Lidia Pirini. Already the Germans are about."

"Where will you go, Uncle?" Elide asked.

"Back to the woods," he said. "Elena waits for me. The Germans will come here today, and there should be no able-bodied people here. We will stay in the woods and come back tonight."

"What of Zia Angelina?" Elide asked. Her aunt lay next to her, babbling in a coma.

"Peppina will take care of her," Attilio said loudly, but just before he walked out with the others, he leaned over and whispered in Elide's ear: "If I see a priest, I will send him."

Tucked alongside his mother, with her skirt covering his face, the boy Fernando Piretti alternated between deep sleep and howling nightmares in the little chapel of Cerpiano. More than once he escaped in his dreams, only to be recaptured by the Germans, and all through the night he heard gunshots, some of them so loud that he thought his ears would burst.

Now it was morning, and the only sound was the soft moaning of the wounded. A gray glow filtered through the single window high above. Fernando felt something hard under his head, and he reached back and touched his cardboard suitcase. They all had carried suitcases or valises when they had been rounded up, in case they were sent away to slave labor. Fernando guessed that his mother had placed his suitcase under his head during the night, so that he would rest better. He turned to see if she was asleep and felt a pain in his right shoulder. He reached inside his shirt and found that the skin was broken and bleeding.

Panicked, the nine-year-old boy turned to his mother. She did not appear to be breathing, and Fernando shook her to wake her up. When she did not respond, he embraced her with both his arms and felt that the back of her head was sticky and broken, and when he slid his hands around to his mother's face, he saw streaks of crimson left by his fingers. He lowered his mother's head gently and stared around the room. Bodies and pieces of bodies covered the floor. The walls were soiled with blood, and bare patches of stone showed where the plaster had been knocked away. Fernando covered his eyes and crawled back under his dead mother's skirt, and slowly he figured out what happened. During the night his mother had been shot, perhaps by one of the carousing Nazis, and a fragment of the bullet had reached his shoulder as he lay cradled against her. Fernando tried to figure how he could have slept through his mother's execution and his own wounding. He bit his lip and tried to reconstruct his dreams. He remembered running from the soldiers in one dream, and grenades exploding uselessly against him in another, and a long fuzzy inquisition by a German sergeant who gave him chocolates. But he could not remember the death of his mother. Somehow, in the infinite procession of his nightmares, the wrong dream had come true.

All through the long night, Sister Benni had stayed motionless in the little sacristy of the chapel, her wounded arm jutting into the air between the bodies that had fallen on her. As daylight came, she began to hear German voices outside. Once she heard a pair of soldiers having a giggling fit, and several times she could make out the unmistakable clink of glasses and bottles. Her own injuries bothered her little—she had flesh wounds in the elbow and the thigh—but she could hear the others moaning, and she wondered how the Germans could remain unaware that there were ten or twenty people alive and suffering in the oratory. Late in the morning Sister Benni heard her fellow teacher, Anita Serra, cry out, *"Sentinella! Sentinella!"* Sister Benni heard the door open, and Maestra Serra saying: "For charity, let us go! We have suffered enough! You must let us out of here." The door shut and a few minutes later reopened, and a voice shouted in Italian, "What is going on?"

Maestra Serra said, "Can you not see what we have suffered? Think of your own loved ones. Then you will find the charity to let the rest of us go."

A rolling peal of laughter came from the man at the door. "Let you go?" he said in faulty Italian. "I will show you how we will let you go. In twenty minutes, *tutti kaput!*"

Almost hidden under the bodies that pinned her, Sister Benni heard the Germans bustling around the outer walls of the chapel. Then she heard the door thrown open again, a loud shout, a sequence of clicks, and a blast of noise that felt as though it had pierced both her eardrums. "Jesus Christ, *misericordia!*" she said to herself. "*Questa è la mia!* This is my end!"

The firing went on in bursts for ten or fifteen minutes, and when it was over, Sister Benni could feel or hear nothing. Her head rang with the echoes of the machine gun, and her ears were in such pain that she was not even positive the firing had stopped. She sniffed an offensive gas, but she was not afraid that she would sneeze or cough; she lacked the strength for either. She lay as she had lain before, under the bodies, and prayed harder than she had ever prayed, and when her wits slowly returned to her, she discovered that somehow she remained alive, no more injured than before.

She did not move for an hour or two, and at last got up the courage to peep through the sacristy curtain at the scene in the oratory. Nothing moved, nor was there the slightest sound. Sister Benni was reminded of the abattoir in Bologna. Maestra Serra lay on top of a pile of bodies in the middle of the chapel, and she was cut in half at the waist. Arms and legs and heads were strewed about; Sister Benni had to turn from the sight. Soon she heard the door open again and something that sounded like farmers walking on melons. Five or six soldiers had come into the room, and they were removing valuables and firing an occasional *coup de grâce*. Once again, Sister Benni waited for the end. She tried to remember if she had worn her gold pierced earrings, but her senses were dulled, and she could not recall. She would know soon enough, when the Germans reached her side. She had her purse; the strap was looped up there on her rigid arm, like a quoit on a stake. The Germans could have it, and her life, too, for that matter. She had now survived forty or fifty hand grenades and thousands of rounds of machine-gun bullets and six or seven tours of the room by drunken soldiers with drawn pistols, and instead of becoming convinced of her own indestructibility, she had simply had enough. She could not endure another trial. She closed her eyes and lay motionless and said her act of contrition to herself.

A hand gripped her rigid arm. The grip relaxed and tightened again. Perhaps her arm was cold from being pressed between bodies for so long, Sister Benni said to herself, and perhaps it was not, in which case she would be shot through the head. She waited. She felt the soldier unloose her hand again, and then her purse was wrenched away. She heard the tinkle of soldi and a muttered exclamation, and then the purse was flung in her face. A hand brushed across her ear, and Sister Benni tensed, but she must not have been wearing earrings, because now she could hear the German moving to the next body. After a few more shots, she heard the door shut again, and the room returned to half-light.

Sister Benni dozed and dreamed, and she did not know how much time had passed when she heard a child's voice. "All dead?" the voice was saying. "Even Mama? Even Grandmother Giovanna? Even Grandmother Rosina?"

"Yes," another child answered.

"And are you sure? Is my brother Giuseppe dead? Oh, are you *sure?* And my Aunt Anita? No, you must be wrong. They cannot all be dead."

"Come, Paola," the other child said. "We must get out of here."

"I cannot move," the girl answered. "My mother has fallen over my legs."

"I will help you."

Sister Benni heard a sound from outside, and she called through the ripped and riddled curtain of the sacristy, "*Zzzzzzt!* Stay quiet, stay good, and we will leave when it gets darker."

Soon the door opened again, and a man's voice began to cry out, "Look at the slaughter! The swine! What barbarians they are!" At first, Sister Benni thought she was saved; the man spoke in the local dialect, and his voice sounded familiar. But then she remembered all the times the Germans had come into the room to make sure everyone was dead, and in her defenseless and debilitated state she suspected a trick. The man called, "Is anyone alive?" Sister Benni did not answer.

When the machine-gun firing had started again, Fernando Piretti had managed to hide himself completely under his dead mother, and he stayed there until the shots stopped and the door was slammed shut. But he could not remain where he was; he could hardly breathe, and his shoulder and neck were covered with a gum of blood. He wriggled like a snake until he had extricated himself, and then he laid his head on the cardboard briefcase in the position his mother had selected for him before she had been killed the night before. For a time he slept, and then he became aware that the Germans were back in the room, removing valuables and killing off the few remaining survivors. He waited for the bullet to rip into his skull; each time he heard a shot he thought it was his. He kept anticipating the impact of the bullet. He could hear the squashing sound as the Germans stepped on the bodies, and their yips and cries when they found something valuable, and their hoarse curses when they did not. And then, without knowing how, he knew that someone was straddling him. He held his breath. A hand slid under his head and lifted it off the suitcase. Fernando's body twitched in a conspicuous involuntary spasm. Now he knew he would be shot in the head. He waited. The suitcase was pulled out from under him, and he felt his head being lowered gently to the stone floor. Now it *must* come. But a few minutes later Fernando heard the soldiers leave the chapel, and he breathed again.

He did not move for hours. Once he thought he heard a small voice nearby, but he dared not open his eyes to check. When he did open them a slit and saw that the light had dimmed with the approach of the dusk of Saturday, he became terribly afraid that the Germans were coming back. He knew that he could not survive another of their visits, and he slowly pulled himself to his feet and wobbled toward the door. As he was about to step outside, he heard a whimper behind him, and he turned to see six-year-old Paola Rossi, niece of Maestra Serra, sitting against the wall, her face covered with blood. "You are still here, Paola?" he said wonderingly.

"You are still here, Fernando?" she said in a voice he could barely hear.

Paola wanted to know exactly who was dead, and Fernando had to tell her that everyone was dead, that no one else survived in the little chapel, and Paola insisted on running down the list of her relatives, name by name. When Fernando told her that they had to leave because the Germans would be coming back, Paola said, "I cannot move. My mother has fallen over my legs."

"I will help you," Fernando said, but he discovered that it was not just her mother's body that imprisoned Paola; several others had fallen on her. He pulled and shoved at the dead weight, but he could not free the wounded girl. Desperate, he ran to the door to see if there was anyone outside who could help him, and just then he heard a voice from the sacristy, back behind the curtains along the altar. "*Zzzzzzt!* Stay quiet, stay good," Fernando heard, and he ran back to his mother's side and lay down and shut his eyes.

He dozed again, and he was awakened by a loud male voice. "Mother," the voice was calling. "Mother! Where are you? I know you are here, Mother. Speak to me!" The man began crying hysterically, cursing the Germans, mourning his mother, crying out at the sight of the dismembered bodies. Fernando heard him gasp and then scream out, "Mother! Where are your legs? What have they done to your legs?"

Fernando lay silent as the voice moved to a far corner of the chapel. "Do not worry, Mother!" the man said. "I will find them."

For at least ten minutes Fernando listened to the hysterical man slipping and sliding around the chapel, carrying on long conversations with the body of his mother, and finally Fernando raised his head and cleared his throat. The man jumped back, and Fernando said, "Do not be afraid. It is only me: Fernando Piretti."

The man approached slowly. "Well, at least you are saved," he said, reaching out to touch Fernando's face.

"Another one lives," Fernando said. "Will you help me free this girl from her mother?"

The two of them pulled the bodies from Paola, and the man looked at her wounded face, and said, "Child, you are going to lose your eye!" and started to cry again. Paola tried to stand, but her legs would not support her, and the man picked her up. The three of them were starting to leave in the dusk when they heard a shrill voice from the altar: "Children! Stay here! Do not trust that man! He may be a Fascist."

The man said, "I am not a Fascist!" and broke into tears again.

"Stay, children!" the hysterical voice called. "We will leave alone, when it is darker. That man is a Fascist!"

"No!" the man cried out. "I am not a Fascist! I am a worker from Vado! My mother is lying dead here! Do not say that I am a Fascist!"

The conversation with the frantic voice from the altar continued for several minutes, and at last Fernando saw a form slowly climb to its feet, sink back, and stand up again. He recognized Sister Benni, the teacher of the *asilo*. "How did you save yourself, *Signorina?*" Fernando asked, and the teacher said, "It must be that God did not want me now."

Fernando went to help her, and when the circulation had been rubbed back into her legs, the four of them slipped out the door and started down the road that led from Cerpiano. Fernando kept looking in all directions, but he saw no Germans. "We will go to the air-raid shelter in the woods," Sister Benni whispered, and Fernando held his breath until they reached the end of the lane and dropped into the forest. There was an earthen cave only fifty yards away, and if the Germans had not already discovered it, the shelter would protect them for the night. As they approached the entrance, the man from

Vado began shouting, "Barbarians! Assassins! Murderers! They killed my mother!"

"Please," Fernando said, "do not raise your voice now!"

"You have saved us, and we thank you," Sister Benni said. "Do not give us away now!"

The man quieted, and as they came up to the entrance of the shelter, Fernando peeked inside and recognized five or six people. He ran from person to person and at last fell into the arms of his father, Maximiliano. Minutes later the sound of gunfire came from the chapel at Cerpiano. The Germans had returned.

The fifteen-year-old Lidia Pirini had tried all kinds of positions on the sodden ground of the cemetery, but no matter how she composed her limbs, the pain from her shattered hipbone suffused her body. Attilio Ruggeri and the others had gone to safety hours ago, and patrols of Germans had been marching by all morning, and Lidia doubted if anyone would come to help her now. For a while she had listened to vague moanings from the mound of the dead, but now even those sounds had ceased, and as far as Lidia could tell, she was the last living person in the cemetery. Then two events coincided: the old lady Gatti screamed again, and a German patrol passed by. Lidia could hear the soldiers chattering excitedly among themselves, and there was no doubt that they had heard the old lady's outcry. Like a snail, Lidia pulled herself across the ground and under the pile of bodies, just as a grenade whistled into the cemetery and exploded. The *vecchia* kept on screaming, and the Germans threw more grenades over the wall. When all was silent, they moved on, but Lidia could hear the old lady whimpering. She called out but got no answer, nor would she have known how to help if Signora Gatti had responded.

By Saturday noon a steady stream of German patrols was passing outside the gates, and now and then a few soldiers would step in to survey their handiwork. Lidia stayed under the pile and tried not to breathe, but sometimes the *vecchia* Gatti would cry out and draw more grenades. Still the Germans were not able to kill either of them, and Lidia remained under the bodies. She wondered how long it would be before the soldiers would grow weary of the game and come in with final bullets for both of them. The way the old lady was moaning and screaming, she seemed to be asking for a release from her pain.

Lidia decided not to die passively. When it was quiet outside the walls and the old lady was barely moaning, she crawled painfully from under the bodies and looked around. No living humans were in sight, although it was almost impossible to distinguish living from dead or men from women in the mound of bodies. The grenades had ripped and torn, and it was inconceivable to Lidia that anyone remained alive. She climbed to one foot and began hopping from tombstone to tombstone till she had reached the front gate. As she was getting up courage to go to the entrance, she heard a strange voice call from the bodies. "If you see my mother, tell her to come and get me," a young male said almost nonchalantly.

"Who is it?" Lidia called.

"Me, Dainesi. I am paralyzed."

Lidia recognized the voice of Albertino Dainesi, a fifteen-year-old refugee who had been staying with his mother at Cerpiano. "I will tell her," Lidia said, and crawled away as fast as she could.

In the woods, she found a forked stick, and using it as a crutch, she headed for the brook and Cerpiano, the last place she had seen her family alive. She could only move a few feet at a time, and then she would have to sink to the ground and rest. She could not put an ounce of weight on her bad leg; it felt as though the thighbone had torn from the socket and was jabbing into her insides whenever she moved. It took her an hour to reach the road to Cerpiano through thickets of brambles and acacia trees, and she stopped at a stone watering basin for a drink. By now it was clear that she would never make it to Cerpiano if she had to keep fighting the underbrush. All that lay between her and her family was 100 yards of narrow road, hung over on top and sides by a long tunnel of trees and vines. Lidia decided to run the risk.

She had not taken ten tortured steps along the road when she heard a clanking sound in rhythm, approaching from straight ahead. To her left there was a high wall of earth topped by trees, and to her right an impenetrable mass of brush. The sounds grew louder, and Lidia considered how she would appear to anyone who saw her now. Her wound had reopened, and a crimson rivulet ran down her leg. Her face was streaked with mud and gore, and her feet were bare and laced with deep scratches from the brambles. Her matted hair stuck out in bloody spikes. Standing on the side of the road with all her weight on the forked stick, she had no chance to pose as anything but what she was: a survivor of Casaglia, a witness to the massacre. She waited.

A squad of SS men came into sight, marching in metallic cadence, their camouflage uniforms heavy-laden with grenades and bombs and their arms brushing their sides in unison. Lidia moved as close to the edge of the road as she could, closed her eyes, and waited for the shot. The Germans clicked and clanked nearer and nearer, and now Lidia could feel them abreast of her. She assumed they would stop and ask a few questions before shooting her, or maybe they would just shoot her without a word. But even while these thoughts were racing through her head, the Germans had marched past, and the clanking was moving away. Lidia realized that they were going to stop down the road, line up in a firing squad, and shoot her in the back. She turned to face her executioners and waited, and then she realized that she could no longer hear a sound. She opened her eyes just in time to see the last soldier dipping over the hill and out of sight.

Lidia limped on toward Cerpiano. Halfway to her destination she passed an opening in the brush, and a shot rang out from the direction of Ca' Dizzola, up the hill. She turned and saw a single German soldier sighting through his rifle in a field about 100 yards away. She crawled madly across the road and dug a path through the brush and into the woods, ripping her nails and tearing her fingers in the thorny underbrush. She lay motionless in a cradle of bushes and weeds for two or three hours, and then she headed for the air-raid shelter of Cerpiano. She was only 40 or 50 yards away from the earthen cave, but she had lost her crutch in escaping from the German sniper, and she had to make her way on two hands and a knee. It took her an hour to reach the black mouth of the shelter, and she waited quietly outside to make sure no Germans were there. After a long silence, she screwed up her courage to look inside. She began to cry when she saw that the cave was full of her friends.

All day Saturday the wounded Lucia Sabbioni and the other three women stayed together in their woods hideout near Casetta di Casaglia, waiting for help. Lucia was crying and moaning from her pain, and the others were telling her that she would draw the Germans down upon them. They were hungry and thirsty and on edge from the constant gunfire that resounded from all around, but they hesitated to leave for fear that help would come and they would not be there to receive it.

Late in the afternoon Imelde Vegetti said to her daughter, Bianca, "I think we will go now, you and I. No one is coming to help us."

"And you intend to leave me with this screaming one?" said the middle-aged Clelia Monti, rising quickly to her feet.

"Please!" Lucia cried. "Please do not leave me!"

"How can we stay with you when you cannot keep quiet?" Bianca said.

"I will be quiet. I promise I will be quiet."

"You have been making that promise for twenty-four hours," the Vegetti woman said. "Now we can stay no longer."

Lucia tried to stand up. "I will walk with you!" she said. "You can not stop me from walking with you!"

"How can you walk?" Signora Monti said. "You cannot even stand."

"If you walk on that wound, you will get an infection," Imelde Vegetti said.

Lucia sprawled in the dirt and raised her arms beseechingly to the three women. "If you leave here, you murder me!"

"And if we stay here, you murder us!" the Vegetti woman said.

The three moved out of the clearing, and Lucia screamed after them: "Traitors! Assassins! Murderers!" She lay alone in the copse of trees for several hours and then began a slow journey on hands and knees and improvised crutches a mile to the valley below. More dead than alive, she reached the safety of a village where miraculously there were no Germans, and there she heard the news. The three who had left her in the woods were caught by the Germans and shot.

All through the morning Elide Ruggeri lay on the mattress in her kitchen and listened to the sounds of torment. A partisan had come and taken eight-year-old Vittorio Tonelli away, and now Elide's cousin Giuseppina Paselli was the only able-bodied person left in the room. Elide's aunt, Angelina Paselli, lay alongside on the mattress, and Giuseppina was trying to minister to her, but gradually the woman's condition grew worse. The dotted line above her knees had begun to turn an ugly purple, and blood still seeped out of the bullet holes, and the forty-nine-year-old mother was going in and out of coma.

Vincenzo Soldati lay on another mattress, and on those rare occasions when the five-year-old boy opened his eyes, he did not seem to know who he was or where he was. He had wounds in the leg and thigh, and the whole side of his head was discolored from concussion. He lay quietly, his breathing rapid and shallow, like a puppy that has run too fast.

Elide's own wound was painful, but by now she had poked and probed at herself enough to realize that the bullet had passed cleanly through her hip, missing the bones and the vital organs. There was no hot water to treat any of the victims, because they were afraid to light a fire, but Giuseppina brought clean water from the well and wiped away the clotted blood with clean rags. Elide knew that Attilio and Elena would be back after dark, and her cousin Cornelia Paselli was somewhere in the valley looking for help, and if the Germans would only stay away, she had a chance for life.

But the Germans came back. It was just before noon on Saturday, and Angelina had come out of her coma long enough to repeat over and over, "Cornelia is dead. I know Cornelia is dead," when there was a noise at the door.

"Hush, Mother," Giuseppina said. "Someone is outside." When the woman continued to moan, the fifteen-year-old girl clamped a hand over her mouth. Elide heard someone enter and walk through the stone hall, and all at once there were six Germans in the kitchen. Elide recognized the leader of the patrol. It was the blond officer who had interrupted his killing in the cemetery to make her comfortable against the wall. "There you are!" he said in heavily accented Italian. "I was wondering where you were hiding."

One of the soldiers asked the officer for instructions, and Elide noticed that he called the officer "Doctor." While the others rummaged through the house, the officer sat on the mattress and asked Elide how she felt. She said they all needed medicine for their wounds and asked if he was really a doctor. "Yes," he said, smiling and leaning over her, "and I have the best medicine for you." He opened his canteen and poured Elide a cup of broth. "Now do not worry," he said. "I have told you that no one will hurt you. We must go now, but as soon as I get a chance, I will come back to help."

"What of the others?" Elide said, pointing toward Angelina Paselli and the Soldati child.

The doctor did not move from the bed. "Time and rest are the best physicians," he said.

After a half hour the patrol reassembled in the kitchen, and the doctor spoke warmly in German to his men. Then he turned to Elide. "I told them they would not believe how much you look like my fiancée," he said. She did not comment, and the Germans prepared to leave. Before he walked out the door, the doctor leaned over her and whispered, "Do not worry, I will return to you."

In a few hours another group of Germans came into the house yelling and shouting and backed Giuseppina into a corner. When they loudly demanded her documents and she answered that she had lost them the day before, one of the Germans began shouting. "Always the documents are lost the day before!" he said. "Come with us!"

One of the Germans went outside to stand guard, and the other three shoved Giuseppina up the stone stairs to the second floor of the house. Elide heard the slam of a door and muffled voices. Then Angelina Paselli blinked back to consciousness and said softly, "Peppina?"

"She is not here, *Zia,*" Elide said. "She has gone for water."

Angelina raised her head and looked about the room. "She is dead!" she said. "Dead like Cornelia!"

Elide was trying to comfort her aunt when the first scream came from above them.

"Peppina!" Angelina called out, and there was another scream, followed by a loud call of "Mama!"

"That is my Peppina!" Angelina said. "What is happening to her?" She tried to stand but fell back heavily on the mattress. Elide tried to soothe her, but the screams from upstairs were growing louder and louder, and soon a hysterical colloquy was going up and down the floors between mother and daughter. The Germans stayed for three hours.

The nine-year-old Maria Tiviroli wandered through the woods all Saturday morning looking for her brothers, but they did not answer to her soft calls in the familiar hiding places around Steccola, and she thought they must have been killed in the *rastrellamento* like the others. Several times she started to return to the heaped bodies at Prunaro, but she was afraid that the Germans would fire on her again from the ridge above, and anyway she could see from a distance that nothing had changed: the dead were still dead.

Late in the morning she was walking on the path to Cadotto when she heard outcries from the other side of a grove of trees. She climbed away from the sound until she had a vantage point and recognized a young *contadino* of Cadotto, Mario Cioni, trying to make his way through the woods. He had improvised a crutch from a forked stick, but he seemed barely able to move. He would take a step, rearrange his whole body, and then thrust himself forward on the crutch, all the time sobbing loudly.

Maria ran to his side and tried to give him support from her own tiny body, and together they made their way 50 yards to an abandoned hut that once had been used for making charcoal. Cioni fell heavily to the floor of the hut and seemed to lose consciousness, and Maria found a rusty can and ran to the brook for water. She splashed part of it in the injured man's face and poured the rest into his lips, and when he revived, he rested for a while and then told his story. He had been in the house at Cadotto when the Germans attacked the partisan headquarters. Most of the partisans had got away, but four or five families of civilians had been massacred. He had jumped from a third-story window and hurt both legs. While he was dragging his useless limbs into the brush, two bullets had drilled through his shoulder, and he had spent the last thirty hours putting distance between himself and Cadotto, 300 yards away.

By midday, the wounded *contadino* and the small girl were famished, but a search of the surrounding area showed Maria that there were no chestnuts, no mushrooms and no berries to be found. "What do you have in your air-raid shelter back at Steccola?" Cioni asked. When Maria told him that there were emergency stocks of food hidden in the shelter, he begged her to go.

Maria followed the grown-over path through the woods until she could see the mouth of the shelter that the family had spent the summer hacking out of the mountainside. "A lot of good it did us," Maria said to herself, as she crouched in the brush and studied the opening. So far as she could see, nothing moved. She walked closer and watched again, and this time she thought she heard a small sound. She circled around until she was on the flank of the mountain above the opening, and then she crawled on all fours until she was exactly above the shelter entrance. Gripping the base of a *ginestra* bush by her feet, she stuck her head over the edge and took an upside-down look into the shelter. In a corner she thought she saw movement, and she quickly pulled her head back.

"Now what am I supposed to do?" she asked herself. "If I go inside the shelter, I will be killed. If I go back to the hut with nothing, we will both die of starvation."

She pondered the problem for several moments and made a decision. She crawled down from the mountain and stood about ten yards in front of the handmade cave, crouched like a sprinter on the blocks, and dashed for the entrance. If there were Germans inside, she would be killed instantly, and it would be over neatly and efficiently.

She burst into the cave, stopped, and waited. Nothing happened. As her eyes became accustomed to the dim light, she saw that everything was as they had left it the day before, and the shelter was unoccupied. Quickly she filled a *sporta,* a small wicker basket, with bread and cheese and added some rags for bandages, and on her way out she grabbed a heavy red and green blanket and towed it behind her. As she was hurrying along the path that led back to the hut, she was surprised to hear shots fired from the ridge above. She knew she was not completely concealed, but she had thought that the thin border of trees and brush was enough to keep the Germans from spotting her. As she lay in the weeds alongside the path, trying to shrink herself into a smaller target, she glanced behind her and noticed that she had been dragging the blanket red side up. Lying on her stomach, she turned the blanket over to the green and continued on her way.

Maria's stern older brother, Leonardo Tiviroli, and the other men of the ruling family of Steccola had fled southward to Monte Termine, one of Monte Sole's subordinate peaks, and from the shoulder of the mountain they had a clear view of the hundreds of fires that dotted the valley below, including one enormous blaze that came from the direction of their own *podere*. "You see, Father," Leonardo said to old Silvio Tiviroli, "we brought in more hay this year than any other farm."

The remark was lost on the patriarch. "If it were only hay that we lost," Silvio told his son.

Monte Termine lay directly on the route from Monte Sole to the front lines, and as the refugees from Steccola waited in the brush for the *rastrellamento* to end, they saw scattered bands of partisans fleeing south. From the direction of Monte Salvaro, minor skirmishes were breaking out, and Leonardo realized that the Germans must have sent patrols up from Grizzana to head off the exodus. Now and then one of the fleeing partisans would stop to talk for a few seconds, and by late Saturday morning the Tiviroli men were well aware of the extent of the massacre and their own loss. Leonardo wanted to go back to Steccola, but from where the men sat, they could see new fires being set along the ridge, and far in the distance uniformed patrols were visible.

The situation had not changed by Saturday afternoon, and Leonardo turned to his younger brother, Antonio, and said, "Now we go, you and I." On their way, they picked up a few hand grenades dropped by the partisans. When they drew near Steccola, Leonardo told Antonio to hide behind a tree while he made a *giro* of the ruins of the *podere*. In the backyard of the house he saw a pig and a cow wandering loose. Near the *casa colonica* he could make out the outline of the opening to the air-raid shelter, and he wondered who had put a blanket over the entrance. Taking out a grenade, he crept closer and now discerned the silhouette of a man sitting inside the flap in front of a reddish glow. Leonardo tiptoed to the corner of the hole and barely lifted the flap. The man sat with a rifle across his knees in front of a fire and a bucket of water. Leonardo recognized him as a partisan who had often stayed in the loft at Steccola.

He brushed the flap aside and walked in, and when the partisan jumped up and cocked the rifle, the former *Bersagliere* knocked it from his hands and said, "You will not need that here."

He saw that the partisan had begun to rummage in the lockers where the family linen and dishes were stored, and the idea of anyone's trying to vandalize the air-raid shelter in the wake of the German raid enraged Leonardo. "Look," he said, "I have no time for partisans. They are all a bunch of thieves, and you are no exception. I see you are interested in acquiring some new linens."

"I was only looking for food."

"Well, get out of here!" Leonardo snapped. "Everything in here is mine. Go steal from somebody else."

The partisan picked up his rifle and backed toward the door. "We must help each other, *Signore*," he said. "All the others are dead."

"What do you mean?"

"They killed everyone who lived here."

Leonardo took the man by the throat and hustled him out the entrance. "They are not *all* dead!" he cried. "It is impossible."

"I have heard that one little girl got away," the partisan said as he hurried off.

"Which little girl?" Leonardo called.

"I do not know her name," the partisan said, "but she lived in this house here."

Leonardo rushed back to the tree where he had left Tonino. "Someone lives!" he said. "It is Maria or Gina. We must look." They searched for an hour and found no one, and more than once they had to break for the woods when German patrols opened up on them from the ridge toward San Martino. At last Leonardo said, "We must get help. There are too many places to look." The two brothers returned to Monte Termine and led the other men of the family back to Steccola.

As they came in sight of the ruined farmhouse, old Silvio ran ahead and began folding a sheet that had flapped loosely in the backyard. Leonardo felt something snap in his distraught brain, and he called out harshly, "*Babbo!* What is wrong with you?"

"Che?" his father said, dropping the sheet.

"The whole mountain is on fire and our house is gone and everybody is dead, and you run around straightening the yard?"

"Yes, my son, I understand," Silvio said hoarsely. "It is only that I wanted to have something to do." While Leonardo stood helplessly, his father covered his face with his hands and turned away.

Although he could not see San Giovanni, where his wife and two sons were lying dead with fifty others in front of a pile of manure, Giuseppe Lorenzini had a clear view of the *podere* at San Martino from his hiding place on the side of the mountain. He had seen dozens of people going into Don Ubaldo's church at San Martino, and he knew of at least eleven of his own relatives who were inside. It puzzled him that there was so little German activity around the village. The bell tower of the church could be seen for fifty miles, and the walled cemetery stood conspicuously on the ridge, and there were several large buildings covered with yellowish *intonaco* stucco, including a three-story *casa colonica* and a barn and several stables and hayricks. If the Germans were after partisans, San Martino should have been one of their prime targets. Until Lupo had shifted the partisan headquarters to Cadotto and the *poderi* along the valley between Monte Sole and Monte Salvaro, San Martino had been the partisans' favorite place. But now it stood in a sort of limbo, totally surrounded by burning villages and busy German raiders.

The question puzzled Lorenzini all during the morning, but slightly after noon the matter was resolved. As he looked across 300 yards of open field, Giuseppe saw a patrol of twenty or thirty Germans march into the courtyard of the church. One of them slammed his gun butt against the door, and a horde of people spilled out. As Lorenzini watched with amazement, the people of San Martino tried to make a break for it, streaming in all directions across the fields, but other Germans were deployed in a ring. After a terrifying succession of howls and screams and several hundred rounds of machine-pistol bullets fired into the air, they succeeded in bringing everyone to the courtyard of the big house. Giuseppe could hear sporadic bursts of gunfire, and now and then someone in the crowd appeared to be tussling with the Germans, but in a matter of minutes some four or five dozen people were lined up against the wall of the *casa colonica.* Quickly the machine guns began, and when Giuseppe looked back at the scene, several SS men were walking along the row, shooting survivors with pistols.

After the Germans took a break from their labors, sprawling on the cobblestones and smoking cigarettes, they began stacking the bodies carefully, until they had a neat pile as tall as a man, and then they stuffed wood from a nearby cart into the spaces between the bodies to form a wall of flesh and wood. Giuseppe saw them pour fluid over the stack and ignite it, and the whole mass burst into flames twenty feet high. Once again he looked away, and when he turned back toward the pyre of his relatives, the Germans were gone, and the whole village was on fire.

Guerrino Avoni, a partisan of the *Stella Rossa,* made his way down from the top of Monte Sole on Saturday afternoon with a small group of survivors of the heavy German bombardment. If he had not known better, Guerrino would have sworn that the Germans had zeroed in on Zone X long before the raid began. They seemed to know the exact location of the partisans' emergency rendezvous, and heavy guns, including a railroad cannon fired from Vado, had sent shrapnel tearing through them all through the day and night, killing at least twenty and wounding others. Now a few partisan survivors were headed for the front lines, foraging for food as they moved, but as they approached San Martino, they could see that the village was a smoked heap. Guerrino took three or four men and reconnoitered the village where he had so many friends, and he saw that there were no Germans around. He waved the other partisans up, and together they walked into the village. They saw a large sign crudely lettered on the front of the church: THIS IS A WARNING TO THE ANTI-NAZIS AND THE ANTI-FASCISTS. A few feet farther on, the partisans found a charred heap of bodies, almost all of whom seemed to be women or children. As far as the partisans could tell, there were forty-five or forty-six.

Guerrino walked up and down the line, muttering to himself. He saw that four of the women had been pregnant, and their stomachs were laid open vertically and the fetuses exposed. Guerrino turned away. "Please," he said to the others, "have we not seen enough?" The group assembled quickly and returned to the woods in double time.

Duilio Paselli, Knight of Labor, and his grown sons, Antenore and Francesco, were hiding in the tall broomstraws near Le Scope for the second day in a row, and they had had no news about the loved ones they had left behind in the church at San Martino. It seemed to Antenore that ever since they had left the rectory the day before, *Babbo* had been on his knees praying. He had interrupted their flight several times to pray, and as soon as they had dug into a concealed burrow in the broomstraws, Duilio had knelt to speak to his various saints. All night long Antenore had awakened to hear the monotone of his father's prayers, and now that it was daylight on Saturday, Duilio continued. Antenore heard him addressing the Madonna and asking for clemency and salvation for the eight members of the family who had remained behind at San Martino. "I do not make any impossible promises just to impress," Antenore heard his father saying, "because I am an old man and there is a limit. But if my loved ones are spared, Blessed Virgin, I will do everything that my age and my power will allow. I am trying to be honest, Mother Mary. I am not promising more than I can do. I hope you will understand that."

When the sun was higher on Saturday, and gunfire had begun again in the distance, Duilio interrupted his prayers every few minutes to ask his sons, "Is there no way we can help them?"

And one of the sons would have to say, "No, there is not, *Babbo,* unless we want to get killed." From Le Scope the brothers had heard the massacres at Prunaro and Cadotto and Vallego, and they knew better than most that they were ringed by Germans who were killing everyone in sight.

Late in the afternoon the three Pasellis were met by a man from San Martino who had witnessed the massacre and now was headed for the front lines. While old Duilio sat trembling with anguish from head to foot and the brothers listened openmouthed, the man said, "They lined them up against the house and killed them, every last one, even a young man with his leg in a cast."

"That was my brother Dante," Antenore said, as Duilio set up an awful wail. "We had to leave him behind. He had an infected leg, and he could not walk."

"He was standing there with the rest of the people against the wall and when he said something loud to the Germans, one of them walked up and shot him in the head, and when that happened, a woman standing next to your brother with a baby in her arms ran out of the line and began calling them cowards and assassins. An SS man answered her in dialect and shoved her back against the wall. That is when the machine guns started."

"They were all killed?" Duilio asked.

"Not yet," the man said, "but then the Germans shot them with pistols and stabbed some of them with bayonets and stacked them up and burned them."

After a while the man made his farewells and went on toward the front, and Antenore and Francesco were left to cope with their distraught father. Duilio was lying full length on the soft earth while a new light mist of afternoon fell on him. "*Babbo,* are you praying?" Antenore asked.

"I will never pray again," his father said. "Never again." His eyes were red, and he looked one hundred years old. Antenore dropped to his father's side and took the hand of the old Knight of Labor. "Be courageous, *Babbo,*" he said.

"Antenore?" the father said.

"Yes, *Babbo?*"

"Do we have a pistol?"

Antenore was surprised. "You know we have no pistol, *Babbo.* We have never had a pistol."

Duilio was still for several minutes, and then he said, "Antenore, do we have a pin?"

"A pin?"

"Yes, a pin, a pin that holds your clothes up."

"What would you do with a pin, *Babbo?*"

The old man's face began working, and he tried to talk, but no words came out. He opened his mouth and pointed inside. "You mean you would swallow the pin?" the brother Francesco asked in disbelief.

"I would eat it," the old man mumbled, "and it would open a hole in my insides, and I would die, and my grief would be ended." The brothers left their father to his misery; they did not know what to do to comfort him. And they had no pin.

In the big square farmhouse at Ca' Roncadelli, a five-minute walk across the fields from the valley village of Sperticano, Vittoria Negri puttered about as though this were just another day. At twenty-six, Vittoria was the strength of her family: her slight frame and her button nose and her delicate pierced ears and her long black hair with highlights of auburn made her look the ultimate female, but everyone on the farm knew that Vittoria thought nothing of hefting a fifty-pound sack of flour and carrying it up the stairs or belting an over-ardent Casanova in the nose. She was the type of woman who walked down the road in the exact center, and when bicycles came whirling along, they swerved out of her way. She took life exactly as it came, becoming neither enthusiastic about the good times nor depressed about the bad. For example, she was going to marry Raffaele de Maria, and he was abroad with the Italian Army, but no one saw Vittoria weeping about it. More and more, as the young men of the family had gone to war or started spending their days hiding in the woods, Vittoria's old parents had come to lean on their strong, imperturbable daughter. Vittoria was aware of their dependency, and on this Saturday morning, September 30, 1944, when rumors filled the air and everyone who passed the house had a different horror story, she went to great pains to go about her duties in a routine manner, so as not to excite the *vecchi*. "Pay no attention to all that rumor!" she told her seventy-seven-year-old father, Gaetano. "It is not good for your health, *Babbo*."

The *podere* at Roncadelli had known some trying times lately, with Germans stomping through the neighboring village of Sperticano and taking hostages, and Blackshirts running around collecting impossible taxes, and corn and wheat lying unharvested in the fields because the able-bodied men had been terrorized into hiding. But Vittoria had never known another morning like this one. Just after dawn she had gone into Sperticano on an errand; and there she talked to Corina Bertacchi Fornasini, the sister-in-law of the parish priest, Don Giovanni Fornasini, and from Corina she learned that there was a big battle on top of Monte Sole.

"I can see nothing," Vittoria said, looking toward the peak. "How do you know?"

Corina explained that her poor husband, Luigi Fornasini, had been on the mountain the morning before, tending the family's sheep at San Martino, and wound up with a partisan band fleeing from the Germans. They had gone to the peak of Monte Sole, and there they were bombarded all day by German shells. Luigi had made it safely home, Corina said, and now he was in total hiding. Vittoria knew what *that* meant. Lately Giovanni Casalini, an old bricklayer of Sperticano, had developed a technique for making false walls on a moment's notice, and "total hiding" meant that Luigi Fornasini was sealed behind a brick wall in the basement of the rectory or the *contadino*'s house next door. The technique had saved many lives in Sperticano when the Germans were looking for young men to execute.

Vittoria asked where Don Giovanni was, and Corina explained that the priest had given up his bed to a wounded partisan named Socialista at about four in the morning, and just when Don Giovanni had made himself comfortable on a couch in the rectory, a hysterical woman had arrived and asked him to intercede for her husband, who had been picked up by the Germans in the mill town of Pioppe di Salvaro, a few miles to the south. That had been the last anyone had seen of Don Giovanni, and there were even rumors that he, too, had been arrested by the Germans.

Vittoria kept all this information to herself when she returned to Ca' Roncadelli. "A partisan passed by and said that the Germans were killing everyone!" her old mother said breathlessly as Vittoria came in the door.

"Yes, I met that partisan on the road," Vittoria said. "He is a liar."

Shortly after noon Vittoria heard faint gunfire from far up the mountain, but she said nothing about it, only exchanging meaningful glances with her three brothers, Fernando, Orfeo and Dante. But after an hour or two the shooting could be heard distinctly, and Vittoria called the family together. "There is no point in getting all excited over nothing," she said, "but there is also no point in letting them carry our men off to Germany. You boys must go into the woods and not come back until tonight. The rest of us will be in no danger." When the brothers left, Vittoria counted eleven in the big *casa colonica:* her own family, plus a few refugees from Bologna.

As the sounds of shooting began to move closer, Vittoria's sister-in-law, Olga Lolli, a highly nervous twenty-year-old, became hysterical and had to be put to bed in a back room. When shots came from the adjoining *podere* of Tagliadazza, Olga rolled on the bed and moaned, "They have killed my husband! I know it! He cannot run with his crippled leg. Oh, I just know it! Orfeo is dead!"

"Your *husband* Orfeo may be dead," Vittoria said sharply, "but my *brother* Orfeo is not." She softened her tone. "Now just be calm, Olga, and they will pass us by, and Orfeo will be back tonight."

Olga asked for her purse, and, crying and moaning, stuffed a handful of bills into her bodice. Several members of the family came in to sit around the bed and comfort the upset woman, and Vittoria went back into the living room to see what she could do for her aged mother and father. As she was telling them not to worry, there was a loud noise from the front door and four men in the uniform of the SS spilled into the house, led by an officer who carried a pistol. Old Gaetano sprang up, and the German grabbed him by the belt and stuck the pistol in his throat. Quickly Vittoria jumped between the two and put on her sweetest company manner, and the German stepped back and gave a smile of his own. "We have found your horse up the road," he said in Italian, "but we cannot find the saddle."

To herself, Vittoria said, "They found the horse themselves; let them find the saddle themselves." It was upstairs in a storage room, but she was not going to give them the satisfaction of leading them to it. She shrugged her shoulders as though to say that she knew nothing about the matter.

"Then you will not mind if we search?" the officer said.

"No," Vittoria said. "We will not mind."

The officer waved three soldiers up the stairs, and Vittoria followed them two steps at a time. Behind her came Egla Stefani, a refugee who knew a few words of German. The two women exchanged looks when the soldiers went straight to the storage room as though they had lived in the house for years. They ripped open the door, and there was the saddle on its pegs, the most conspicuous object in the room. One of the soldiers turned his pistol on Vittoria and said, *"Kaput!"* but another one interceded, and the search party walked into one of the bedrooms, with the two women still following. "What is this?" a German shouted. He had found the hat of Vittoria's brother Dante, left on the post of the old iron bed when Dante had fled the house.

"My brother's hat," Vittoria said in Italian.

"Dov'è fratello?" the German said. "Where is brother?"

Vittoria knew the German word for "writing," and she thought it would make an impression on the soldier if she spoke in his language, so she said, "He is *schreiben* at the municipal building in Marzabotto."

"No," the German said. "He hides. He is a partisan."

Egla Stefani said softly in dialect, "Vittoria, tell them he is fighting with the German Army. Tell them he is a comrade-in-arms."

"Camerata!" Vittoria said, pointing to the hat. *"Il mio fratello è camerata."*

The soldiers led them downstairs, and now Vittoria could see that eleven or twelve of their neighbors from Tagliadazza had been brought into the house at the point of the German machine pistols. The officer who had threatened her father pointed to the roomful of frightened people, beckoned Vittoria aside, and said not unpleasantly, "You have it in your power to save the lives of all these people. Are any of them related to you?"

"Almost all of them are related to me," Vittoria said.

"Then you will be happy to save them. You only have to tell me where the partisans are."

"I have no idea where the partisans are."

"Then *tutti kaput!*"

Remembering that her brothers were hiding outside the house,

Vittoria said, "The partisans are high on the mountain. We have no partisans around here."

The officer began to show annoyance. "What are these?" he said, pointing to a row of framed photographs of brothers and loved ones in uniform.

"Members of our family serving in the military."

"No, they are not!" the officer shouted. "They are partisans! Where are they? Go get them!"

Vittoria did not know how to answer, and the officer lined everyone up in two rows and began to count. There were twenty-two, and he ordered the soldiers to enclose them in the bedroom where Olga Lolli was moaning. When they all had been squeezed into the room with kicks and shouts and threats, the door was shut, and Vittoria heard the officer shout, "Anyone who leaves will be shot!"

At once the dialogues broke out. "As long as we stay in here, they cannot do anything to us," a voice said.

"Remember the count: twenty-two," another said. "Every one of the twenty-two of us must stay together."

A few of the children were crying, and over the noise came the sobs of Olga Lolli, now forced back against the headboard of her bed by the press of bodies. "Poor Olga!" someone said, and Vittoria heard another answer, "Poor all of us!"

After an hour or so in the close atmosphere of the room, Vittoria begged everyone to be completely quiet, and she put her ear to the heavy door. *"Zzzzzzt!"* she said again, and waved her hands for silence. She listened for two or three minutes and then told the group, "They are gone! There is not a sound out there!"

"But we must stay in here, Vittoria," her mother said. "The commander told us."

"We will stay for a while and see what happens," Vittoria said.

A single small window in the back of the bedroom faced the corner of the barn and a haystack, and daylight was beginning to fade when a refugee woman peered out into the shadows and said, "*Zzzzzzt!* Germans!"

Vittoria looked out and saw a group of eight or nine heavily armed soldiers marching into the barnyard from the direction of Tagliadazza. "We must stay absolutely still!" Vittoria whispered. "Do not make a sound."

One of the Germans flipped a lighted match into the haystack. "They are burning!" the nervous refugee at the window said frantically.

"Remain still!" Vittoria said in a loud whisper.

When one of the soldiers tossed a red bomb into the barn, the whole *podere* seemed to break out in flames, and the nervous woman stood up and shouted, "We will be burned alive!" Before Vittoria could stop her, she had stuck her head out the window and screamed at the Germans to save them.

The soldiers looked up with surprised expressions, and seconds later a pair of them in camouflage suits and belts of grenades and carrying machine pistols came to the door and ordered everyone out. They seemed to be in a hurry, and even before the last of the captives were hustled out the front door of Ca' Roncadelli, one of the soldiers threw an incendiary bomb on the stone floor of the hallway. The last few stragglers stepped around the sputtering round ball and into the dusk. Two Germans were standing just outside, ordering everyone to move along, and two others stood at the edge of the stone courtyard, beckoning the group toward a narrow brook 50 or 60 yards away. Vittoria looked for a way to escape, but there were armed Germans on all sides, even down below in the field. She heard a commotion and turned to see two of the soldiers dragging a struggling young woman into the group.

"Let me go!" the woman said. "I am doing nothing wrong. I am only going to buy eggs."

Vittoria recognized a young bride, Lina Casalini, carrying a basket on her arm. Apparently she had been walking up the path to take food to her husband, hiding in the brush. The Germans shoved her in with the others, and the group became twenty-three.

"Raus! Raus!" the Germans were shouting, and Vittoria stepped to the front and began walking toward the brook. The others followed slowly, and Vittoria noticed some soldiers matching them stride for stride in the field 2 or 3 yards below the upraised path. She hurried along, and two ten-year-old boys, Nino Amici and Sereno Zagnoni, caught up and clung to her skirts. Behind them stretched the disorganized group, with her aged parents bringing up the rear. As Vittoria looked over her shoulder, a rifle cracked from below and behind the stragglers, and her father fell heavily. A second shot spun

her mother to the ground, and the people in front of these first victims increased their pace and brought the whole group into a swarming, hysterical mass.

Now they were almost to the brook, and Vittoria could see two soldiers sitting behind a machine gun on one side of the path. The brook came down a steep earthen slope, ran flat in the open for about 6 yards opposite the gun, and then dipped into a heavily wooded ditch about a yard deep. Vittoria and the two boys were the first to reach the open space, and they jumped across the brook ahead of the swarm of terrified people. As the mob closed up like a human wall between them and the machine gun, she shoved the boys into the ditch, and at the first sounds of machine-gun firing, she broke up the slope of Monte Sole. She had gone about 30 yards through a vineyard when the first bullets began pinking into the earth around her like hailstones. As she kept running higher and higher, she heard the machine gun stop momentarily, and then the blast of a grenade, and then the machine gun again. She hid behind a hillock, but bullets began to come at her from another direction, and she raised her head to see. Level with her but 50 yards away on the slope, a German rifleman sighted on her. Vittoria heard a shot and a snapping sound from the trellis, and then she saw that the German had lowered his gun and was starting to run across the vineyard in her direction. As she ran, she heard another shot, and her thigh felt as though a giant bee had stung her. She knew she was wounded, but the pain only had a stimulating effect, and she climbed Monte Sole faster than she ever had before. She had gone something like 200 yards up the steep slope when she tripped and fell, and when she discovered she could not regain her feet, she rolled into a shallow ravine and waited for one of the bullets to find her. The earth was erupting in gray spurts around her, and she could hear the ripping sound of machine pistols from the path below. She buried her face in the dirt and tried not even to breathe, and she kept saying to herself, "Which one will get me?" She had asked herself the question about ten times when the firing stopped.

Fat old Gaetano Rosa was grumbling in the house at Colulla di Sopra, high above the cliff overlooking Ca' Roncadelli and the village of Sperticano. For two days now, the best card player and wine drinker on Monte Sole had been unable to leave the house to play *brescla* in the inn of Sperticano, and his patience had grown short. "Listen," he said to his foster son, Mario Zebri, "I am seventy-five years old. What do I care if I run into some German idiots on my way down the mountain?"

"The rest of us care, *Babbo,*" Mario answered. "There has been shooting around here all day, and I am told there has been killing, too."

"Which way am I to die?" Gaetano asked. "Of shooting or of thirst?"

The argument resumed sporadically throughout the day, and finally Mario said to the old man, "*Babbo,* let us talk of it no more. Sometimes it is wise to be afraid."

"It is not wise to be afraid of idiots," old Gaetano said, and he climbed heavily up the stairs to visit at the bedside of his paralyzed wife, Enrica Quercia, and belabor this captive audience with his hardships.

It was about three in the afternoon of Saturday, September 30, 1944, and the skies were poised between rain and overcast, when Mario saw soldiers coming around the mountain from the direction of Abelle. "They are here!" he shouted to his twenty-four-year-old son, Pietro.

The Germans drew closer, and Mario and his son watched through the window to see whether they would take the turnoff toward the house. When they did, Mario's wife and daughters and eleven-year-old son, Bruno, set up a clamor. "Get out!" they shouted. "Hide! They will take you both off to Germany!"

"How can I leave with German soldiers on their way?"

"They will not harm us," his wife said, shoving Mario and Pietro out the back door. "It is you men they are after. Go! We will see you tonight."

Father and son ran across the field to a ditch about 100 yards from the house. The ditch was shallow and exposed, and they dared not raise their heads for fear they would be seen. After a few minutes they heard a long, piercing scream. "Who was that?" Mario whispered.

"Mama," Pietro answered.

The postman lay in the weeds above Ca' Roncadelli, cursing softly to himself. He cursed the mountain, the rain, the Germans and the day of his birth. Only a few months before, the postman had reckoned himself the luckiest of men, with a lovely wife and two beautiful children, a pleasant job and hundreds of friends who pressed food and wine and gifts upon him. And now what did he have? Scratches from head to foot, rings of fiery, itchy redness where the nettles had assaulted his ankles, and a stomach that was tied in a knot from hunger. He did not even know if his wife and children were safe back in Sperticano, although he had never heard of any German cruelty to women or children. The rumor had gone out two nights before that there would be a major raid against the male population, and ever since then, the postman had been lying in this inhospitable patch of brambles above the Negri house at Roncadelli. His wife had brought him some food this Saturday morning in his mail pouch, and since then he had been alone.

It distressed the postman that the whole region of Monte Sole could change overnight from a Garden of Eden to a wet hell where innocent men had to run and hide in the rain for no reason whatever. He shook his head, thinking of the speed of the metamorphosis. Only six months before, on the night of the Monday after Easter, the postman had gone up this same mountain with forty of his friends from Sperticano. Everyone had a bottle, and as they climbed toward Caprara, they sang "The Bridge of Bassano" and knocked back their delicious *negrettino* and played the game of *chiamaloste*. Someone would throw a *boccie* ball into the crowd, and the one who was nearest and the one who was farthest had to pay two soldi each, and then the next one threw the ball, and two more victims had to pay, and so the revelers went up the mountain, accomplishing the one-hour climb in three hours flat. There was not a sober face in the crowd of men who reached Caprara. There they found 150 eggs on a table, and within seconds they converted them into a pile of shells. Every man bought a new bottle of wine from Luigi Massa, and the game began all over again, and finally the forty men from Sperticano and another forty men from the mountainside lurched and wobbled back down the mountain to the fountain of Sperticano, and when the postman staggered out of his bed to deliver his mail the next morning, he found the square littered with empty bottles and paper hats and discarded shoes.

Could all that have happened only six months ago? The postman watched a drop of water form on the tip of his nose and drip on his soaked shirt. Another question came to mind: How could a man call himself a man and put up with this all-day humiliation? For one of the few times in his life, the postman found himself on the brink of rage. He had always hated the war, but that was a sort of concealed, restrained hatred, fully under control and shared with his comrades. The rain and the spasms in his stomach and the fire around his ankles and the scratches on his hands confronted him more directly, and at last the postman wriggled to his feet and shouted at the sodden trees around him, "Enough! I have had enough!" He picked up his leather mail pouch, squared his soggy gray cap with the red stripe and the tinny medallion, and marched toward Roncadelli and the road toward home.

"Now I am alive again," the postman said to himself as he walked down the mountain. "Anything is better than sitting up there alone and stupid." He stepped out of the brush and onto the road and almost tripped over three men in German uniforms.

For an instant the postman thought of turning back the hands of time by the simple expedient of stepping into the woods and returning to his hiding place and pretending that he had never left. But one of the Germans, his middle sagging from a belt of grenades, said, "Where are you going?"

"I have just finished delivering my mail," the postman said. "I am going home."

"Soc' me!" the soldier said in dialect. "Suck me! You are not going anywhere. Come with us!"

The postman walked in the middle of the three men, and as they approached Roncadelli, he could see that another patrol was herding twenty or twenty-five people down the path toward the brook. "You will take us to the place where we can cross the river!" the soldier who spoke dialect announced. "Then you will see what we do to partisans!"

"I am no partisan," the postman said.

"Soc' me!" said the other.

Now they dropped to a lower field and out of sight of the people of Roncadelli. They walked quietly for several hundred yards, until they intercepted the narrow road that led from the house at Roncadelli to the village of Sperticano. The postman had heard a few scattered shots, and as they reached the road, he heard a long burst of machine-gun fire, and his head snapped to the left, toward the place where the Germans had been leading their prisoners. Down a narrow lane of grapevines, he saw that the Germans were firing into a crowd of people. The postman stood fixed to the ground, shocked, and when the first long burst ended, he heard the cry of a small child. He watched three-year-old Marisa Amici toddle out of the mound of bodies and start to crawl up the mountain. As the postman watched, the ground exploded around her, and she fell on her side and did not move.

"What are you waiting for?" the Italian-speaking man said. "Soon it will be dark, and we have to be away from here."

The postman led the way toward Sperticano, and as they rounded a bend just below the church, they came upon four bodies. The postman recognized Tommasina Marchi and Mercede Bettini and their children, and he saw that they had been bayoneted to death. Another patrol of five or six Germans was preparing to fire a towering pile of hay. Once again the postman stopped involuntarily, and one of the Germans said, *"Komm! Komm!"*

The four men marched into Sperticano, and when they were passing his house on the main street, the postman was horrified to see his wife and two children standing in the entranceway. When they saw that he was surrounded by German uniforms, they set up a loud caterwauling, and the postman wished they would suddenly evaporate into the air. "Who are these?" he was asked.

"My wife and children," the postman said.

The German hesitated, looked back and forth from the postman to the others, and then said, *"Komm!"*

A few hundred yards down the hill they came to the temporary wooden bridge that had replaced the old cable bridge of prewar years, and the postman said, "There is your bridge."

The Italian in SS uniform shoved him against a mound of dirt and said, "Now admit you are a partisan!"

"I am no partisan," the postman said. "I am in the postal service. Here is my identification card."

The soldier grabbed the card and was studying it when one of the Germans, a sergeant, pointed back up the road and said to the postman, *"Raus! Raus!"*

The postman did not understand.

"You heard the sergeant!" the Italian said. *"Avanti!"*

The postman ran toward Sperticano so fast that he was not even aware of his feet hitting the ground. At first, he had expected a bullet in the back, but when nothing happened, the tears began to stream down his face, and crying and running, he reached his house in a few minutes. His wife and children were still at the door, and when they saw him, they started wailing twice as loud as before. "Angelo, Angelo," his wife said, falling on his neck, "we were sure you were on your way to Germany." The postman beckoned his family inside the house and bolted the heavy door with trembling hands.

When the shooting stopped, Vittoria Negri lay on the mountainside high above Roncadelli for several minutes without moving, as her normal senses gradually returned, and then she began to hear outcries from the brook below. She decided to stay where she was until there was no question that the Germans were gone, but after fifteen or twenty minutes she said to herself, "*Babbo* and Mama are dead. I saw them die. Nothing remains for me. I might just as well be down there as up here. If I die, I die." Clutching the sides of her head with her hands, she staggered down the mountain toward the brook. By now it was almost dark, and the first person she ran into was her thirty-two-year-old brother, Fernando, who had watched the scene from the top of a nearby oak tree. As Vittoria stumbled out of the brush, scratched and bleeding, Fernando said, "How does it happen that you are alive?"

Vittoria did not answer. For the life of her she could not remember how she had escaped from the pile of bodies that now lay in disorder in the stream running red with blood.

"Qui tutt' mort'," the brother said softly in dialect. "Here all are dead."

They heard a sound from the wooded wall where the stream dropped down a ledge, and Fernando ran to help his crippled brother, Orfeo, over the side. "I cannot walk," Orfeo said. "I was hiding in such a cramped space, my bad leg is now useless."

The three of them peered at the bodies. "Did you see my Olga?" Orfeo said.

"Here," Fernando said. Three big wooden vats had been soaking in the brook, closing their seams for the grape harvest, and alongside one of them lay the body of Orfeo's wife, Olga Lolli, the woman who had been hysterical even before the German arrival. Vittoria helped Fernando pick her up, and they could see that she was chopped almost in half at the stomach. Intermingled with bits of flesh Vittoria could see the sliced remnants of reddish Italian bills bearing the picture of King Victor Emmanuel.

"Wait!" Orfeo cried out. "Someone lives!"

Fernando and Vittoria hurried to his side, and the two ten-year-olds, Sereno Zagnoni and Nino Amici, rose dripping and trembling from the ditch where Vittoria had thrown them. Then a sound came from the bodies, and a pale arm reached out toward the little group of survivors. "Help me!" a voice said, and Fernando and Maria pulled aside some bodies to find eleven-year-old Marisa Tomesani only slightly wounded in the shoulder. They pulled her out, and as they did, Maria saw that the child's mother was lying dead alongside. Both her breasts had been shot off, and it looked as though she had shielded her daughter from the worst of the gunfire. Marisa's thirteen-year-old brother, Anselmo, lay groaning and groping at wounds in his stomach and his knees, and a red foam bubbled from his mouth. Before Vittoria could move him out of the brook, he closed his eyes and stopped breathing. Seventy-seven-year-old Rita Santini was alive upside down in one of the vats, but she died almost as soon as they could pull her out.

Vittoria and her brothers began to separate the bodies into two rows: the dead in one and the living in the other. Vittoria hesitated at nine-year-old Annamaria Amici. The child's eyes were open, and she was trying to talk, but her chest was caved in by bullets, and Vittoria knew she would die. She laid the child in the row of the living. Another child, Emilia Carboni, Vittoria's niece, was pulled out wounded, but alive. Fernando retrieved the body of a cousin, forty-two-year-old Maria Negri, and saw that her face was covered with blood and one eye bulged half out of its socket. "Which row are you going to put me in, Fernando?" Maria Negri said, and Fernando gently laid her with the living.

When they had finished separating the bodies, Fernando and Vittoria left their brother Orfeo to watch over the wounded and hurried back to the house for sheets to make bandages. On the way they came to the solitary bodies of their mother and father. "Look at them," Vittoria said. "Our two old ones. They brought up twelve children, and this is how they end."

As brother and sister walked in the rainy darkness toward the house, Fernando began to cry, and Vittoria put an arm across his shoulders. "In all the world I have never heard of things like this,"

Fernando said. "This did not happen, sister. Such things do not exist."
"D'altro mondo," Vittoria said. "It is of another world."

Augusto Massa, brother of the storekeeping Luigi and the *contadino* of the church's land at Casetta di Casaglia, did not sleep at all after he learned that his wife and two children had died in the cemetery. With his remaining sons, Pompilio and Dante, Augusto spent the night wandering in search of consolation, and toward daybreak on Saturday he was reunited with another of his brothers, Giuseppe, who had lost his own wife and daughter at San Giovanni. The bereaved brothers left the two young boys in a heavy thicket near Cerpiano, and as soon as they stepped out of their hiding place to look for food, Augusto and Giuseppe Massa were captured by the Germans.

They were thrown down the steps of the *palazzo* at Cerpiano, and they stayed in the dark basement for five hours, until just before noon, when they were haled before a German officer holding court in one of the classrooms. Several soldiers carried on a rapid-fire conversation with the officer, while the brothers were ignored. After about ten minutes of discussion the Massas were taken outside on the piazza, where a detachment of some fifty German soldiers had lined up. Neither Augusto nor Giuseppe had ever seen so heavily armed a group. Half the soldiers carried machine pistols, and the other half was armed with rifles, grenades and mortars. Two of the soldiers carried flamethrowers.

While they were gaping at the helmeted soldiers in their camouflage suits, a corporal led the brothers to a stack of boxed mortar shells and ordered each to load up. The detachment moved off with the Massas staggering under the weight of the heavy ammunition. They marched from Cerpiano to Ca' Dizzola to Bergadella and back to Cerpiano, but they found no living being, and except for the firing of an occasional haystack, there was nothing to break the monotony of the work.

After the soldiers had stopped to eat, ignoring the two exhausted brothers, they moved over the western edge of Monte Sole and began picking their way down toward the terraced *poderi* at Colulla di Sopra, Colulla di Sotto, Abelle, Tagliadazza and Roncadelli. An officer ordered a halt just below Abelle, where the Marchi family lived, and while most of the troops relaxed and smoked and whispered among themselves, sentries were posted, and the two brothers saw a squad of seven or eight Germans creep toward the house. Machine-gun fire rang out, and then the big rectangular *casa colonica* burst into flames.

After a while the soldiers who had gone ahead to Abelle waved a signal toward the ones waiting below, and the support detachment moved on to Colulla di Sopra, the Zebri *podere,* where they again waited 100 yards down the mountain while the advance squad went straight to the house, fired their guns and set everything ablaze. The pattern was repeated several more times. While the big detachment stood guard with their flamethrowers and mortars and other weapons, the killer group went ahead and scorched the earth. By nightfall the Germans and their two Italian bearers had reached the Reno River and the town of Pian di Venola, where a convoy of German trucks pulled up in a cloud of exhaust and waited with motors running while the soldiers jumped aboard. A Blackshirt was helping direct the traffic, and Augusto and Giuseppe heard him say that the Allies had broken through the lines to the south and every German soldier was being rushed to fill the gap. The trucks slammed into gear and raced down the highway, and the brothers Massa ducked into a hedge and ran back to their hiding place near Cerpiano.

Augusto's sons lay quietly in the thicket where their father and uncle had left them. *"Babbo,"* Pompilio said. "We are dying of hunger. Where have you been?"

"We were detained," Augusto said. "We will try to eat tomorrow."

Mario Zebri and his son Pietro lay unmoving in the ditch until late in the afternoon, or long enough to hear shots and screams from their own *podere*. The sounds were the same all afternoon; a short time later, they would be repeated farther down the mountain. The terror seemed to follow the contours of the land—the *podere* below theirs at Colulla di Sotto, the one around the ridge at Abelle, and the lower farms of Tagliadazza and Roncadelli—and smoke and flames marked each stop on the trail.

As Mario tried to get comfortable in the shallow ditch, it troubled him that he had kept his old foster father, Gaetano Rosa, from making his daily trip to the *osteria* in Sperticano. At the time he had only been trying to protect the old man from the *rastrellamento* that was in progress. It seemed safer in the big *casa colonica* than on the path to Sperticano. But now he wondered. If anything had happened to the old man, it would go hard on Mario's conscience. Mario had been a thirteen-month-old baby lying in an orphan's home when Gaetano and his wife, Enrica Quercia, adopted him, and he had never known any other parents. In every way, he had been treated as a child of their blood.

By an effort of will, he shifted his thoughts from the prospect that his devoted foster parents were dead, along with almost everyone else he loved. He forced himself to think about more pleasant times, and when one memory came back to him, he even managed a little laugh. Don Giovanni Fornasini, the priest of Sperticano, had visited the Zebri home only a few days before, and he had told Mario, "You know, I am not supposed to reveal what is said in the confessional, but I am going to break the rule once. Your old *Babbo,* Gaetano, was in to see me yesterday, shouting out his sins so half the church could hear, as usual, and when he finished I said to him, 'You know, Gaetano, you need a lot of good deeds to get into paradise.' He said, 'Tell me, *Reverendo,* when somebody makes a perfect wine, an exquisite wine, would you consider that he had done a good deed?' And I thought, and I said, 'Well, I suppose in one sense you could say that he had done a good deed, at least for those who would drink the wine.' And your *Babbo* threw back his head and laughed so loud that he could be heard at the fountain, and he said, '*Whay, Reverendo,* then I will be catapulted into heaven. I have drunk more good deeds than anyone in my time! I have drunk thousands of good deeds,' and he walked out without another word."

Mario's memories were interrupted by Pietro. *"Babbo,"* he said, "I am not staying here a second longer."

"Where do you want to go?" Mario asked.

"I want to go home."

Father and son headed across the field in the late afternoon, but Pietro was almost running, and soon Mario found himself twenty or thirty yards behind. The son reached the raised front yard of the house and ran up the embankment, and suddenly Mario saw him stop. Slowly Pietro backed down the terrace, motioning for his father to halt. When Mario kept walking, Pietro called out, "Do not go up there! Stay, *Babbo!*"

"Why?"

"Everyone is dead."

Mario hurried up the embankment. There were seven bodies. Gaetano lay about ten yards from the others, as though he had tried to run, and there was a hole the size of a fist in his chest. The old man was on his side, and his knee was raised in futile self-defense. Mario straightened his foster father's legs, and as he did he saw that a bayonet had pierced through the wallet that Gaetano always carried in his vest.

When he had rearranged the body, Mario went to his eleven-year-old son, Bruno, and for a moment he thought the boy still lived. Blood flowed from Bruno's nose, and as Mario tried to pick his son up to help him, the body came apart in the middle.

"Babbo!" he heard Pietro shout from below. "Come away! Stop, *Babbo!* You cannot help them now."

Mario stepped to the body of his seventeen-year-old daughter, Bruna. She had been pregnant, and he could see a large hole where her abdomen had been. Next to Bruna was the body of seven-year-old Vittoria Paganelli, a niece who had been staying with the family as a refugee.

"Come, *Babbo,*" Pietro said.

"Let us at least be sure no one is alive," Mario said.

"No one is alive," Pietro said.

No one was. The crumpled bodies of Mario's wife, Florinda Gigli, and his foster sister, Clelia Rosa, both forty-two years old, and his oldest daughter, Mathilde, nineteen, lay in a neat line, with three or four empty machine-gun belts at their feet.

"And what of *Nonna?"* Mario said. "*Nonna* is not here." They approached the house to see if they could get to the room where the old lady had been confined with paralysis, but the whole inside of the house had tumbled into the basement, and all that was left was a shell.

Bruno pointed into the smoldering ruins. "Someday we will find her there, *Babbo,*" he said. "There is no place else she can be."

"I will pray every chance I get," Mario said, "that she was dead before they burned the house."

Father and son sat on the edge of the courtyard and watched the last flake of sunlight slip from Monte Sole. A damp breeze had sprung up, and clouds were assembling in the west. Now and then one of their pigs or cows would wander by, sniffing the air and bawling, but neither man made any effort to round them up. After they had sat with their dead for a while, they occupied themselves for another hour improvising a fence of charred boards around the bodies, to protect them from the animals.

"Pietro," Mario said when they had finished, "I know this will sound peculiar, but I want to find someone else to talk to."

"Where can we go, *Babbo?*"

"Anyplace," he said, and choked back his sobs, "anyplace where there are people."

The two men began to walk toward the foot of the mountain. The first *podere* below them was Colulla di Sotto, where fourteen members of the Laffi family lived with four refugees from Bologna. As the two Zebris approached the home of their neighbors, they saw that the place glowed with coals, and they heard a persistent whacking sound, as though someone were chopping wood on the far side of the house. Pietro called out, "Ettore! Marina! Primo!" and when there was no reply, the two men stepped up to the raised patio and saw that the house had fallen in on itself. No one was in sight, so they walked around to the barn. Eighteen bodies lay charred and bare alongside the hayloft. Some of them had blown up to twice their size from the heat. None of the bodies had any remaining hair, and their color was a dull red. As the two men hurried away, they heard a groan. They turned back to look for the source of the sound, but all the bodies looked dead, from the sixty-year-old patriarch to the newest of the Laffis: twenty-four-day-old Giovanni.

"Let us go away from here," Pietro pleaded again. "Whoever it is will be beyond help soon enough, no matter what we do."

As they walked from the barnyard toward the back of the *casa colonica,* the woodchopping sound seemed to grow louder, and in a pigpen they found an old sow standing by her ten scorched piglets, butting her head over and over again at the locked gate. Her skin was pink where the fire had seared off her bristles, and her little eyes rolled wildly in her head. Long after the two men had wandered across the ridge toward the next *podere* at Abelle, they could hear the old sow trying to escape.

At Abelle, they found another smoking house and more bodies. On the edge of the raised cobblestone courtyard, the young woman Argia Monti sat on a rock with her arms cradling her head. "Argia," Mario called, "what are you doing out here?" When there was no answer, he gave the girl a shake by her shoulder, and she toppled over and looked past him with eyes that did not blink. Nearby were the bodies of two young women, Giuseppina Balugani and a refugee whom Mario and Pietro did not know. Both women were naked except for a string of elastic that clung around their middles like tattered belts: the remains of their underpants. The Balugani woman's three-month-old child, Iole Marchi, lay in two pieces next to its mother; the unborn child of the other woman had been ripped from her body and torn to pieces. One part lay between the woman's legs, another against her naked breast.

"What are we doing here, *Babbo?*" Pietro asked his father as they stood on the courtyard in the early evening darkness.

"We came to find someone to talk to," Mario said.

Pietro swept his hand toward the five bodies on the courtyard. "There they are," he said. "Do you want to look for somebody to talk to at Ca' Roncadelli?"

"No," Mario said.

Father and son walked the mile to the church at Sperticano, but the priest, Don Giovanni Fornasini, was not at home.

A leaden sun came up on the morning of Sunday, October 1, 1944, the third day of the *rastrellamento,* but it did not warm the inside of a livery stable in the mill town of Pioppe di Salvaro, where sixty men prepared to begin their third uncomfortable day of imprisonment. Gioacchino Piretti, a powerfully built machinist with a crew cut, oversize ears like parchment, and light-hazel eyes, started the day by thanking God that at forty-five years of age he was still fit and healthy. Others in the group were not, and some of the older men were beginning to weep in an almost irrational manner. So far, no one had been killed, but Gioacchino did not doubt for a second that the Germans would open fire on the whole room if they were provoked.

He wondered what his wife was doing and how he could get a message to her. But there was only one window in the place, and it was too high in the wall to reach. Besides, he knew what would happen if he moved. A sentry at the open door had a stack of empty wine bottles, and whenever one of the prisoners started to rise to his feet or even craned his neck to see over the other heads—*zing!*—an empty wine bottle would come whirling at him and splatter against the wall. The game seemed to titillate the Germans. No one had been hit, but the floor was covered with broken glass, making it all the more vital that the men remain stationary in their squatting positions.

As the early morning light filtered in through the small window and the opened door, Gioacchino could make out the silhouettes of some of his fellow captives. He knew there were at least three priests in the stable, and a few men he had known in his childhood, and at least one wounded man, whose name, in dialect, was Barcein. The wounded man emitted small moans from time to time, but since they were all under threat of death if they uttered so much as a single word, Barcein managed to swallow most of his pain.

To Gioacchino, the scene was further proof of a proposition he had long defended: that although the men in charge of war operations may be brave, self-sacrificing and patriotic, mostly they are simply stupid. The Allies were advancing only twenty or twenty-five miles to the south, and here at Pioppe a crack detachment of SS was wasting days of its time torturing a bunch of aging civilians, within whose ranks were men like himself who had critical war jobs. Some worked in the hemp mill at Pioppe, where woven war matériel was turned out, and others worked in the artillery factory at Vergato, where Gioacchino tooled brass gunsights for the very cannons that were helping keep the Americans and the British at bay.

When the SS had picked up the men two dawns before, there had been a lot of shouting about partisans. *"Raus!"* the Germans had said to him when they hauled him out of the apartment just south of Pioppe where he and his wife had been living for a year. "We are going to teach you partisans a lesson!"

"I am no partisan," Gioacchino said, relieved that it was simply a case of mistaken identity. He reached into his wallet and extracted the pass signed by Marshal Kesselring, issued to all critical war workers—the pass that caused German sentries to click their heels and salute smartly. But these SS men were different. As Gioacchino held out the pass, the German just turned away, and no amount of entreaty could get any of the soldiers to pay the least attention. *"Tutti partigiani!"* the Germans had said as they lined them up and marched them toward the stable. "All partisans!" If Gioacchino had not been feeling sick to his stomach from the lack of breakfast and the morning chill, he would have laughed. The "partisans" around him averaged about fifty-five years old, and some of them were men of God, and a few were cripples. It made no sense: even an SS man should have been able to tell that these were not partisans.

But then there was very little that seemed to make sense to Gioacchino anymore. Two years before he had been happy in Bologna with his wife and his teen-age son, Bruno. Gioacchino had held a good job as a machinist, but when the Allied bombers knocked down the factory, he suggested that the family move south to Pioppe, the region of his childhood, to escape the danger. Just before they moved, Bruno was drafted, and Gioacchino and his wife took a small apartment below Pioppe near Calvenzano, not far from the artillery gunsight plant where his skills were welcomed. Hardly had husband and wife settled into their new quarters when they received the notice from the government: Bruno's parachute had failed to open in a practice jump at Viterbo. That was September 7, 1943, the day before Italy's unilateral surrender.

A year later, on the first anniversary of Bruno's death, the bereaved Pirettis were even deprived of religious consolation. There was no lack of churches; there were three within a few miles of where they were living. But each church was closed for the duration or opened only rarely. The Allied bombing was so heavy that people would not go to mass; already several churches had been destroyed, and a few of the worshipers killed as they knelt in their pews. Now and then word would circulate that a priest was saying mass in a thicket of woods a few miles up the mountain, and the people would make the difficult trek to the service. But more often there would be no religious succor whatever. On the anniversary of Bruno's death, both Gioacchino and his wife inquired around the apartment house if anyone knew of services to be held that day, but already Allied attack bombers were up and down the valley, and everyone was lying low. Gioacchino asked a Blackshirt sentry behind a barricade of sandbags if it was permissible for him and his wife to go to the neighboring cemetery to light a candle, and the Fascist looked at him as though he had escaped from the "institute." "If you keep on standing here," the sentinel said, "you will certainly go to the cemetery." Gioacchino walked to the shop to buy flowers and a candle to put in front of Bruno's picture, but the shop was closed, and when he heard the drone of approaching aircraft, he hurried back to the apartment. He and his wife sat together holding hands through the afternoon of that first anniversary of their loss, and instead of a religious service, they exchanged remembrances of their son.

Now it was three weeks later, and Gioacchino was sitting on his own sore legs on the floor of a stable, wondering what he had done to deserve the punishment that the SS was meting out. The stall was only about fifteen by twenty feet, and with sixty men crammed inside, there was no room to sit in a normal manner. One of the guards had come in and demonstrated how to sit, with the feet tucked under the buttocks. By sitting exactly in this manner, all sixty managed to jam shoulder to shoulder into the stable. The guard explained that they would have to remain in precisely that position, in total silence, on pain of death. "The slightest noise, and *kaput!*" the guard said, and smashed a wine bottle against the wall for emphasis.

Pondering his two previous days of imprisonment, Gioacchino still found it difficult to see a pattern in the German behavior. Just when he would reach the conclusion that they were devils incarnate, the guards would do something merciful like allowing one of the wives to pass food inside to her husband. But if a man asked the guard for permission to go outside and relieve himself, the guard would shout, *"Nein!"* Then, an hour later, another German would enter the room and point his finger at four or five men and order them to the outhouse, whether they had to go or not. As a result of this quixotic behavior, some of the old men on the floor had lost control of themselves, and the odor mingled with the leftover smell of the horses and made Gioacchino slightly sick. The SS men would poke their heads in the door and shout, "Pigs! You are all pigs! You even *smell* like pigs!"

So far no one had been searched, and Gioacchino felt the family fortune, about $160, tucked in a wallet attached to his suspenders under his vest. On the one occasion when the Germans had allowed his wife to pass him some food, the Pirettis had held a whispered discussion about throwing the money out the window, where she could pick it up later, but she had said, "No, *caro,* that will only get you killed." Gioacchino was glad he had not taken the chance. As this Sunday morning grew older, certain occurrences gave Gioacchino hope that he would be home before nightfall, money and all. Once a German officer came to the door of the room, pointed to a man named Medardo Benini, and said, *"Raus!"* When Benini limped to the door, the officer put a sprig of thorny acacia in the man's pocket and told him to leave. The symbolism of the act was lost on Gioacchino, if indeed any was intended, but perhaps the Germans were beginning to feel ashamed now that the Sabbath had arrived.

Shortly after Benini was released, the priest of Calvenzano, Don Venturi, broke the rule of silence and shouted hysterically that he had to go to Bologna. Gioacchino waited for the wine bottle to come sailing toward the priest's head, but instead an officer appeared at the entrance and beckoned to Don Venturi. The officer said, "If you must go to Bologna, then by all means go! But go in your naked feet, as befits a man of the cloth!" The priest sat down and removed his shoes. Gioacchino heard loud laughter as the barefooted Don Venturi walked gingerly up the road toward the north.

No one else was released, but the prisoners sensed a relaxation on the part of their captors, and a few whispered conversations began. *Splat!* A wine bottle shattered against the wall, and the men fell silent again.

Shortly before noon, a soldier pointed at Gioacchino and ordered him outside. He did not know if he was going to be released or killed, and as he got up from the squatting position, he almost fell back on his companions. *"Raus!"* the German was saying. *"Raus!"* Gioacchino balanced himself and picked his way to the door. The soldier handed him a pair of muddy boots and a shoe shine kit, and Gioacchino went to work with his machinist's hands. He polished and brushed and buffed until the boots gleamed, and then he handed them back to the soldier, who took one quick look and flung them at Gioacchino's feet and began screaming at him in German. Gioacchino started over again, and this time the boots shone like polished bronze when he handed them to the soldier. Again they were flung at his feet with an accompanying tirade. Gioacchino felt like crying. His chance to gain some goodwill was evaporating simply because he could not please this unreasonable soldier. "What is the matter?" Gioacchino said in his most respectful tone. "What am I doing wrong?"

The German turned one of the boots over and tapped loudly on the sole.

Gioacchino scraped and buffed and waxed the soles until they were as smooth as the uppers of the boots, and after a half hour of shining and reshining until he could see his own face in the bottoms of the boots, he succeeded in satisfying the soldier. "Now may I go to the outhouse?" Gioacchino asked, and the German answered with a kick that sent him sprawling back inside.

Just before dawn on Sunday, Angelina Paselli gave a great sigh on the mattress where she lay next to her niece Elide Ruggeri, and all the participants in the death watch of Pudella came rushing to her bedside. Cornelia, Angelina's oldest, still had not returned from her mission to seek help, but there were Angelina's daughter Giuseppina, who had watched over her mother for two days, and Attilio and Elena Ruggeri, who had come back to the house to sleep Saturday night, and a few other *contadini* who had taken refuge in the old *casa colonica.* Someone lit a candle, and in the darkness Giuseppina leaned over her mother and studied her face. Then the fifteen-year-old girl turned away and began to scream, "Mama! Mama!"

"You look at her, *Babbo,*" Elena said to her father, and Attilio leaned over the form on the bed. As Elena turned away, she saw a giant shadow of her father against the kitchen wall. He was making the sign of the cross.

At about the same hour of Sunday, Antonio Tonelli pitched and tossed under a raspberry bush not ten feet from a path heavily traveled by the Germans. There was a possibility that his noises could be heard from the path, but such possibilities did not trouble Antonio. Without stopping to reason it all out, he had worked up a set of ground rules for his behavior. Self-slaughter was a sin that condemned one to hell, no matter how exemplary one's previous behavior; but what if a man happened to stray close to a German sentry, and the sentry happened to kill him? Or suppose a man was in the woods looking for chestnuts to fill his aching stomach, and a German patrol came along and shot him?

Ever since the massacre, Antonio had followed his plan for joining his wife and nine children. He had deliberately selected this bivouac near the road, where he could be seen easily. During the day, he had roamed the woods looking for food, taking no pains to conceal his movements or to walk quietly. Once he was picking berries not more than two yards off the road that ran from Cerpiano to Casaglia, and he heard the approach of marching feet, and he backed closer to the road and kept on picking, closing his eyes as the Germans came abreast so that he would not have to see the gun that killed him. And after all his trouble, the patrol did not even slow down. "I suppose," Antonio said to himself, "I am not important enough to kill." But as his morale recovered from this new humiliation, he told himself that no one could look for death for very long without finding it, especially with the SS around. Another day or so, another night in his bivouac, and the family Tonelli would be together again.

At the first light of Sunday, Antonio raised his head from the earth and looked around. He had thought there was a movement in the bushes but realized it was his imagination. There it was again, and now he heard a soft voice, hardly audible, calling, "Toni. Toni!"

He recognized the voice of his friend Antonio Ceré of Vado, and he replied, "This way, Tonino, over here."

"I have brought you something to lighten your load," Ceré said as he reached Tonelli's side.

"What is there that could lighten my load?" Antonio said, and just as the words came out, he saw his eight-year-old son, Vittorio, standing in the bushes. Father and son embraced, saying each other's names over and over.

"My friends," Ceré said, "hold on now! You are making so much noise with your laughing and your crying that you are inviting the Germans."

"Where did you find him?" Antonio said. "Some women told me he was alive in the cemetery, but I could not believe it, and then I was told that all were dead."

"He has been staying at Ca' Pudella with the Ruggeris," Ceré said. "I found him there yesterday, and I told them I would take him to you."

"God bless you for returning my son, Antonio," Tonelli said, and put his arms around his friend. Then he turned back to Vittorio. "Your mother," he said, "how did she take all this?"

"She did not suffer, *Babbo,*" the boy said, but Antonio could tell that he was holding back. Little by little the father extracted the whole story. "Just before the firing, *Babbo,*" Vittorio said, "Mama took a step toward the gun, and I heard her say, 'You do not have the courage to kill us,' and just then the firing started. Mama is up there now. You will see that she is lying in front of the others. She took the bullets that were meant for me."

"But did she suffer, Vittorio?"

"She did not suffer, *Babbo*. She fell with the first burst. Bruno was at her breast, and they fell together. I saw them go down, and then I was knocked off my feet. One of the Sabbioni girls was next to me, the mute one, and her mouth was open, and she was screaming in my ear."

"She cannot speak," Antonio said.

"She was screaming in my ear," Vittorio said again.

Antonio became obsessed with the need to see the remains of his family. Already the daylight was edging around the woods, and he said to his son, "Come, we must hurry!"

The two of them rushed to the cemetery at Casaglia, saw that no one was visible outside the walls, and stepped inside. At once, Antonio was sorry he had come. The body of his wife lay, as his son had told him, in front of the others. The eight-month-old child, Bruno, was sprawled alongside in two pieces, and the mother's blouse was open as though she had been nursing him. Antonio leaned over both the bodies and kissed them. Then he went to the mound of the dead and began looking for his other seven children. He found a few and gave them a final embrace. Then he remembered that his wife had the moneybelt, and he returned to her side. Her stomach had bloated, and he had to rip the belt loose. The family's savings of $20 were intact. As Antonio was rearranging his wife's clothes, a volley of shots came from the mountainside. "Run, Vittorio!" he shouted. Unhurriedly, he folded his wife's mutilated arms over her naked breast and then stood erect over her, his eyesight blurred by tears.

"Toni!" a voice cried. "Toni!" Antonio turned and saw a skinny arm poking out of the pile of bodies, just as another fusillade of bullets ricocheted off the tombstones around him. "Toni," the voice went on. "Give me a drink, I beg you!"

Antonio went to the mound and peered into the half-hidden face of old Artimesia Gatti, the caretaker of the church at Casaglia, lying under some bodies. "I will come back to help you," he said. "They are shooting at me, and my son waits outside." He turned and rushed from the cemetery.

"How are your wounds?" Maria Tiviroli, the golden-haired princess of Steccola, said when she awakened in the abandoned charcoal hut between Cadotto and her home.

"My wounds do not trouble me as much as my hunger," the *con-*

tadino Mario Cioni told the child. "Is there nothing you can give me to eat?"

"We ate the bread and the cheese yesterday," Maria said, "and when I went back to the shelter for more, it was gone."

"Are there no grapes in the fields?"

"There are a few black grapes in the first vineyard, but if the Germans have come and taken the food, they must have taken the grapes, too."

"Go see, Maria, I beg of you. If I could walk, I would help you."

Maria already had made two trips back to Steccola. Once she was fired on as she returned to the hut, and the second time she found that all the provisions had been stripped from the shelter. Now she was convinced that a third trip would lead her straight into the hands of the Germans. "I cannot go, *Signore,"* she said. "I am too afraid."

"Here!" Cioni said, digging into his pocket. "Go to the nearest grapes and cut some bunches for me. You do not have to go to the shelter." He handed her a brown-handled pocketknife.

"Oh, *Signore,"* Maria said. "I am so afraid!"

"Why are you suddenly afraid?" Cioni said, taking the little girl's hand. "For two days you have been afraid of nothing."

"Yes, but I have had time to think. I see the German faces all the time. If they caught me again, they would not have to shoot me. I would look at their faces and die."

"Stay in the woods," Cioni said. "Do not use the path. And when you get to the vineyard, stay on the outer edge. That way you will be able to see the Germans long before they can get to you."

Maria put the knife in the wicker *sporta* and walked slowly toward her family's abandoned *podere* at Steccola. She lingered on the edge of the first vineyard for several minutes, but there were no signs of the Germans. On the ridge where the soldiers had held sniping positions behind Prunaro di Sopra and Le Scope, nothing was visible. Still trembling, Maria edged into the vineyard and looked for grapes. There were scattered, desiccated bunches hidden under the leaves, and as she reached into the *sporta* to get the knife, she discovered that it had dropped out. Working quickly, she began stripping the grapes with her hands, but all that she was able to put into the *sporta* was a soggy mess of skins, seeds and crushed pulp. Signore Cioni would be disgusted with her. Her hands began to hurt from the toughness of the stems, and she cried with frustration.

It seemed like an hour before Maria had filled the *sporta* with the ruins of several dozen bunches of black grapes, and she hurried back into the woods to return to the hut. She found the knife lying on the edge of the vinepard, and she picked it up disgustedly. To her surprise, the wounded *contadino* thanked her profusely as he stuffed the pulpy mixture into his mouth, and he even managed a smile at the story of the lost knife. Maria tried a few of the grapes, but she was too upset to enjoy them. "Come, come, my child," Cioni said, "you must put something in your stomach," and she ate some grapes without tasting them. She knew that she had to eat to live, but she was not sure that living mattered anymore. Perhaps if she could find the other members of her family, it would be different, but who knew whether they were alive or dead? If the Germans killed women and children and old grandfathers, how much more likely were they to kill able-bodied men like her father and her brothers?

Cioni had fallen into a half sleep, and Maria lay on her back and watched a company of red-tinged clouds slowly moving across the sun. She remembered an old saying of the region: *nuvola rossa o che piscia o che soffia.* (Red clouds mean rain or storm.)

The sun had barely shone since the day of the Germans' arrival, and now the gloomy rain was going to take over another day, and it mattered not at all to the princess of Steccola. She pulled out her saints' pictures and was staring hard at them when she heard someone approaching. She woke Cioni and ran around the back of the shed to hide, but soon they both recognized the voice of a *contadino* from neighboring Ca' di Dorino, calling for his father and brothers. "Have you seen my family?" Maria asked.

The man said, "I am sorry to have to tell you—"

"I know about the dead ones," Maria said. "But have you seen my father or my brothers?"

"Yes. They are hiding near Monte Termine, but the Germans are killing again, and I would not leave here if I were you."

Maria begged the *contadino* to tell her family where she was hiding, and he promised. It was only an hour or so later that she heard her big brother's voice calling her name from the woods.

Leonardo Tiviroli had searched for a sister all morning, not knowing whether he would find Gina or Maria, but until he ran into the *contadino* of Ca' di Dorino, he had walked in fruitless circles. The survivors of his family were in a new hiding place in the thick broomstraws around Le Scope, just above the ashes of Steccola, and Leonardo had told his brothers to keep a watch in case the girl appeared in the valley below. He found Maria shortly before noon and took her back to the rest of the family. Then he returned to the hut to treat Mario Cioni's wounds with some old rags and vinegar salvaged from the ruins of the basement of a farmhouse. Leonardo told his friend Cioni to remain in the hut until he could get help. As he was climbing back toward Le Scope, he saw to his horror that the members of his family were filing slowly toward the massacre site at Prunaro di Sopra. He raced up the side of the ravine and when he got close enough to attract attention, he waved madly at them to get back in the brush. "What has happened to everyone?" he said as he tumbled breathlessly into the weeds alongside the others. "Because we have suffered, do we have to turn into lunatics?"

His father Silvio explained that they had heard the story of the massacre from Maria, and they were on their way to pay their respects to the bodies of their loved ones. "Pay your respects?" Leonardo said. "There are Germans all around! Do they have to be sitting on top of you before you can see them?"

Leonardo saw that the older ones were crying, and he knew that they were beginning to lose control after three days in the open and the shock of learning how their families had died. "Sit here in the brush," Leonardo said gently, "and I will go see what is to be seen." He went to Prunaro di Sopra, and on his way he passed the bodies of his sister Gina and the Grani boy at the stream. "It is as Maria said," he told the family when he returned. "They are all dead."

The remnants of the families Tiviroli and Grani beat down the weeds at a new place on the ridge above the mound of their dead and prepared to spend another night in the open. They were lying under clouds when a wailing and moaning sound came from the woods behind them. Leonardo said, "Let me see who it is!" and returned with Marino Stefanelli, a neighboring *contadino,* thirty-nine years old.

"Gone, all gone!" Stefanelli shrieked. Slowly Leonardo and the others calmed him and learned how he had hidden in the woods, how he had only come out after two days of listening to screams and shouts and gunfire, and how he had discovered the bodies of his wife and children on the mound below. "All the time I was hearing those noises,

I thought it was partisans fighting Germans," Stefanelli cried. "In my wildest thoughts, I said to myself that my wife and the children might be afraid, hiding in the house and listening to all that noise. But I never thought they would be gone."

"Nor did we," old Silvio said to his neighbor. "We did not know the SS."

After a while Stefanelli lay down, but suddenly Leonardo heard a scream and jumped up to see the distraught *contadino* standing and crying. "For charity, try to control your grief, *Signore,*" Leonardo said, but Stefanelli did not acknowledge the comment. Instead, he began ripping at his hair and talking so loudly that there was a danger the Germans would hear him.

"Be quiet!" Leonardo ordered in his harshest *Bersaglieri* tone, but Stefanelli shouted, "I have to bury them! They must be buried in the cemetery! It is not right, it is not decent, to let them lie in the rain!"

Stefanelli began running along the ridge toward the mound of bodies. Leonardo followed, but the man was going too fast, headed for the funeral mound behind Prunaro di Sopra, and soon Leonardo could only crouch down and watch. He saw Stefanelli hurl himself upon the pile of decaying bodies and begin burrowing. He saw the man pull out the body of a small boy, and Leonardo realized that it must be five-year-old Gaetano Stefanelli. He watched as the man slid the child's body away from the others and pulled the tiny arms around his own neck as though to bring the body back to life. There was a shot from the ridge above Steccola, and then another, and Leonardo saw Marino Stefanelli fall on top of his son's body.

On Sunday afternoon, Elide Ruggeri's heart almost jumped from her body when she heard poundings on the door of Ca' Pudella and the guttural sounds of German voices. She watched as a familiar group of four or five SS men trooped into the kitchen, but she relaxed a bit when she noticed that the doctor was not among them. "Where is the old mother?" one of the Germans said, pointing to the empty space on the mattress next to Elide.

"She died this morning," Elide said, but the Germans did not understand, and Elide repeated, *"Morta. Morta."* When she said, *"Kaput,"* the Germans put on long faces, and one of them sat on the end of the mattress and said several times, *"Triste, Triste.* Sad. Sad."

Giuseppina was hiding in a closet, and Elide recognized one of the Germans who had taken her cousin upstairs the day before and made her scream. "Nobody here!" Elide said. But the Germans only went into the kitchen and removed the last remaining eggs. When the squad had dined to its satisfaction, the leader returned to the mattress and began a long, rambling conversation in Italian and German and gestures, and it was many minutes before he had managed to communicate his message. As best Elide could understand, the SS man was telling her that other German soldiers would soon be in the area, that they were not of the SS but of a common army called the Wehrmacht, and that no member of this new army must be told what had happened on Monte Sole. "We have taken care of you, and our doctor has ordered that you be spared," the soldier said, "and in return for that you must tell the Wehrmacht that you were shot by partisans. *D'accordo?*"

"Sì, sì," Elide had said. Anything to get them out of the house before Elena or Attilio returned or Giuseppina made a noise in the closet. *"Ja, ja,* I agree."

The Germans had hardly left when her Uncle Attilio and Cousin Elena walked into the house. "Here he is," the kindly uncle said. "He is not dead. He has just been indisposed."

Elide raised her head from the mattress and saw the handlebar mustache of her stern old father, Giulio. He leaned over the bed and gave her a peremptory kiss on the forehead, a lavish sign of affection for one so reticent and disciplined. *"Babbo!"* Elide said, "where have you been?"

"When the shooting began," Giulio said, "I found a hole below the roots of a tree. The next thing I knew a German sentry was standing in front of me, so close that I could have bitten his shoe. For three days there was a sentry there. Now I am hungry." He walked to the cupboard and began nibbling at an apple.

"Who has been here today?" Attilio asked.

"The Germans again," Elide said. "They made me swear to tell the others that the partisans shot me. *Zio,* what am I to do? Every day the rest of you hide in the woods, and I must lie here and face the Germans. That sickly doctor comes in and breathes in my face, and the others search the house over and over again, and whenever I see them, I think of the cemetery again. *Zio,* I cannot spend another minute in this house!"

Attilio called a council of the family, and it was decided that there were too many Germans trooping in and out of Ca' Pudella. Elide's father and uncle brought in the wooden ladder that had been used to carry the dying Angelina Paselli from and to the cemetery, and in the lengthening shadows of dusk the brothers bore Elide to a safe place in the woods. "We are unprotected, and the rain will fall on you," her uncle said apologetically.

"Better the rain than the Germans," Elide said, and lying on the ground with a screen of leaves for a roof, she fell into her first deep sleep in three days.

By late afternoon, Corina Bertacchi Fornasini was in a state of nerves. The Germans had been buzzing around her home, the rectory at Sperticano, for three days; the night before they had set up machine guns in the piazza of the church. The trim-figured black-haired Corina had locked the shutters and hidden in a closet when she saw trucks driving into the courtyard, and when she looked out later, she saw at least two dozen mounted machine guns facing the wall. With the dawn of Sunday, the guns remained in place, and Corina did not know where to turn for advice. Her husband, Luigi Fornasini, was still entombed behind the false wall that old Casalini had bricked into the basement of the schoolhouse alongside. Corina's brother-in-law, Don Giovanni Fornasini, had gone down the road to Pioppe on Friday when a woman had asked him to intervene with the SS on her husband's behalf, but Don Giovanni had not come home for two nights now, and Corina feared that at last the priest had gone too far with the Germans.

Corina remembered how Don Giovanni had dared the Nazis and the Blackshirts to kill him over and over again. When the SS came into the villages and lined up hostages for execution, the priest would run in front of the guns and say, "Shoot me! I have no family. These men have children!" His intervention had saved the lives of dozens of local men, and he thought nothing of jumping on his bicycle and riding to other parishes when he heard that the Germans were killing. Don Giovanni had become a familiar sight in all the regions of Monte Sole. He wore black Army shoes, and when he rode his bike, he would tie his cassock around his waist and a big black balloon of cloth would follow him down the road. The Germans had come to know him all too well, and more than one officer had warned the twenty-nine-year-old priest to stop meddling. Twice Don Giovanni had succeeded in getting executions postponed long enough to cycle all the way to Bologna and return with notes from Field Marshal Kesselring canceling the bloodletting. And when the Germans took hostages and killed them and displayed their bodies in the public square, Don Giovanni would sneak back at night and cut the bodies down and take them to the nearest *camposanto* for Christian burial. Everyone on Monte Sole knew that this bold behavior would get him in trouble with the Germans one day, and Corina Bertacchi feared that the day had come at last.

Late in the afternoon she grew tired of waiting around the rectory and walked across the bridge of Sperticano and down the main road toward Pioppe. It was possible that there had been trouble, and Don Giovanni had not been able to communicate with his family, although Corina had to admit to herself that the possibility was remote. Even when her brother-in-law could not come home, he always sent word so as not to alarm his old mother, who lived with them in the rectory.

Corina had walked a half mile down the road when she saw the outlines of two priests hurrying toward her from the direction of Pioppe. She recognized her brother-in-law, but it took her a few minutes to recognize his companion, Padre Collia, the pastor of Pioppe. When the two men drew abreast, she could see that both were breathing heavily, and it seemed to her that Don Giovanni had never looked so distressed.

"Corina," he said without slowing down, "a terrible thing is going on at Pioppe. The SS has imprisoned fifty or sixty men and threatened to kill them because of the trucks the partisans destroyed the other day."

"It is worse here," Corina said. "There are dead at the Colullas and Abelle and Tagliadazza and every *podere* up the mountain."

"No!" the priest said, stopping in his tracks. "Did you hear that, Padre Collia?"

The older man nodded.

"How many died, Corina?" Don Giovanni asked.

"No one is sure, but it was half the congregation, I am certain of that."

"Half the congregation!" Don Giovanni said, his face turning pale. "Then they killed more than one hundred."

"Many more," Corina said, "and on the whole mountain, more

than one thousand." She glanced down and discovered that her brother-in-law was wearing no shoes.

"The Germans took them when they let me go at Pioppe," Don Giovanni said. "They also took the shoes of Don Venturi of Calvenzano, but he left long before us. Padre Collia and I were held separately in a little room, and they kept threatening to shoot us if we did not tell them where the partisans were, and then one of the officers said we could go if we would remove our shoes. I took off my old shoes, and they threw them into the dirt. But Padre Collia was wearing a new pair of *così così* shoes, and the officer exchanged them for Army shoes with holes in them."

By now the three had covered half the distance to Sperticano, and Don Giovanni said to his sister-in-law, "Corina, do not ring the church bells for mass in the morning."

"Oh, but I must, Don Giovanni," she said. "The people need the mass. They have suffered so!"

"Others suffer still," the priest said. "Even now I am afraid the Germans are killing at Pioppe, and probably they are still killing all over the mountain."

"But why can there be no mass?"

"Because we are walking to Bologna. We are going to the Curia to ask for help. It may be a few days before we return."

"And what good will that do?"

"Maybe no good. Maybe we will not be believed, but we must try."

"And what of all the funerals?"

Don Giovanni stopped to remove a pebble from between his toes, and when he was finished, he covered his face with his hands and said in a voice that Corina could hardly hear, "First the living, dear sister Corina." He paused. "Half the congregation?" he whispered. "Come, *Padre,* we must hurry!"

Corina Bertacchi watched until the two black figures blended into the night.

Late that Sunday afternoon an officer appeared at the door of the stable of Pioppe di Salvaro and told the machinist Gioacchino Piretti and the other prisoners to prepare themselves for their release. The men stood up, but some suffered leg cramps and fell to the ground again, and only after ten or fifteen minutes was the group able to line up outside the stable at the German command. Even though he had been one of the first on his feet, Gioacchino felt daggers in his muscles, and he leaned over to rub his thighs and calves. It was as though hot mercury had been infused into his veins, and he did not understand how some of the older men, the ones in their sixties and seventies, were able to stand up at all.

"Achtung!" a German voice cried out. "We are going to take a collection for war invalids. You will remove everything of value from your person and throw it here." Soon there was a pile of watches, rings and wallets. Gioacchino toyed with the idea of keeping his wallet, but when German soldiers began passing among the men patting them down like criminals, he quickly pulled the wallet from his suspender clip and tossed it on the pile.

When everything had been collected, an officer walked slowly up and down the ragged line of men and selected a dozen or so. "You men will get in that truck!" he ordered. "You look strong enough to be of help." When the able-bodied men had been driven away, the officer scrutinized the others. "You men are old and useless," he said. "But we will see if we can find something for you to do at the mill."

The hemp mill was a quarter mile from the stable, and the Germans kept after the old men to march in double time. After they had crossed the bridge over the Reno River and nearly reached the mill, a soldier shouted, *"Halt!"* A murmur of fear swept through the forty-nine prisoners. "You will sit down and take off your shoes!" the German snapped. When all the men were barefooted, the Germans marched them a few feet farther to the edge of the *botte* of the hemp mill, a cement-lined tank in the ground about twenty feet square and ten feet deep. Years before, the *botte* had been used to store water for the mill, but now it was empty, except for a foot or so of stagnant water and gray silt in the bottom.

Gioacchino saw that two machine guns had been set up at the front edge of the *botte,* one at each corner, and helmeted German gunners were seated in place. A small catwalk led under some electric wires along the left edge of the tank, and a metal gate bore a sign: CHI TOCCA MUORE. (Who touches, dies.) Two of the Germans broke the gate open with their rifle butts.

"Avanti!" an officer said, and the forty-nine men headed slowly across the catwalk, with Gioacchino deliberately straggling along be-

hind. A wailing and moaning began among the men, but the narrowness of the catwalk and the busy rifle butts of the Germans kept them in line, and soon all forty-nine had reached the far edge of the tank, where they stood facing the machine guns. A single German soldier attempted to line them up in precise military rows, and while this was going on, Gioacchino tried to figure out how to save himself. He decided to fall with delicate timing just ahead of the gunfire.

The soldier who had been tending them quickly walked back across the catwalk, and before he had even reached the gate, the firing started. With the first shot, Gioacchino allowed himself to drop to the edge of the tank, and another man fell hard on top of him. Gioacchino lay there for what seemed like ten or fifteen minutes, while the machine guns fired off and on, and then he heard footsteps coming across the catwalk. There was loud talking in German and then a splash, followed by more loud talking and more splashes. Gioacchino realized that the soldiers were throwing the bodies into the *botte*. He held his breath as he felt himself being picked up by the seat of the pants and the back of the neck and pitched ten feet straight down into the water and mud. He hit with a heavy splash and lay perfectly still.

By now it was nearly dark, and Gioacchino could hear bodies flying through the air and landing all around him. He was stretched out facedown in the water, playing dead, with his fingertips barely supporting his weight on the clammy bottom of the *botte* and his nose a fraction of an inch above the surface. When the last splash had sounded, Gioacchino heard the Germans clomp back across the catwalk, and out of the corner of his eye he thought he saw a metallic gleam. "Holy Mother!" he said to himself. "Now come the bombs!"

He heard something splash into the *botte,* and quickly he ducked his head below the surface. He thought his eardrums would burst with the noise, and just as he lifted his head out of the water, he heard a click, and he shoved his head back under for another burst of compression. The grenades rained into the *botte* for five or ten minutes, or until Gioacchino reckoned that his eardrums had been shoved halfway through his skull. He did not know how long it had been since the Germans had stopped throwing the grenades when he finally realized that it was quiet above. He pushed himself up on his fingertips again, and to his surprise discovered that he remained unhurt except for the sharp pain in his ears. It was totally dark now, and Gioacchino dared not move until he was certain that the last German was gone.

Then he heard a voice. A man was speaking German excitedly, almost screaming, and to Gioacchino it sounded like the word he used most often was "Italian." Every few seconds the voice would hit a peak, and Gioacchino would hear a responding cheer. It sounded like a miniature of one of those newsreel scenes of Hitler addressing 100,000 screaming Germans. Gioacchino could hardly understand a word, but the tone was clear. The man was offering congratulations, and the men, in turn, were cheering his words.

Gioacchino waited until the ceremonies had ended, and then he lifted himself to his feet and looked for a way out. A new sound from above sent him slipping back into the mud, and soon he felt himself being bombarded by shoes. The Germans had decided to discard the pile of shoes—Gioacchino knew that most of them were soled with cardboard anyway—and the logical place to fling them was in the *botte* with their former owners. Gioacchino balanced on his fingertips and kept his nose just above the water level and prayed that he would not be hit in the head by an old boot. There was a limit to what he could take without crying out: he had endured trial by bullet, water and grenade, but he was not sure that he could endure trial by boot. His head hurt so that he thought it would burst if anything touched it. When the last shoe splashed into the water next to him and the German footfalls died in the distance, Gioacchino stood up once again and discovered that he was nearly naked. Somehow in all the intensity of the German firepower, his clothes had been ripped to threads, and it seemed to him nothing less than a miracle that his body remained unmarked except for a few cuts and bruises.

Gioacchino peered into the darkness. There was no sound. The old men were heaped up in piles of two and three, and circles of blood eddied out from their bodies. Gioacchino saw that there was no one alive. Afraid that the Germans would return any minute, he waded through the sucking gray mud toward an intake pipe that pierced under the road and the railroad embankment and another twenty or thirty feet to the river beyond. Gioacchino knew that the cement mouth of the pipe had been enlarged by Allied bombs several days before in a big raid that had set the mill on fire, and the river water had been diverted by a sluiceway. He knew the pipe was safe, but he did not know what would greet him when he came out. Perhaps the Germans had had the foresight to post another gunner at this exit. A single soldier with a pistol could have prevented any escapes.

Gioacchino entered the slimy innards of the pipe on his hands and knees, crawling very slowly so as to make no noise. The darkness was total, and it took him five or ten minutes to reach the center. When he found that he was breathing hard from his exertions, he paused in the blackness to regain his strength, and then he heard the distinct sound of someone coming up behind him.

Gioacchino discarded reason. Gulping for air and slipping and sliding along the slime of the bottom, he propelled himself to the other end with the speed of a sewer rat, and when he looked up and saw a gray screen of clouds, he pulled himself painfully to his feet and ran up the hill. He had only gone a few yards when he came to a bush, and he crouched in panic with his eyes focused back toward the exit hole of the pipe. Soon a man appeared at the opening, slowly came out of the pipe, and began crawling toward Gioacchino with his hand clutching his middle.

"This way, my friend!" Gioacchino whispered. "Let me help you."

The man crawled a few yards farther up the hill, still holding himself, and Gioacchino stepped out to meet him. He saw that the man had been cut horizontally across the abdomen, and he was trying to keep his intestines from slipping out. "Wait!" Gioacchino said. "Sit down here!" He ripped some vines from the side of the railroad embankment and attempted to tie them around the man's belly, but it was no good. Vines that were thick enough were impossible to tie, and the others were too small to cover the hole. Gioacchino despaired of solving the problem with vines, and summoning up his last reserves of strength, he picked up the old man. "We will try to get to the watchman's shack up there," he told the old man. "I know it is empty."

They entered the bombed-out hut just above the tracks, and Gioacchino stretched the man on the floor as gently as possible. The man's eyes were still open, and his hands clutched his abdomen, but Gioacchino realized that he would soon die. "Can you hear me, old man?" he said as he leaned over the prostrate form. The man nodded. "Look, there is no way I can help you," Gioacchino went on. "I lack even clothes to share with you."

The old man began talking in a voice that surprised Gioacchino for its clarity. "Do not worry," he said. "You have done enough. Go, and save yourself!"

Gioacchino thanked the old man and stood up to leave, and then he heard sounds coming from the boarded entranceway to the hut. First there would be a footstep, and then a loud clomp, and then another footstep and another clomp. Gioacchino ducked behind the door of the shack and watched a man limp inside. It was his childhood friend, Aldo Ansaloni, the amputee who lived in the same building with Gioacchino and his wife at Calvenzano.

"Aldo!" he said. "It is me: Gioacchino."

"Gioacchino?" Ansaloni said painfully. "I am wounded twice in the neck and once very badly in the ass and once again in the leg, Gioacchino, and how many bullet holes do you think there are in this damned wooden leg? *None!*"

Ansaloni rooted around the cupboards of the watch hut and pulled out an ancient half bottle of vermouth. "Here, try this!" he said to Gioacchino, and the two took steps to rebuild their strength. The old man on the floor had shut his eyes, and his breathing was jerky and shallow. "Gioacchino," Ansaloni said heavily, "I do not think I can get back to the house. Will you tell my family to come for me?"

"How can they come, Aldo?" Gioacchino said. "There are Germans everywhere."

"Then will you help me, my friend?" Ansaloni said. The two men clutched each other for support and staggered from the hut. Stopping often to pull at the vermouth bottle, they crawled and walked the half mile uphill to their home. Gioacchino's wife screamed when she saw him at the door, and when she asked him what had happened, he opened his mouth, but no sound came out. She led him to the bed, and when she asked him again what the Germans had done to him, he could only shake his head from side to side. He shivered and trembled in the bed, and it was many hours before he could speak.

Gilberto Fabbri, twelve years old, had wandered around Monte Sole for three days, bleeding from the furrows that had been plowed up and down his right side by the first grenade that came through the window at Caprara. Now his strength was nearly gone, and he lay alongside the little stream that ran from the shoulder of the mountain down toward Gardeletta. The boy told himself that he was lucky he had found the stream. At least he was able to bathe his throbbing eye with cold water.

As the day went on, he drifted in and out of sleep, and he saw again the dead bodies that he had been wandering past for what seemed forever, and he heard again the screams and moans that had come from all around him on the mountain. He did not know how long he had slept when he realized that he was being carried through the woods. "Who?" he asked.

"We are your friends," a voice said. "We know your brother. We are taking you to the valley for help."

"Grazie," Gilberto said. "Thanks. It is kind."

On Sunday night the moon flitted in and out of dark clouds, and toward midnight it disappeared altogether. Adelmo Benini and his father-in-law, Sassolein, and the pilot from Florence were out foraging, and when the mists began, Adelmo was reminded of two days before, when he had hidden in the chestnut tree and watched through the rain as his wife and two daughters were shot to death. He was hungry and cold, and this new rain seemed to him to be the last test he could endure. "Go on without me!" he said to the other two. "There is no food here anyway."

Sassolein, the old man who had been known on the mountain for his capacious drinking and little else, put his arm around Adelmo's shoulders, as he had numerous times during the three days of their wanderings, and said softly, "We must go on, Adelmo. No one can say there is no food. We must help one another, or we will perish like the rest."

"Forgive me, *Babbo,*" Adelmo said. "You have kept me going, but now it is the end. Now I have no more desire."

"Stay here and rest yourself, and we will bring you something to eat," Sassolein said, and walked into the night with the lieutenant.

Adelmo leaned against a barren chestnut tree, closed his eyes and let himself slip to the ground. With the moon gone, there had never been a blacker night. He could not see ten feet through the woods, and as he sat on the wet earth and allowed the raindrops to roll down his face, he thought he discerned images in the darkness, as though he were in the cinema he had once attended in Bologna. He closed his eyes and opened them again, and the images remained. Gradually they took form, and Adelmo could see his wife and his two little daughters running hand in hand through the trees, stopping now and then to lean over and put something into a *sporta.*

Adelmo jumped up and ran toward the figures, but they dissolved in front of his eyes. *"Babbo!"* he shouted. *"Babbo!"*

Sassolein materialized out of the darkness. "What is it, my son?" he asked.

"I saw them! Norina and the children, walking through the woods."

"They are dead, Adelmo. You know they are dead."

"They are alive, *Babbo!* They were here a minute ago."

The two men argued briefly, but the distraught Adelmo would not be convinced that he had been seeing things, and finally, the pilot and the old man agreed to accompany him to the cemetery to see if the bodies were still in place. While the two others stood guard at the gate, Adelmo walked inside. The bodies had begun to decay, forcing Adelmo to hold his nose, and in the darkness he studied the faces. When he had examined all the bodies that were visible and still had not found his loved ones, he was encouraged, and slowly began to pull the cadavers aside to see who was lying underneath. He had only removed a few when he came to his wife. She was arched over backward with the two children under her arms. Then he saw Artimesia Gatti. The old lady was propped up against the wall watching him, and Adelmo found himself almost unable to speak.

"Is it you, Adelmo?" the old lady said hoarsely. "I beg you, Adelmo, give me a drink. I am dying of thirst."

Adelmo knelt at the old lady's side. "How did you get here, *Signora?"* he asked in a quivering voice.

"I was with the others in the pile," the old lady said. "Some partisans pulled me away today, but the Germans came, and no one has been here since then."

"Where are you wounded?"

"Across the thighs. But it has stopped hurting. If you could only give me a drink, Adelmo."

"I will try to find water, *Signora,"* Adelmo said. He stood up, and as he did, he heard the voice of his father-in-law: "Adelmo! Run! The Germans!"

His legs had turned to broomstraws from fear, and he dashed out the gate. Halfway up the wooded hill he found the other two, and they crouched in the brush and looked down to see flashlights playing about the walls of the cemetery. The Germans left after a few minutes, and Adelmo saw little pencils of light bobbing on the path toward Cerpiano. When the lights had reached Cerpiano, 500 yards away, Adelmo said: "The *vecchia* Gatti is alive in the cemetery."

"You are imagining, Adelmo," Sassolein said.

"No, *Babbo,* I am not imagining now," Adelmo said. "I can tell you what I saw. Norina and the girls are dead. But Signora Gatti lives against the wall. I promised to get her something to drink."

The three men walked softly along the mule road that ran around the shoulder of the mountain, heading for a watering trough that lay between Caprara and Casaglia. As they walked, they stepped across dead animals; the Germans had taken target practice on the beasts they had released from the *poderi.* "Wait!" Sassolein said as he halted in front of a cow. "This one is not dead."

Adelmo looked into the animal's face, and as he did, the cow raised its head and let it drop heavily back to the ground. "Give me that can!" Adelmo said.

His father-in-law handed over a rusty can that the three men had been using for water, and lying on the ground next to the fallen cow, Adelmo began milking. There was barely enough fluid in the cow's udders to cover the bottom of the can. "This will have to do," Adelmo said. "I will take it to the *signora.*"

While Sassolein and the pilot stood guard again, Adelmo walked to the back of the *camposanto* and pressed the can against Artimesia Gatti's old lips. She took a sip, but then Adelmo noticed that the milk was dribbling down her chin. *"Signora,"* he said, "you must drink!" But the old lady would not open her mouth. She lay against the wall staring at Adelmo, and even though he begged her to take just a sip more, she made no motion. *"Signora!"* Adelmo cried. "Are you all right?" Artimesia stared at him, and Adelmo was relieved to see her blink her eyes. He reached out and touched the gravedigger's widow on the shoulder. "We will come back to help you," he said, and ran from the cemetery.

"Listen," Sassolein said when the three men came together outside the gate, "we are in our own backyards now, and while the Germans sleep, it is a good time for us to get some food." Only a few hundred yards down the road was one of the richest vineyards on the mountain. It sloped down a hill from Poggio di Casaglia, the *podere* of the Laffi family, and more than once Adelmo had stopped at the vineyard to sample a few of the *contadino*'s prize grapes.

The three men reached the vineyard long after midnight and began feeling along the vines for grapes. "There are none," the pilot said.

"You Florentines do not know how to look," Adelmo said, sharing a tiny handful of gnarled, half-fermented fruit.

The three scavengers worked from the edge of the vineyard toward the center, and after a while Adelmo thought he could see the faint outline of a scarecrow through the darkness. Scarecrows were not a common sight on Monte Sole; most of the *contadini* hung up stuffed dead rabbits or snippings of twirling tin to frighten the birds. Adelmo stepped closer for a better look. As he approached, he could see that the scarecrow was a small one, and when he was alongside, he saw that it was dressed in kneepants and a little country jacket, and then he realized that he was looking at the body of a small boy, impaled on a stick six feet high.

He crashed through the vines and trellises to get out of the vineyard. "What is it?" Sassolein cried, but Adelmo kept on going. They caught him on the road between Casaglia and Caprara, and when he told them what he had seen, they agreed that they must return to their cave high on the mountain; there was too much danger here in the center of the massacre zone.

As they were heading back, they passed through the remains of Caprara, and there, on the outer edge of a chestnut grove, they found the bodies of three young women tied to trees, their feet off the ground, their dresses over their waists, in the position of crucifixion. Nearby were the remains of two pregnant women; one of the unborn children had been torn from the abdomen and laid against its mother's cheek; the other was sticking out of the body cavity by the legs, and Adelmo was surprised to see such small toes. "Look, *Babbo,*" he called in a quaking voice, "I think the baby has no nails on its toes."

Sassolein touched him on the shoulder. "But, *Babbo,*" Adelmo repeated, "the little baby has no nails on its toes!"

Sassolein and the pilot pulled him away from the sight and led the hysterical man down the road.

Survivors

THROUGH the three days of the *rastrellamento*, Luigi Massa and his wife, Maria Comellini, and their nineteen-year-old daughter, Emma, stayed in the farmhouse at Poggio Comellini, and the good angel who had shepherded Luigi out of the sharecropping business and into the ownership of the general store at Caprara had remained with them. Within a few hundred yards of their house, farms were burning, and *contadini* were dying in agony, but Poggio Comellini seemed to be just beyond the boundary of the area selected by the SS for immolation. Luigi would look out his windows at Nazi patrols marching harmlessly past, while just over the ridge to the west he could see a long string of destroyed *poderi*.

By the morning of the fourth day, Monday, Oct. 2, 1944, the destruction of Monte Sole and especially its southwestern slope seemed almost complete, and the German activity slowed except for occasional patrols. Here and there the *contadini* who had fled were returning to their smoldering farmhouses, and early in the morning one of them stopped to exchange information with the family Massa.

"I am thankful to God that we were left entirely out of it," Luigi said.

"But you were not," the visitor said. "The Germans killed in your store."

The report disturbed Luigi for no reason that he could understand. The Germans had killed elsewhere; why not in his store? But as the morning went on, he found that he could not take his mind off this latest piece of news, and he decided to see for himself. Against the wishes of his wife and daughter, Luigi headed over the ridge toward Caprara, a mile away. He saw no Germans on the way, nor, for that matter, anyone else. He passed several gutted farmhouses, some with stone walls intact, some imploded into a heap of rock. But the change that struck Luigi was the almost total absence of haystacks. Usually he made his way from Poggio to the store by going from stack to stack. Now all these useful landmarks were gone. Even the center posts had been burned, and in the charred circles that marked where the stacks had been, Luigi saw a few blackened bodies lying like dress patterns against the earth.

As he came into sight of Caprara, he noticed that the silhouette of the village was almost intact. But as he drew closer, he saw that the two large farmhouses showed the scars of fire, and the stone walls had collapsed in a few places. Luigi's *tabacchi* seemed the least disturbed. He stepped inside and found that bottles were broken, tables overturned and closets rifled for the meager stocks he had left in the store four days earlier. The scene registered on Luigi's mind, but it did not disturb him. He was looking for bodies. It seemed to him that he could not bear the shame of having his store converted into an execution chamber. He ran frantically from room to room, and when he had checked the last closet and found that there were no bodies and no signs of killing, he leaned his head against a doorjamb and found that he was drenched with perspiration.

Outside, Luigi was certain that he could smell death in the air, and he was afraid, but his curiosity overcame his fear. He stepped quickly into the first house in the row. It belonged to the family Carboni, Luigi's good customers and neighbors, and he could see the marks of fire through a hole in the front wall where stones had fallen away. He stepped through the hall and looked into the kitchen, and there he saw a mound of burned bodies. He blinked once and ran.

Back home, Luigi tried to tell his wife and daughter what he had seen, but it was a long time before the words would come. Over and over they asked if he had recognized any of the bodies, and he had to tell them that he had seen a few members of the Calzolari family, some of the Iubini family and a Tondi or two, but he could not be sure about anything. He guessed that there were from thirty to sixty bodies in the pile, and he explained that they had been burned and the skin hung from most of them in sheets, and his glance had been so short that he was certain of nothing beyond the fact that the Germans had not killed in the *tabacchi;* they had killed next door.

Long before dawn on Monday morning, the refugees from the Ruggeri home at Ca' Pudella decided to return to the big *casa colonica* and take their chances on being picked up by the Germans. "Look," crusty old Giulio had said, "we know we are safer here in the woods, but can we stay in the woods forever? Elide, you are wounded and it is not good for you in this wet weather. And what of the Soldati boy, lying in the house alone?" They had had to leave five-year-old Vincenzo Soldati, wounded in three places, including the head, lying on a mattress when they fled.

"We can go back and help him from time to time," Elide said.

"No, I say the killing is over," Giulio said. "I say we return to the home that is ours."

Attilio said, "I agree with my brother. We can return to the house at night, and each day the men can hide in the woods. At least we will sleep under our own roof."

The brothers piled Elide back on top of the rung ladder, and the whole group headed for Ca' Pudella in the darkness. In addition to the brothers and their daughters Elide and Elena, there now were others. The two members of the Menarini family, Maria and thirteen-year-old Giorgio, who had escaped from the church with Elena, had been joined by another brother, Dario, and the old father, Augusto, returned from their hiding places in the woods. Antonio Ruggeri, Elena's twenty-year-old brother, had escaped from the German artillery trap on top of Monte Sole, and now that his partisan brigade had been routed he had come home. The fifteen-year-old Giuseppina Paselli was gone; with the death of her mother, she had headed for the refuge at Cerpiano, looking for her sister, Cornelia, and her father, Virginio. As the clans Ruggeri and Menarini stepped into the family home to join the dying Soldati boy, Attilio counted noses. There were ten.

Shortly after sunup, someone rapped on the farmhouse door, and while the men ran swiftly into the basement and hid themselves behind the rows of demijohns and vats, Elena answered. A man in civilian clothes identified himself by a Fascist *tessera* and asked if he could come in. "What is your business?" Elena said.

"I speak for Major Reder, the commandant of the SS troops here," the Fascist said. "I bring the message that you may proceed with the burial of the bodies. It is the wish of Major Reder that all bodies be buried as quickly as possible."

"I cannot bury bodies," Elena said, "and there is no one in this house except my wounded sister and a five-year-old boy who has been unconscious for two days."

"As you wish, *Signorina,*" the Fascist said. "I only bear the message. Anyone who chooses to assist in the burial of the bodies will not be disturbed." He tipped his hat and disappeared down the path toward Ca' Dizzola.

Elena watched until the Fascist was out of sight and then called everyone up from the basement to hear the news.

"It is a trap!" Dario Menarini said. "They know that some of us got away, and this is the way they will finish the job."

"Trap or not," Attilio said, "our loved ones lie in the rain. It is a sacrilege to leave them there."

"We will bury," Giulio said.

A work party consisting of Elena and all the able-bodied men left Pudella in search of bodies. They found a blackened Don Ubaldo Marchioni stretched out in front of the altar at Casaglia with one foot burned off. The crippled Vittoria Nanni was found in the bell tower along with two other bodies. Just behind the gravedigger Gatti's hut, Elena found her mother, shot in the back. Apparently she had slipped away en route to the cemetery from the church and been killed later. Farther down the road, near Poggio, the search party came upon a scene that puzzled them. The wizened body of Artimesia Gatti lay like a dead sparrow next to a half-dug hole that was ringed by the bodies of four young men. It was only later in the day that the Ruggeri burial party learned what had happened. Around dawn on Monday, four fleeing partisans had heard the old lady moaning in the cemetery. They were carrying her away when she died in their arms, and they were digging her grave at Poggio when a squad of SS killed them all.

The Ruggeris spent most of the day collecting bodies and burying them where they lay. They found the three crucified women at Caprara and the scarecrow boy in the vineyard at Poggio, as well as a dozen or so bodies along the road. When they had finished burying the scattered dead, they returned to the cemetery and began to dig a common grave for the six or seven dozen who lay against the burial chapel. Putrefaction had begun, and the men worked with wet rags over their noses, and still they were only able to stay in the cemetery for fifteen or twenty minutes at a time. By nightfall the grave was barely big enough for three or four bodies, but work went faster when the diggers were joined by others who had learned of the truce. Luigi Massa, for one, worked like a man possessed, making the dirt fly from the *camposanto,* nor did he lay down his shovel and run into the woods for periodic breaths of fresh air like the others. On his way, he had dug some onions from the garden at Cerpiano, and he worked with a whole onion clenched between his teeth. His tears went unnoticed; most of the men were crying as they worked through the night to bury their dead.

Two days after the Germans had gone up and down the western slope of Monte Sole killing everyone in sight, more bodies were laid to rest. Mario Zebri and his son, Pietro, buried their family in a common grave in the vineyard. The families of Abelle and Tagliadazza and Colulla di Sotto were buried in the same way. Each group of survivors had sent someone to Sperticano to ask for Don Giovanni Fornasini's help at the burial, and each had been told that the priest was in Bologna on a mission to the Curia. Vittoria Negri waited at Ca' Roncadelli for Don Giovanni to return—she had made up her mind that her old parents and the other victims would be buried in the *camposanto* at Sperticano and that a priest would preside—but by Monday she realized that she could wait no longer. The bodies lay under sheets, and the wet autumn air stank of them.

One cow had wandered back to the *podere* after the killings, and Vittoria borrowed another from the survivors of the neighboring Rubini family. She hitched the two animals to a large flatbed cart and began loading the bodies with the help of her brother Fernando and a few Rubinis. When about half the bodies were loaded, Vittoria hit the cow with a switch and started on the ten-minute walk to the church at Sperticano. She had hardly gone fifty yards when four Allied planes came out of the high cloud cover and began strafing on both sides of the river. "For charity!" Vittoria said, shaking a fist skyward. "Do you think I am the SS?" The SS headquarters sat halfway up a neighboring mountainside at Villa d'Aria, and the planes were bombing and machine-gunning the headquarters and anything that moved.

The cows panicked at the noise, and Vittoria was afraid they would dump the eight bodies. She tied the animals to a tree, finishing just as one of the planes began a strafing run and pelted the area with bullets. She climbed into the tree and waited for the plane to disappear, but everytime she untied the animals and tried to go on, another attack would begin, and she was only able to cover fifteen or twenty yards at a time. In this manner the ten-minute walk to the cemetery took two hours.

In the walled burial ground of Sperticano, Vittoria laid the bodies on the earth and covered them with sheets. An hour later she returned with the last of the dead, and she discovered that relatives had quietly assembled in the cemetery for the burial. An exasperated Vittoria started to ask where they had been while she was hauling the bodies, but she held her tongue. Don Giovanni was still absent, and the group said prayers for the dead and lowered them into a common grave.

By Monday night apprentice seamstress Cornelia Paselli had been forced to remain in the air-raid shelter near Vado for three days. She had screamed and cried and begged the men in the shelter to let her go. She had told them that her mother needed help in the cemetery of Casaglia and that others were lying wounded, and the answer was always the same: "We cannot let you go, because the Germans will force you to tell where we are hiding."

Just before dawn on Tuesday morning, a young man named Tristano crept to Cornelia's side and said, "Come! They are asleep. I will go with you to your mother." The pair sneaked out of the narrow opening and ran through the woods until they were in the clear.

"I know a stream bed that leads straight to Cerpiano," Cornelia said, but Tristano led her to another path, closer to Vado and less likely to be known to the Germans. When they had climbed to within sight of Cerpiano, Tristano took his leave to return to the shelter, and Cornelia struck out through the woods. Near Cerpiano she saw a familiar face: a *contadina* of the area. "You are still alive!" the woman said with incredulity. "Everyone thought you were dead."

The *contadina* explained that there were groups of survivors everywhere: fifteen or twenty in the air-raid shelter below Cerpiano, ten or twelve at Ca' Pudella, a few in the shelter at Caprara, and dozens holed up in caves near the summit of the mountain. "We go out each day and look for food," the woman said, "but there is not much to look for."

"And where are my sister and my mother and father?" Cornelia asked. "The last I saw them, they were in the cemetery."

"Your sister is safe in the shelter at Cerpiano. I have not seen your mother and father."

The two women walked through the woods toward the air-raid shelter at Cerpiano, and when they passed near the chapel where Cornelia had heard the screaming and moaning four days before, she said, "I must look inside."

"No, you must not," the woman said. "I beg you not to look in there!"

Something in her voice made Cornelia veer away, and in the dugout shelter below Cerpiano she was reunited with her fifteen-year-old sister, Giuseppina. "And Mother?" Cornelia asked.

"She died Sunday morning at Ca' Pudella," Giuseppina said. "There was nothing anyone could do."

Cornelia began to cry and berate herself for not getting help, and her sister embraced her and said, "Cornelia, you do not understand. You have not been here to see. There was no help for anyone. If you had brought someone to Mother, even if you had brought back a doctor, he would only have been killed. Can you not understand?"

By Friday the survivors who had jammed into the earthen shelter below Cerpiano were *in extremis*. There were eighteen or twenty inside a cave that had been designed to hold eight or ten, and all the food for miles around had been scavenged until there was no more. Now the old people were moaning, and the children were crying, and the two or three able-bodied men in the shelter could see that a change had to be made.

"Come!" Maximiliano Piretti said, grasping his little son, Fernando, by the hand. "We all return to Cerpiano. Even if the SS is there, it cannot be worse than this." Slowly the group assembled itself and began the procession through the woods, with Maximiliano and Fernando in the lead. There were Sister Benni and the fifteen-year-old wounded girl from Murazze, Lidia Pirini, and Lidia's old uncle, Felippo Pirini, who had lost his wife and six children, and a dozen or so more.

There were no signs of life from the conglomeration of buildings at Cerpiano. The bodies in the chapel had already been buried at night by Maximiliano and a burial party led by Luigi Massa, and for some reason the Germans had not tried to burn the place. "Come!" Maximiliano said brightly. "We will go inside and enjoy a breakfast."

The survivors trooped into the four-story building, and immediately their noses were assaulted by a stench. "Wait here," Maximiliano said, and he and Fernando walked through the first floor of the big building. In the kitchen they found the foodstuffs of the house dumped on the floor. There were sticky puddles of mulberry jam, piles of flour and rice and *pasta,* and a soggy mess of broken eggs next to the barrel in which they had been stored in powdered chalk. There was not so much as a speck of edible food left on the shelves or in the cabinets. On top of every vestige of food, the Germans had moved their bowels.

Now it had been more than a week since the beginning of the *rastrellamento,* and more and more men had come out of the woods and taken nightly refuge in the Ruggeris' big house at Pudella. Several forces had driven them from hiding. They were hungry, and hardly anything edible remained in the woods. Although the Germans were carrying out isolated killings each day, there were no conspicuous massacres on the order of Casaglia or Roncadelli, and it seemed to the isolated groups of hiding men that the raid might be over. And finally, the front was moving northward, and so many German soldiers were descending on the mountain that there were few places to hide. The men of Monte Sole knew that Ca' Pudella was highly visible to the Germans and that the Germans visited there often, but it seemed like the best of a number of dangerous places. There were women to do their cooking, and a roof overhead, and the respected brothers Ruggeri to serve as leaders and advisers. If there were also Germans in the vicinity—well, there were Germans everywhere.

Early on the morning of Friday, October 6, the first week's anniversary of the *rastrellamento,* four men in SS uniforms arrived at Ca' Pudella and politely asked who was inside. Most of the men had fled with the daylight, but there were five or six in the house, and Elena told the soldiers there were only women and a critically injured child. "I know you are not being honest with me," an SS major said, "but my men and I do not want to be unpleasant. Please tell your men to come out here, and I give you my personal word that no one will be harmed." As the officer bowed politely, Elena was surprised to see that one of his hands was missing.

"Please wait," Elena said, and she shut the door and whispered the major's words to the others.

"Come," Giulio said. "They will only find us anyway."

One by one the men assembled on the front courtyard of the house, where they were told that they were needed for a work detail. There were Giulio and Attilio, seventy-year-old Augusto Menarini and his son, Dario, and two valley men whose names Elena did not know. *"Scusi,"* Attilio was saying, "my niece is inside with a bad wound in her hip, and I must remain home to care for her."

"Do not trouble yourself about that, *Signore,*" the major said in a friendly manner. "I see at least three fine women here who can care for your niece, and anyway, this work assignment will only last for a few hours."

Dario Menarini said, "Major, look at my father. He is seventy years old. Surely you will not force him to work?"

The major beckoned with his good arm. "Go back inside, old man," he said. "We have four or five other volunteers, and you will not be needed."

As the work party marched up the road toward Casaglia, the one-armed officer turned and shouted to Elena, "Remember! Two hours, and then they will be returned!"

Back inside the house, the women chattered about the incident, and concluded that they had nothing to worry about. "The raiding is over now," Aunt Maria said, "and now it will be live and let live. They have no further need of killing. The partisans are gone."

Early on the same day Antonio Tonelli and his eight-year-old son, Vittorio, sneaked back to the shambles of their house at Possatore di Casaglia to try to find some food. As soon as they approached, they noticed that the barn door was open, and when they entered the half-burned kitchen, they found that the remains of their flour had been eaten. Motioning Vittorio to wait, Antonio climbed the ladder to the upstairs and found his seventy-eight-year-old uncle, Achille Moli, shoveling a pasty flour-and-water mixture into his old mouth. *"Zio!"* Antonio said, embracing the old man who had been missing since the first hours of the raid. "I was sure you were dead!"

"Dying of hunger, *Nipote,*" old Achille said, "but not yet dead."

"A few people are near the *portico* trying to make bread without getting caught," Antonio said. "They would welcome your skill."

Antonio and Vittorio took the old man to the outdoor bakers and resumed their foraging for food. They had almost reached the path leading toward Ca' Dizzola when they heard shouts and cries. They ducked into the thick brush and watched as a German patrol herded eight or nine men along the path with gun butts and kicks and bloodcurdling SS cries. Antonio recognized Attilio and Giulio Ruggeri, Dario Menarini and a few men from the valley. He held his finger to his lips to signal Vittorio to remain quiet, and when the patrol had passed, he said, "Vittorio, we must warn the Ruggeris that their men have been captured."

Father and son passed near the *portico* and the bread bakers on their way to Pudella, and they heard a man screaming, "Toni! Toni! Help me!"

"It is *Zio!*" Antonio said, and they rushed to see what was going on. Through a clearing in the brush, they saw two German soldiers carrying the aged uncle, his feet barely touching the ground. Antonio and Vittorio followed at a distance, and they could hear the Germans loudly demanding food and money.

"Niente!" old Achille cried. "I have nothing!" The squirming threesome disappeared in the direction of Possatore, and after they reached the house and disappeared inside, Antonio could still hear the Germans shouting and complaining. Every time Antonio heard his uncle try to speak, the German voices would interrupt, and soon the old man's voice died away altogether.

Antonio and Vittorio remained in the bushes for many hours, but they heard nothing more, and at nightfall they crept toward the house to see what had happened. The old man was hanging from a tree in the front yard. Then and there Antonio decided that nothing but evil could come from staying around the old home. Their loved ones were buried; the food was gone; the house was a wreck—there was nothing to keep them in this cursed place. Antonio decided to go over the ridge to his sister's house at Creda. Little Vittorio was following close behind when two German soldiers stepped out on the path and told Antonio that he would be needed for a work detail.

By late Friday morning Sister Benni and the Pirettis and all the others who had returned to Cerpiano had finished cleaning the mess the Germans had made in the kitchen of the *palazzo*. Then the door opened, and dozens of German soldiers piled in. For a moment, both groups seemed puzzled, but a German officer with a missing hand stepped to the front, pointed to the door leading to the basement, and said, *"Civili raus!"* When Maximiliano Piretti lagged behind to ask what was going on, he was lashed with a rifle barrel and sent tumbling to the bottom. The door was shut, and the surprised refugees huddled together in the darkness and tried to decide what to do.

"Maybe we can just walk away," said Felippo Pirini, Lidia's aged uncle. "At least we can try." He opened the door leading directly to the outside and walked into a German sentry. "Why do you hold us here?" the uncle asked.

"Because you are partisan spies," the German said. "If you try to leave, you will be shot."

The noises from upstairs indicated that the Germans were installing themselves in the twelve big rooms of the *palazzo*, and after a while one of the officers came down and asked for women to help clean a pair of geese and prepare a meal. He grabbed the wounded Lidia Pirini, but she held up her hands imploringly and said, "Oh, please, you cannot make me work. I am wounded!"

"How were you wounded?" the German asked.

"I have a hole in my side and a dislocated hip," the girl said.

"I want to know *how* you were wounded, not where," the German said.

Lidia did not want to stamp herself as a survivor of Casaglia. "The Americans!" she blurted out. "The Americans dropped one of their bombs, and the shrapnel hit me."

"Let me see," the German said.

"It is a personal matter," Lidia said.

"Let me see!" the German snapped.

Lidia raised the edge of her dress as carefully as possible, making sure to keep the rest of her body concealed, and showed the German her festering wound. "That is not a shrapnel wound," he said. "That is the wound of a bullet."

"Maybe it is," Lidia said quickly. "But it happened when an American plane was attacking."

The German stepped back and looked at the fifteen-year-old girl coldly. She dropped her eyes. Finally, he turned away and said, "We will see about you, young lady." He poked Sister Benni and two other women in the basement. *"Avanti!"* he said, and hustled them up the steps toward the kitchen.

The postman Bertuzzi and his family stayed in hiding in the river town of Marzabotto for a week after the *rastrellamento,* but there was no news of any sort from the mountain, and they decided to return to their home in Sperticano. They found that German troops occupied their house, the rectory of the church, and half the other houses in the village. Angelo and his wife and the two little children knocked on doors until they found a dwelling that was unoccupied, and there they took up residence. The postman donned his gray cap with the red stripe, shouldered his leather bag and walked off to deliver the mail that had accumulated in Marzabotto in his absence. He marched past several groups of flabbergasted German soldiers, and headed up the mountain.

The postman approached San Martino shortly after noon, and the woods seemed to him uncommonly silent. There was no cry of *"Whay, Postein!"* from old Gisetto's house; in fact, Gisetto's house now consisted of three walls toppled against one another. There were no bird whistles from the little glade at Poggio di San Martino, and for one of the few times in his life, the postman walked through the whole wood without flushing a rabbit or a grouse.

As he came into sight of San Martino, he could see that there had been a fire, and it had left behind a peculiar odor, more like garbage than smoke. Walking by the ruined *casa colonica,* he thought he saw an arm hanging out a window, and farther down the road, he came upon several bodies in a state of decay. As he turned the corner toward the church, he saw that forty or fifty half-burned bodies were lined in a neat row on one edge of the piazza. A big sign was posted in front of them.

The postman did not stop to read. He ran all the way down the mountain, past the same groups of German soldiers, and into the house where he had billeted his family. "It is terrible!" he shouted as the door shut behind him. "It is horrible. It is like going from heaven to hell!" His wife calmed him, and Angelo ordered the children from the room while he told her what he had seen.

"And now what do we do, *caro?"* she said when the story was finished.

"I do not know," Angelo said. "We are here, and the Germans are here, and I would not dare take you and the girls back to Marzabotto through these swarms of killers."

"Then maybe it would be better for you to take up your duties," his wife said.

From then on Angelo made his regular morning bike ride to the main post office at Marzabotto and picked up what mail there was. Usually it consisted of a few letters from Italian prisoners of war writing to their families on Monte Sole. Angelo would bring the letters to the house and go over them with his wife. There was a law that required that all deliverable mail be held for one year and then macerated, but whenever he could, the postman attempted delivery. Failing that, he would send the letter back with a short personal note or put it aside to be handed to the soldier when the war was over. Every day he walked his old route: from Sperticano up to San Martino and then to the other side of the ridge at Casaglia and back past the flattened *tabacchi* and down the mountain to his home. He was showing the Germans that he had a job, an official function: carrying letters for the dead.

Attilio and Giulio Ruggeri did not return in two hours or two days, nor did any of the other men who had gone off to work for the amiable one-armed major. Soon after their departure, the five-year old Vincenzo Soldati died, and a burial party consisting of Elena Ruggeri, seventy-year-old Augusto Menarini and his thirteen-year-old son, Giorgio, laid the child to rest. With the death of Vincenzo, Elena grew fearful for her cousin Elide. Three wounded persons, Angelina Paselli, little Vincenzo and Elide, had been brought into the kitchen infirmary at Ca' Pudella, and now two of them were dead. It mattered little that their wounds had not been major. There were only vinegar and water for medicine and ripped-up clothes for bandages, and under those conditions the slightest injury could kill. Old Angelina had died mostly from loss of blood, and Vincenzo from a shallow scalp wound that turned gangrenous. Elide could be next.

Her cousin's peril was on Elena's mind when she answered a knock early one morning to find that the tall blond German doctor had returned after an absence of a week. "So?" he said. "You remain at home? And how is your lovely cousin this morning?" He pushed through the door and went straight to the kitchen, where Elide lay, as usual, on her mattress.

"Ah, how much you look like my fiancée this morning!" he said as he knelt alongside the wounded girl. Elide did not answer.

"Let me see your injury," he said, and when Elide hesitated, he said, "Come, come, now! This is your doctor speaking. I have brought you medication."

Elena caught her cousin's eye and nodded slightly. Better medication from an SS doctor than death from an infected wound.

The doctor cleaned and cauterized the injury, working with skilled fingers, and applied a white cream and bandages that encircled Elide just below the waist. "There!" he said. "You will survive this accident, dear child, and just to make sure, I will return every few days to change the dressing." Elide looked at her cousin wanly.

On Sunday, a week after the massacre, the boy Fernando Piretti was in the courtyard of Cerpiano watching the Germans shoot the heads off the chickens that they planned to have for dinner. His shoulder hurt from his wound, but his father had been cleaning it each day with vinegar and water and bandaging it with pieces of bed sheet, and Fernando could tell by the itchy, pinching feeling that the wound was healing. He was not so sure about little Paola Rossi's wound. Her injured eye bulged from its socket, and sometimes blood and a whitish fluid seeped from the corners. Maximiliano had no idea how to treat such an injury, and the German doctor refused to examine any of the Italians living in the basement. Sister Benni had a slight wound, too, in her arm, but that was progressing nicely under daily treatment.

Now one of the Germans was emitting shrill SS yells and chasing a rabbit across the barnyard, and when the rabbit turned the corner into a cul-de-sac, the German skulled it with a heavy stick. Fernando felt like pointing out that the domestic farm rabbits did not have to be hunted down so ferociously; they only had to be picked up and put to death gently. But he held his tongue. He did not want to jeopardize his standing with the Germans. They had made him a sort of mascot, allowing him the run of the place, sending him on minor errands like getting water, and giving him their worthless Italian coins until he had a stack of them hidden under his bed. Sometimes they even joked with him and patted him on the head, and at nine years of age Fernando did not know what to make of such behavior. All the troops at Cerpiano were of the SS: you could tell by the death's heads on their hats and the parallel bolts of lightning that looked like crooked 44's on their uniforms. Fernando remembered that it had been the SS that had lined them up outside Cerpiano and tortured and murdered them for a day and a half.

Try as he might, Fernando could not reconcile the various actions of these uniformed foreigners. He recalled that certain members of the SS had been kind to him even before the massacre. They had questioned him pleasantly and given him chocolates, and just when he had come to trust them, they had thrown everyone into the death chapel. Fernando decided to accept their new kindness but never to turn his back on anyone wearing the crooked 44.

Sister Benni strolled into sight from the direction of the kitchen, where several of the women had been pressed into service. Fernando never knew what to say to Sister Benni. His parents had not sent him to her *asilo,* and therefore, he had not established a close relationship with her, and he found her difficult to understand. For one thing, she was almost always smiling and cheerful, and sometimes Fernando wanted to shake her and say, "Sister, Sister, we are in a bad spot here," but he knew that if he did, she would only tut-tut him and smile the problem away. So he said, "Well, today is Sunday."

Sister Benni smiled and said, "Yes, and what a beautiful Sunday it is, too."

Fernando looked up at the dull glow of dirty orange that signified the sun on this cloudy morning and said, "What is so beautiful about it, Sister? It is going to rain again, and we are being held prisoner, and we just finished burying all our dead. How can you say it is a beautiful day?"

"This is the day that our Lord gave us," Sister Benni said. "This is *His* day, and therefore, it is beautiful."

"To me, every day up here is the same," Fernando said.

"I understand, my child," Sister Benni said, "but when you get older, you will learn to rejoice in what the Lord gives you."

"What does He give me?" Fernando asked, but Sister Benni had already started walking toward the kitchen.

"They do not like me to leave the sink," she said over her shoulder. "I will speak with you later, Fernando."

That night they all reassembled in the dark basement and tried to get to sleep. The basement was vast and broken into several rooms. In one, the furniture of the *palazzo* had been stored for the duration, and in another were the big vats and demijohns of winemaking. Some of the women would crawl into the old armchairs and sofas and sleep. The wounded Lidia Pirini had found herself a small cot, and she slept with the blanket over her head. Fernando and his father and old Felippo Pirini leaned against one another for warmth on the floor at the bottom of the steps. They were talking softly about their plight when the door above them opened with a bang and a flashlight beam dazzled their sleepy eyes. *"Donne! Dov'è donne?"* a big German shouted. "Women? Where are the women?"

Maximiliano, the unofficial spokesman for the group, climbed the steps slowly to deal with the German, and Fernando saw the door shut and heard loud voices. A few minutes later, his father came stumbling down the stairs. "They want a woman upstairs," he said. "I hate to ask, but who will go?"

Fernando looked around in the darkness. Sister Benni was missing; he had heard noises from the winemaking room, and he suspected that she was hiding in one of the big *tini*. Lidia Pirini had pulled the covers even higher over her head, and Fernando could see that both her hands gripped the edges. Three or four other women, whose names Fernando did not know, lay mute on the stored furniture of the basement.

"Do I have to tell them that no one will join them?" Maximiliano said. "They promise it is only for a party."

There was silence in the basement. "I understand, ladies," Maximiliano said, and resumed his place on the floor next to Fernando.

Fernando said, *"Babbo—"*

"Shut up!" his father said. "This is no business of yours!"

After a few minutes the upstairs door was flung open again, and Fernando heard the sound of boots descending the stone staircase. "Well?" a German officer said to Maximiliano. "Where are they?"

Maximiliano did not answer. The officer took two steps to Lidia Pirini's cot and grabbed at the blanket. It did not yield. When he pulled harder and still the blanket remained in place, the officer backed off and shouted at the top of his lungs, *"Genug! Basta!* Enough!" He walked to the place where the furniture was stored, shook one woman hard, and said, "Will you come to our party?"

"No," the woman said.

He shook another. "And you," he said, "do you refuse to join us?"

"I refuse," she said.

The German stalked across the basement floor and climbed the steps two at a time. He returned within seconds with several burly SS men, and three of the women were dragged up the stone steps and flung through the open doorway. Fernando heard a German voice shouting excitedly and answering laughs from six or seven others. For the life of him, he could not understand what was happening. No one could argue that the Germans were pleasant or lovable men, but one did not have to find them lovable to join them at a party. A few drinks, a dance or two, and the women would return safely to the basement.

Fernando did not dare ask his father to explain what was going on, and he fell asleep thinking about it. He did not know what time it was when he heard a scuffling noise from the stairs and sat up to see.

"Turn yourself away!" his father ordered.

"Why?" Fernando asked.

"Because I tell you to!" Maximiliano said.

The nine-year-old boy peeked anyway. At the top of the stairs he could see three figures silhouetted: one was a naked woman, and the other two were Germans, one of whom Fernando recognized as the doctor. The woman was screaming and thrashing about, and the Germans were trying to get a grip on her. As Fernando watched, the soldiers stepped back and kicked the woman down the stairs. The door slammed shut, and Fernando could hear the sounds of laughter retreating in the hall.

This SS headquarters at Cerpiano, on the southeastern face of Monte Sole, was soon matched by another SS outpost at Sperticano, far around the mountain at the bottom of the northwestern slope. Germans were billeted all over the village, but the command post, under the direction of a stubby little captain, was in Don Fornasini's church. The school was lined with cots for thirty or forty enlisted men, and three or four rooms of the rectory were occupied by the officers and their orderlies. A first-aid station was set up around the *fontana* in the middle of the churchyard.

At first, the arrangement posed few problems for those who lived in the rectory. There were Corina Bertacchi Fornasini, wife of the priest's brother, Luigi, the priest's old mother, two or three refugee women from Bologna, and Don Giovanni himself, home from his mission to the city. The other men were hiding in the woods, and Don Giovanni was all that stood between the women and the soldiers.

To Corina, the priest seemed like a changed person. He hardly spoke, refused to explain what he had accomplished in Bologna, and in general acted like a man in permanent shock. The Germans kept him under virtual house arrest, and his infrequent requests to leave the zone on church business were uniformly denied.

But except for the depressed behavior of her brother-in-law, Corina had little to complain about. The Germans had been rigorously correct. A few of the soldiers had acted flirtatious, but no more so than the typical young *contadino,* and Corina and the other women had no trouble fending them off. Every night there would be sounds of wild shouting and carousing from the direction of the church school, and the next morning Corina would have to find room for twenty or thirty empty wine bottles, but the Germans seemed satisfied to get drunk by themselves.

On the afternoon of Thursday, October 12, nearly two weeks after the opening shot of the *rastrellamento,* a delegation of German soldiers walked into the rectory for a word with the priest. Don Giovanni escorted them into his office, and took down his German-Italian-German pocket dictionary. The soldiers announced that today was the birthday of their captain, and they asked if the priest would object if they held a small observance. Standing in the hallway listening, Corina wondered why the soldiers were asking for permission; they held wild parties every night without consulting anyone. "We would like to invite a few of the ladies," one of the Germans said.

"You are free to invite them," Corina heard Don Giovanni answer coldly.

Promptly at seven in the evening, a trio of scrubbed and scented German soldiers entered the rectory and issued a blanket invitation to Corina and a pair of refugees named Anna and Carla. All three answered politely that they were busy with their household duties. "If you stay here, you insult our captain!" one of the soldiers said loudly. "We will take this one, this one, and this one!" He pointed to all three women, and Corina quickly said, "Oh, but I cannot go. My baby is deathly ill!" The Germans grabbed the other two and hauled them toward the church school. Just as they left, Corina turned and saw Don Giovanni slipping into a pair of shoes.

"What are you doing?" she said to her brother-in-law.

"I am also invited to the party," he said, and hurried out the door.

All evening long Corina could hear loud noises from the church school, and she was unable to rid herself of a sense of doom. She knew that the combination of twenty or thirty German soldiers, two handsome young girls and a parish priest was volatile. Even when laughter came across the courtyard and an accordion began butchering a medley of Italian street songs, Corina could not relax. At midnight she heard loud voices coming from the entrance to the school, and a few minutes later the two girls burst in the door of the rectory. "What is it?" Corina called.

The girls told her that an argument had been raging off and on through the evening. Whenever a drunken German would attempt to fondle one of the girls, Don Giovanni would quickly step in between and say, "What are you doing to my niece?" After this had happened several times, the captain loudly ordered Don Giovanni to mind his own business, but the priest persisted in protecting the two young women from the increasingly abandoned advances of the soldiers, and finally he had instructed Anna and Carla to go home. *"Bene!"* a German soldier said. "We will see them to the door."

"*I* will see them to the door," Don Giovanni said. "It is only thirty feet away."

At that, the fat little captain lurched across the schoolroom, and a hush fell upon the others. "So it shall be!" the captain said. His face had turned from red to purple, and the two girls had thought he was going to strike the priest. "You walk the girls home, Father! Allow no harm to befall them, by all means! And the instant they are safely inside, *you are to return here!*"

"I am sleepy," the priest said. "I must say mass in the morning."

"You will return here!" the captain screamed. He turned to a couple of soldiers. "Go with the father, and make sure he returns!"

When Corina Bertacchi heard the whole story, she tried to calm the two young women, but she felt no calmness within herself. "You know how men are," she said. "That is all that is going on: men being men. They will shout at Don Giovanni and have a few more bottles of wine, and then all will be friends."

Corina went back to bed, but once again she could not sleep. Loud noises came from the church school, and now and then she would hear the sounds of glass breaking, followed by raucous laughter. She could not make out Don Giovanni's voice, but there was so much noise that no individual voice was audible, not even the loud little captain's. Against the background of racket, Corina finally dozed off.

The next morning she was surprised to see that the captain was right on time for his eight o'clock coffee, but before he sat down, he told one of the young women, "Go upstairs and awaken the father and tell him it is time for our appointment."

By the time Don Giovanni came down the stairs, rubbing his eyes and carrying his prayer book, the captain had finished the coffee and gone out. "Sit down to breakfast, Don Giovanni," Corina said. "You need something in your stomach."

Don Giovanni brushed past his sister-in-law almost as though he had not seen her. "I must go to San Martino," he said in a flat monotone. "I must do my duty."

"What are you talking about?" Corina said. "Sit down to breakfast."

"There is no time," the priest mumbled. "I have been praying all night. I have been told there are dead in the cemetery." His voice was hardly audible as he added, "Many dead." He instructed the women to prepare a container of holy water and to get his *asperge,* the wand for holy water. "Go into the church," he said to the girl named Anna, "and prepare some of the host for me to take." When the girl had returned with the holy bread, the priest's old mother came into the room and asked Don Giovanni where he was going.

"To San Martino," he said in that same flat, subdued voice. "I must bury the dead."

His mother threw herself upon him, crying, and said, "You cannot go, my son. I have heard about San Martino. It is not safe there."

The priest disengaged her gently. "I must go, Mother," he said. "Do not try to delay me."

"Who is waiting?" Corina said.

"They are waiting," the priest repeated vaguely, and stepped outside.

Corina ran behind him, and she could see that her brother-in-law was saying his beads in Latin as he approached the steep path toward the mountain cemetery. "Please, please!" she cried. "Do not go to that unsafe place!"

"My defense is the rosary," Don Giovanni said, and turned to climb the mountain.

After Vittoria Negri had buried her dead, the people of Ca' Roncadelli were hard pressed. The Germans had moved into Sperticano in force, distributing themselves all over the village and turning the church into a command post. Ca' Roncadelli was only a short walk across the fields, and the big *casa colonica* was highly visible from the valley. There were wounded in the house, and a handful of able-bodied men, and a few uninjured women. As usual, Vittoria had taken charge. She made arrangements with the priest of Marzabotto to send a rattletrap old car to take her wounded aunt, Maria Negri, to the hospital in Bologna. The aunt was the only victim of the massacre to be accorded such treatment, and she survived, though losing an eye. Emilia Carboni, Vittoria's thirteen-year-old niece, stayed at Ca' Roncadelli, where Vittoria patched up her minor flesh wound, and Marisa Tomesani, the eleven-year-old refugee from Bologna, also stayed behind with a bullet hole through the shoulder region. The men returned to the big house to sleep each night, but in the daytime Vittoria would shoo them off to the woods. Orfeo, with his crippled leg, was the only man allowed inside the house by daylight, although brother Fernando was always prowling around in violation of the rule. At the slightest unexpected sound, Fernando would sprint out the back door or shinny into the air space around the chimney.

Food supplies were low, and all that remained in any quantity was flour. But flour had to be made into bread, and although Vittoria made several attempts, she was not able to produce a loaf. If there were Germans in the vicinity, she could not even start the fire, for fear of attracting them to the house. Twice she had begun baking only to have to run for the woods when the Germans approached, and another time she was about to mix the dough when an Allied air attack sent everyone sprawling into the basement.

Several dozen men, survivors of Roncadelli and the other *poderi* up the mountain, were roaming the woods like wild animals, and as they grew hungrier, they grew bolder. All day long Vittoria would be running back and forth to the door, answering the loud *Zzzzzzts!* of vermin-infested beggars, some of whom she did not even know. At first she would have a bit of food for each, but as the siege continued, she had barely enough to feed herself and the two wounded girls. The big sacks of flour tempted her, but the danger was too great.

Then one morning Vittoria arose in the chilly darkness before dawn and announced to her brothers that she was disgusted with the life they were leading, and her stomach was hurting from hunger, and she was not going to slink around in terror of the Germans any longer. "Fernando," she said to her older brother, "you go down to the chestnut trees at the end of the path and watch for soldiers. Dante, you go a few hundred yards up the mountain and watch from the other direction. Orfeo, you watch the fields by the river. And remember! Do not disturb me unless the Germans are heading this way. I have important work."

With all the sentries posted, Vittoria went to the basement and lifted the heavy sacks of flour. "Marisa!" she said. "Emilia! Get some kindling! We are firing up the stove."

All morning long Vittoria prepared the dough for the traditional two-pound *pagnotte* of the region. When the stove was hot, she slid the first mounds of dough inside, and the fresh smell of baking bread was wafted on the air of the mountainside. Two or three men showed up at the back door, and Vittoria ordered them away. "They are not ready," she said. "Wait another hour. They must cool before you can eat."

By early afternoon, thirty-five loaves were cool and ready, and Vittoria sent word to her brothers on sentry duty. Within minutes, there was a loud breadline of bearded men at the back door. Vittoria flung open the door and shouted sarcastically, "If you can only make a little more noise, we can have the SS as luncheon guests!" The men quieted, and Vittoria handed out loaves of the rough-textured, grainy bread of the mountains. In the afternoon, others showed up, some of them sprinting down the mountain, grabbing a loaf and lurching back to their hiding places. Then the earlier arrivals began returning for seconds and thirds, and by late afternoon the thirty-five *pagnotte* were gone. "Sorry," Vittoria said to a knot of late arrivals, "we will have more bread when I get bold and foolish again."

A few days later Vittoria and little Marisa were laying bed sheets across the bushes to dry when three German soldiers appeared on the path not twenty yards away. The eleven-year-old child began to tremble violently. "Come!" she said to Vittoria. "We must run for our lives."

"Remain still," Vittoria said softly. "Act as though nothing is happening."

The child started to cry. "We must run," she said. "They will shoot me again!"

"Put your faith in God," Vittoria said as the Germans were almost upon them, "but first shut up!"

The young soldiers were smiling and friendly, and one of them said, *"Komm, komm,"* and motioned them toward the house. Vittoria talked loudly as they walked along the path. She knew that her brothers Fernando and Orfeo were inside, and she was trying to give them a warning. She slipped out from under the grasp of one soldier, who tried to put his arm around her, but she tried to remain amiable so as not to annoy the soldiers. Inside the house, the German friendliness turned to brutishness. Two of the soldiers grabbed Vittoria by the arms, and another took the child and hustled them up the stairs and into a bedroom. "You will wait here while we decide what to do with you!" one of the Germans said, leering at the handsome auburn-haired woman. The door slammed and the lock clicked.

Marisa began to cry, and Vittoria said, "For charity, child, if you do not calm yourself, we are both dead, or worse than dead." Vittoria could see the future clearly. The soldiers would rip up the kitchen looking for food. Then they would find the few bottles of wine that remained in the basement and sit in the kitchen drinking. There was not a German soldier alive who could drink more than a glass or two of the local wine without getting drunk, and once drunk, their behavior was always the same. Vittoria knew she had to work fast.

There were two doors in the bedroom. One led directly down the stairs and into the kitchen, where already she could hear the Germans tearing the doors off the cabinets. The other door was hidden behind a six-foot-high armoire, placed there to provide a little privacy for the Bologna refugees who had been renting the next room. Vittoria opened the armoire and began tearing at the wood panels in the back. If they could get into the other room, they could get down the back stairway into the pantry and from there out the door to the yard. One of the boards of the armoire came loose, and Vittoria began ripping the back out without arousing the attention of the Germans below. Luckily, they were shouting and laughing; apparently they had already found the wine. One by one Vittoria tore the panels loose until the door to the next room was exposed. As she expected, it was locked. The doors of the old *casa colonica* were thick and heavy, and Vittoria knew she could not make a dent in the wood with her hands. She walked to the other side of the room, got up a head of steam, and threw her entire weight against the heavy door. The wood did not give, but the old lock burst, and the door banged open.

Vittoria waited for the Germans to come see about the noise, but there was no interruption in the bacchanal below. She motioned to Marisa to come with her, and as they were tiptoeing toward the back stairs, they heard a male voice say, *"Zzzzzzt!* Vittoria!" It was Fernando, wedged tightly into the air space above the fireplace.

"Here," Vittoria said, "take the child!" Marisa disappeared up the hole. "Do you have room?" Vittoria asked.

"Just enough," Fernando whispered.

Vittoria opened the door leading to the stone staircase that ran down to the pantry. She slid full length down the steps like a snake and continued on her belly through the pantry and past the door to the kitchen, where the Germans were now singing lustily. She opened the back door slowly and saw that a sentry had been posted ten yards away near the barn. Each time he turned his back, she opened the door another few inches, and finally, there was a crack wide enough for her to slip out. Wriggling across the yard so close to the ground that her clothes tore in strips from her body, Vittoria made it to the edge of the brush leading toward the top of Monte Sole. She kept going until she was out of the brush and into the woods, and then she climbed into a chestnut tree to hide. She stayed thus, naked except for a ragged collar of cloth around her neck, bleeding from hundreds of scratches, burning and itching from the nettles she had slid through, until nightfall, and then she walked down the mountain toward the house. As she reached the path leading toward Ca' Roncadelli, she saw two men of the neighborhood, but they ran pell-mell as she approached.

"Stop!" Vittoria shouted. "Help me! It is Vittoria!" The men doubled back and approached her from another angle, and soon Vittoria recognized the owner of the *osteria* in Sperticano and a man she knew only as Neroni.

"There were Germans at the house," Vittoria said. "Are they gone?"

"We saw Germans walking back toward Sperticano just a short time ago," Neroni said. "They caught your brother Dante as he was coming up the path, but when they were trying to tie him to a tree, he knocked one of them down and ran. I think he is hiding in the brush. They shot at him, but they were so drunk I think they must have missed."

Vittoria ran to the house and found Fernando and Marisa standing in the kitchen removing their damp clothes. "Mercy!" Vittoria said. "What has happened here?"

Fernando embraced his younger sister. "Vittoria!" he said happily. "Once again you are safe and alive when we thought you were dead!"

Fernando said that the Germans had come up the stairs to reclaim their female prizes almost as soon as she had left, and they flew into a violent rage when they saw that she was gone. Huddled in the chimney space with the little girl in his arms, Fernando listened to a series of SS war whoops, loud rippings as one of the soldiers thrust his bayonet into the armoire, and finally the sounds of furniture being flung against the stone walls. When the Germans stepped through the broken armoire and began sniffing around the fireplace, Fernando became so frightened that he lost control of his kidneys and drenched both himself and the child. The two of them had remained in the chimney until dark.

At about three o'clock the next morning, Vittoria's crippled brother, Orfeo, and her other brother, Dante, returned to Ca' Roncadelli, and Vittoria tended to a bullet hole that had gone through the fleshy part of Dante's arm. When the first aid was finished, the brothers and Vittoria sat down to a council of war. "We are no longer safe in our home," Vittoria said, "but what do we do next?"

"I think we go to Bologna," Fernando said.

"But why?" Vittoria asked. "Even if we could get to Bologna, we would be hunted down. By now they know who we are, and other survivors have been killed because of what they saw."

"I do not believe those stories," Dante said.

"I do," Vittoria said. Several days before, a woman from Sperticano had come by the house at Ca' Roncadelli with tales of refugees from Monte Sole being arrested and tortured at an SS detention camp up the road at Colle Ameno. A few had escaped, and they reported that nineteen of the others were taken before a firing squad. Anyone who had any knowledge of the massacre of Monte Sole was being executed. The woman had brought a page from *Il Resto del Carlino,* the Fascist newspaper in Bologna, and Vittoria had read the "official" story of the massacre:

> The usual uncontrolled voices, typical products of galloping fantasy in wartime, were telling us until yesterday that in the

> course of the police operation against a band of outlaws a good 150 women, old men and children were shot by the German troops in a raid in the commune of Marzabotto. We are able to refute those macabre voices and what they have had to say, and to the official denial we will add what we have learned during an investigation of the place. It is true that in the zone of Marzabotto there was carried out a police operation against a nucleus of rebels, who suffered strong losses, including their dangerous commander. But fortunately it is not in the least true that the raid produced the decimation and sacrifice of well over 500 civilians. We find ourselves face to face with the usual thoughtless talk bordering on the ridiculous. Anyone who takes the time to interview any honest inhabitant of Marzabotto or the adjoining areas will have an authentic version of the facts.

Sitting with her brothers in the chill stone farmhouse as the first light of dawn began to slip through the narrow windows, Vittoria reminded them of the newspaper article. "That is the official version of what happened on Monte Sole," she said. "Can you not understand that anyone who threatens that version must die? The SS has already killed hundreds. What are a few more?"

"I believe the executions are over," Orfeo said. "The Wehrmacht is moving in, and soon this will be a battleground. There will be no more attention paid to civilians when the fighting starts."

"Well, my brothers," Vittoria said, "you may do as you please. I am going to find the Americans."

Several days later the family broke up for the duration. The brothers headed north with the injured children, and Vittoria cast her lot with three women from Sperticano who had decided to breach the front lines, now only a few miles to the south. The women walked through the woods all night, and at dawn they ran into an American patrol. They were taken to an Allied command post at Grizzana, a small town just below Monte Salvaro, and trucked to the Allied refugee center at Florence, fifty air miles away. There they were brought before an Italian-speaking U.S. officer for routine interrogation, and when Vittoria tried to tell him about the massacre of Monte Sole, he said, "Never mind. We know all about it."

The sisters Paselli, Giuseppina and Cornelia, hid out in an air-raid shelter not far from Railroad House No. 66 for several days after they were reunited at Cerpiano, and gradually they began to hear reports and rumors about their father, Virginio, the trackworker, missing since the first morning of the massacre. "Your father is alive and wandering around Monte Sole," one refugee told them, "but he is half-crazy. He thinks you were all killed, and he speaks of killing himself." Another told the sisters that Virginio had been captured and killed by the Germans on the first day.

"I do not care about these stories," Cornelia told her sister. "We are going to find *Babbo*."

A string of air-raid shelters had been carved all around the mountain, and every one of them was full of refugees from the massacre. Giuseppina and Cornelia visited dozens of the shelters looking for Virginio, and at each one they left word that they could be reached themselves in the refuge at San Mamonti. One night, as they were bedding down on their sleeping mats, a familiar bald head appeared at the entrance to the shelter, and the two girls almost knocked their father down with the force of their greeting. When all the crying and hugging were finished, old Virginio said softly, "Tell me, my *bimbe,* what of your mother?"

"She was killed in the first burst," Cornelia said.

When Giuseppina started to say something, Cornelia interrupted quickly and said, "She died instantly and without pain." Giuseppina kept quiet.

"And the twins?" Virginio said.

"It was the same with them," Cornelia said.

Four days later Virginio told the girls to wait for him at the refuge while he returned to Cerpiano to dig up some of the family's valuables behind the *palazzo*. Every family on the mountain had buried its silver and dishes and bed linens, and Virginio explained that he did not want them to flee to Bologna without retrieving their valuable possessions. Cornelia was against the return trip to the mountaintop. "The Germans will capture you, *Babbo!*" she cried, and held her father by the arm.

"I will only be gone a few hours, and I am going by way of the woods," Virginio said. "The Germans will never see me."

Cornelia became almost hysterical. "Please, please, *Babbo!*" she begged. "We can get our things later. Please, *Babbo!* You will be killed!"

Virginio extricated himself gently from his daughter's grasp. "I will not be long," he said, and headed up the path.

But night fell, and Virginio did not return, and then a whole week of nights fell without a trace of the father. Gradually the refugees in the shelter moved north out of the battle area, and one day the girls woke up to find that they were alone in a mountain cave, waiting for Virginio. Not far to the south, the heavy guns of the Allies could be heard ripping into the flanks of Monte Sole. When the battle approached their shelter, the girls walked several miles to the home of an aunt in the valley, but soon the retreating Wehrmacht arrived and evacuated them to Bologna. On the first day in the big city, Cornelia went to the refugee hospital seeking information about her father. She found several men of Monte Sole who had been injured by Allied shells while on forced labor parties on the mountain, and one of them said that Virginio had been picked up and put to work carrying ammunition for the Wehrmacht.

From then on, Cornelia and her sister haunted the hospitals of Bologna, and even hospitals farther out in the country, to the very limits of safety. They left descriptions of Virginio and their own address everywhere they went, and one night a young German soldier told them that their father was twelve miles away at Villa Stella, a country mansion that had been converted into a hospital. "But I was there two days ago, and he was not on the register," Cornelia said.

"He is there now, *Signorina,*" the German told her.

Cornelia walked to the hospital in four hours, and when she asked for Virginio Paselli, she was handed a cloth bag tied at the top. Inside was Virginio's wallet, his identification card from the railroad, a pair of rough trousers and a white woolen undershirt that Cornelia recognized immediately. It had been knitted from the wool of Tay-a by their mother. "And now can I see my father?" Cornelia asked.

"Oh, I am sorry," the attendant said. "I thought you had been told. Your father was hit by American shrapnel. He died this morning."

Gioacchino Piretti stayed in his apartment at Calvenzano for several days, or until he was able to recover the composure he had left in the bottom of the *botte* of Pioppe di Salvaro, and then he went to see the secretary of the local Fascio for advice. They were boyhood chums, and Gioacchino knew there was not the slightest chance that the secretary would turn him over to the Germans. "You are in a bad position, Gioacchino," the man said. "The SS thinks that everyone died in the *botte*. The next night they opened the valves and flushed all the bodies down the river. Now there is no evidence except you."

"Another one or two survived," Gioacchino said. He had heard that a man named Pio Borgia had escaped by climbing up a grate, and his one-legged friend Aldo Ansaloni was recovering.

"Do not tell me the names!" the secretary said. "You are all in terrible danger. You will be killed on sight if the SS finds out about you."

Gioacchino and his wife and his friend Ansaloni waited until late at night and succeeded in reaching a seminary to the north, where they were secreted in a second cellar by the priests. But after two weeks they decided that death was preferable to this dank cell in the earth and crawled out. Moving only at night and hiding from German patrols by day, they made their way slowly and painfully toward Bologna.

Two weeks after the massacre of Monte Sole, American artillery had triangulated the SS headquarters at Cerpiano, and shells began to arc toward the building from emplacements on the opposite bank of the Setta. Late one afternoon, in the middle of an intense shelling, the one-armed SS commanding officer rushed into the basement and shouted, *"Civili raus!"* He pointed toward the other door, the one that led to the fields outside, and when a few of the older refugees were slow to understand, the major kicked the door open and began shoving them through.

"Why are we to leave?" Maximiliano asked.

"Because, dumbhead, we need the basement for ourselves," the major said.

A dozen survivors of the massacre straggled across the pockmarked fields behind Maximiliano and Fernando. A few of them, like Lidia Pirini, still limped from wounds, and they were consoled and assisted by Sister Benni, who ran from front to back of the procession telling everyone to believe in God and not to worry. A few carried knotted neckerchiefs full of valuables, but after enduring the massacre and two weeks of imprisonment in the basement, they retained little enough of value. Fernando had a pocketful of the worthless Italian coins the Germans had given him, but Maximiliano had only the clothes on his back. The four women who had been taken up the stairs night after night were no longer with them. Two had escaped by running naked across the fields early one morning, and two others had simply vanished. Fernando did not dare ask his father what had happened.

As the survivors made their way across the stubble of wheat, the shells fell all around them. It was almost as though the Americans could see them making their slow way and thought they were soldiers. They had walked about a quarter mile from the buildings of Cerpiano when the shelling became so intense that Maximiliano herded the group behind a haystack and told them to lie down. Seconds later, a smoking cylinder of red-hot metal came flying through the air end over end and landed in the hay. "Stay away!" Maximiliano shouted, and as Fernando moved a step closer for a better look, his father grabbed him by the shoulder and yanked him back sharply. The refugees watched transfixed as the piece of metal set the haystack on fire, and they were obliged to run through open fields to the ruins of a farmhouse. "We will all have to stay here," Maximiliano said.

That night the shelling subsided, and Fernando and his father went out to look for food. They found a bonanza: a sack of potatoes hidden away in a nearby earthen pantry. For two days and two nights the group lived on the find, but the bombardments grew worse, and soon the walls of the farmhouse were being splattered regularly by Allied shrapnel. To Fernando, it sounded like hail.

"We cannot stay in this house," Maximiliano said to the others.

"There is no place to go," one of the refugees said.

"Everyone may do as he wishes," Maximiliano said, "but I prefer to remove my son to another place. The war has caught up to this one."

Leaving the rest to decide for themselves, father and son struck out into the night. The bombardment was heavy from the south, and every now and then the whole sky would turn incandescent, and the two of them would have to stop and put their hands over their eyes. Once Fernando slipped into a ditch, and his father pulled him out and said, "A slit trench. The footsoldiers are here already."

A barn gave them shelter for the night, but there was nothing to eat, and by dawn they began a mad search for food. In a drainpipe that carried animal urine to the outside, Fernando found a moldy crust of rye bread, and he scraped at it with his fingernails and shared the bread with his father. That night at another ruined farmhouse they found a bladder of lard, and they heated it over a straw fire and drank it like hot, oily cocoa.

The next night they were picked up by the Germans, and Maximiliano was assigned to a work detail that was scarring the long flanks of Monte Sole with trenches and barbed wire. Fernando was allowed to follow his father, and when Maximiliano's assignment was changed to hauling supplies and ammunition on his back, Fernando even tried to help. The Germans thought nothing of working the fifty-three-year-old man from five in the morning till midnight, and Fernando could see the lines of strain etched into his father's face. One night they were handed a cup of soup and led back to work by German soldiers. "I hope I cause us no trouble," Maximiliano whispered to his son, "but I cannot carry any more. My arms are too heavy."

The Germans handed him a field radio and a case of food, but the nine-year-old Fernando quickly took the food from his father and balanced it on his shoulder. He thought the case would break his back, but he struggled manfully as they went from post to post in the black of night, with the Germans calling out the password and papers being checked and the two refugees waiting all the time with their heavy loads.

Fernando guessed it was about two in the morning when they came to the sticky mud, and he had only taken a few steps into it when he fell and dropped his load. When he tried to reposition the case on his shoulder, he found that it had suddenly become too heavy. Maximiliano stepped quickly to his son's side and added the case of food to his own load. A short time later Maximiliano fell flat and did not move.

"Komm!" one of the Germans shouted, pushing at the inert form with his boot. *"Komm! Avanti!"*

Fernando knelt and saw that his father was unconscious and breathing heavily. "Please!" he said. "He is sick. Can you help him?" The Germans angrily picked up the mud-covered cases and slogged into the night.

Father and son lay in the open till morning, when Maximiliano was able to stand. They made their way downhill for several hundred yards until they ran into another German patrol, and this time they were loaded on trucks with others and taken in the direction of Bologna. In Marzabotto, where the Wehrmacht had set up headquarters, the Germans served them minute portions of rice topped by a sweet sauce made of crushed grapes, and Fernando was unable to keep it on his stomach. At the next town a priest rushed to the open truck and handed out crusts of bread, and father and son wolfed it down. As they proceeded northward, they passed three bodies hanging in a public square, and Fernando could make out the words on a big sign THIS WILL BE THE END OF EVERY PARTISAN. A German soldier who was riding with them in the back of the truck pointed, and said, "I hope none of you are partisans, because that is exactly what will happen to you when we get to Mongardino."

Mongardino was a small village off the main road, and the refugees were led into cells by soldiers of the SS. The next morning their dungeon was opened and Fernando and Maximiliano were led outside. "Where do you want to go, old man?" a German soldier asked.

"Only to our home in Gardeletta," Maximiliano said, "on the other side of Monte Sole."

"Go where you wish!" the soldier said, scribbling out a pass. "You are no good to us."

Fernando hardly believed what he had heard, and he grabbed his father by the wrist and began to pull him away. No one bothered them, but as they walked past a barn, the last building in Mongardino, they saw two SS men dragging a young man whom Fernando recognized as one of their companions in the work details on the mountain. "You are a partisan!" a soldier said in perfect Bolognese dialect. "I saw you with the partisans a month ago."

"I remember you," the prisoner said. "And I remember when you and the other partisans came to the house. But I was not with the partisans. I *lived* in that house."

The prisoner was shirtless, and Fernando heard the SS man say, "You like the Red Star so much, let us see how you like a red necktie." He pulled out a knife and slashed the man's neck on each side, and the two rivulets of blood combined down the man's breast to form a perfect red *V*.

"Come!" Maximiliano said, hurrying his son along. They heard two shots, and Fernando looked back to see the SS men kicking the body into a ditch.

"Babbo!" Fernando said. "Where are we going?"

"Where there are no Germans," Maximiliano said. Several days later they arrived on foot at the town of Medicina, where Maximiliano's married sister lived, and they were welcomed and given a room on an upstairs floor. A few days after they arrived, a company of German soldiers pulled into Medicina and began seeking billets around the town. Several moved in with Maximiliano's sister. "Where do we go now, *Babbo?*" Fernando asked.

"We stay here," Maximiliano said. "There is no place left to hide."

It was of no great consequence to Sister Benni whether she remained in this uncomfortable and dangerous farm ruin or was conducted by American shells into the hereafter; whatever happened was God's will, and she would accept it with equanimity. But for the moment she was concerned about the small children who had entrusted themselves to her. Two of them were bleeding from shrapnel wounds, and five-year-old Paola Rossi's wounded eye was beginning to look gangrenous. "Come, children, we are leaving," Sister Benni said, trying to make her voice as pleasant as though they were getting ready to play *giro, giro, tondo* in the *asilo*.

They headed over the hill toward an air-raid shelter, and there they found several dozen refugees waiting out the bombardment. They stayed the night, and the next morning they made their way to another shelter a few miles to the north. In this fashion, traveling from refuge to refuge, Sister Benni and the four children in her charge approached the sanctuary of Bologna. During an air raid one night, they were huddled together in a tiny crack in a cliff when a German soldier rushed up and told them to get out.

"The bombs are falling," Sister Benni said. "We will be killed."

"Jesus Christ, woman," the German said, snuggling into the tiny shelter, "my mother is dead, my father is dead, and my whole family is dead. What in hell do I care if you live or die?"

Sister Benni and the children hurried away from the blasphemous soldier and took refuge against the wall of a bombed-out house. All night long she held Paola in her arms while the other children snuggled against her sides, and in a few days they managed to get a ride on a German truck into the middle of Bologna, where doctors removed the little girl's eye. A few more days, the nurse told Sister Benni, and Paola would have died of infection.

One morning when the shelling was intense and he thought his ears would burst with the noise, Angelo Bertuzzi told his wife and two children to get ready to leave. "It is only a matter of days now," he said, "and Sperticano will be the front lines."

"But the Germans are picking up men for work detail," his wife said.

"Let them pick me up," he said. "It is better than staying in this house and dying under a shell. Besides, I have an idea."

He donned his official kingdom of Italy postal hat, put some food into the bottom of his brown leather bag and covered it with a layer of undelivered letters, and led his family out the door. They were stopped ten times before they reached Marzabotto, two miles away, but each time the postman acted unruffled, showed his identification card and pointed meaningfully to the bulging bag on his back, as though he spent every day delivering mail in the company of his wife and two children.

"Avanti!" each guard said, and the postman gave a little bow and continued with his family up the road. It took two days, but they covered the fifteen miles to Bologna without incident.

Adelmo Benini, his father-in-law, Giovanni "Sassolein" Migliori, and the pilot from Florence, Luigi Cesare, left their cave after a few days because they were afraid the Germans had spotted it, and for a month they wandered through the wooded areas of Monte Sole, trying to avoid the war that exploded around them. Every day was the same: they would comb the woods for chestnuts, hardly ever looking to the trees anymore, but concentrating on the earth below, where a few nuts in advanced stages of disintegration were still to be found. At night, they crept into cornfields and frisked each stalk for stray ears. Sometimes they would search the charred rubble of farmhouses, and once they came up with a super-cooked salami for their pains. Toward the end of their ordeal they began begging at farmhouses in the valley and along the northern border of the mountain zone, where neither the massacre nor the front had reached. Often they were chased by terrified *contadini;* the three of them were living like wild dogs, and they had begun to look the part. Their clothes, kept damp by four weeks of nearly constant rain, were holed and ripped; their beards were long and untrimmed; their bodies stank.

For a time the three refugees were joined by the blacksmith of Quercia, Augusto Moschetti, the man who owned the thresher that gave Adelmo part-time employment, but after five days Moschetti announced that he was going to try to cross the front lines. Adelmo and the other two watched him disappear down the mountain, still carrying the wooden case which contained all his financial accounts. Sometime later the body and the case were dug out of the dirt wall of a cave by a work party that had taken refuge from the rain. Toward the end of October, the refugees were joined by a man named Nino, son of a *cantoniere* (road keeper) of the Setta Valley, but by now there was hardly any food to share. One night Adelmo said, "I have not wanted to leave, because my loved ones are here, but now we have no choice."

"I have a choice," Sassolein said. "I stay."

"But, *Babbo,* there is no food, and we grow weaker," Adelmo said. "You are the oldest, and the weakest. Look at you! You have lost one hundred pounds!"

"Come with us, Sassolein," Cesare said. "We will get through the front lines, and then we will have hot food and dry beds and water to bathe in and shave."

The four men headed for the front under cover of darkness, but after a short walk Adelmo said, *"Zzzzzzt!* Stop!"

"What's the matter?" the pilot asked.

"Sassolein is gone," Adelmo said.

They backtracked up the mountain and found the old man sitting at the base of a tree. "Come, *Babbo*!" Adelmo said. "You are slowing our journey."

"I lack the strength to leave Monte Sole," Sassolein said. "You must go without me."

"But you cannot survive alone, *Babbo,*" Adelmo said.

"Perhaps you are right, my son," Sassolein said, "and if that is true, then I die here."

"And if we stay with you, *Babbo,* we *all* die here."

"That is so, Adelmo, and therefore, I ask you to leave. Better that one worthless old man should die than three young ones like you."

Adelmo hesitated. "Go! Go," Sassolein said, waving his hand toward the river below, the dividing line between Axis and Allies, "and maybe you can send a patrol to pick me up."

Adelmo put his arms around his father-in-law. "Stay here, *Babbo,* and we will send for you." As he rejoined the others, Adelmo found that he was crying, "Why did I have to deceive him?" he said to the pilot. "No patrol would come through the front lines to save an old man."

"You did not deceive him, Adelmo," Cesare said.

Soon the three men were within several hundred yards of the Setta. Adelmo held a finger to his lips. "From here on we will be walking between German positions," he whispered. "Follow me, and do not say a word!" Two minutes later he led them into the center of a chestnut grove where a German sentry was lighting a cigarette. Adelmo and the *cantoniere*'s son saw the flash, and they dropped back into the brush, but the pilot bumbled ahead and almost knocked the sentry down.

"Halt!" the German said. "Where do you go?"

"Only for a walk," Cesare mumbled. "I was not able to sleep."

The soldier clapped the Italian on the shoulder. "Stay away from the front lines, my friend," he said. "The enemy is shelling. Go back to your bed. You will be safer."

"Yes, your honor, I think you are right," Cesare said. He touched his head in a clumsy civilian salute and backed out of the grove.

The three men resumed their slow descent toward the river. Once they heard a patrol of Germans coming up the path and hid in the brush until the way was clear. At last they reached a long cornfield that sloped down to the *direttissima,* and Adelmo knew that the Setta ran along the embankment on the other side. The corn had been cut, and all that remained was the stumps, and the three men got down on their hands and knees and crawled toward a drainage exit across the field. A German head popped out of the earth, and Adelmo shouted, "Roll!"

The three men rolled and slid the remaining hundred feet down the hill while bullets whistled all about them. They scurried through the narrow cement drainpipe and splashed one by one into the Setta on the other side. The water was up to their chests, dirty and roily from the accumulated rains. "Grab hands!" Adelmo shouted, and the three men headed into the river. Nino slipped on a rock and went under, but the other two held on and waited while the *cantoniere*'s son regained his balance. Adelmo slipped into a pool that was over his head, but he quickly backed out and led the way to another route. The water was licking at their chins as they walked through the channel, but then they felt a slope under their feet and clambered up the other side.

"Now what?" Cesare asked.

"Up this hill lives my friend Augusto Nerozzi," Adelmo said. "We will see if his house is safe."

It was midnight when they came into sight of the house, and they had been on the move for seven hours. The house was dark; it lay in full sight of the German positions on the other hill across the Setta. "Let us watch for signs of life," Adelmo whispered. The three men sat for an hour, and at last they were rewarded by the sound of the front door opening and closing in the wet darkness.

"I will see who it is," Adelmo said. He had crept to within fifteen feet of the place when he heard a voice shouting orders. He did not understand a word; the texture of the language was Germanic, but Adelmo heard none of the familiar words like *"Achtung!"* and *"Heraus!"* and *"Halt!"*

He put up his hands and said, *"Italiano!"* and his heart sank as someone answered in German, *"Komm!"*

As they walked into the blacked-out little house, Augusto Nerozzi stepped out of the shadows and said, "Adelmo!"

"Augusto!" Adelmo said, and he saw that Nerozzi was crying. "Augusto, what are you doing here with the Germans?"

"These are not the Germans, my old friend," Nerozzi said, sobbing on Adelmo's shoulder. "These are English soldiers."

"Then why did that one say, *'Komm'?"*

"Oh, Adelmo, where have you been? He did not say, *'Komm.'* He said, 'Come.' That is English."

The two men embraced and cried together, and finally, Adelmo went back into the darkness to fetch the others. They stayed with Nerozzi and the English until morning, and then an American patrol took them to a headquarters position far behind the lines. Adelmo and his two friends remained with the Americans for a month, carrying ammunition and helping wherever they could. Several times Adelmo was questioned by American intelligence officers. "What happened to you?" they would say, and Adelmo would answer, "Nothing much. The Germans killed my family and burned my house."

"Nothing more?" the officer would ask, and Adelmo would say, "Nothing more." He did not go into details because he did not think anyone would be interested.

The relatives of Don Giovanni Fornasini stayed in the church at Sperticano while the battle ebbed and flowed around them. Half the little village had been leveled by Allied artillery and aircraft, but the family stayed on for two reasons: they felt safer in the shadow of their church, and they were waiting for Don Giovanni, who had never returned from his walk up Monte Sole toward the cemetery of San Martino. Several times the priest's brother, Luigi, suggested that it was time to leave, but his mother always said, "No. I forbid it! We will remain here until Don Giovanni returns."

"And if Don Giovanni is dead, Mama?" Luigi would suggest.

"Don Giovanni is not dead!" the mother insisted. "He is on the mountain doing his duty. We will do our duty by waiting."

Luigi went to work for the Germans, reporting each day to an officer who assigned him a work detail. It did not please Luigi to be in uneasy alliance with the same army that had wiped out half the civilians of Monte Sole, but it was preferable to hiding in the woods or behind Casalini's dummy wall. One by one Luigi's friends in hiding had been dragged out and shot to death, worked to death or sent up the road to Colle Ameno, where the SS maintained a small concentration camp for the men of the region.

Early one morning a dirty and disheveled partisan knocked on the door of the rectory and explained that he brought a message from GAP, the partisan command in Bologna. "Don Giovanni Fornasini is alive in a refugee camp in Florence," the partisan said. "It is his wish that you leave the battle zone and take refuge in Bologna. He hopes that you will all be reunited after the war." On Christmas Eve, 1944, Luigi, his wife, Corina Bertacchi, and his old mother packed their belongings, padlocked the rectory, and struggled up the road toward Bologna.

Sitting in the little kitchen at Ca' Pudella, Elena Ruggeri was almost certain that the last hour of her existence had arrived. One month had gone by since the massacre of Monte Sole, and now the sole residents of the house were Elena, her old uncle, Augusto Menarini, his wife, Maria, their son, Giorgio, thirteen years old, and the wounded Elide, who lay on the mattress, still unable to walk because of her hip wound. Now Aunt Maria and Uncle Augusto sat under a table, holding their ears, and Giorgio hid in a closet. The Americans had shelled the mountain every day for two weeks, but this bombardment was the culmination of all the bombardments of history. Thousands of rounds of heavy shells whistled through the air and landed all about the stone house, and in the slight lulls between shells, waves of Allied aircraft came in low to plant their bombs on every last habitation on the mountain.

Just after dark, three German soldiers burst in from the front lines, now only 100 yards away, and ordered Elide out of the bed. "She cannot walk!" Elena cried, and one of the Germans, blood dripping from the remains of his hand, shouted, "Well, she can slide!" and nudged her rudely off the mattress and onto the stone floor. Elena could see that the soldier had lost most of the fingers on one hand. The other two men were slightly wounded, and they sat on the mattress with their comrade.

At nine that night the bombardment stopped after six hours, and a group of German medical corpsmen came to the house and removed the wounded men, carrying the one with the missing fingers on a stretcher.

"Now we must leave!" Elena shouted. "If we stay here, we will not last another day. If the Germans do not get us, the bombardments will!"

"But I cannot walk," Elide said. "How are we to leave? And anyway, where are we to go? The war is everywhere."

The five civilians huddled together in the darkened kitchen until two in the morning, when another group of Germans came into the house and began saying, *"Raus! Raus!"*

"This is our house," Elena said. "My cousin cannot walk. How can you put us out?"

"The wounded one may remain," one of the soldiers said, "but we need the house for ourselves. Everyone else will have to leave."

"I will not leave," Elena said as the three Menarinis crouched behind her. "Where my cousin stays, I stay."

"If you do not leave, you will be shot," the soldier said.

"Elena!" Aunt Maria said. "Do not argue! Come!"

With her aunt pulling at her sleeve, Elena stared hard at the soldier of the Wehrmacht. In the days since the massacre of Monte Sole, she had learned the difference between these regular troops of the German Army and the death squads of the SS, and she felt utterly unawed by this young soldier who stood in front of her trembling at his own words. "Where do you want to hold my execution?" she said. "In here or against the wall outside? If it is to be outside, then please wait while I get my shawl."

The German said, "Wait! I must consult with the sergeant."

A sentry was posted at the door to Ca' Pudella, and the five civilians waited inside till six A.M., when a different party of soldiers arrived, leading a mule. Elide was loaded aboard like a sack of potatoes, and the rest followed behind as a trio of German soldiers led them a half mile across the woods to the command post at Poggio. From there they were transported to Sperticano in the valley of the Reno, and when the war swept through that village, they made their way on foot to Monte San Pietro, to the northwest, where they lived as refugees and waited for the liberation.

Gianni Rossi and three or four other partisans, one of them wounded by shrapnel, limped slowly toward the Allied lines and finally crossed into British positions. "Who are you?" a subaltern asked in Italian.

"I am Gianni Rossi, vice-commander of the brigade of the *Stella Rossa,*" he said. "My brother Gastone and my leader, Mario Musolesi, lie dead on Monte Sole. We ask permission to continue our fight against the Germans."

"Come along," the young officer said brusquely, and the remnants of the *Stella Rossa* found themselves detained in various rudimentary habitations behind the front. The British treated them with marked suspicion, took no steps toward utilizing their fighting ability or their knowledge of the region, and in general ignored them. When the British moved off after several days, Rossi and the others hurried toward the American lines.

There they were welcomed as allies, and Rossi became the close friend of several Italian-American soldiers, who explained to him that the Tommies were only acting under orders from the British high command. Too many "partisans" had turned out to be spies and informers, and the British had decided to continue the war without the aid of the Italian irregulars. The Americans acted under a looser policy, and Rossi and his partisan companions were issued boots and helmets and integrated into the patrols without rank or arms.

Antonio Tonelli had been carrying ammunition for the Germans for a month, and every footprint he made on Monte Sole was overstamped by his eight-year-old son, Vittorio, following along behind. Shells and bullets whistled about the ears of father and son as they continued in their roles of beasts of burden, but at least, like beasts of burden, they were fed twice daily and kept alive by their masters. One day near the end of October they were carrying provisions through the Fosse di Galiberti, a ravine near Vado, when the allies began a thunderous bombardment from across the Setta. Antonio was slipping and sliding hurriedly through the muddy ravine when he felt a blast, and all at once he was sitting in the mud watching a fountain of blood pour out of his arm. He reached up and touched his eye and found that it was bleeding, too, and then he turned around to see Vittorio lying on his side in the ravine. There was a chestnut in the boy's hand, and his mouth was open, as though he had been just about to dine. There were no visible wounds on the boy, and as Antonio stared back and forth from his own wounds to his son, he wondered why the boy did not get up. "Vittorio!" he cried. "Help me! I am hurt!"

When his son did not move, Antonio slithered through the mud on his hands and knees and turned the boy over. The eyes stared up at Antonio. He laid his ear on the boy's chest, but in the bombardment he could hear nothing. His own blood was spurting all over his son, and once again he said, "Vittorio! Wake up! We must get away from here." The boy continued to stare, and all at once Antonio realized that the last of his nine children was dead.

He reached down, closed the boy's eyes and kissed him. "I am sorry," Antonio said, blood and tears dripping from his face, "but I cannot stay with you, Vittorio." Slowly he pulled himself to his feet and, stumbling and falling on the mountain, managed somehow to reach his sister's house three miles away at Creda. The house was empty and half-destroyed, but Antonio found his sister and a few of her neighbors in the air-raid shelter in the rear.

When the bombardment ended, everyone returned to the shambles of the house, and Antonio's sister put a tourniquet on his arm and bathed his wounded eye with hot water. After several days a German doctor took a look at Antonio and said, "*Niente buono*. This is not good." He warned that Antonio would lose both his eyes, the wounded one *and* the healthy one, unless something was done about infection.

"Can you not give him something?" the sister asked.

"Verboten," the doctor said. "It is forbidden. There is nothing to do but dig his grave."

Antonio remained in bed until nightfall, and then he grabbed a blanket and some old shoes and walked straight into the woods. He wandered all night from copse to copse, and in the morning he ran into a bearded man with bloodshot eyes and tangled hair. It was Guido Musolesi, brother of the partisan commander, his own wounded foot wrapped in rags, and the two of them joined forces to evade the Germans and hunt for food. But after several days Antonio could hardly think for the pounding and the burning in his eye. "How does it look, Guido?" Antonio would ask, and Musolesi would only say, "It looks like death."

One day they were joined by a wandering woman whose fingers had been cut off by shrapnel. She said her name was Norina Quadri, and she was from Vado, and like Antonio, she was slowly dying of infection. One night Guido said to the two of them, "I would like us to remain together, but you are both going to die unless you get medical aid."

"And which of these trees is going to help us?" Antonio said weakly, his hand gesturing toward the thorny acacias that surrounded them.

"There is nothing for you to do but head for Bologna," Musolesi said. "Otherwise you are both dead within a week."

"And what about your foot?" Antonio asked.

"My foot is wounded, but it is not infected, thank God," Guido said. "It will not kill me."

Antonio, naked except for his blanket and a pair of soleless shoes, headed down the mountain with the fingerless woman toward the valley road that led to Marzabotto and the north. They had almost reached the outskirts of a small village when a German patrol stopped them. The soldiers seemed to be a little drunk, and one of them twirled the blanket from Antonio and left him standing naked in the road. *"Partigiano!"* the German said, and Antonio said, *"Niente partigiano!"*

They were taken to a field hospital that had been set up in the church of Marzabotto, and Antonio saw that several dozen wounded German soldiers lay on cots in front of the altar. To one side a wood fire blazed away, and other soldiers were chopping the pews into kindling. Now and then a truck would pull up outside, and more wounded Germans would be carried in on stretchers, and soon the place was crowded with injured men whose screams reverberated around the walls of the old church. Antonio pulled his blanket around him and began to pray. He prayed to God and to Jesus Christ and the Virgin Mary, and when he had prayed to every saint whose name came into his tortured mind, he began praying to his loved ones, telling them not to worry, that they would soon be together. As the long night went on, Antonio found that he was strengthened by the conversations with his dead.

In the morning, the two refugees were loaded on a northbound truck, and when they were about six miles from Bologna, a German shouted, "End of the line! All greasers get out and walk."

It took them two more days to make Bologna on foot and turn themselves in at a hospital for refugees. "We will have to remove your eye," a doctor told Antonio.

"Go ahead and remove," Antonio said. "There is nothing on that side of the world that I want to see, or in the other side either."

The doctor smiled at the little man's joke, and wheeled him toward the operating room.

A few of the partisans of the *Stella Rossa* had turned toward Bologna, instead of the front lines, and there they made themselves available to the formations that were busily sabotaging communications and waylaying Nazis in the city streets. One of the groups of refugee partisans was led by a man who called himself Maio, and one day Maio received an anonymous communication to the effect that a young man named Giuliano De Balzo could be reached at a certain address in Pianoro, a small town to the south of Bologna. By now, Maio and his men knew some of the details of the treachery at Monte Sole, and he blinked his eyes when he read a postscript to the note: "De Balzo also calls himself Cacao."

Maio and three other partisans knocked softly on the door of the address in Pianoro at four o'clock the next morning, and a little old lady appeared. "If you make a sound, you are dead!" Maio said, shoving her back into the house with his pistol.

"What do you want of me?" the woman said.

"You have a son?"

"Yes, I have a son. He is far away."

"Do you know someone named Giuliano De Balzo?"

The old lady threw her hands in the air. "Yes, I know that delinquent. He is somebody else's bastard, and the state gave me money to care for him. But no amount of money could repay me for the pain he has caused me." The old lady paused. "Why do you ask? What has he done now?"

"Where is he?" Maio asked.

"Upstairs in the front room, sleeping."

The four partisans tiptoed up the steps, and there in the bedroom, his face under the sheet like a little boy trying to fool his parents, lay the traitor of the *Stella Rossa,* the gold-toothed blond who called himself Cacao. "We are here," Maio said, tapping his pistol barrel on the young man's forehead. "We have come to visit you."

"Why?" Cacao blurted.

"Lupo has asked us to congratulate you because you were such a good partisan."

"Why do you come in the middle of the night and wake me up?" Cacao said, ducking his head from the hard taps Maio was administering.

"Because we thought it was time you knew how much we respected you," Maio said.

Cacao sat bolt upright. "Let me alone!" he said. Maio pulled back the hammer on his automatic pistol, and Cacao began to scream. "Time to sleep now!" Maio said, and pulled the trigger at a range of about an inch.

"What have you done to him?" the old lady said calmly as the partisans bounded out of the house.

"Less than we should have done," Maio said. "Your foster son died in bed."

Homecoming

THE postman and his wife and three-year-old daughter, Edera, walked, and two-year-old Ermano alternated between the arms of his mother and his father, sometimes toddling a few steps before complaining in baby talk that he was tired. As they passed through Casalecchio, two hours down the road from Bologna, the postman said for the twentieth time, "Let my arms fall off from fatigue! What does it matter? We are going home."

"And what will we find when we get there?" his wife said. "That is what troubles me."

"What will we find?" the postman said. "The trees. The *fontana.* Monte Sole."

The route lay along the river Reno, and as they walked, they had to give wide berth to the American and British military traffic lumbering northward toward Bologna. There were tanks as wide as the road in strings of forty and fifty at a time, and strange vehicles that looked like tanks in the rear and trucks in the front. Troop carriers with dark-green canvas tops crawled along in low gear, and sometimes the postman would shout, "*Whay,* Yank!" and instruct the family to wave at their liberators.

"Angelo!" his wife said. "You make us fools!"

"Excuse me, *cara,*" the postman said, taking off his gray cap and shaking it at one of the trucks. "It is only that I am filled with happiness. The war is over, and we are alive." He waved his cap high in the air and shouted, "*Whay,* Yank!" and when one responded, the postman pointed to the badge on his cap and cried, *"Postino!"*

South out of Sasso Marconi, where the Setta and the Reno joined, the travelers caught their first glimpse of the massif of Monte Sole.

"There!" the postman said. "Take a good look, *cara.* Has it changed?"

Now, after walking and carrying the baby for five hours, the postman and his wife should have been exhausted, but the sight of their mountains in the distance gave them strength and they pushed on in two more hours to Marzabotto, capital of the Monte Sole area and less than one hour's walk from Sperticano. The postman wanted to stop at his old post office, but his wife reminded him that there would be plenty of time. They continued down the road and suddenly reached a world they did not recognize. The first missing landmark was the little Etruscan museum just south of Marzabotto on the left. It lay in ruins. *"Aspetta!"* the postman said to his wife. "Wait!" He walked to the site where he had spent many hours admiring the handicrafts and statuary of his predecessors on Monte Sole, and as he approached the crumbled walls, a bearded man scuttled out of the wreckage like a rat. The postman did not recognize him. "What happened here?" the postman asked.

The old man said, "First the SS came and smashed all the artifacts. Then they mined the staircase, and in the Allied bombardment the whole place exploded. Do you have a soldo?"

The postman handed the old man a few coins and rejoined his family. They climbed slowly up a hill and finally reached a point where the whole western valley of Monte Sole was in sight. As far as the eye could see, there was not a house standing, nor a bell tower to mark a village. Fields that had stretched green and brown and yellow lay untended, rank with weeds, pocked with shell craters with oily films of stagnant water at their bottoms. Groves of trees were burned; the trunks of giant oaks were split down the middle, and the insides were dark and ragged. The scars of tank treads crisscrossed the fields, and litter was everywhere, and in the silent air there was a stink that the postman remembered from seven months before, when he had climbed the mountain and found the first bodies.

"Come!" the postman said, and they resumed their walk toward home. They had gone only a few hundred yards when the postman stopped again, took off his hat, and scratched his head. "There is something wrong," he said. "What is it?"

His wife looked across the ruptured walls and blackened fields of Monte Sole. "What do you mean, *caro?*" she said. "Everything is wrong, not just something."

"No, no," the postman said. "There is something especially wrong." He turned and sniffed the putrid air, stepped to the top of a broken stone wall and peered toward Sperticano, and then hopped back to his little family. "Have you seen a bird?" he asked.

"A bird?" His wife paused. "No, not one," she said.

"That is what is wrong," the postman said, relieved and disturbed at the same time. "It has been an hour since we left Marzabotto, and we have neither seen nor heard a single bird."

They walked in silence into the village of Sperticano. Almost all the houses were down. The church where the SS had made its headquarters was flattened by shells and bombs. Their own house was little more than walls. The postman and his wife and children made themselves as comfortable as they could in the ruins, and the next morning he slung his brown leather bag across his shoulders and headed up the mountain. He went no farther than his usual first stop: San Martino. Bodies were strewn along the narrow path, and as the postman came out of the blackened grove of trees at Little Hill of San Martino, he stopped and blinked his eyes. Ahead, where there should have been a church and a village and several big barns and haylofts, there was nothing. The land was flat. All that marked San Martino were a baptismal font lying in a ditch and a few piles of stone and the jagged walls of the cemetery.

The postman looked across the flank of the mountain toward Caprara, but where the ancient capital of Monte Sole had stood there was now only a grove of scorched and ripped trees. Farther along the ridge toward Casaglia, he saw nothing but fields laced with trenches and heaped with earthen barricades. He turned and hurried down the mountain. "Well," his wife said. "Who did you find on your old postal route?"

"My old postal route," the postman repeated, wiping his eyes. "It is gone, *cara.* I have no postal route." Later he went to the post office at Marzabotto and told the authorities that there was no one to send or receive mail on Monte Sole. They gave him a new route in the valley, and he never climbed the mountain again.

Acacci "Rugi" Ruggero, the man who stood fire guard in the hemp mill, did not know what to expect as he turned off the valley road and walked up the hill toward his in-laws' house at Maccagnano. He had not seen the place since his wife had chased him and her father up the mountain with a warning that the Germans were around, and a few hours later everything had gone up in smoke. The winter had been cold, and there was the possibility that the bodies would be there, but in what condition? Had they been burned alive in the house? Rugi tried to dismiss such ideas.

He came into sight of the ruins of the house, and as he stepped up to the cobblestones of the front yard, he saw a dozen bodies. His wife and his three-year-old daughter, Luisa, lay together, their bodies bloated and sieved with bullet holes. Luisa's head was gone; Rugi supposed that an animal had taken it. His wife's mother and two other women of the family lay alongside, and next to them were seven members of the family Bevilacqua, who had lived in the other half of the farmhouse.

Rugi laid his dead in a neat line and went off to find wood for boxes in the litter left in the wake of the war. He made two coffins, but when he tried to stuff the bodies inside, he found that they would not fit. He built a big bonfire with the wood of the battlefield and piled the adult bodies on top. When the fire had burned to ashes, he shoveled the remains in one of the boxes, and placed the headless body of Luisa in the other, and gave them burial in the field.

Attilio Comastri was on his hands and knees scratching at the rubble of Creda when he saw his old friend Rugi climbing up the road from the valley. The two comrades put their arms around each other and cried for a long time. They composed themselves, but they both cried again when Rugi told how he had found the bodies of his loved ones, and they cried once more when Attilio said, "Do you see this mess, Rugi? Under it are the bodies of mine."

Creda was a junkyard of crumbled walls, scorched timbers, litter and half-rotted cadavers. The Allies had set up a command post in the ruins of the *casa colonica,* but now there was nothing left of the post but a stack of empty K-ration containers and a stinking outdoor latrine, adding its odors to the gases of putrefaction coming from the ruined barn. Here and there an arm stuck out, or a leg, and as Attilio and Rugi worked to remove the timbers from the seventy or eighty bodies that lay underneath, they coughed and covered their noses with rags.

"It is no use, Attilio," Rugi said after they had dug at the ruins for several hours. "We will never get them out, and even if we did, how would we know which are yours?"

"Someone has to bury these bodies," Comastri said. "They have a right to be buried."

Hidden in the earth alongside the broken wall of the old barn, they came upon a wooden box with a wire leading from it. "That is a tripping wire!" Comastri said. "When a tank crosses the wire, it explodes the mine."

"Yes," Rugi said. "The box is a mine, and the wire is the detonator. But how do you explain this?" He pointed to a pair of conspicuous treadmarks over the top of the wire a few feet away.

"The mine is a dud," Attilio said. "It failed to go off. We will blow it up ourselves and help clear away some of this rubble."

The two men tied the end of the wire to a long cord, backed into the woods, and gave the cord a yank. Nothing happened. They tugged again and broke the cord, but the mine did not explode.

"We will burn it," Attilio said. The two men walked into the valley and returned with a container of gasoline. They poured it on the mine, made a trail of gasoline to a wall several hundred feet away, and dropped the match on the liquid path. The box burned and sputtered for several hours, but nothing happened except that the wooden case burned away and exposed the metallic innards of the mine. When the ashes of the fire were cold, the two men poured gasoline directly on the mine and set it afire once again, but the mine remained inert. "To hell with it!" Attilio said, and the two men resumed their digging about fifteen feet away.

They had worked for several more hours when Attilio heard Rugi shouting, "Run! Run! It is sputtering!" He wondered if Rugi had gone crazy.

"We burned that thing," Attilio said. "It cannot go off. You must be talking to the dead."

Just then the whole place lifted three or four feet into the air in a tremendous explosion, and Attilio felt a bolt of metal slash into his thigh. He fell and lost consciousness, and when he awakened, he discovered that he was being carried down a mountain road on a stretcher. As they were loading him into a truck, he heard a familiar voice shouting, "Where is Comastri? Where is Comastri?" He turned his head and saw Rugi lying on another stretcher, his arm bandaged and splinted. "Here I am, Rugi," Attilio said. "Do not worry." The two cronies were carried to the hospital together.

In the early weeks of liberation the extent of the massacre was unknown. Communications were shattered, even the word-of-mouth communications that had served the *contadini* so well in the past. Those who returned to Monte Sole were afraid to take a single unnecessary step toward a neighboring *podere* for fear they would step on mines. Each family had its list of the dead or missing, but each kept its records a private matter. Bodies were found and buried quickly, without ceremony or investigation. High on a ridge near Ca' Dizzola, the desiccated remains of Attilio and Giulio Ruggeri and the other men of their work party were found at the bottom of a ravine. The putrid body of old Gino Cincinnati, covered by seething sheets of flies and maggots, was found under the rubble of the *palazzo* at Cerpiano; apparently he had hidden when the Germans ordered everyone out, and within days he had been pinned by falling timbers from the Allied bombardment. The old man was still clinging to a piece of wood, and there were no wounds on his body. Perhaps he had starved.

The family of Don Giovanni Fornasini returned to the ruins of the rectory at Sperticano and continued their seven-month vigil for the priest. Don Giovanni had not been waiting for his family in the refugee center at Florence, as the partisan messenger had promised, and now the Fornasini family could only hope that he had taken refuge elsewhere. But only a few days after they returned to Sperticano, an old woman tapped on the door and said that she had heard that the body of a priest was lying near the cemetery of San Martino. Luigi Fornasini hurried up the mountain, and in thick weeds outside the back wall, he found bodies. One was a man named Moschetti, sixty-seven years old, an invalid veteran of World War I. His crutches were propped neatly against the wall. Alongside was the body of a priest, separated from its skull by a few inches. Luigi was not certain that this was his brother; other priests were missing on the mountain. He went through the pockets and found a German-Italian-German pocket dictionary and a book of the prayers for the dead in Latin. Under the body was an *asperge,* the wand for distributing holy water, and a small gold chain with a tiny replica of the Madonna. Luigi recognized these effects, and he walked down the mountain to tell his wife and mother that the long wait for Don Giovanni was ended. The priest's body was buried the next day in the cemetery at San Martino.

Wherever one turned, the dead were littered about. Lupo was found in a field a half mile from Cadotto, lying in a hole with his hands folded across his breast like someone waiting patiently for the end. The old father of Don Ferdinando Casagrande returned to the mountain and found the bodies of his son and daughter, both shot in the neck at close range. They joined the old man's other three children in burial at San Martino. One day a wagon tipped on its side in a field near Gardeletta, and the *contadini* dug into the rut to find five bodies in shallow graves. Two of them were recognized as Desiderio Sabbioni, grandfather of Lucia, and Enrico Coramelli, but the rest were beyond identification.

The people of Monte Sole had strong beliefs about the formalities of burial, but now bodies were being thrown hastily into the earth wherever they were found. For a time the *contadini* could not believe their own discoveries: they were finding dozens and dozens of male bodies that could not be identified. Where had all these strangers come from? The mystery was solved when it was noticed that several of the corpses were clothed in simple jackets of the type issued to prisoners of war. Apparently the Germans had brought in work parties of prisoners during the heavy fighting with the Allies, and when the prisoners had outlived their usefulness, they had been shot in the back and left in the fields. For months after the liberation, Monte Sole was visited by *Milanesi* and *Lucchesi* and others from surrounding places, looking for their relatives who had been taken away by the Germans. Some of these searchers were lost to the mines as they wandered about Monte Sole, bringing the postwar mine casualties on Monte Sole to an estimated fifty or sixty.

Cemeteries were quickly filled. Above grave no. 27 in the *camposanto* of San Martino, a wooden cross bore the rough-carved name Maria. No one knew who Maria was or how she had come to be buried there. Around the ridge at the cemetery of Casaglia, a simple stone marked the common grave of the people who had huddled in front of the burial chapel and waited for the Nazi machine guns to open fire. Off to one side a cross bore a roughly inscribed 84, the number that were believed to lie below. One day notices went up all over the valley, telling those who had lost loved ones at Casaglia to assemble up at the cemetery on a certain afternoon. Four laborers from the *munici-*

pio in Marzabotto put on masks and gloves and started opening the grave in the early morning. By midday they had laid out a long line of bodies and portions of bodies. The number was ascertained by counting heads. There were seventy-five, including one that could not be identified.

Adelmo Benini was among the witnesses; he identified his wife and one daughter by their skulls, and he told a black-coated clerk from the *municipio* that the count was wrong. The clerk told Adelmo not to become upset, that all the counts from all the common graves of Monte Sole were wrong. There was no way to take an accurate census of the dead. The census of the living showed that the population of the region had dropped by nearly 2,000, and most of the missing were women and children. Some of the bodies would not be found for years; some would never be found. Adelmo returned to his rented room in the valley and his new job at the paper mill in Lama di Reno. Like the postman, he would never go up the mountain again.

Raffaele de Maria, soon to marry Vittoria Negri of Ca' Roncadelli, was on his way home after two years of soldiering in the Italian cavalry and nineteen months of forced labor at a German shipyard at Königsberg. He was a little green-eyed sparrow of a man with a pack on his back and the tattered components of three armies covering his skinny body. The bus driver at Bologna had given him a big argument, claiming that he was filthy and lousy and ineligible for rubbing elbows with the fine customers of the bus company, and Raffaele had argued back that he had been deloused by the American Army the day before, and if he was filthy it was because he had been traveling for two weeks after fighting on behalf of such trash as this bus driver, and as a compromise they had agreed that Raffaele could ride with the luggage on the roof.

As the smelly bus passed through Marzabotto, only a few miles from his home in Sibano, Raffaele had a fine view of the foothills of the Apennines. He smiled broadly; he was looking forward to riding into his home village and waving to the cheering crowds who would be lining the street for the hero's return. But as he passed the Etruscan town of Misa and the villages at the base of Monte Sole, he began to shake his head. Nothing seemed alive here. Where were the dogs that used to chase the bus from stop to stop? The houses were gone, and the churches, too. Raffaele studied the ruins as the bus chugged on in a cloud of black smoke, and his soldier's eye recognized that a major battle had been fought in this valley.

He wondered how his old mother was and what had happened to Vittoria, but he wondered more about his field, the twelve acres that lay across from the house in the Reno Valley. To Raffaele, the field was Italy. In it grew wheat, corn, grapes, cherries, apricots and hemp. Along its edges there was a stream where he had learned to swim. Night after night he had thought of the field, with the apricots full and bursting from the tree, and the stalks of wheat bending to the ground under their golden loads, and the scent of the grapes sweating in the sun. As much as he wanted to see his mother, as much as he wanted to see the woman he was going to marry, he wanted to see the field more.

The bus jerked to a stop in front of the *tabacchi* in Sibano, and Raffaele climbed down. Two friends of his childhood, Celso Elmi and Desiderio Marzari, met the bus, and as the returning hero walked up, they stared blankly at his German pants with the rip in the seat and his French Army jacket splattered with food stains and his broken American service cap. Raffaele stuck out his hand and called his friends by name, and the two shouted simultaneously, *"Whay,* Rafflein!" using his dialect name, and lifted him up and spun him around and almost smothered him with their welcome. Then they let him go and stood back, and Raffaele saw that they were crying.

"What is the matter?" he said. He had endured too much to cry now.

"Nothing," Elmi said. "After what happened around here, we cry when we see anyone."

"Is my mother all right?"

"She is fine," Marzari said, "and your brothers wait for you, too."

It was after dark when Raffaele reached the little home and nearly midnight when the family stopped kissing him and hugging him and asking him to repeat his glorious adventures over and over. He was up before dawn the next morning, into his clothes in seconds, and out the front door headed for the field. He was shocked by what he saw. The field that he had remembered night after night of the war was gone. In its place was a no-man's-land of holes, uprooted trees, leafless vines, trash and litter.

Raffaele walked all the way to the middle of the field, mentally calculating how many months, maybe years, he and his brothers would have to work to return it to shape. When the sun came up and made the scene look even worse, he sat on the stump of a tree that had once showered him with cherries. He was still sitting there brooding when a loud voice came across the field: "Rafflein! For the love of God, do not move!" Raffaele looked up to see a neighbor, Augusto Barberini, leaning from an upstairs window in his nightshirt.

"What is wrong?" Raffaele called back.

"The field is full of mines!" the man cried. "If you move, you will be killed!"

It took Raffaele twenty minutes to walk back to the road. Sometimes he stayed in his old footsteps, and sometimes he walked on top of the smashed grapevines, being careful to plant his foot where roots of the vine entered the ground and not an inch to either side. When he finally reached the road, the whole neighborhood was there to greet him, and once again there was a tumultuous welcome.

"You should have warned me!" Raffaele said to his brothers, who were slapping him on the back and hugging him as though he had returned from the dead.

Later Raffaele and the *padrone* filed an official report to the government, and Italian Army sappers arrived at the field with metal-detecting equipment. From the twelve acres they removed 299 mines.

After the liberation the Ruggeri cousins, Elena and Elide, went to live with their aunt, Maria Menarini, in Rioveggio, southeast of Monte Sole in the valley of the Setta. There they learned from a *marachale* of the *carabinieri* that the bodies of their fathers had been found at Ca' Dizzola, and they buried Attilio and Giulio in the family plot at Casaglia. The cousins decided to make a final trip to Ca' Pudella to retrieve some of the valuables they had buried in the earth the morning of the first day of the massacre, but when they reached a high spot on the mountainside, they were at a loss to find their own homestead. They were almost on top of the house before they discovered it: a pile of rocks and weeds. It was impossible to take two steps in any direction without falling into a shell hole, and the sisters realized that the Allies must have marked their house as a priority artillery target. Perhaps the Germans had been using it as a command post. They stepped carefully into the backyard, where they had buried sheets and linens and tablecloths, but the shells had churned up the earth and allowed air to get in, and everything was rotten.

Antonio Tonelli did not return to Possatore at all. When the officials at the refugee center in Bologna asked the one-eyed man where he wanted to go, he was momentarily taken aback. Finally, he managed to blurt out, "To Montorio." His old mother lived there; perhaps she had survived the war and would take him in. Antonio was loaded on a bus, and when the bus led its own cloud of oily smoke down the Setta Highway toward Montorio, he realized suddenly that he was going to pass Monte Sole. "Please!" he said to another refugee in a seat across the aisle. "Will you change with me?" The arrangement was made, and as the bus lumbered past the mountain of his losses, Antonio stared with his one eye in the opposite direction.

The survivors of the Piretti family were barely reunited in the remains of their home in Gardeletta when old Maximiliano had to be rushed to the hospital in Bologna. The months of forced labor in all kinds of weather had brought on pneumonia, and as the weeks went by, his condition grew worse. Fernando, now ten years old, begged rides to be at his father's side, but soon Maximiliano had wasted away to a shadow, and there were times when he did not recognize the son who had followed him all over the mountains. One day Fernando's big brother put him on the handlebars and cycled all the way to the hospital; Maximiliano had been calling for his sons during the night. Fernando threw himself on the bed and put his arms around his father, but by now the old man lacked the strength to open his eyes. Three days later he was dead.

When war hero Mario Cardi and his friend Quinto Marzari reached their home *podere* of Creda after a fifty-mile walk from the refugee center at Florence, Mario ran to the rubble of the barn and began crying hysterically. "Come, Mario," Quinto said, putting his arm around his friend and leading him away. "It is too soon." The next morning Mario returned to the place where his family had been executed and began digging with his bare hands. When he had hollowed out a space about six feet deep, he dropped some hay into it, climbed down and pulled a broken door over the top. "This will be fine," he told himself. "This will suffice."

For three weeks Mario lived in the hole in the ground alongside the corpses of his family. He ate the remains of K rations, lying around him in the fields. He would get up with the sun, remove rubble with his hands until long after dark, and crawl back into his hole to sleep. His friend Quinto had an old Army rifle, and they used it to detonate mines at long range.

Gradually the bodies came into view. Most of them were shrunken and shriveled from the fire, and others were in pieces or crushed beyond recognition. One day a journalist from Bologna pulled a cadaver out of the ruins and leaned it against the broken wall for a picture, and when Mario started to put the body back, he recognized the earrings of his twenty-one-year-old sister, Lucia.

By now he had been joined in his daily labors by a few of the *contadini* of the area, and as he worked for sixteen and eighteen hours of each day, he felt power flow into his being. It seemed to him that he had never been more alive, here among the dead, and he could not explain it to anyone except his friend Quinto. "I know I am not supposed to feel this exhilaration," he told Quinto one night before he climbed down into his hole to sleep, "but I feel satisfied, complete. I work harder and harder each day; it excites me. I have some kind of unreasoning feeling that my family will return here, and I will be able to say to them, 'Look around you! See? I was the first one home, and I did my duty. Everything is in its place. I was the first one home, and I had this responsibility, and I accepted it.' Do you understand that, Quinto?"

"I understand, Mario," Quinto said. He had been engaged to one of Mario's lost sisters, and the two men had been together so long that they almost thought as one.

When the last mummified human remnant had been sifted from the ashes of the barn, Mario and Quinto walked to the river and began ripping apart a wooden footbridge constructed by the German engineers. From this salvage, they fashioned six oversize wooden caskets. Into five of them they put the bodies of sixty-nine persons, and into the sixth they put leftovers: arms and hands and legs and feet that did not match up. The *contadini* brought candles and prayers, and one by one the heavy caskets were carried on peasant shoulders to the cemetery at Salvaro.

A few days after the services, Mario received a request to visit the Lelli sisters, who owned the ruined farm at Creda. "We know what you have done," one of the sisters said. "Now we would like you to move into a room in the small house down the hill and take over the farm. It will be what you make of it." Mario paid a visit to his fiancée, Bruna Manfredini, and suggested that they get married.

"And what are we to eat?" Bruna said. "Your Merit Cross?"

Mario begged a live chicken from a friend and returned to his fiancée. "This!" he said, holding the squawking bird by the feet. Two weeks later they were wed.

Luigi Massa, the storekeeper of Caprara, waited until he heard that the road from Bologna to Monte Sole was safe, and then he headed on foot for an inspection trip of the family's holdings. Luigi's wife, Maria Comellini, and his nineteen-year-old daughter, Emma, wanted to come along, but Luigi explained that he could walk faster, and he would return to Bologna that night with a report. Later, when all was shipshape at the *tabacchi* in Caprara and their farm at Poggio Comellini, they would go down the road to Monte Sole together.

As he sidestepped the military vehicles rumbling toward him from the south on his five-hour walk through the valley of the Setta, Luigi was stricken again with the feeling of guilt that had remained with him ever since the massacre of Monte Sole. He had lost nothing but money, and money was something that could be replaced, especially when one owned the only store for miles around and a fertile farm for good measure. The Massas had taken 20,000 lire with them when they fled to Bologna, but the Germans had appropriated Maria's purse on the way north and with it half the family fortune. Luigi had spent the remaining 10,000 lire to house his family in Bologna. The loss was not insignificant—20,000 lire would buy six oxen—but as usual Luigi felt a twinge of conscience as he dwelled on the money. He knew that there were men on Monte Sole, some of them his good friends, who had lost ten or fifteen members of their family. He had heard, for example, that the wife and nine children of Antonio Tonelli had died, and Tonelli himself had lost an eye. Luigi wondered what kept the man going, how he would survive. Children were the only wealth of Monte Sole; a childless man looked ahead to slow starvation. Luigi wondered how he could face a man who had suffered such a loss. He hoped that it would not be held against himself and his family that they had had the good fortune to survive, but he found that on one level of his thinking he even held it against himself.

Luigi walked straight up the mountain toward the family home at

Poggio Comellini, and by the time he had passed the ruins of other familiar farmhouses, he was prepared for the scene that awaited him. The *casa colonica* at Poggio was reduced to foundations and cellar. When the family had fled, they had filled a small room in the basement with their most valuable possessions: silver, linen, tablecloths and their best clothes, and in front of the door they had put a mattress stuffed with corn leaves. Luigi slipped over the foundation and into the remains of the basement and saw that the room had been opened and emptied.

The *tabacchi* at Caprara was only a short walk, and Luigi was quivering as he hurried across the fields to his last remaining property. At first he thought he had made a wrong turn when the walls of the *tabacchi* failed to come into view, and then he saw all at once that Caprara had been pulverized. The stump of a single wall remained, and already weeds and wild vines were covering it up. Luigi stood alongside his store and cried.

In the little state warehouse at Vergato where he had gone so often to stock up on monopoly goods, Luigi was told to forget about his *tabacchi* on Monte Sole. "You are still the license holder," a clerk said, "and legally it is your business, but take my advice: if you opened the store tomorrow, you would fail in a week. The mountain is covered with mines. The homes are wrecked. The farmhands are dead. No one will stay on Monte Sole anymore. You say you are without a building. I add to that: you are without a customer." Luigi filled out the retirement form and walked back toward Bologna, carrying in his hand the paper that gave him official permission to hang on the ruins of his store: CLOSED TILL FURTHER NOTICE.

But if the *tabacchi* was lost, the earth of Poggio Comellini remained. Luigi found lodgings for his wife and daughter at the nearby home of Luigi Piretti in Gardeletta and soon moved the family down from Bologna. The house was full of men: there were six or eight Pirettis, including little Fernando and his brothers, and several male refugees from the mountain. The Massa mother and daughter were welcomed; they cooked and kept the house. Each day Luigi looked for work, and one day he was hired as a railroad track laborer. The family put aside every soldo that could be spared; someday they would use the money to rebuild at Poggio.

No one had been able to enter the cellar of the Piretti home since the liberation; it was jammed with sticks and junk left by the Germans.

When everything else was cleaned up, they would tackle the messy basement. But one day the family learned accidentally what the Germans had stored below. A spark from an outdoor oven ignited a haystack, and windblown hay drifted through a broken cellar window and fired something in the basement, and a few minutes later the house blew up. Luigi's wife, Maria, and his daughter, Emma, died a few hours later in the hospital at Bologna.

Luigi hardly missed a day's work on the railroad. Trembling and alone, he beat at the ballast with his pick and watched his tears flow into the rocks. He dared not think about his loss. He talked to no one; his pick was his consolation, and when the ten-hour day on the railroad was done, he would go to Vado and do odd jobs. Each day he worked himself into fatigue and fell into bed to regain his strength for the next. Once a track foreman said to him, "Luigi, you are a courageous man to go on like this."

Luigi looked up and said, "You do not understand."

One day it entered his mind that his wife's memory demanded that the farm at Poggio should not be allowed to lie fallow, and picking his way among the mines that he now knew lay all about, he climbed the path to the ruined old home. That night he rearranged a few of the stones of the house and positioned a wooden trellis that had fallen. The next evening he returned and began studying the land for mines. He found several, and he sent a letter to the authorities asking that the mines be exploded. He began dividing his time between the railroad and the farm, and soon he had constructed a small stone house with his own hands, and planted crops, and started to feed a calf. One day the rehabilitation of Poggio was complete, and Luigi returned to the *podere* where he had spent the happy years with his loved ones. Against advice, he refused even to consider remarriage, explaining to his well-meaning friends, "When you have been so well coupled as Maria and I were, you cannot think of another. Every day we looked at the world, and all we could see was ourselves and our children."

Vittoria Negri walked to Ca' Roncadelli from Florence, and the closer she got to the ancestral family home, the lighter her feet became, and the faster her heart pounded. She raced through Sperticano like an Olympic walker, and then she rounded the corner of the fields that she had worked with her brothers. Where the house should have been, there were two tall pieces of wall, and she could look right between them at the back side of Monte Sole. The barn appeared to be intact, but as she approached, she could see that the walls were only supporting themselves; the inside of the barn was hollow, and the roof had fallen in.

"Well," Vittoria said aloud, "we will begin at the beginning." She found a shattered piece of wood and began digging into the earth where the family valuables had been buried. She worked until the frock that the Americans had given her was drenched with perspiration, and then she worked some more. She was only a few inches from the cache when she heard voices coming from the lane that led to the Bologna road. She turned and saw her three brothers, Dante, Fernando and Orfeo, walking toward the house. As they saw her, Fernando and Dante broke into a run, and Orfeo struggled along behind on his game leg.

"Vittoria!" Fernando said, and for the third time in seven months, he said, "How is it that you are alive?"

"It is a long story, brother," Vittoria said, embracing the men one by one, "but here we are, all of us alive together!"

"Siamo ancor' viv', a neg briz' un poc'," Fernando said in mangled Italian and dialect. "We are alive, and that is no small thing."

Just then a white rooster hopped into sight, and Fernando raced through the brush in futile pursuit. He returned, panting and smiling broadly. "We have our land, and we have one rooster," he said happily. "What more do we need?"

"Work!" Vittoria said. She handed him the piece of wood she had been using for a shovel.

When Duilio Paselli and his sons returned to the family's big *casa colonica* on the hillside near Gardeletta, the old patriarch wasted no time in ordering formal death notices for his loved ones. Since he lacked a familiarity with anything but the *dialetto bolognese,* Duilio dictated the wording of the notice to his son Antenore, and Antenore wrote it out in Italian. Soon people for miles around were receiving the black-bordered notices bearing eight pictures and two crosses to represent the infants who had died unphotographed. The announcement said:

> The barbarous Nazi-Fascists in the certainty of defeat became crazed, and the flowered, prosperous zone of San Martino was

> converted on the thirtieth of September, nineteen hundred forty-four, into a cemetery, where two thousand innocents were sacrificed to the Nazi-Fascists' unlimited evil. To rid himself of a pain which has no limit for the loss of his faithful wife, Ester, and for his two adored daughters, Fidelia and Malvina, and for his dearest son, Dante, and for his most affectionate daughters-in-law, Anna, Lisetta and Anna, who were burned in a holocaust holding their three children, Anna, Claudio and Franco, tightly to their breasts, Duilio Paselli invokes for all of these a prayer, believing that they have gone to glory as martyrs, and asks God to alleviate his pain and the pain of all the other survivors.

For months and months old Duilio sat around and mourned his losses. No one else in the family could console him. Just down the road, at Railroad House No. 67, Bruno Pedriali mourned his own grief, and often the two men would walk arm in arm to the common grave at Ca' Beguzzi, where Pedriali had returned after a narrow escape and found his wife and three children dead on their sleeping mats.

"Babbo," Antenore said one day, "why do you go to Ca' Beguzzi with Pedriali? You only add his suffering to your own."

"I cannot bear to see him sitting by that grave alone," Duilio said. "We share the pain. He will not eat, but sometimes I can get him to take a little wine."

Pedriali was soon carted away to the hospital at Bologna, a victim of jaundice brought on by malnutrition, and Duilio suspended his pilgrimages to Ca' Beguzzi. His relatives noticed that the old man began spending hours sitting in the sun, and one day Antenore glanced out the window and saw his father staring straight into the sun's rays, his eyes narrow slits and his face set in a mysterious smile.

Antenore rushed outside. *"Babbo,"* he said, "what are you doing? You will hurt your eyes."

Duilio turned away, blinking, and said, "Have you ever thought about the sun, my boy?"

Antenore said he thought about the sun occasionally.

"It rises at the same place every morning, is that true?" Duilio did not wait for an answer. "It sets at the same place every night, is that true? And even when the clouds get in the way the sun remains. Is that true?"

Antenore agreed.

"The sun warms us," Duilio went on, "and it makes our crops grow, is that true? Has it ever occurred to you, Antenore, that the sun is *the only thing we can regard with complete and absolute faith?"*

It was not long afterward that Duilio took a shovel to the farthest corner of his orchard and dug a deep hole, and into it he dropped his statues of the Virgin Mary and Saint Anthony and his Christs on the Cross. When he had tamped the last shovelful of dirt back into place, he went into town to the stonecutter and ordered a marble plaque for the outside wall of the house. It bore the words "Duilio Paselli, Knight of Labor, here makes a remembrance of his loved ones," and showed a young girl and a young boy kneeling in front of a rising sun. Before he died, the old man explained to his friends that it was an emblem, a declaration of faith in mankind, a message of hope for the coming generations.

Epilogue

DRIVING up the Autostrada del Sole from Rome today, one passes through the Apennines with their cluttered villages and battered farmhouses sometimes extending far up the flanks and almost to the summits of the mountains. At an exit marked RIOVEGGIO, a subtle change comes over the landscape to the west. Big brown-orange farmhouses are wedged into the sides of the mountain, just as they have been for several hundred miles, but a closer look shows that they are empty. The windows are dark. The fields are untended. The vines are dead, the trellises rotting into the earth. There is hardly any color, not a piece of washing, or a dot of cow, or a splotch of ripening orchard. The land is grayish brown. Immediately alongside the *autostrada,* in the rich lands bordering the *torrente* Setta, there are a few homes and farmlands. But from there to the top of the massif, there is no sign of life. A few miles farther, at an exit marked MARZABOTTO, the usual pattern resumes: farms, homes, cultivated land, cattle, oxen, all the way to the scalloped peaks of the mountains.

Those few motorists who venture off the Autostrada del Sole and climb the narrow dirt roads between Rioveggio and Marzabotto quickly find that everything is dead. Monte Sole exists nowadays only as a lifeless geological lump, shadowed and silent. A single *contadina,* an old lady who was widowed in the massacre, lives with her son at San Giovanni, and the richer *poderi* along the river bottoms on both sides of the mountain are still farmed, but there is no one at San Martino, at Cerpiano, at Caprara, at any of the mountainside villages where the postman used to deliver his mail and collect his snacks and play his jokes. At Casaglia the walls of the church are holed and pitted by shells, and one must be careful not to step into the basement, overgrown like the rest of the church by brambles and bushes. The walls of the cemetery of Casaglia are falling into the ground; the chapel where the victims were grouped together is one wall away from extinction, and the inscriptions of most of the headstones are worn off. Ahead and to the left as one passes through the rusty iron gate, one sees a tilted slab of flat stone that once bore the names of the victims of Casaglia. Now it is smooth and illegible, and the common grave where the *contadini* buried their dead in darkness appears only as a slight depression in the sandy soil. Bushes and weeds cover everything; periodically the proud young priest of Gardeletta shames his parishioners into climbing the mountain to pull out the weeds in the graveyard, but the battle is a losing one. The people of Gardeletta have too much to do already; there is no time to tend yesterday's history.

A short distance down the road, a stump of rock shows where Luigi Massa's *tabacchi* once stood, and there are a few empty stone houses, rebuilt and then abandoned, but the rest of the village of Caprara is pulverized and overgrown. Around the bend of the ridge road, the flattened village of San Martino has disappeared under siftings of humus; one can scratch off the dirt and find the cobblestones that marked the piazza of the village. Neither the church of San Martino nor the big *casa colonica* nor the many outbuildings are visible in any form. A single wall remains under a jungle of weeds; the baptismal font of the church lies on its side in a ditch. Nearby, the cemetery is intact, its tombs and its walls pitted with gunfire, but behind the rear wall only an impenetrable entanglement of brambles and vines marks the place where the bodies of the war invalid Moschetti and the priest Don Giovanni Fornasini lay together in death through the long winter of 1944-45.

The brick and fieldstone chapel of Cerpiano stands roofless except for a single arch that somehow remains in position in defiance of the laws of physics. Every inch of the floor where Sister Benni and her two small friends played dead is covered with weeds and brush; columns are broken off, plaster chipped and broken, the altar an indistinguishable remnant. A lizard crawls up the wall in the sun. The *palazzo,* the big four-story mansion of Cerpiano, has vanished, nor are its foundations visible. An enterprising farmer from the valley below climbs up to Cerpiano to collect berries and chestnuts, but no one lives there. Nor does anyone live at Le Scope, Vallego, Cadotto, Prunaro, Casetta, Poggio, almost all the other *poderi* of the mountain. The sites are marked by rotten walls, empty center posts of unformed haystacks, brown and desiccated vineyards where only weeds grow, and the black holes of uncovered wells.

After the war, wild and unbelievable rumors circulated in northern and central Italy: it was said that the Nazis had killed a vast number of innocents in the mountains near Bologna. Now and then someone who purported to be a survivor would come forth and tell lurid tales about the massacre of hundreds of women and children. One-eyed Antonio Tonelli reported to the authorities that his wife and children had been murdered along with 80 or 90 others at Casaglia, but his *denuncia* was filed away; it was unsupported by physical evidence. Besides, Italians knew that their countrymen from Emilia-Romagna and Tuscany tended to exaggerate. If the Bolognese were saying that thousands had been slaughtered on Monte Sole, perhaps hundreds had been killed, maybe dozens. What was so astonishing about that? The SS had liquidated 200 at Vinca, 335 in the Ardeatine caves of Rome, 200 or so at Bergiola, thousands throughout the rest of Italy.

The authorities were busy with postwar survival problems like feeding the homeless and stemming disease. The massacre of Monte Sole, if indeed there *had* been a massacre of Monte Sole, would have to wait. And wait it did, for another reason—the Communists exploited the matter, and automatically the Italian right wing hardened against the fact of Monte Sole.

Right after the war the Communists were engaged in a struggle to win Italy, as they had won Yugoslavia, and they very nearly succeeded. They had hundreds of natural leaders; almost every partisan in Italy had fought under Communist direction, in brigades and groups organized and controlled by avowed Communists. A rare exception was the *Stella Rossa,* formed by a Fascist along with an outspoken anti-Communist, and backed up by a hard core of *carabinieri,* loyal only to the king. If there was a single Italian partisan brigade for which the Communists could not claim credit, it was the brigade of the Red Star.

Even so, the name of the brigade proved irresistible to the propagandists. All over Europe, one began to hear the legend of the "Communist" Red Star Brigade. One hears it still. In this distortion of history, the final attack of September 29, 1944, became the Battle of Monte Sole, when in fact, it was no battle at all but a rout, with the raggedy *Stella Rossa* fleeing from the Germans in the best tradition of partisan warfare. The historians of the Communist Party wrote of the "four divisions of German troops" which vanquished the Red Star Brigade, when in fact there were something less than 1,000 SS men on the mountain at maximum. According to the Communists' Newspeak version of the events, the partisans dug in and fought almost to the last man, losing hundreds of valiant Red soldiers to the combined German infantry, tanks, airplanes and artillery. And what did the Germans do after they had won this great battle by sheer force of arms? *They killed several thousand civilians.*

Where did the truth begin, and where did it end? The Reds had made the *Stella Rossa their* brigade, the massacre of Monte Sole *their* massacre. The Catholic politicians, battling the Communists for control of Italy, had no choice but to dismiss the entire story—a conclusion, incidentally, that found support in certain German quarters, coinciding, as it did, with an understandable German reluctance to admit that soldiers of the land of Beethoven and Goethe could have carried out such atrocities.

Not until 1949, when the political situation had become somewhat stabilized, could the martyrdom of Monte Sole be recognized. The Gold Medal, Italy's highest decoration, was presented to the entire commune of Marzabotto, with posthumous individual gold medals to Mario "Lupo" Musolesi, Gianni Rossi's brother Gastone, and the priest Don Giovanni Fornasini. An ornate marble *ossario* (bone crypt) was built in Marzabotto, and the names of all the known dead chiseled into plaques, and the place began calling itself the "martyr town"—an appellation lampooned by certain neo-Fascist writers who charged with accuracy that next to nothing had happened in the town of Marzabotto during the war, conveniently failing to spell out the difference between the *town* of Marzabotto and the *commune* of Marzabotto, whose communal limits embraced the abattoir called Monte Sole.

As late as 1951 only one person had been brought to account for the massacre. Field Marshal Albert Kesselring, the career soldier who had told his troops that squashing the partisans was more important than remaining within "the normal limits" of warfare, was sentenced to death by the British for assorted war crimes in Italy, including Monte Sole, but his sentence was reduced to life imprisonment and finally commuted altogether. Kesselring lived to write his memoirs in the privacy and comfort of his home and to tell an Italian journalist nonchalantly that the Monte Sole action was a "war operation," neither more nor less. So astute a military commander must have known better. There can be little doubt that Kesselring knew the exact makeup of the SS troops he sent to secure Monte Sole. Almost to a man, they were veterans of the eastern front, where excesses on both sides had made the simple killing of civilians a commonplace—a normal "war operation." For weeks before the Monte Sole massacre, these same SS troops had been slaughtering and butchering noncombatants in Italian cities to the south. Twenty-four years after the fact, it remains difficult to believe that such organized, conspicuous atrocities took place—could be permitted to take place—without the knowledge, if not under the direction, of Field Marshal Kesselring and his staff.

Six years after the end of the war, the Italians got around to trying the one-armed major of the SS, Walter Reder, for war crimes including the massacre of Monte Sole. Reder was another with long experience in mass killings. The son of an Austrian industrialist who went bankrupt, Reder at nineteen was linked by the Austrian police to the assassination of Chancellor Engelbert Dollfuss. The same year, 1934, found him admitted to the academy of the SS in Berlin, where Hitler was training an elite corps. When war broke out, Reder was already a veteran officer of the SS, and as such he was involved in the extermination of Jews and Communists in Poland, partisans in the Ukraine (where he lost his hand), and women and children in the troublesome mountain zones of Italy. Before descending on Monte Sole, he had carried out any number of mass slaughters. In one, his handpicked troopers posed 107 men, women and children before hooded "cameras," then whipped off the hoods and machine-gunned the group to death. A little girl, shielded by falling bodies, lived to tell the story. In another of Reder's actions, 53 Italian men, singing their native songs as they rolled in trucks toward a "labor camp," were put to death by strangulation and hung on a barbed-wire fence for the *contadini* to see.

After the liberation of Bologna, Reder had fled north with the German troops and was arrested by the Americans in Salzburg on routine charges of war criminality filed long before by Marshal Pietro Badoglio. The SS major was shunted from the Americans to the British to the Italians and finally convicted by an Italian military court in Bologna in 1951. Many of the victims of Monte Sole testified against him. Sister Benni and Elena and Elide Ruggeri were among the prosecution witnesses. SS men were interviewed in Germany (they were noticeably unwilling to come to Bologna) and their depositions made a part of the trial record. The Italian military prosecution, adhering to the normal practice of prosecutors everywhere, introduced heavy testimony only in the cases in which Reder was overwhelmingly guilty. As a result, the ex-major was formally found guilty of only about half the atrocities on the mountain. The sentence was life imprisonment in any case.

With the pronouncement of Italy's harshest penalty, cries of anguish came from the German-speaking world. The Germans and Austrians assumed that the Italians had rigged the trial and used Reder as a scapegoat. Tens of thousands of signatures demanded his release. Official protests were issued on the floor of the Austrian Parliament. Packages and gifts and banknotes were showered on the victimized major in his oversize cell at the military prison in Gaeta, where he enjoyed the use of a kitchen, a balcony with a view, and an occasional female visitor. An organization called the League of Austrian Fighting Men canceled its official participation in a reunion of the veterans of the Battle of Monte Cassino, hoping thereby to stimulate international interest in the miscarriage of justice. As late as 1957 an organization of former SS men—the Cooperative Mutual Aid Society—was circulating petitions demanding Reder's release.

In support of Reder, a Bavarian writer named Lothar Greil wrote a paperback called *The Lies of Marzabotto* in which he argued that the massacre never took place. A British writer named F. J. P. Veale also insisted in two books that Monte Sole was a Communist hoax and claimed that Reder was railroaded by an anti-German Italian court. In sole rebuttal was a slim book, of some 100 pages, consisting mainly of interviews with survivors, by Dr. Renato Giorgi, a librarian and scholar of the Monte Sole area. It was called simply *Marzabotto Speaks,* and when it was published in Germany (*Marzabotto Spricht*), it was attacked as a network of Communist lies.

After *Il Monco* (The Mutilated One), as Reder was known on Monte Sole, saw his hopes for pardon dashed by vote of the survivors of the massacre, the mayor of Marzabotto received a letter telling him that he would be shot if the major were not released. Nevertheless, Reder remains at Gaeta Prison, where his cellblock neighbor is Herbert Kappler, the SS commandant who carried out the reprisal massacre of 335 Romans in 1944. Petitions for the release of both SS officers continue to appear in Germany and Austria and even England, and periodically there is another addition to the neo-Fascist literature "proving" that Reder is an innocent victim and the whole affair a fiction.

There will never be an official count of the exact number of those killed in the massacre of Monte Sole. At the trial of Reder, the Italian Army used the figure 1,830 as an educated guess. One bone crypt in Marzabotto bears the remains of 1,200 identified victims, and another the bones of 300 unidentified. This includes most of the war dead of the commune of Marzabotto during World War II, with the exception of Fascists and spies. There was a terrible uproar when the bones of a known Fascist were inadvertently put in the *ossario* in Marzabotto.

There are other reminders of the massacre of Monte Sole. In Pioppe di Salvaro, where flowers are placed in vases by relatives, there is a plaque that reads: "October 1, 1944. In these mountains, where hard work was all the people had, the barbarous German with unequaled ferocity took the lives of people who were guilty of loving only their families and their country." There are 41 names listed; on the bottom is added: "and four others, one of Pisa and three Lucchesi."

In Sperticano there is a marble relief of a swastika-bearing soldier stabbing a baby held in his mother's arms. A man and woman are lying on the ground, with the man's arms upraised beseeching mercy; in the background a house is burning down. Listed above the bas-relief are the names of 116 known dead.

Down in the valley of the Reno, near the little town of Pian di Venola, the Nazis creosoted a swastika on a shack to mark the site of an execution, but now it comes into view only after a rain, when it seems to glow and fade in ghostly alternation. Up the road at Colle Ameno, where some of the men of Monte Sole were imprisoned and then executed, one can still read penciled messages in the stone dungeons of the ancient villa. A prisoner signed his name and added, "In utter misery." Over a group of names is the inscription: "Companions in misfortune." A faint message from "C. E., Nov. 18, 1944," says: "I leave it for you who enter to look for any hope."

Miles away in the city of Cuneo, there is a testament in marble, addressed to Field Marshal Kesselring, written by the late Professor Piero Calamandrei, rector of the University of Florence and founder of the political and cultural journal *Il Ponte*. In part it says:

> You will have, Comrade Kesselring, the monument you demanded of us Italians. But we will decide of what stone it will be built. Not of the scorched rocks from the defenseless villages you outraged and destroyed. Not of the earth from the cemeteries where our young brothers lie in peace. Not with the inviolate snows of the mountains, where for two winters they challenged you. Not with the spring of these valleys that watched you flee. But only with tortured silence, which is harder than any boulder. Only with the rock of this vow, sworn by free men, who willingly gather, in dignity rather than in hatred, to redeem the shame and the terror of your world.

Two decades after the last shot had been fired and the Allies had liberated Monte Sole, a little boy picked up a red metal ball on the banks of the river Reno and was blasted to pieces. More years will pass before a hunter or farmer or perhaps another child will detonate with his last footfall the final unexploded shell or mine or booby-trap, and the massacre of Monte Sole will be over.

Appendix

Reder, Walter, prisoner of war, serving sentence, Military Prison, Gaeta (Latina).

GAETA, APRIL 30, 1967

DEAR HONORABLE MAYOR,

The undersigned, Reder, Walter, condemned to life imprisonment for the mournful deeds committed in Marzabotto takes the liberty to set forth to you, First Citizen of Marzabotto, the following:

The mother of the undersigned, now over eighty years of age, has already lost three children. The first died at a very tender age. A brother, Rudolf, died in 1930 in an accident. A sister, Martha, who was married in Verona to an Italian engineer and lived in Paris, perished together with her husband in 1941.

Numerous appeals for mercy, initiated for the most part by the mother of the undersigned, by the undersigned himself, and by numerous personages, have had no success.

Honorable Mayor:

Deeds already done and blood already spilled cannot be erased, and the memory will always be alive in the hearts of those who have suffered so greatly, as it is alive in the ever-more acute remorse of the one who has committed them.

But above all stand the virtues of mercy and forgiveness, which are the prerogative of strong and noble souls.

A mother who has lost three children, broken by sorrow, extends her hands toward Marzabotto and begs forgiveness for her last son. No longer able to travel because of age and poor health, the mother of the undersigned has but one hope: to be able to embrace her son before she dies after having obtained for him the forgiveness of Marzabotto and a pardon from the President.

Those who gave the orders which brought about such odious deeds have been free for many years now, for example, Marshal Kesselring, sentenced to death, General Simon, and others.

All the nations who were then in the war, even the Soviet Union, released, a long time ago, all the Austrian war criminals condemned either to life imprisonment or to extremely long detentions.

In December, 1966, the Town Council of the martyred city of Marzabotto launched a very noble appeal for peace in distant Vietnam.

Having said all this, the undersigned turns to you, most Honorable Mayor, spontaneously beseeching that the people of Marzabotto, through you and the Town Council of Marzabotto, grant me

Pardon

for the blood shed and for the destruction inflicted on the population of the martyred city.

This pardon would be a demonstration of the highest virtues of nobility, mercy, and pity.

WALTER REDER

STATEMENT BY THE TOWN COUNCIL ON THE OCCASION OF A SPECIAL MEETING CALLED IN MARZABOTTO AFTER THE REFERENDUM REQUESTED BY REDER

We believe that we have done our duty and nothing more than our duty in calling the survivors of the massacre of Marzabotto—the families of the deceased, all those who have crosses in their homes, those who suffer ineradicable sorrows—to reply to Reder, whose name will remain forever linked with one of the most horrible massacres of humanity, a carnage about which even we of Marzabotto do not know all the details yet.

Our decision was clear and unanimous even from the beginning; our representatives and administrators were of the same mind: a pardon is unthinkable. Reder must carry out his full sentence where he is until the end of his days. He may and must ask for forgiveness of himself, not of Marzabotto, not of Italy, not of those who have suffered so much during the interminable years of the war and of martyrdom.

Toward the families of the deceased, toward the survivors, toward the young who want to and must know, we have the responsibility and the duty to give proof of the dignity and the moral strength of our people. How could we consider ourselves worthy representatives of these people if we did not respect, if we had not respected fully its will? What we want is that it never be forgotten that it was not an act of war that was committed here, as Kesselring said, but a horrendous massacre, an inhuman reprisal against unarmed peoples, an act of cowardliness and of hatred and nothing else. For this reason, we said, that pardon is unthinkable.

These were our thoughts, but we had to hear, we *had* to ask the families of the martyrs for their judgment. And their judgment now is known. The verdict is final. But it does not apply only to Reder; it would be absurd to claim that it did. It applies to Nazism, Fascism, war, violence, intolerance, racism, hatred for any nation, all that hinders the path toward peace, the peaceful coexistence among all nations. It applies to Reder and all the Reders who now exist, or who may emerge in the world; all those who hate people and their most simple and noble feelings.

It applies to Reder, Nazism, and Fascism, and not to the German people or the Austrian. In Auschwitz, in Mauthausen, monuments have been erected in memory of those Germans martyred by Nazism; there were hundreds of thousands. Here we have mourned a German soldier killed in Creda by Reder because he failed to fire on the people. Don Tommasini, the chaplain of the partisan brigade of *Stella Rossa* has spoken on television of a German soldier killed because he was caught in a gesture of mercy toward one of the victims. We honor them! We consider them our sons.

There is no hatred in Marzabotto!

Extended hands and open arms toward all men that are men, toward all those who have and will perform, even in the most dramatic moments, a human gesture.

Reder has no nationality. Nazism has created him, has deprived him of all human feeling, has turned him into a perfect synthesis of Nazism, of Fascism, of war.

They may as well not bother to wait for him in the Alto Adige; Reder will not come to start new massacres. Don't look for him in the Nazi beer halls of Munich, where they are still raising the swastika.

Reder will not come.

He will remain where he is.

To the President of the Republic we will bring the vote of Marzabotto, the vote not only of the Italian people, but of all peoples who want peace, and fight for it.

WORLD WAR II MAGAZINE PRESENTS

THE WORLD WAR II READER

With an introduction by ROBERT LECKIE

ISBN: 0-7434-2387-9

It was a war that defined a generation of the world, a war that saw America transform itself from an inward-looking isolationist nation to an arsenal of democracy whose reach spanned the globe. *The World War II Reader* presents in one extraordinary book the thrilling story of the greatest generation in its finest hour in the best essays from the world's most distinguished historians compiled by *World War II* magazine, the only magazine that brings the history and drama of the 20th Century's defining conflict to life.

The World War II Reader includes insightful essays on the larger-than-life leaders who made life-and-death decisions that shaped grand strategy and crucial battles. In addition, this book cuts through the fog of war and presents thought-provoking revelations of little known events that had far-reaching consequences, including the Niihau Incident, that tragically affected the fate of Japanese-Americans in Hawaii and mainland America.

The World War II Reader is a must-have for every history enthusiast, and for the person searching for the one book that not just tells the story of America's greatest conflict, but makes World War II come vividly alive as if it happened yesterday.

With an introduction by Robert Leckie,
best-selling author of the World War II classic
Helmet for my Pillow

HELMET FOR MY PILLOW
By ROBERT LECKIE

ISBN: 0-7434-1307-5

The true, incredible story of the U.S. Marines in World War II, the toughest fighting men the world has ever seen, in their finest hour.

Robert Leckie, one of America's greatest military historians, was both an eyewitness and participant to some of the greatest battles in the Pacific. This is Leckie's vivid account of combat and survival in World War II.

In January 1942, in the aftermath of the infamous Japanese sneak attack on Pearl Harbor, he enlisted in the United States Marine Corps. From boot camp in Parris Island to the bloody war in the Pacific, Robert Leckie experienced it all. The booze, the brawling, the loving on sixty-two-hour liberty; the courageous fighting and dying in combat, as the U.S. Marines slugged it out, inch by inch, island by island across the Pacific to the shores of Japan.

SPECIAL TO THIS EDITION: "The Battle of Tenaru" a never-before-published piece by Robert Leckie commemorating those who fell in one of Guadalcanal's bloodiest battles.

THE B-17: THE FLYING FORTS
By Martin Caidin

ISBN: 0-7434-3470-6

There is no such thunder in history—nor ever will be again—as the deep-throated roar of the mighty, four-engined B-17s that streamed across the skies in World War II. The long runways are silent now, the men and planes are gone.

But out of the massive files of records available, and the memories of the men who flew, Martin Caidin has assembled this dramatic portrait of America's most formidable heavy bomber of the war.

The B-17: The Flying Forts recreates a vanished era and a great and gallant plane—a plane that could absorb three thousand enemy bullets, fly with no rudder, and complete its mission on two engines. A plane that American pilots flew at Pearl Harbor, Tunis, Midway, Palermo, Schweinfurt, Regensberg, Normandy, and Berlin, in thousands of missions and through hundreds of thousands of miles of flak-filled skies. A plane that proved itself in every combat theater as the greatest heavy bomber of World War II.

THUNDERBOLT! THE P-47

By Robert S. Johnson with Martin Caidin

ISBN: 0-7434-2397-6

They were outnumbered and underrated. They were fresh from the training fields in America and ordered to fight an enemy that had rewritten the book of war and brutally controlled a continent and the air above it. But the men of the 56th Fighter Group had courage and, more importantly, they had the P-47 Thunderbolt.

This is the incredible story of the U.S. 56th Fighter Group as told by one of its best pilots, Robert S. Johnson, who would rack up a score of twenty-eight kills against the Luftwaffe and become one of America's top aces—one of a special breed of men who changed the course of history.